D1007897

JENNIFER ARMINTROUT

blood ties book four:
all SOULS' NIGHT

MIRA

MIRA®

ISBN-13: 978-0-7783-2537-6
ISBN-10:   0-7783-2537-7

BLOOD TIES BOOK FOUR: ALL SOULS' NIGHT

Copyright © 2008 by Jennifer Armintrout.

www.MIRABooks.com

Printed in U.S.A.

To everyone who has stuck with Carrie and co.
to the bitter end.
See you next time in the Lightworld.

.

ACKNOWLEDGMENTS

This series would not have been possible without the people in my life who love me, support me and understand that while I might not be writing about something "important," I am writing something worth reading.

And as always, big thanks are owed to the fast food and beer industries.

Also, the Fourth Coast Cafe in Kalamazoo, Michigan, where a large portion of this book was written and revised.

Prologue: Daymare

Some days, I dream of the time that I spent in Marianne's soul. Or is that the time that she spent in me? In reality, it was horrible, but in the dreams, it feels wonderful. Powerful. Another soul gliding over mine like silk, whispering in my head.

I stand over Nathan. He's still restrained, babbling, senseless with fear and the spell his sire had cast over him, bleeding from the wounds scored deep into his flesh by his own hand. Marianne leans tenderly over her husband, kisses his mouth, calms him. And then the power swells up inside me, and she screams for mercy in my head. All I know is blood and tearing flesh. Darkness and warmth with the copper-tinged smell of slowly ebbing life urging on my bloodlust.

I don't even consciously drink. I don't feel or taste the blood, and though I know, somehow, that I am dreaming, I find it unsettling, as if some understanding is just out of my reach. If only I could see the greater picture.

I consume without drinking, reach my fill without satisfaction. And when I raise my eyes to the evaporating darkness, I see the ballroom where Marianne met her fate. All around me are the bodies of people I know: Nathan, Max, Bella, even old friends long since dead, like Cyrus and Ziggy. Their blood is on my hands. Their life in my veins. Their tortured screams rolling through my head like the sweetest symphony I've ever heard.

And then Jacob Seymour is there, seated at the head of the massive dining table. He wears a crown of thorns and the blood that drips from his wounds is black tar, staining his white hair and shining golden robes. A huge, silver-domed platter covers the table, and I remember—in that dream memory that doesn't quite see reality the way it happened, but still manages to catalog every horror you've ever known—what will come next. Clarence appears, as if from nowhere, his dark, regal face a mask disguising the hate he feels for the task, and removes the cover. On the platter, arranged in a way that is familiar, yet shocking, is Dahlia, her skin pale and mottled blue with death, a carpet of rose petals beneath her halo of red curls.

And then, with the voices still screaming in my brain, I laugh. Blood flows from my mouth, splashing to the tabletop, my hands, my lap that is suddenly and inexplicably dressed in a voluminous gown to match Jacob's attire, and I laugh.

But when I wake, I'm screaming.

One: A Shot In The Dark

This day, when I bolted upright in the bed, throat tensed, vocal cords poised to emit a scream as soon as the gasping breath I'd drawn forced its way out, a hand clamped over my mouth. Nathan was already awake.

Don't make a sound, he warned through the blood tie, his body rigid with tension that jumped through our mental connection, filling me with his anxiety.

Something was seriously wrong. In the past few weeks, since we had fled Grand Rapids and come to Max's Chicago penthouse, Nathan's entire focus had been my recovery. I'd gone mute and practically catatonic after Cyrus, once my sire, then my fledgling, had died. After I'd wake from one of my many nightmares—daymares, I supposed, since we vampires are third-shifters on account of that pesky sun thing—Nathan would hold me and try to reassure me that it had all been a dream, that he wouldn't let anything harm me. Now, though, I felt his irritation and acute distraction through the blood tie, the telepathic and empathic connection that coursed between a fledgling vampire and their sire, and I knew something wasn't right.

Before he could explain, I heard a thud and some violent cursing upstairs.

There's someone in the apartment, I practically screamed into his head, and the pressure of his hand on my jaw subsided slightly.

I know. That's why I said not to make a sound. I'm going to check it out. He let go of my face and threw back the blankets. I could tell from the faint light outlining the heavy curtains that it was still the middle of the day, but Max's apartment was specially designed to be dark as a tomb and just as protected from unwanted sunlight.

Be careful, I warned. As if someone could be careful apprehending an intruder in their home. At least Nathan would be armed.

Crap. He wasn't armed.

"Nathan!" I whispered after him, so the cause of the disturbance wouldn't hear me. Unfortunately, neither did Nathan. He was probably halfway up the stairs by now. Rolling my eyes, I got out of bed and pulled on the jeans I'd discarded the night before, realizing how ridiculous a silk camisole nightgown looked with jeans. Good thing this wasn't a fashion show. I grabbed a stake from the drawer in the bedside table. *Forget something?* I shot across the blood tie, letting him feel all my aggravation at having been pulled out of a comfortable bed. I hoped it would cover the fear that pounded through my veins.

Besides pants? he quipped. He was scared, joking with me to disguise it.

We'd been sleeping in the room I'd used when I'd

stayed with Max, after the spell we did to free Nathan from his sire's possession went all sorts of haywire. No, that wasn't true. The spell had worked perfectly. It was our relationship that had gone all kinds of haywire. I'd left with Max to try and sort through the disaster of my personal life, but—as seemed to be the case ever since I'd become a vampire—the preternatural world didn't slow down for boyfriend-girlfriend drama. Nathan's sire, the Soul Eater, was still out there, trying to become a god and turn the world into his own personal feeding trough.

Though I'd spent a lot of time in the penthouse, I still wasn't familiar enough with the halls to navigate in the dark. The place was huge and, as huge places often were, decorated with lots of expensive and sharp-edged little tables bearing fragile objects that held the potential for lots of noise if they came crashing down. The guest rooms were on the first floor. Who or whatever had broken in would have had to access the place through the main entrance on the second floor, or the roof door on the third. I felt along the wall, recoiling whenever I encountered the shape of a painting or a light switch. My toes painfully found the bottom step of the stairs to the next floor, and I wondered why I hadn't heard Nathan tripping and falling over himself on his way. I gripped the rail and went slowly up the stairs, quelling the urge to race up, making heavy clomping sounds on each step. There was no light at the top. I'd just keep on going until there weren't any more stairs, I supposed.

Or, until I ran into something. Nathan turned abruptly as I collided with him. He grabbed my arms as if to flip me onto my back, but stopped before I even needed to tell him it was me. *Don't do that,* he admonished through the blood tie.

"Sorry," I whispered, craning to see past him in the dark. We were at the top of the stairs. The marble floor of the foyer gleamed in the faint glow from the recessed wall lights set at shin level around the perimeter of the room. When Max's sire, Marcus, had designed this place, he'd obviously done it with daytime stumbling in mind. Too bad he hadn't employed that feature in the rest of the house. In the darkness, a shadow moved, fast, from the bottom of the stairs to the third floor to the kitchen door.

Well, there's at least one, Nathan told me grimly. *You stay here.*

I pressed the stake into his hand and watched him go, wondering how long I'd have to wait before following him. He knew me well enough that he'd expect me to disobey his command, but if I waited long enough he'd be too busy with the intruder to stop me.

The kitchen door opened and light spilled out. No burglar I'd ever heard of turned on lights. Well, at least, they didn't in the movies. But burglars didn't break in during the day, either. Unless this burglar knew who and what he was dealing with.

How did they find us so quickly? my mind screamed as I watched Nathan disappear behind the door. It swung shut and I was left to adapt to the darkness again. *It isn't fair. We haven't had any time.*

And just like that, fair blew right out the window. There was a shout, not Nathan's, and the clatter of metal-on-metal that seemed to go on and on. A grunt, a thud, something hit the wall. I charged up the stairs, my heart in my throat, a distinct feeling of having done something very like this many times before fogging my brain.

I pushed through the door. Nathan's stake lay on the pristine white tile. The rack of pots over the kitchen island was half-empty, most of its stock scattered on the floor. The island itself was completely bare, like a body had been thrown or dragged across it. Nathan's body, from the looks of things on the floor. His assailant had him pinned, no small feat for a human fighting a vampire, and he was definitely human. I could smell his blood, and his fear. The man lay across Nathan's chest, the muscles of his back straining against his black T-shirt. Judging by the V of sweat growing there, he would tire soon. And judging by the shape of the gun tucked in the waistband of his jeans, he'd come here betting on a fight.

I knew why Nathan was losing. He didn't want to hurt a human, even if they were out to hurt us. I, on the other hand, didn't care all that much when the human in question could be one of the Soul Eater's day staff. I grabbed one of the pans off the floor, a heavy, copper-bottomed saucepan. I'd just raised it up when Nathan's gaze met mine and knew my intention. He gripped the intruder's wrists and forced them down, then pushed him off. His strength was enough to send the man flying across the room, safely out of my range. He didn't want me to kill a human, either.

Nathan was on his feet in an instant, charging as I screamed, "Nathan, don't! He's got a gun!"

The shot rang out before I'd noticed the man had climbed to his feet. Nathan crumpled to the floor, and there was a second of horrible silence before he rolled onto his back, groaning and whimpering. The intruder stood, face drawn in shock. I leaped after him, easily clearing the corner of the island between us, and knocked him to the floor. His fingers tightened around the gun. I had to slam his closed fist into the floor over and over, until the tile cracked under his knuckles and he howled in pain, releasing the weapon. I hated to give him credit, but the guy was *tough.*

I grabbed the gun, hoping my shaking hands and the way I held it didn't mark me as a total novice. *A novice can still pull a trigger,* I thought, and, through his haze of pain, Nathan admonished, *Squeeze, Carrie, not pull. You squeeze a trigger.*

I rolled my eyes and pressed the point of the gun into the stranger's forehead. Imagining a bullet lodging and blossoming in fatty brain tissue, I pulled it back, just in case my trigger finger squeezed when I didn't mean to.

"Don't move," I barked when he cradled his bleeding hand to his chest.

"Shouldn't you check on your friend there?" His voice had an appealing, everyman tone to it. Like the professor I had who'd been from upstate New York and could make a pharmaceutical lecture sound like a retelling of a soft-ball game victory. It was a dangerous quality in an armed assailant, because it put me slightly at ease.

I'll be fine, Nathan sent on a wave of agony. It was a little hard to believe when he was writhing on the floor and making strangled cries as though he'd just hit a ten on the pain scale. I turned back to my captive. "He'll be fine. Who sent you?"

"Well, no one. I'm here once a month." He nodded to

the refrigerator. On the floor beside it was a small cooler, white with a red top that swings back, the kind that you'd pack a transplant organ in. "I'm Max's blood supplier."

I lowered the gun a little. "Right. And you just waltz in here all the time."

"Well, once a month," he corrected with a shrug.

I was about eighty percent sure he was lying. "Sorry. I think that Max would have mentioned you to me. Or, at least, that I would have seen you before."

"No, I'm quiet. And I've got keys. How the hell else do you think I got in here? There's a doorman and great security." He ran his uninjured hand through his sandy-colored hair, his gaze flicking to Nathan, still on the floor. "Listen, I knew your friend there was a vampire, or I never would have shot him."

"Right." Trembling, I moved to tuck the gun into the back of my jeans.

"I wouldn't do that. Not with it ready to fire and the safety off." He held out his hand for it. I turned, fired a hole into the side of the plastic wastebasket, then looked for the safety switch and pushed it before sliding the gun into my waistband. I felt oddly empowered with a gun in my hands, and very grateful that the bullet hadn't ricocheted and wounded me.

I knelt beside Nathan and tried to roll him onto his back. He resisted, arms clamped tight around his stomach. "Let me see," I said, urging his hands away from the wound.

"Don't…you should…tie him…." Nathan managed between wheezing breaths.

"I'm not moving. Trust me." The stranger paused. "Just like I'm trusting you guys not to eat me."

"I'm not really hungry at the moment," I snapped. "If you move, I might change my mind."

Nathan reluctantly let his arms drop to his sides. Blood gushed, and I quickly replaced his hands with mine. "Burglar, get me a towel or a pot holder or something."

There was a noise of rummaging, then a blue-and-white checked towel thrust in front of my face. "I'm not a burglar."

"I don't care. Go back to where you were." I snatched the towel. The bullet hole in Nathan was perfectly round, identical to the one in the trash can, but for the torn flaps of skin around it. It looked like some kind of diseased tropical flower. I pressed the folded cloth to it and held it, noting the time on the clock. With my other hand, I reached up and touched Nathan's face, clammy with sweat. "When the bleeding stops, I'll give you something for the pain."

"He can heal from this, right?" our visitor asked. "I swear, I thought it would just slow him down."

I nodded. "It will slow him down. And he can heal from it. But not the way you see vampires do it in the movies, where the bullet oozes out and the wound closes up instantly. If you'd gotten his heart, he would be dead now."

The guy made a noise of self-loathing. "God, I'm sorry. But you understand my position, right?"

I did. If I had been a human fighting with a vampire who could have easily killed me with his bare hands, I would have used any method at my disposal to stop him. Understanding didn't stop me from being pissed off at the guy who'd shot my sire. I turned back to Nathan. "Do you think you can walk?"

He gave a shaky laugh. "Oh, I could run a mile. Just point me in the right direction."

"Do you think you can walk *with help?*" I fixed him with a no-nonsense glare. *The medical kit is downstairs, and I don't want to leave you alone with him.*

Then tell him to get the hell out, Nathan said, his gaze flicking to the stranger. *He's the one who broke in and shot someone. I'm not worried about hurting his feelings.*

Neither am I. But the bullet needs to come out so you can heal faster. I helped him sit up, intending to get him on his feet and downstairs, so he could rest.

"You stay right where you are," I ordered the intruder. "I'll be back."

The hell you will. I'm not going anywhere, Nathan argued.

"You have a recently fired piece registered to me, with my fingerprints on it. I'm not leaving," the burglar assured me. "You want help getting him wherever he needs to go?"

"Stay where you are," I repeated, and, to Nathan, *Yes you are. You're going downstairs, away from the crazy man who shot you.*

Before I could get him on his feet—and before he tried to argue with me—he stabbed two fingers into the wound and, barely restraining his grunts of pain, pulled the bullet out himself. When he withdrew his fingers, a cold, wet jet of blood shot out, and I clamped the towel over his stomach with a curse.

"What the hell were you thinking?" I scolded, reminding myself firmly that any of the various germs and bacteria he'd just introduced into the wound wouldn't affect him.

"Now the bullet is out," he said, infuriatingly calm despite the beads of sweat standing out on his forehead. His teeth chattered and he sagged against me. "And I'm staying right here."

Swearing, I pulled him to rest against the wall, his legs dragging two wet trails of blood after him.

"You're an idiot," I muttered, placing his hand to hold the towel over the wound. I turned back to the assailant. He'd remained exactly where I'd expected him to be, nursing the knuckles I'd bloodied.

"Is your friend okay?" he asked, with enough grace to appear genuinely remorseful.

"He'll be fine." I leaned hard on the word "fine," so he'd know I was still dangerously pissed off. "What were you doing here?"

"Dropping off blood. Max pays me to come by and stock the place—the mini fridge in his room and the big one here. I do it once a month. Sometimes he pays me between visits to drop in and give the bum's rush to any overnight guests that might be…disinclined to leave without saying goodbye." He shrugged. "I've got a key, and you can ask Dolores, the morning doorman. She thinks I'm the cleaning lady."

I arched a brow at him. "Okay, cleaning lady. What's your name?"

"Bill. William. Bill." He reached behind him. So did I, looking for the gun. He smiled. "Don't worry, I'm just going for my wallet."

"I don't need to see ID, Bill." Interrogation was harder than I'd imagined. I wished Nathan was up to the job. It seemed that in the movies the questions all flowed in a seamless pattern of logic. My thoughts were all over the place, would probably come out all scattered. "So, if you and Max are so chummy, why do you carry a gun when you come to his place?"

Bill shrugged. "I always carry a gun."

"Why?" I had definite issues with people who just carried concealed weapons around. I wasn't a card-carrying member of the NRA for a reason.

He snorted, as if I couldn't possibly be serious. "Why not?"

I didn't want to get drawn into a gun-control argument with someone who just exercised his second amendment right in Max's kitchen. Staring him down, I crossed my arms and waited.

"Well, for one, it's kind of like my sidearm. I was in the Marines for twelve years, and I just never got used to not having a gun with me. I also need it, in my line of work. Max isn't my only client. But this is the first time there have been other vampires here that he didn't tell me about. Usually, he'll give me a heads-up when blood-sucking guests are going to be here. That's why I attacked you guys, because as far as I know, you're not supposed to be here."

"Well, you're wrong. Max offered us a place to stay. But still, a gun? Why not a stake?" I realized I still had him cornered on the floor. There was a small first aid kit in the odds-and-ends drawer in the island—nothing that could help me with Nathan's wounds—and I retrieved it. "Have a seat, and I'll bandage your hand."

"Thanks, I'd appreciate that." He slid onto one of the stools, glancing ruefully over the pots and pans littering the floor. "Hell of a fighter, your boyfriend."

"He's my sire," I said, not elaborating any further on the messed-up nature of the relationship between Nathan and I. The guy might have just ambushed us in our sleep, but he didn't deserve that kind of punishment.

I opened the first aid kit and took his hand in mine. His knuckles were swollen and split, and I felt a little sick knowing I'd caused the damage. Still, Nathan was far more damaged. I looked to him, and he gave me a weak wave from his spot on the floor. His face was gray, but he'd dropped the towel and I saw that the bleeding had stopped. I faced Bill again. "You haven't answered my question."

"I don't carry a stake because it's not a sure thing. A gun, I can shoot and take someone down, at least long enough to get the hell away from them. With a stake, you've got to hit the heart. I'm not a doctor. I don't know where somebody's heart would be." He winced as I swabbed the blood from his hands with a disinfectant pad. "I mean, really, do you think you know where the human—sorry, vampire—heart is?"

"Yes. But I'm a doctor." I dabbed at a particularly nasty cut and reached into the first aid kit for some bandages. "So, you deal with vampires you don't trust and feel the need to arm yourself. Sounds like you should make a career change."

He chuckled, and there was an edge of bitterness to it. "This pays better than anything I could get. The job market is tough."

"So is the market for blood donors, I guess. Since you have to service more than one vampire." I eyed the cooler. "So, exactly how much blood do you have left in your body, if you don't mind my asking?"

He grinned. "You're a smart lady. Okay, you caught me. It's not all my blood. I get it from other donors, ones who don't mind providing so long as they don't have to deal with actual vampires. I take it, and give it a little markup for my troubles."

I shook my head. Was nothing sacred anymore? "You profit from trafficking human blood?"

"Got by honest means." He nodded to his injured hand. "And really, it's not like I don't have my fair share of trouble trying to deliver the stuff. What are you two doing here, anyway? Where's Max?"

"Max is…" I hesitated. Not knowing exactly what kind of guy Bill was, I didn't want to tell him that Max was the first vampire in known history to father a baby, or that he'd used that awesome power to knock up a werewolf. "Indisposed. I don't know when he's coming back. There are some strange things happening in the vampire world lately, and Nathan and I needed a place to hide out."

Good girl, Nathan sent across the blood tie. He had a way of saying something like that without sounding completely patronizing. My heart, which was slowly thawing out from the death of my fledgling, warmed a little at Nathan's approval.

Apparently, Bill accepted my answer. He cleared his throat and asked, "So, Nathan is your sire and your name is?"

"I'm Carrie." I frowned down at his hand. Bandages never stuck right to joints.

"I'd shake your hand, but you've already crushed my other one." He looked around the kitchen. "So, if you're staying here, you need blood. I can cut you a good deal."

I shook my head. "Even after we beat you up?"

"I don't know what fight you were watching, but I had your sire pinned. Human on vampire, that's got to count for something."

"I was suitably impressed." It was very strange, how easily he had gotten me to trust him. He was either a genuinely nice person, or a master manipulator. The thought made me uncomfortable. "Listen, the other vampires you…service…are they affiliated with the Voluntary Vampire Extinction Movement, by any chance?"

He nodded. "Some of them *were*."

"They haven't had any communication from other members, either?" My heart sank. Scores of Movement vampires out there and no way to contact them. And if they were anything like Nathan had been when he'd been under the Movement's control, they would just sit tight and wait for word, as they'd been trained to do.

The Voluntary Vampire Extinction Movement had been the final word in the battle between good vampires versus bad vampires—until a really bad vampire blew it up. But before their headquarters went *kablooie,* vampires had two choices: join the Movement and follow their rules, or don't and they'd kill you. In return for the privilege of not being killed, Movement vampires killed the vampires who didn't follow the rules. If we could find Movement members who were still committed to the organization's ideals, we could put together a fighting force capable of wiping out the Soul Eater and any of his cronies who might be hanging around. But the Movement had never established any kind of communications system outside of their own records, and with good reason. When a vampire went bad—and some did—they didn't need to have the names and addresses of their new enemies. Still, in an emergency like this it made it impossible that we'd find enough support to even put a dent in the Soul Eater's plan. There was no way to prove that a vampire we might meet worked for the Movement, or the Soul Eater. Of course, I was a non-Movement vampire, and so was Nathan. But I knew we were okay. When it came to networking, hearing someone was aligned with the Movement was like a seal of approval. Non-Movement vampires could be good, but they could be very, very bad, and I liked to err on the side of caution.

Nathan pulled himself to his feet, wincing, and shuffled over to the island in a stooped-over kind of walk. I wanted to admonish him for not resting, but his signature look of single-minded determination stopped me from saying anything. "We need you to supply us with the names of your customers," he said, so curtly that I wanted to tack on a "please" to soften the sharp edges of his command.

Bill appeared to be of the same mind as me, because he snorted at the request and shook his head. "No. Even though you asked so sweetly, I have a privacy policy with my clients that I can't break. It would ruin my reputation and my business."

"Listen, you were the one who came in here, armed, and shot me." Nathan gestured to his stomach, where the wound was now pink and tight and shiny. "Maybe you should give us, the injured parties, some kind of recompense. And as for confidentiality, you have no idea the kind of danger we're involved in. Just knowing that we're here, well…let's just say we vampires have our own ways of keeping our affairs private." He changed his face, though I could see it took a lot of his already taxed strength, and stepped closer to Bill.

I knew Nathan would never kill a human. He might knock one out and throw him out the door, maybe scare him a bit, but not kill him, no matter how we'd been threatened. It wasn't Nathan's way. But Bill didn't know that. He paled a little, then regained some of his confidence. "Buddy, I was in the Corps. You're not going to intimidate me with a pair of fangs and a few threats."

A smile twitched at the corner of Nathan's mouth. "Yes, I see you're a very tough guy. Especially when taking on an unarmed vampire."

There's a point in every tense situation where someone loses their stomach for the argument and gives in. Bill had reached his. Nathan took my seat at the kitchen island while I went to the refrigerator—to get some blood for Nathan, to replace what he'd lost, and something, preferably alcoholic, for Bill, whose hands trembled as he drummed his fingers on the tabletop.

"I'm not usually in the habit of attacking people," Bill said apologetically. "But since the Movement fell apart, it's been a little like the Wild West in the city."

Nathan made a casual shrug, but I saw how he watched Bill. He would note every breath, every twitch, to analyze later.

Bill continued, oblivious to Nathan's scrutiny. "I'd lay even money that Chicago isn't the only place getting weird. Am I right?"

"You're probably right. We've only been here, and

where we came from." Nathan shrugged. "Which is why I could really stand to talk to some of your other customers."

"I don't know." Bill took a swallow of liquor. "I'd have to find someone willing to talk. But you guys…how do I know you're not going to bust in and kill them? I mean, I just met you." He stopped, a wry smile on his mouth. "I'm not sure I want to vouch for you. I don't know you all that well and maybe I don't want to be involved in whatever you're involved in. I've already heard rumors of some Soul guy trying to become a supervamp. I really don't want to get tangled up in that."

"Supervamp?" I blurted, at the same time Nathan shouted, "You heard what?"

Bill looked back and forth at the two of us, frozen in indecision. "I'm not sure who I should answer first."

"What do you know about Jacob Seymour?" Nathan asked, overlapping my, "When did you hear this?"

"I don't know him. All I know is that every vampire in the city is either working for this Soul guy, or they get killed by him. And the last time I heard mention of him was a couple of days ago, at a bar downtown." Bill shook his head vehemently and said, "I don't want to get involved."

"You became involved when you shot me," Nathan said, reaching to squeeze the other man's shoulder in a gesture of camaraderie. "Now, you just have to decide your level of involvement. If you give us the names of your clients and leave, you're not too involved."

"And yet there's still the problem of losing my liveli-hood." Bill laughed. "No, thanks. Look, I'll do some work around here for you, same as I did Max. He's still paying me, after all. And I'll spy on my other clients. But

I'm not going to hand over their names and compromise their safety. I work for good people."

Nathan leaned back, letting his arm drop. "Fair enough. Let's set down our terms." He opened a drawer on the island, then looked dismayed that it contained only kitchen gadgets. "Carrie, do you have a pen?"

"I'm sure there's one in the mess on the dining room floor," I said, backing to the door. I wanted to keep an eye on Bill for as long as possible. "Scream if you need me."

I wasn't sure I trusted Bill. He had that smooth, friendly way about him that most con men worked hard to perfect. Maybe I was just being cynical, but I never trusted people like that. Plus, something he'd said had set off alarms in my brain. Every vampire in the city was either working for the Soul Eater or had been killed by him. Which meant if Bill was still in business, he was working with the Soul Eater's goons.

I found a pen in the rubble of the dining room, and paper in a drawer of the sideboard. I hurried back to the kitchen, where Nathan drew up a list of "terms" for both sides. He requested that Bill not breathe a word of our presence in the city, and promised to match anyone's offer of payment for that information. Of course, we had no money, but there was no reason to tell him that. I suggested that Bill make us a priority over his other clients. And Bill asked simply that we "not act like assholes."

"Good idea," Nathan agreed.

"Most of my clients don't talk business in front of me. In fact, most of my clients don't talk *to* me." Bill glanced from Nathan to me. "I'm a little intimidated by the idea of spying. Not that any of them would do anything to me. They're all as meek as kittens."

"I'm sure," Nathan agreed drily.

Bill spread his hands. "I just don't want you to think I'm going to waltz in here with a ton of information in two weeks."

"We'll cross that bridge when we come to it," Nathan told him, sounding menacing and reassuring at the same time. "But if you tell anyone that we're here, and what we've asked you about, I can guarantee you'll come away from this place with more than a bruised-up hand."

Since we'd pretty much covered everything and made all the threats we could reasonably make, we all sealed the deal with an awkward three-way handshake.

"What do you think?" I asked Nathan later as I stood at the windows in the library, watching the traffic pass on the street below. The sun had set, but twilight kept the sidewalk around Grant Park bright with a diffused glow. In the reflection in the glass, I saw myself, just as blond and pale and plain as ever, and Nathan, coming to stand behind me, all brooding dark, like an undead Heathcliff with his mussed black hair and hard, chiseled features.

He wrapped his arms around my waist and leaned his face close to mine, so that his deep voice, softly accented with his native Scots Gaelic, stirred my hair and tickled my ear. "I don't know. I think that we will either find information that will be helpful to us and get us into a lot of trouble, or we'll find information that isn't helpful to us and we'll still get into a lot of trouble."

"Trouble is inevitable." I turned and stepped out of his embrace, putting some distance between us. Being close to Nathan always affected my judgment. "Do we really need to find it for ourselves? You've already been shot. Speaking of which, let me look at it." I crossed the space between us and reached for the bottom of his T-shirt. I pulled up the fabric to see the wound, nearly healed, just a paler patch of white against his normal pallor. "It looks okay. Thank God."

He pulled his shirt down, a little reluctantly, as if he didn't want to break the contact of my fingers against his skin. "It's like any wound. Nothing to be alarmed about."

"Nothing to be alarmed about? Nathan, I would be worried if you had a paper cut, let alone a gunshot wound." I rubbed my temples to ease a headache I didn't have, but I suspected I would later on. "I'm worrying needlessly, aren't I?"

"It's nice to be worried about," he assured me. The corners of his eyes crinkled when he fake smiled the way he was now. "Really, it's just nice to know you still worry about me."

I didn't respond with more than a smile. He wanted a different answer, that much was clear. But I wasn't in a position to give it to him.

It was the story of our relationship, it seemed. From the moment we'd met, we'd both been on very different pages with each other. At first, he'd been in love with his dead wife, and I'd been enthralled by Cyrus, my first sire. When I'd finally gotten over that—and Nathan had accidentally resired me and saved my undead life by giving me his blood after I was attacked by Cyrus—Nathan realized he wasn't anywhere near finished grieving for his lost wife. Then, when he finally was, Cyrus had come back into my life, and departed it just as quickly and painfully. Every day I began to appreciate more the way Nathan must have felt when I had pressed him again and again to give me love he just hadn't felt. I wasn't whole enough to give him love now, but I could certainly give him sympathy.

"Ah, well," he said to break the awkwardness between us. Still, I couldn't think of anything to say, so I was relieved when Nathan's cell phone chirped.

"Nathan Grant," he said after he'd flipped the phone open. I'll never understand why men always seem to answer the phone that way, stating their names instead of just saying "hello." I shook my head as I turned toward the fireplace. *A fire might be nice, in the morning.*

I heard the soft drum of something falling to the carpet, and I turned. Nathan stood, empty-handed, the phone still open on the floor. He stared at it as though it were a talking frog or a shimmering mirage, something you hear about but never see. A mixture of fear, disbelief and, strangely, happiness warred on his face.

As he made no move to pick up the phone, I knelt and lifted it to my ear.

The voice through the speaker was tinny and broken by static, but a chill of recognition ran up my spine. "Hello? Hello? Nate, are you still there? Dad?"

It was Ziggy.

Two: Unhappy Returns

"Scusilo, dove è il deposito di pattino?"

"That sounds terrible. Your accent is all wrong."

Max turned from the mirror and pulled his headphones from his ear, hitting the pause button on his iPod. "You know, your 'helpful' criticism really isn't helping. We've been here three weeks and I still can't talk to anyone. It doesn't hurt to try and learn something new."

With a sympathetic look, Bella held out her arms, and Max crossed the bedroom to join her on their bed. The French doors to the balcony stood open and afternoon sunshine poured in. He stepped around a band of it on the floor, forgetting, as usual, that he no longer needed to fear it. Taking a deep breath, he walked through the warm rays and slid onto the crisp white bedspread.

"Why do you always do that?" Bella asked, her voice still rough from sleep. She slept all the time lately, but Max couldn't fault her for it. It was common, apparently, for pregnant women to be exhausted, and he guessed that doubled for pregnant women who were recuperating from nearly mortal injuries, as well.

"I don't know," he admitted, turning his gaze back to the sunlit windows. "I just always have my fingers crossed."

His full change from vampire to half-vampire, half-werewolf hybrid creature—the word *lupin* was as hated as he'd expected it would be in a werewolf pack, so he never used it—had been more gradual than he would have liked. The worst part was, they'd had no idea what traits would stick until after he'd actually shifted into his wolf form. After that, a whole world of weirdness opened up to him, and between hairier legs and a sadistic urge to pull riders off their bicycles and devour them, the vampiric aversion to sunlight had somehow vanished.

It had been a fortunately happy accident that they'd discovered it at all. From the moment they'd arrived to, in Max's opinion, a hostile welcome in Italy, members of Bella's family had made it very clear that no concessions to his vampirism would be made. And, since the family—the entire family—lived in the same, window-covered villa on a sunny, sun-drenched cliff, he'd found himself confined to Bella's bedroom every day. Only when one of Bella's "well-meaning" aunts had come into the room while they slept and opened the curtains, flooding the room with frying light, had he realized that he no longer had to worry about such "well-meaning" people burning him to death with UV rays.

He'd also realized that it would take a lot more than Bella's love for him to convince her family he was an okay guy. Hence the studying Italian, so that he could fit in and also, admittedly, so he could tell what they were saying about him.

More importantly, he'd realized that he really didn't give a damn about what they might try to do to him. He was actually, really, truly in love with the woman who was carrying his child, and, despite having to drink blood and change into a wolf at the full moon, he felt more normal than he had in years.

He dipped his face to sniff Bella's neck and planted a kiss on her sleep-warmed skin. Rather than simply patting his thigh and rolling away from him, as she had been doing for the past few weeks, she stretched her neck and writhed her body against his. *Jackpot.*

He loved her. God, did he love her. And he understood that pregnancy could be rough on a woman, even one as strong as Bella. But it had been a long, long time, and he was only...not human.

"So, is this official, or are we just getting my hopes up to dash them again?" He smiled against her neck and gave her jaw a playful nip, so she would know he was half joking. And he ground his hard-on into her hip, so she would know he was half-serious, too.

Bella laughed, a sound that was so oddly delicate coming from a creature that was all dark and smoky. "If I told you now, that would spoil the fun."

"You're a devious bitch, aren't you?" He slid one hand down the length of her body, bunching the white satin of her nightgown higher by fractions, revealing the tight, olive-tinged skin over her thighs. He danced his fingers from her hip to her knee, watching her face for any flicker of change. "Can you feel that?"

She moaned a little and gave a nod, and relief clutched in his chest. The car accident that had paralyzed her while they'd been in pursuit of the Oracle had at first left her with no feeling below the waist. The doctors who'd examined her in Italy had warned him that the loss of sensation might be permanent, and Max, stupid, stupid man that he acknowledged he was, had only been worried about whether or not she would be able to have sex again. He knew he wouldn't want to live a life condemned to never getting off again, that was for damned sure.

Luckily, they'd already discovered that wouldn't be a problem for her.

Moving her legs gently apart, he pushed the nightgown to her waist. Her fingers worked fast, undoing the button and then the zipper of his jeans, letting him spring eagerly into her soft, warm hands. He almost came right then, just from being touched after so long. "I have to be inside you," he groaned, and she whimpered her agreement into his ear as he leaned over her. The tip of his cock was poised, trembling, at the glistening pink core of her and he pushed in, taking it slow, just a centimeter at a time it seemed. So painstakingly slow that he ground his teeth to keep from ramming hard into her. It took more willpower than he'd known he had to ignore her pleas to go faster. There was no way he was going to mess this up, not after the wait he'd had. Just a few moments more and he'd be home, encased in her sweet, clutching body. All he needed was infinite patience…

A voice and violent banging on the door brought everything to a crashing halt.

Infinite patience, and for all of his in-laws to die in a horrible explosion that rained body parts all over the picturesque Italian countryside.

"Oh, no," Bella said softly, though her voice held more disappointment at the interruption than dismay over the words muffled by the door. "My father needs to see you."

"Now?" He thought they called Italian a romance language. Words to summon him away from imminent sexual pleasure shouldn't even exist in it.

Bella gave him a sympathetic nod and he reluctantly withdrew, reminding himself firmly that grown men do not cry. "Fine. Tell this guy I'm on my way."

If there was one thing he'd learned about pack life, it was that when the *paterfamilis* called, you answered, or else…well, there was no "else." You just did it.

Bella yelled something to the door, and the banging stopped. "You should hurry. He is not in a pleasant mood lately."

"I wonder why," Max muttered, pulling her nightgown down so that she was decently covered again. He let his hand linger a moment on her stomach, which had been flat before and now bowed just slightly out in a hard little bump. It was hard to imagine a whole person fitting in there, even one that looked like the tiny shrimp he'd seen on the ultrasound picture.

He stood and zipped his jeans, hoping his erection would calm down, fast. Nothing got on a man's bad side faster than obvious, physical evidence that you'd just been fucking his daughter. "Do you need anything before I go?"

Bella smoothed her nightgown, repeating Max's action of petting her stomach. "Send for my cousin. Maybe I will take a walk."

Max arched an eyebrow at her.

"I will take a wheel, then," she said with a laugh, and threw a pillow at him as he retreated through the door.

The man waiting outside, a skinny, swarthy guy in a faded Van Halen T-shirt, was a runner, a lower-ranking member of the pack who carried messages for the family. Usually, Max had learned, runners weren't related to the pack or they were family members in disgrace, and he wondered how long it would be before he ended up an errand boy. "Go get one of Bella's cousins. She wants some company."

The man said something that Max guessed sounded affirmative and went off on his way, leaving Max to his awkward visit.

It wasn't that Max didn't like Bella's father. After all, he'd granted Max safe haven and let him stay with Bella. That alone was deserving of eternal gratitude. But the man knew it, and he was definitely going to cash in the eternal gratitude coupon as much as possible. He had also made it clear that Max was staying on a trial basis, and could be kicked out on his half-werewolf ass at any time.

The house—the "den," as the pack called it—was the kind of place that made Max wish he'd managed his money better, so he could have one all to himself. Not that his digs back in Chicago had been shabby, but this place made the penthouse look like a condemned building full of sick cats. It was built on a cliff overlooking Lake Lugano. From the drive, it appeared to be a long, low, Roman-style villa. For all Max knew, it dated back to actual Roman times. Inside, though, it was way, way bigger, just the tip of an iceberg that carved into the cliff face. Most of the time, you couldn't tell you were underground, owing to the windows facing out at the lake, but the lowest floor was windowless, the walls unfinished rock. Bella's father kept his meeting rooms in that section of the house, and there weren't any elevators, so Max had to trudge down eight flights of stairs, quickly, to get where he was going. The pack leader's meeting room was kind of a throne room, with guarded doors and all that medieval jazz. He gave his name and waited to be allowed inside.

The smooth marble columns flanking the doorway were the last bit of added ornamentation. The meeting room was a cave. Max couldn't tell if it was a natural one or if it had been blasted out to accommodate the pack leader. The furniture was comfortable and modern and very European, but moisture trickled down the walls and the whole place definitely smelled like it was underground.

"Ah, Maximilian." The pack master stood in the middle of the room in his sleek tailored suit, trying hard to look pleased to see his daughter's vampire boyfriend.

Lupin, Max reminded himself, then struck the word from his mental vocabulary again as Bella had taught him. *Vampire-werewolf hybrid.*

"Pack Master," he replied. "You wanted to see me?"

A polite smile creased the man's face as he crossed the room. He looked oddly similar and at the same time very different than Bella. She'd inherited her father's exotic, tipped-up eyes, though hers were golden and his gleamed black. His hair was as midnight dark as hers, but it was white at the temples and wavy. Bella's was as straight as a line. They had the same gestures, which must have been genetic, and the same lithe grace that Max had wrongly assumed all werewolves possessed.

"I did want to see you," the man said, coming closer. "And call me Julian. We are family now, are we not?"

"We are," Max agreed. He would agree with anything Julian said, because to disagree might mean banishment, and banishment would mean being apart from Bella, forever. That was something he wasn't willing to risk.

As if reminded by his own words of their connection, Julian delicately sniffed the air. His expression hardened for a moment, then the mask of expedience glazed his face in false friendship again. "And how is my daughter?"

It was a sick little pleasure, to know the man smelled her on him, to have that sort of olfactory flag to wave and silently shout, "She's mine now." But Max kept his features neutral. "Happy. Happier than I think she's been in a long time."

Julian nodded. "I will go directly to my point, then." He hadn't even asked Max to sit down. "You must return to the United States. Tomorrow."

Max almost choked on the torrent of curses that rose in his throat. All he managed to say was, "Why?"

With a sympathetic smile, Julian shook his head. "Not forever. Do not despair. But the child my daughter carries is a weapon, as you have said. And the man who desires this weapon is still very likely to come into his power and claim the child."

Shit. Of course, the Soul Eater was still out there. And he was still an evil bastard. And he would still want to get his hands on the baby. "I've got friends back in the States who are taking care of that whole mess."

"Maximilian, may I be frank with you?" Julian asked, as if he hadn't been so already.

Max steeled himself for whatever the man would say next. It probably wouldn't be something he wanted to hear.

"You are not one of us. My daughter has feelings for you, and whatever is between the two of you is enough to earn you my mercy. But my concern for Bella's safety, eh, trumps, I believe is the word, any concern for her happiness." He steepled his fingers at his mouth and appeared to consider his next words. "I will not remind you of my responsibility to the pack, and the consequences that would befall them if this Soul Eater were to come after the baby."

But you just did, Max thought irritably. "I understand your concern. But Jacob can't use the baby until he's become a god. He wants her for her destiny, and I'm guessing that destiny won't come into play until at least preschool, right? In the meantime, I don't understand how my leaving Bella when she needs me most will ultimately benefit her. I mean, there is no one in this pack who will fight harder to keep her safe."

Julian's face turned to stone. "I do not think that is correct."

He hadn't come to argue. But he was sure as hell not leaving Bella behind. "No. If I go, she leaves with me."

"Maximilian, this is not permanent." Julian laughed, as if it had been clear from the very beginning and Max had just been too stupid to figure it out. "If you say this vampire will have no interest in my grandchild until after he's become a god, then I believe you. But I wish for you to see that even this small victory for him is prevented. If he is defeated, and if you survive, then you will be welcome to return to my daughter."

So that was it. He was being shipped off in the hopes that he wouldn't return. "I'm not a vampire anymore. I'm a werewolf. Vampire hybrid," he added quickly, before Julian could shoot him down as an outsider. "How do you know anyone is still going to want to include me in their plans?"

Julian spread his hands and smiled, as if he knew he had his prey cornered. Not cornered. Served on a platter. "I trust that you will be able to find a place in this fight. Besides, did you not just assert that you would do anything to keep my daughter safe?"

Max didn't have an answer to that.

"Your plane will leave in the morning. Try and break the news gently to my daughter." And then Julian left. Left Max standing there in the cavernous room, left him holding the bag. How was he going to tell Bella that her father was sending him away to die?

On the other hand, Max thought as he stalked angrily back to Bella's room, *there's no way Nathan and Carrie won't be involved in this thing. And if Julian is making noise about it right now, something is going on.*

He couldn't stand by and let his friends finish what he'd helped to start. But he couldn't leave Bella.

Of course, he knew what she would say if he told her. Go, help them, go where you are needed. Go and be the warrior you are supposed to be. It was a big argument for just not telling her. The argument against not telling her was that he respected her, damn it. It didn't make sense, considering that a few short months ago he would have liked nothing more than to jam a screwdriver into her ear, but now she was the mother of his child. Also, the love of his life. Hell, even memories of his sire had begun to fade gently into the background since Max had realized how much he loved Bella. He had to tell her why he would be leaving, because he couldn't lie to her.

He came to their room just as two of Bella's aunts were on their way out. They gave him shifty looks as he entered and one muttered under her breath, probably complaining that he hadn't knocked on the door, but they looked relieved at the same time. It was starting to appear that his outplacement was a group decision.

Bella was on the balcony, still clothed in her white nightgown, but wrapped in an equally pristine terry cloth robe. Her long, black hair was unbound, spilling down the sides of her face and over her shoulders in dark slashes.

"The wind off the lake is cold," he said, and she didn't startle at his sudden reappearance.

"I like to be in the sun. And the cold does not bother me." She wrapped her arms protectively around her stomach and smiled up at him. "And she is warm enough in here."

She'll be in piss-poor shape if her mother dies of pneumonia, Max thought, but he didn't say it. He didn't want to spend some of what could be their last day together arguing. "Listen, I have to talk to you about something."

"Oh?" Bella gestured gracefully to the other lounge chair, closer to the railing.

Max pulled the chair up close to Bella's, though he wasn't sure he'd ever be close enough to her. The thought of spending mornings away from her, of not waking to her beautiful smile, her warm, clean scent… He pushed those grim thoughts aside. "You know, he's still out there."

He saw her chest hitch in a sharply drawn breath, but

she caught it before it could make a sound and pretended—badly—not to comprehend. "Who?"

Better to do it like ripping off a Band-Aid. "The Soul Eater. He's still out there, and he's still going to go through with the ritual that will make him a god."

"What does this have to do with us?" Bella's voice held a note of steel, as if she could will Max's past to vanish. "You are no longer one of them. It is not your concern."

He smiled and pushed some of her hair off her face. The very first time he'd seen her, she'd been wearing her hair back. She'd always worn it that way, scraped back from her face so severely that her skin had looked tight. It had made her seem hard, and she was, to people who didn't know her. But now Max knew her, and he saw the currents below her deceptively smooth surface. She was frightened for him, and for their child, and she looked as vulnerable and young as he knew she was.

"You're right. I'm not one of them. But I'm half of them," he reminded her, and he dropped his hand to place it over the bump of her abdomen. "And she's half, too. I don't want to take the chance of his goons waltzing in here and grabbing you. I'm going back to the States to get this all sorted out."

She whipped her head up sharply to glare at him. "You will leave me here?"

"I'm not going to drag you into a war zone. I'm sorry." He looked away, to the vast expanse of black water on the lake. "If I don't go, and he becomes a god, I'll be here, trying to protect you from a god. If I go, and we can beat him, yeah, I'll be away from you, but you'll be safe."

"My father put you up to this." She said it flatly, providing no room for him to argue.

And it was damned tempting to say, "Yeah, your father is a real prick and he's sending me to fight the Soul Eater knowing that the odds are pretty good I won't be coming back." But what good would that do? He'd still get sent away, still might die, and then Bella would be estranged from the one person who had the power to protect her. Not that her anger toward her father would stop him from watching over her—in fact, it might make her a virtual prisoner for the rest of her life, and that was something else Max just couldn't accept.

"He didn't put me up to it. We talked out this solution together." It ground his guts to have to make the man look decent through a lie, but Max forged on. "Besides, you know that Nathan and Carrie will still be involved. They'll need me."

"If they are still alive," Bella snapped, then her expression softened. "I am sorry. I do not mean to speak evil thoughts out loud. But you do not know where they are or how they fared in their mission. And you cannot do this thing alone."

They sat in silence, both staring out at the lake, the occasional foam cap peaking on the dark surface. The wind had picked up. Bella's hair whirled in it and slapped against her face.

"Let's get you inside," Max said quietly, and before she could argue he lifted her into his arms.

"You are right. You have to go," she said as he settled her onto the bed. "It would be against everything you believe to leave your friends in peril. And it would be against everything I believe to be with a man who would do that to the people he cared for."

He lay down beside her and took her hands in his, frowning down at his, the way his missing fingers and gnarled scars seemed grotesque against her perfect skin. "I'm glad you have so much faith in me. Because I'd much rather stay with you."

She lifted his hands to her mouth and pressed a kiss to each of his palms. "No. You would go where your friends needed you."

He wanted to argue, but she opened her mouth and sucked one of his fingertips inside, swirling her tongue around it. She laughed at his groan and released him, her hands wandering down, over his chest, to lift his T-shirt.

"Finishing what you started earlier?" Max asked, trying to keep the hopefulness out of his voice. "Because otherwise, this is just cruel."

Her golden eyes glittered as she slipped her fingers inside the waist of his jeans. "I cannot let you leave without a proper goodbye."

He couldn't say he didn't agree.

Three: Resurrected

<hr/>

"Hello? Is anybody there?"

There was no way it was possible. Ziggy was dead. I'd seen him die—or had I? Nathan had told me of his death, but I'd never checked. Still, there was no way he could have survived the injuries. No human could have.

Please, God, no.

Nathan took the phone from my shaking hands. I could hear Ziggy calling, "Are you still there? Is anyone still there?" over the line.

Nathan heard it, too. I covered my mouth and nose with both hands, eyes wide as I watched him. Slowly, he lifted the phone to his ear. I watched his face as he listened. One moment he stood before me, holding the phone, listening to his dead son's voice imploring him to talk to him. The next, his knees shook, collapsing him to the floor. He held the phone like a drowning man clutching a piece of debris after a shipwreck, unable to believe his luck, terrified he'd lose his hold on the one thing saving his life at the moment.

Ziggy's pleading on the line halted. My heavy breathing seemed to only heighten the tense silence. I caught the tinny whisper of Ziggy's voice in Nathan's ear. "Dad?"

Nathan's lips pulled back in a grimace or a smile—I couldn't tell which—as his shoulders shook with silent sobs and he covered his eyes with his hand. "I'm here," he managed, his voice strangled.

"Don't cry. Christ, Nate, don't cry." Even at reduced volume, I could tell Ziggy struggled to follow his own command.

Nathan's emotions overwhelmed him to the point he couldn't stop them from slamming into me like waves in a storm. I'd never stopped to imagine what I would feel if, after believing them lost forever, someone I loved, my parents, perhaps, could suddenly come back into my life. To know exactly how it felt—relief so sharp it cut through the cascade of doubt, hope shadowed by fear, a million questions meshing and conforming until they incapacitated the mind totally—wasn't a gift. It was a burden. I staggered backward a few steps to one of the chairs and fell into it.

Nathan pulled in a shuddering breath, but he still couldn't speak without tears clouding his voice. "Where are you?"

I didn't hear Ziggy's answer, but I felt Nathan's sharp shift in emotion. He was afraid. Terrified. "You have to get out of there, now. The Soul Eater will be looking for me. I don't want him to find you instead."

"He's at the apartment?" I whispered. Of course he would have gone there. But why hadn't he gone home before now?

"I don't care if you think you can handle yourself, get

out of there now!" Nathan growled. It was a little comical, the way he lapsed into full-on dad mode so quickly.

Something horrible pulled at the back of my mind. Some vague, terrible knowledge that wouldn't come readily to the surface, as though I wasn't ready to know it. "Nathan…"

"I'm going to give you directions to somewhere we can meet up." He ignored me. "What do you mean, you can't come right now?"

"Nathan, something about this isn't right." I held out my hand. "Hang up the phone."

He covered the phone with his palm. "No, I won't hang up!" Returning the phone to his ear, he demanded, "Stay right where you are, I'm coming to get you."

I watched with growing dread as Nathan folded up the phone. No goodbye. He couldn't tell his son goodbye, when he'd done it more permanently once before. Turning to me, he said, more gruffly than he probably intended, "Stay here. I've got to go get Ziggy."

As he brushed past me without waiting for an answer, I grabbed his elbow. "Nathan, wait!"

"What?" He jerked his arm back. It hurt me to see the impatience in his eyes, knowing I would have to tell him that I sensed a trap.

"This isn't right. Why didn't Ziggy contact us before now?" I wasn't sure I believed it wasn't Ziggy, but I wasn't sure I believed it was him, either. "Please, think about this!"

"The only thing there is to think about is that my son is alive!" He stalked up the stairs to the second level of the library, where the doors were.

I followed him, pushing words past my puffing breaths as I ran after him. "Exactly! Why do you think he's alive?

There were two other vampires in that room besides us when Ziggy died. Why do you think he's alive now?"

"I know this!" He whirled, catching me off guard, and I stumbled. He didn't see it, though, too focused on the time that was slipping away from him. "Do you think I didn't realize it the moment I heard his voice? But I've got to go, Carrie. He's my son!"

I couldn't argue with that. But it still wasn't right, still didn't make any sense. Why now, after all this time? "Please, don't go. There are other ways of contacting him. But going alone, when you don't know where he's been or what he's been doing…that's crazy, Nathan."

"You think he's going to betray me?" His expression grew colder than I'd ever thought possible. "Do you think my son is going to stab me in the back?"

"I think," I began, choosing my words carefully, "I think that you know as well as I what a sire's influence can make a fledgling do. We know that Dahlia was somewhere on the grounds being turned. She would have been too weak to make another vampire. Cyrus didn't make him. I would have seen it when I sired him. So that leaves the Soul Eater. You said yourself he forced you to do things you didn't want to do."

The war between dying anger and acceptance raged for a few seconds in Nathan's eyes. I prayed common sense would win, but some primal, protective instinct in Nathan forced a curse from his lips and he stalked out of the room.

Something desperate welled up inside me. I didn't want him to go to Ziggy. He could get killed. And I didn't want another person in Nathan's life.

Do you hear yourself, the way you're thinking? I scolded myself. *It's his son. His son!*

But I didn't care. All I cared about was the sadness, the crushing sadness I felt at the thought of him choosing someone else, anyone else, over me. I didn't know where it came from, and I knew better than to try and justify it. I was acting like a big baby. I knew it—anyone who was privy to my deranged thought process would know it— but I couldn't stop myself. And above everything else, I hated being out of control.

I caught up with Nathan in the foyer. He didn't look at me, focusing instead on opening the coat closet and ri-fling through it. "I have to get on the road."

"On the road?" I glanced up at the shuttered window.

"Once I get a few things together. I don't want to leave unarmed." He pulled out a crossbow, one of the weapons we'd spirited across state lines hidden in a spare tire. "I'm going to get Ziggy."

I fought back the urge to tell him one last time not to go. I had to curb this ridiculous jealousy. I'd lost Nathan once—okay, probably countless times by now—and I didn't feel like doing it again.

"He asked me to meet him. Back in Grand Rapids. I'd ask you to go, but as you said, it might be—"

"A trap?" I forced the hands I'd placed on my hips firmly down to avoid appearing too confrontational. "You think?"

"My son is alive. And I'm going to go get him." His eyes were hard, daring me to argue with him further.

I don't respond well to dares. "Don't be stupid! Na-than, how much time has gone by? Why didn't he contact you before now? You know that if you go after him, you're going to end up dead. You're not thinking!"

"No, I'm not thinking about you!" He threw the crossbow down and it bounced with an earsplitting clatter on the marble floor. "You're pissed off because for a moment, my focus isn't on you. I've been Carrie-centric nonstop since the first night we met! How much longer do you expect me to hang on to you while you punish me?"

"Punish you?" The shrillness of my voice startled me. "Why am I punishing you?"

"I don't know! But ever since you came to Chicago with Max you've done nothing but punish me. I'm sorry, okay? Does that end this asinine vendetta you've had against me? I'm sorry that I couldn't love you at first sight and give up my memories of my wife and give up my love for my son. I'm sorry I couldn't get myself together for you on your time!"

"That's not what this is about!" I followed him as he stalked into the kitchen, barely caught the door before it swung back to slam into my face. "What have I done to you?"

He spun, face contorted in rage. "You slept with Cyrus! I'm not an idiot, and I can read your mind. You slept with Cyrus while I was possessed, then you left for Chicago because you thought we needed time apart. And when I came back, ready to tell you that, yes, I love you and I want to be with you, you ran off and you fucking sired him!"

"I didn't have a choice!" The fight had become like some sick exploratory surgery, cutting through scar tissue to see how deep it ran. I'd thought we were finished fighting over Cyrus, but Ziggy's sudden return from the grave seemed to have opened all kinds of old wounds.

I knew what he would come back at me with even as he spoke the words. "You did it because you wanted to. You get so lost and so desperate when the focus of someone else's life shifts from you, and you'll do anything to get it back. If you're constantly pulling me in two directions, begging me to be with you, pushing me away, then you've got your captive audience." His voice dropped, deadly soft in the deafening quiet of the room. "Now, I've helped you when no one else could. I helped you through your change. I helped you when you turned your back on me to go to Cyrus, and it cost me my son. I even helped you mourn his murderer. I've never asked for anything in return from you, but I'm damned sure you wouldn't give it, even if I did. So, I'm taking. I'm taking my focus off of you, to go and get my son and bring him here where he will be safe, with me. You can be as jealous as you want. You can hate me. But I'm not giving you anything else."

He went to the door without his weapons, just blind fury and determination, and left.

I wanted to run after him, to scream at him, but not to warn him of danger or assert that I had been right in the argument. Because just his mention of Cyrus had opened the blood tie I'd had to him in my mind. There was no connection at the other end. Cyrus was dead, lost in the watery blue world where vampires went when they died. It was raw, almost physically painful, like a severed nerve straining to reconnect with its missing end. Coupled with the stress already building in me, it bowled me over. I had to brace myself against the rail as I nearly fell down the stairs to the third-floor guest rooms. Everything was wrong. Surreal.

I stormed into the bedroom and stared in outrage at the curtains, the bed, the television. How dare those objects exist while I was in pain? How dare the drapes hang so perfectly, almost cheerfully stirring in the breeze from the central air?

The last time I'd been in Chicago, I'd been staying with Max, nursing my broken heart over Nathan. I'd been mourning then, too. Mourning my broken connection with Nathan, still mourning the loss of my normal life. And it was here, in this very room, that I'd called Cyrus, heard his voice.

I would never hear him again. Never hear the way his soft, cultured accent turned my name into a sinful prayer against my ear. Never feel his body pressed to mine. But it was more than just a sexual connection. I'd never been able to do the things I'd longed to when he was alive. I wanted to sit and dream of a future with him without thinking I was twisted. I wanted to lie in his arms and feel safe, not as though I should be on guard.

And I wanted Nathan. I would never stop wanting a life with him. I was torn in so many different directions at once, I wanted so many things that I couldn't have, could never have had even if circumstances had been perfect. And it made me angrier than I'd ever been before.

The pain and the rage built up inside me, forcing my mouth open in a silent scream. My chest constricted, allowing only a tiny breath to escape in a thin, high wail. It grew and deepened as the pain deepened, until I *was* screaming, and I rushed at the curtains, yanking them down. They tore easily, too easily, and I turned to the bed, my empty hands spasming open and closed until they fell on the duvet cover. I threw it from the bed, shredded it with my fingers, pulled handfuls of blanket and sheets away from the mattress. All the while I screamed, my chest caving in, my heart breaking all over. It would never end. I would feel this horrible feeling forever, I was sure.

My hands actually trembled from the force of the emotions that had been loosed, and I pressed my forehead to the carpet, feeling my cold breath bouncing back at me to chill the tears on my cheeks. There was more to think of now than my pain. Nathan's words had hurt. Not because he'd said them in anger, but because every one of them was true. I *was* selfish, I *was* jealous. I'd just never realized how deeply.

Had I slept with Cyrus that night in the van because I was genuinely disturbed by Nathan's suffering as he lay, possessed by his sire, upstairs? Or had I done it because I knew, in some dark part of my heart, that he would get better and the whole nasty business would come to light? And when it hadn't, at least, not right away, I'd run away with Max and almost slept with him, as well. And when none of that had worked, when Nathan had still seemed so close to giving me what I'd thought I'd wanted from him, I'd turned one of his worst enemies into my fledgling, brought him into Nathan's home.

All the while, I'd accused him of not being understanding, blamed him for making my life complicated. My God, had I ever been responsible for my own actions? Ever, in my entire life?

I dropped my head in my hands and let the tears come, beat myself down with memories of Nathan's kindness in the face of my selfishness. When I'd run from him, he'd pursued. When I'd destroyed things between us, again and again, he'd always been willing to rebuild. And I'd abused that, pushing further every time, trying to push him past the breaking point.

He'd broken, finally. I'd pushed him far enough, and he'd pushed back. I'd sent him running headfirst into a trap because I couldn't stop being so caught up in my own drama to support him in his.

The buzzer sounded, and my head snapped up. I ran to the foyer, mashed the intercom button and spoke, not caring how desperate my voice sounded. "Nathan?"

"No, it's Bill." He sounded embarrassed for me. "I left my cooler here. Can I come up and get it?"

"Yes, of course." I let go of the button, my mind racing. Nathan had walked into a trap, I was sure of it. And it was time for me to stop being selfish.

It was time for me to save Nathan, for a change.

"Well?" Dahlia tapped her foot. She wore those stupid slippers with the feather stuff around the toes, like she was some old-time movie star.

Ziggy folded up his phone. "He wants to meet at a safe place."

Dahlia snorted, lifting up a couch cushion that had been slashed by something. Probably a knife. Maybe a claw. The thought of those monsters coming here, tearing up the place…

It had been hard enough, coming back. Seeing the

place he'd called home for the tail end of his childhood abandoned and destroyed made it worse. And with Dahlia here. It was like betraying Nate before he *actually* betrayed him.

It's not betrayal, he thought angrily, feeling the sudden need to wipe tears from his eyes. He blinked them back. It wasn't betrayal. He had Jacob's word. All he had to do was deliver Nate, just to talk. No harm would come to him. And then Ziggy got his freedom, and everything could go back the way it was.

Only now, he'd be a vampire. It would make Nate's schedule easier to deal with.

"This place looked a lot better the last time I was here," Dahlia sniffed, arranging the cushions on the couch and sitting. "You know, when I tried to kill your dad?"

"Right. I remember." He squeezed his hands into fists. He wanted to kill her, had been wanting to for a while now. He pushed the rage down. It made him a monster, and he'd been Jacob's pet monster for way too long. "Let's get out of here."

"What? Don't you want to sit and reminisce? Go through your old things?" She paused to glance dramatically around the room. "Oh, gee…I don't see much left."

She wasn't as good at hurting him as she thought she was, but there was no arguing with her. "Shut up, let's get out of here."

"No, I'm curious. I wonder how long it took for him to move her in here, once you were gone." She giggled. "So, tell me, are you real jealous of her? You don't honestly expect me to believe you never had a little crush on dear old daddy."

He had his hand around her throat before she could move. She might have magic, but magic didn't work so well when your head was snapped off your neck, and he was definitely stronger. "If you ever fucking say that again, I'll kill you." He tossed her across the room, easy as throwing a doll. There were advantages to having a powerful sire. Advantages he wished to God he didn't have to know about.

Dahlia gagged and wiped blood from her lips as she stood. "Jacob would never let you. You might be the favorite, but I've got the power. He needs me."

"That's great, Dahlia. He won't let me kill you because you're a tool he can use. You must be real proud. Why won't he let you kill me?" That would get her. Jacob had barely spoken to her beyond giving orders since he'd given up on that stupid potion of hers. And she hated him for it. "Get your fat ass up. We're leaving."

She picked her way through the rubble of ruined books and furniture. "Fine. There's nothing here I'd want to keep anyway. Slut-tastic only wore 'sensible' clothes."

"Nice, Dahlia." He opened the door for her and resisted the urge to kick her down the stairs.

The car was waiting for them, the driver leaning against the door. It struck Ziggy for the first time how many human servants he interacted with every day, and how he never knew their names. Heck, he didn't even really look at them or wonder how the hell they started working for vampires.

"Are you going to open my door, or are you going to just stand there and stare at the man meat?" Dahlia pushed Ziggy aside and grabbed the handle of the door. "You gross me right out sometimes, you know."

I won't kill her. I won't kill her. He repeated the mantra all the way to the highway, leaning his forehead against the cold glass. Grand Rapids seemed empty and alien. It was just knowing that Nate wasn't there. He'd left. Even after the message he'd had Max relay to him. "I'm coming home. Wait for me. I'll be there in five days." How much clearer did he have to be? He knew Max wasn't the kind of guy to forget something that important. He would have at least mentioned, "Hey, by the way, your dead son isn't that dead." So, knowing Ziggy was alive, knowing what Jacob was like, why hadn't Nate waited for him?

Dahlia babbled on and on about something stupid. The girl's mouth never stopped running. When she was in his presence, it was usually "you're a fag this," and "you're a homo that." He could tune that out pretty easily. He'd even been able to shut her up for days at a time when he'd first started pointing out that he'd slept with Cyrus, making Dahlia's first vampire lover a "homo," too. Whenever she was around Jacob, though, butter wouldn't melt in her mouth. It was a perk to being crazy, Ziggy figured. It was easy to be different things to different people when there really were different people living in your head.

It was a trick he needed to learn. Especially around Jacob.

The car pulled off the South Beltline, onto 37, and took a right at the spot where it became a plain old two-lane road. They passed by some small houses, ranch style with aboveground swimming pools and swing sets in the yards. People lived there. Kids lived there. So close to evil, oblivious to its presence. He suppressed a shudder to think of those people and what would happen to them if Jacob got some sadistic whim to toy with them.

He would, eventually. He always had some fun new "game." "Come, play a game with me, favorite son," he would purr, and the game would always be something to make Ziggy feel dirty and used.

Jacob liked to watch.

"What the hell, you're not even listening to me." Dahlia puffed air between her pursed lips. "I swear, you're about the most boring person on the planet."

He snorted, leaning his head against the window. "What side of the conversation were *you* on?"

Dahlia mumbled something unintelligible. If it had sounded like a spell, he would have been more worried. Jacob had laid down some strict rules about her spell casting, but, as Dahlia often liked to point out in these situations, Jacob wasn't there.

They pulled onto a dirt road, lined with cattails and other weeds that warned drivers not to stray from the path if they didn't want their car to be forever known as the swamp buggy.

The new digs Jacob had moved them into weren't as nice as the mansion. But since they'd been infiltrated once, it could happen again, and Jacob was nothing if not paranoid. They pulled off the road onto a little covered bridge that creaked as though it was seriously considering dumping the car into the swamp. It was dark as hell, and that was probably a good thing. He really didn't want to see what condition the wood was in, because he'd have to cross it again sometime. The rumbling of the wheels on the boards stopped and they emerged onto a rutted dirt two-track that wound through the swamp. The house, a sagging farm-house done up in plantation style, gleamed bone white in the moonlight. Two willow trees drooped in front of it, like the tattered edges of a corpse's Sunday suit.

"I hate this place," Dahlia said, and for a moment he felt some solidarity with her, until she followed up with, "It's so far from the mall."

"Yeah, that's the feature it's really lacking."

The car pulled up in front of the broken porch, and Ziggy didn't wait for the chauffeur to open his door. He slipped out and thumped up the steps, his boots ringing hollow on the rotted wood.

"Where are you going?" Dahlia stood by the car, a chubby hand on her round hip.

"Uh, inside. The opposite of outside, where the mosqui-toes are." He slapped at one that had taken an interest in his neck—he wasn't sure if drinking his blood would make a mosquito a vampire, since they already kind of were—to illustrate his point. "I've got to tell Jacob what's going on and get permission to take some of *them* out with me."

"I want to come, too," she said petulantly. "It's not like you can control them the way I can."

Oh, hell no. "No, no way. You're not going along on this one."

Dahlia's eyes narrowed unpleasantly in her chubby face. "Well, we'll just see what Jacob has to say about that."

Ziggy had a pretty good idea what Jacob would say about it. That there was no way in hell Dahlia was going anywhere near his fledgling. Ziggy had already warned their sire of what Dahlia had done to Nathan in the past. "Yeah, let's go and talk to him."

"No. I'll go and talk to him." She smirked and jerked her chin toward the darkness behind the house. "It's your turn to feed them."

Ziggy wished the chill up his spine was from actual cold. But no. There was nothing he would rather not do than go into that filthy, stinking barn tonight. "Fine. Give Jacob my regrets, will ya?"

Of course she would. The bitch. Feeding them would keep him tied up long enough for her to climb onto Jacob's lap and beg and plead and promise all sorts of perverted things in order to wheedle her way into "helping" retrieve Nathan.

The barn sat a comfortable distance from the house, not too far for the old owners to walk to it in the winter, not too close for the smell of the animals that used to inhabit it to reach the house. But these were an entirely different kind of animal, and their stink *did* reach the house on some days. He could smell it now, the ripe, unwashed stench of them and the stale piss odor of their waste. They were awake and restless behind the big sliding door. He strained to move it, but the wood had swelled in the humidity. Sometimes you could get it open without them hearing. Not tonight. Tonight they stood in an uneven semicircle around the door, eyes shining in their unwashed faces, their clothes filthy.

They flinched when he took his knife from his pocket, then relaxed when he rolled up his sleeves. He drew the blade across his wrists and held out his arms. They came at him from all sides, swarming, fighting for his blood.

Bracing himself, he muttered, "Come and get it."

Four: Double Cross

~~~❧❧❧~~~

We pulled up next to the curb in front of the apartment, and I launched myself from Bill's car. For the entire ride from Chicago, I'd imagined countless horrible scenarios. Now, standing on the sidewalk in front of our home, just footsteps from either terror or relief, I almost didn't want to go up.

"Jesus, I hope there's a bathroom up there," Bill groaned as he climbed out. "We couldn't have stopped even, you know, along the highway?"

"Next time, bring an empty coffee can," I sniped, my hands shaking as I fumbled for the keys to the front door.

"You could be a little nicer to the complete stranger who drove you all the way here from Chicago. I was just trying to get my cooler back, lady."

"You're the complete stranger who shot the man we're coming to save. You owed him." I scanned the street. The van wasn't there, but Nathan might have parked somewhere else, to remain inconspicuous. I prayed I would find him in time. I flipped through my keys again, to unlock the door at the top of the stairs. "Back me up."

"Whoa, whoa. You're not going to just charge up there, right?" Bill put a hand on my arm as I stepped through the front door. "I mean, you said he was walking into a trap. Call me crazy, but if someone's walking off the edge of a cliff, you don't go running blindly after them."

"What do you suggest I should do?" Normally, I wouldn't mind advice from someone, but something about Bill's tone rankled me.

I figured out what it was when he moved ahead of me, protectively, as if he were on some kind of macho, soldier-guy autopilot. "Let me go up and check it out first."

"How about no?" I followed him halfway up the steps and grabbed the back of his shirt to stop him. "You're human. I'm not putting you between me and whatever might be up there."

"Yeah, but you're a—" He stopped, wetted his lips, his gaze darting around above my head as he searched for a different word than the one he'd been about to say.

I stepped close to him, getting as in-his-face as I possibly could, with my height disadvantage and the two steps lower than him that I stood. "I'm a what?"

"You're a dead vampire." The voice came from the top of the stairs, and my heart—the only one I had left—stopped beating.

Dahlia stood at the top of the stairs, juggling a bright, blue sphere of light between her hands.

"Holy shit," Bill breathed beside me.

I spoke through clenched teeth. "Run."

"I don't think he's going anywhere," Dahlia said with a laugh, hurling the sphere toward us. Bill turned and tried to follow my directive, but the crackling light hit him square between the shoulder blades. He fell forward, his face bouncing off a step as he landed.

There was no time to worry about helping him. He was likely already dead. But I had myself—and Nathan—to worry about. "Where is he?"

"Where's who?" Dahlia lowered her hands, shaking them as though she were flicking water from them. "You might want to rearrange that. Before it wakes up."

"He's going to wake up?" I shook my head, willing my face to change shape and become a monster's mask.

Dahlia laughed and mimicked me, her face becoming a strange, almost dragonlike countenance with bony ridges where her nose should have been. "Doesn't scare me anymore. Oh, wait…it never did."

"Where is he?" I repeated, advancing up the stairs. She didn't try to stop me, and didn't try another spell. I didn't know if it was because she truly wasn't afraid of me or if she couldn't do more magic again so soon.

"Where is who? Jesus, you think the world revolves around you and your little boyfriend?" She scoffed and turned from the door, disappearing into the apartment.

I flipped Bill onto his side, so his face wasn't smashed into the steps and he wouldn't drown in it if he vomited, since I didn't know the possible side effects of the spell. Then I followed Dahlia.

The apartment had been ransacked by the Soul Eater's men after Cyrus's death. Nathan and I had been hiding beneath the floor of the bookstore in a secret shelter he'd built there. We'd been back in the apartment before fleeing to Chicago, but I'd forgotten how awful it looked. Now, seeing Nathan's prized books on the floor, covered with dirty footprints where they'd been trampled, and our furniture overturned, made me sick to my stomach.

Dahlia standing in the middle of all of it didn't help. She flopped onto the couch, one of the few pieces of furniture that hadn't been tossed around the room, as if I'd invited her to make herself at home. She'd let her feeding face drop. I didn't. I couldn't. I was too angered by her presence. "If you didn't know who I was talking about, then why are you here?"

She smiled and kicked up her feet onto a pile of ruined books. "I like it here. I mean, I never did before. You know, when I was here trying to kill your little sweetie pie? But Ziggy brought me by and it kind of grew on me. I mean, there are enough books here to keep me busy for ages. And yeah, the decor is ugly as all hell and someone left behind some really tacky clothes, but I can overlook all that in favor of having a really cool place to hang out all by myself."

"Get the fuck out of my house." My hands balled into fists at my side. My rational mind knew I shouldn't engage her. She was more powerful than I was, even on my best days. "And if I find out you did anything to him, I swear—"

"You swear what?" She snorted, picking up a leather-bound book by its cover, the binding dangling away from the spine. "You'll get really, really mad at me and I'll end up kicking your ass?"

"I don't remember it going down that way in the past," I reminded her, my voice hoarse and distorted from the shape of my face and the blind fury pushing up in my chest.

She laughed, throwing her head back. There was a scar, fresh, on her neck, and it wasn't made by fangs. It was the shape of a human mouth, opened wide to make a large bite. *Disgusting.*

"Yeah, you wouldn't remember it going down that way," she said, rolling her eyes. "Cyrus was always there to smack me down for you. And he's not here now."

I lunged for her, but she was on her feet, putting the couch between us before I could grab her.

"Ooh, don't like me talking about your little ex-fledgling, do you?" She giggled, the girlish, crazy sound that haunted my nightmares. "You know, the last time I fucked him, it wasn't your name he shouted into my ear. It was *hers.* The little mouse girl. He would never talk to me about her. What happened to her to make him hate you so much?"

It was exactly the kind of remark Dahlia was so good at dispensing. Cruel, cutting.

But she was better at hurting in another kind of way. She could have hurled a spell at me, could have just gone for it and tackled me to the floor, two vamps go down, one comes up. But she did neither of those things.

"What's your game, Dahlia?" I paced a wide circle around the living room, noting that she moved away, keeping the same amount of space between us. "What are you really doing here?"

"What do you mean?" It wasn't like her not to have a smart-ass answer. Posing a question to my question was a sign she was delaying physical aggression. Which meant… "Dahlia, what are you trying to keep me from?"

She giggled, but said nothing.

"It's a trap, isn't it? Ziggy set up a trap." I watched her

from the corner of my eye as she moved behind me. I tensed, listening to her footsteps. If she hesitated, even for a second, I would turn and take her out in a heartbeat.

But she didn't try anything at all. She just wandered past me, to the bookshelf, where she pulled out a leather-bound journal and began ripping pages from it, slowly.

"Fuck it," I muttered under my breath, my heart beating hard against my rib cage. She *was* trying to delay me. And I had to find Nathan.

Where are you? I called out with the blood tie. Dahlia followed me to the top of the stairs, threatening me with words I didn't bother listening to. I was focused too intently on the blood tie, on what might come back to me.

Bill lay at the bottom of the stairs where I'd left him, his eyes squeezed shut, an indication he was conscious. "Jesus…" he rasped. "My head is killing me."

"Get up," I ordered, grasping him under his arms and pulling him to his feet. He could worry about his headache later. "We've got to get out of here."

"You'll never find him," Dahlia called from the top of the stairs, sounding truly angry for the first time since we'd arrived. "He's probably already dead!"

"No, he's not," I retorted calmly, putting myself between her and Bill while he staggered out the door. "If the Soul Eater wanted him dead, he could have done it years ago. He wouldn't need the help of some second-rate witch to do it."

I made it out just as another bolt of whatever spell had knocked out Bill hit the door. I slid into the driver's seat of the car and grabbed the keys from him. "Are you okay?"

"I feel like my skull is going to crack open. I feel like my brain has been in a centrifuge. No, I'm not okay." He leaned his head against the dashboard as I pulled away from the curb. "Where are we going, and who was that?"

"That was Dahlia," I said, scanning the road as I drove for any sign of Ziggy's big, crappy van. "And I don't know."

I hope you brought backup, sweetheart. Nathan's thought shot through my head with an urgency that definitely indicated there was a problem.

I did, but he got a little damaged. Where are you?

You won't believe me....

It was the location that made him doubt Jacob.

Ziggy paced around the alley, the place where he'd first met the only real parent he'd ever had. He'd been a stupid, stupid kid then, thinking he was some big shit who could hunt down vampires. Only then, a real vampire had shown up, and it had gone from being a cool game where the bigger kids included him to a life-or-death situation. And he'd lucked out. It could have been someone like Cyrus, out to find a kid to feed off, or torture to death. But it had been Nate, out to scare the hell out of stupid kids who thought it would be cool to hunt for vampires. And he'd taken a stupid kid out for pie and coffee, and then home to a normal life.

Now, to repay that, Ziggy was going to return Nate to his sire? Jacob had made it seem like common sense. "Bring my son, my true son, home to me," he'd said, and he'd looked so pathetic and sad and pained. Something inside Ziggy had ached to comfort his sire, to do the right thing. He'd thought of being separated from Jacob for so

long, imagined the immense effort it would require to seal
himself off from the blood tie the way Nate had for something like seventy-five years. It would be hell on earth,
and Jacob had made it seem that tricking Nate into coming home was something necessary for Nate's happiness.
Now that he was here, though, and Nate was on the way,
Ziggy wasn't so sure.

*So why are you still selling him out? Why don't you get
the hell out of here and stay away from him forever?*
Ziggy forced the voice away. His conscience had never
worked before, so why the hell did it think he needed it
now? He wasn't hurting Nate. He was saving him.

On the street outside the alley, he heard the squeaking
hubcap from when he'd driven the van over the curb in
front of the apartment. The engine sounded a little better—
Nate probably changed the oil when he was supposed to—
but the driver's side door still screeched when it opened.

Nate was here. He was here, and Ziggy couldn't stop
panicking. What the hell would happen? Would he be
glad to see him? Would he still be ashamed? Jesus, was
he just coming to pass judgment again?

And then Nate was in the mouth of the alleyway, and
Ziggy saw him, and they both froze.

"Ziggy?" It was a whisper that ended like a shout, and
Nate ran at him.

Since he'd run away from home, he'd wondered a
thousand times how things would have been different if
he'd never left. Now, with his dad's arms around him—
and Jesus, was he crying?—he realized nothing would
have been different. Nate would still love him. He still did.

"Hey, come on. Don't cry." He stepped back a little, his

arms on Nate's shoulders, worried that if he didn't hold on he'd crash to the ground. "Come on, Dad. Don't cry."

"I can't believe you're alive." Nate staggered back, sniffling, as though he was crazy or drunk. Or standing in front of a person who was supposed to be dead. "I held you. While you died."

"I know you did." Now Ziggy's throat felt tight, like he was going to start blubbering, too. "I remember."

"I never would have left you. If I had known—"

"I know. I know." *But if he'd taken you with him, you would have died. He didn't turn you. He wouldn't. He was going to let you die.* Ziggy hated his sire's voice in his head. And he hated that he was right. Nate could have saved him, but he didn't.

It helped him overcome some of his guilt at tricking him like this. "Listen, I wanted you to come here for a reason."

"Of course. But we'll talk about it on the road. It's not safe for you here." Nate grabbed his wrist, but Ziggy stood firm.

"No." He took a deep breath. Somewhere, he'd heard that the moment a guy really becomes a man is when he first hits his father. No way in hell was he going to hit Nate. But he wasn't going to let him walk off. Not now. "No, you're not going anywhere."

"Ziggy, you can be honest with me. For Christ's sake, it's me. What's going on?"

Stay strong. Ziggy cleared his throat. "You can't leave. You're supposed to come back with me."

"Come back with you?" Nate's brow crumpled with confusion, but the trust never left his eyes. "Where?"

"You know where. To our sire. You're supposed to come

back with me." If he kept his fists clenched, the tension could support his whole body, and he wouldn't crumble.

Even when he realized what Ziggy was talking about, Nate still didn't look angry or betrayed. It was a low blow. "You're supposed to take me back so he can kill me? Why would you agree to that?"

"He's not going to kill you!" Ziggy rushed to clarify. "He just wants you back home."

"Ziggy, he has to consume the souls of every vampire he's sired before he can become a god." Nate did sound angry now. "I don't know what line he's been feeding you—"

"No, listen! It was a mistranslation. He doesn't need you. He needs someone else. He's got it taken care of, and he's going to let us live." He swallowed. Why did it sound so implausible now? "He wants you back because he misses you."

"And you believe that? I raised you better than that." Nate turned, as if he was going to leave.

Ziggy looked up, signaled to the tops of the buildings on either side. They waited up there, hungry and mindless. "Oh, yeah. You did a good job raising me. Why, exactly, am I a vampire now?"

When Nate turned back, they made their move.

Jacob's human soldiers were disgusting, filthy, stinking and strong. A steady diet of vamp blood did that to a human. Made them dangerous, addicted and loyal. Twenty of them dropped from the rooftops, landing on their feet, ready to fight rather than howling in pain with broken legs. They formed a circle around the two vampires, blocking off Nate's escape.

Please don't let them hurt him, he pleaded to no one in particular. *I'd have to kill them and he would know I can't really force him to go back.*

"Ziggy," Nate began, and there was panic in his voice.

Good. It gave him strength. "I'm not a kid anymore, Nate. And you're coming with me."

Turn left off Cherry Street. Do you see it?

I scanned the street frantically for the sight of the van. It was parked in the shadows, across from a building I knew too well. *I see it.*

"I see it," Bill said, pointing ahead. "Why are you slowing down? It's right there!"

"I know it's right there," I snapped. I pressed the gas pedal, suddenly aware that I had slowed.

Club Cite was a squat brick building with a peeling coat of black paint. All the goth kids and wannabe vampires hung out there. I knew, because it was the place I'd first met Dahlia. And the place Nathan had first met Ziggy.

"How could he have not known this was going to be a trap?" I whispered, shaking my head in disbelief.

Carrie! I need help!

I pulled the car up to the curb and hurtled out before it was fully in Park. I heard Bill yell out behind me, but I cut him off, barking, "Stay in the car until I call for you!"

I rounded the building, to the alley where Nathan and Ziggy stood, surrounded by…junkies?

The people closing in on them were not vampires. I could tell by the smell of their blood. As disgusting as it sounds, humans smell like food, and they were definitely food. But when one grabbed Nathan and he spun, landing a punch squarely to the thing's jaw, nothing happened. Well, a close approximation to nothing. Its head snapped back the way anyone's would when taking a punch. But these…people, for lack of a better term, looked half-starved. Their dirty skin showed through ragged clothes, their eyes were sunken, skin tight across the sharp bones of their skulls. They looked like famine victims. Nathan is strong, even by vampire standards. The one he hit should have ended in a shower of exploded skull and bits of brain.

The surprise on his face mirrored my own when the skeletal man shook off the pain, wiped the blood from his nose, and repaid the blow with a right hook that came so fast and hard I heard the bones of Nathan's face crack.

I rushed forward, a stake drawn. Even if they weren't vampires, a stake to the heart will kill most things. Ziggy caught sight of me and held his hands out in front of himself, as if from the distance he stood he could stop me. "Don't!"

I ignored him, my stake sinking into the back of the creature that had hit Nathan. The man screamed and fell forward. His body stiffened up, the wounded muscles contracting to lock the stake in place. I had to plant a foot in the small of his back and use both hands to jerk the weapon free, releasing a tremendous arc of blood.

Going in, my intent had been to save Nathan. I don't know if I thought it would be enough to cause a distraction, or if I thought killing one would scare the others off, but neither plan panned out. As I stepped back from the dying creature, two more attacked me. I killed the first easily, jamming the stake in her throat as she charged me.

The second grabbed my shoulders from behind, holding me in a punishing grip. My flesh turned to pulp under the squeezing fingers, my bones audibly cracked. I couldn't fight. I could barely breathe from the pain. I watched as the others caught Nathan and dragged him, struggling, to the other open end of the alley, and Ziggy followed.

"Bill!" I screamed, taking a deep breath to gear up for another when the creature holding me let go, dropping me to the pavement with a blow to the back of the head. I managed to keep my face from smashing into the ground, but I couldn't get up. The world spun, and in the white-outs of light from the pain exploding in my skull I saw the taillights of a car at the other end of the alley.

They didn't want to kill Nathan. They wanted to take him.

Behind me, I heard the squeal of tires, and the sound sent pain like jagged glass through my brain. I focused on Bill's voice shouting, "Get up, we're going to lose them!" and managed to climb to my feet and to the car. My door wasn't completely closed yet when Bill hit the gas. The tires squealed and the car jolted after the vehicle in front of us.

"We don't have enough…" I cradled my head in my hands and searched for the words between the flashbulbs of pain popping behind my eyelids. "We can't go after him alone. They're going to the Soul Eater."

"I hate to tell you, but we *are* alone. I don't know anybody around here, and your crowd is apparently not too friendly." He dropped his speed and changed lanes, putting at least four cars between us and the car carrying Nathan.

"What are you doing? You're going to lose him!" I leaned forward, gripping the dashboard as if the pressure from my hands could make the car go faster.

Bill glanced at me sideways, an annoyed kind of look. "I'm not going to lose them. I know how to follow people without being obvious. Believe me, they'll think we lost them, and they'll be wrong."

I settled back reluctantly, keeping my eyes on the car as it zoomed ahead of us. "I don't know what I'm worried about. If they get away, I can always get directions from Nathan."

"Yeah, that's a handy trick," he said offhandedly as he barely squeaked through a yellow light. "Do you know where we're headed?"

"We're going south." I shrugged. "Pretty soon we'll run out of city, so keep an eye on them. Wherever they're going has to be within a few more miles."

But it turned out I was wrong. They skipped all the major numbered streets and just kept heading south on Division Avenue, until there were no more streetlights and the buildings gave way to swamps and trees. Soon, we were the only cars on the road. There was no way they didn't know we were following them.

"What's the plan, Stan?" Bill asked, jerking the wheel to make a hard turn onto a dirt road. The car ahead of us roared and shot farther from us.

"We have to get Nathan before they get him to the Soul Eater." I closed my eyes. "I just wish I knew how to do that."

"Well, I could run them off the road," Bill suggested, clearly uncomfortable with the idea. "It's dangerous. But it's not like they're going to stop to get gas out here and we could just grab him then."

I nodded, remembering something Nathan had told me when I'd first become a vampire, that a car crash could kill me if the damage done to my body was bad enough that I couldn't heal it quicker than it killed me. He'd used it as an example back then. I'm sure he didn't expect that I'd be using it to brace myself mentally for ramming a car he was riding in off the road. "Let's do it."

I suppose I should have felt more guilty for endangering a human, but things went so fast. Bill hit the gas and we swerved as the tires resisted the pull of the loose gravel. We caught up with the other car fast enough that we nudged them with our bumper, but it wasn't enough. I watched, wary, as the needle of the speedometer went higher and higher.

Seventy on a dirt road. Might as well have shot ourselves in the head right then.

It took two tries—bumping, scraping, screeching tries—to edge past the car enough to make a good hit. Before I could revise the plan, Bill shouted, "Hang on!" and jerked the wheel hard to the right, crashing us against the other car. They pushed back, just for a second, before spinning across the road. As the driver, another of the skeletal superhumans, struggled to turn the vehicle, Bill reversed, revved the engine and shifted into Drive, T-boning the car and spinning it into the ditch.

We both got out, Bill drawing his gun. "More effective than a stake," he said with a shrug, and I couldn't argue with him, though I didn't think a bullet would stop those things in the car.

"Nathan? Are you okay? Can you hear me?" I eased down the bank and wrenched the back door open.

"I can hear you," Nathan said as he pulled himself out.

Inside the car, the humans were either unconscious or dead. At least something could hurt them.

Nathan's face was bruised and misshapen where he'd been hit, bleeding where a shard of broken glass protruded from his forehead just below his hairline. "You couldn't think of a better way to rescue me?"

I threw my arms around him. I knew but didn't really care that one of those superfreaks could wake and we'd have another fight on our hands. I just wanted to touch him, to make sure he was okay. Well, aside from the gash across his forehead.

He put his arms around me for just a moment, squeezing me tight. Then he let me go and gestured up the bank, to where Bill stood, his eyes wide as he surveyed the damage he'd done. Nathan gestured to the open door, and Ziggy's unconscious form inside. "I need your help, my son is in the car."

I stepped aside while they pulled him out. It took some maneuvering from all three of us to get him up the steep slope, but we managed to get him into the backseat. The car groaned as we pulled away, and something squeaked ominously, but Bill assured us we could make it back to the bookshop.

"Before sunrise, if you don't mind," Nathan added. He sat in the back with Ziggy, cradling his head in his lap.

"What happened?" I asked, my heart still aching with relief. I didn't want to believe what I couldn't deny was true. Ziggy had set Nathan up.

Nathan looked down at his son's face, a shadow of hurt crossing his battered features. "He was trying to take me back to the Soul Eater. Jacob has him brainwashed into believing that he doesn't want to hurt me, that he wants us all to be a family. He's Ziggy's sire."

A lump of tears I couldn't shed formed in my throat. Of all the things Nathan feared, his sire was number one. And now, the Soul Eater had his son. "What are we going to do?"

Nathan shook his head, stroking the hair back from his son's face. "I don't know. It's up to Ziggy. I can't force him to turn his back on his sire." He laid his hand gently, almost reverently, on the front of Ziggy's T-shirt and frowned.

"What?" I asked, leaning over the seat, though I had a terrible inkling of what Nathan had felt there.

With trembling hands, Nathan jerked the fabric of Ziggy's shirt up, exposing a long, puckered scar bisecting his torso from his collarbones to his navel. My breath froze in my chest. I knew what that scar was. I had one, myself. So had Cyrus, when he was alive the first time.

"Jesus," Bill said, his eyes fixed on the rearview mirror. His skin paled, and he turned his gaze back to the road. "That must have been some serious injury."

But he had no clue how serious it was. Nathan and I did. The Soul Eater had taken Ziggy's heart.

My eyes filled with tears as they met Nathan's. "What are we going to do?"

"I don't know." His voice was tight, hopeless. "I don't know."

Five: Heartless

Ziggy was still unconscious when we returned to the bookshop.

"Stay with him," Nathan ordered, motioning me into the backseat. "If he wakes up…knock him out again."

It wasn't the most tender, fatherly suggestion, but he was right. If Ziggy could, he would go back to his sire.

On the chance Dahlia was still inside somewhere, Nathan searched the bookstore. When it was clear, they carried Ziggy downstairs, to the hidden shelter that Nathan kept below the shop floorboards.

"I can't say I'm glad to see this place again," I muttered as I followed them down the steep few steps.

There was a thud, and Bill swore. "There isn't much head clearance down here," Nathan warned belatedly.

The hideout was a short, narrow space with a dirt floor and stone masonry walls that were crumbling. The sleeping bags, medical kit and camping lantern we'd left behind were still there, as well as the empty bags from the blood we'd consumed while in hiding. But we didn't have any blood now, and Bill was human. "We're not going to be here long, I hope?"

I'd whispered the question to Nathan, but the space was too crowded and confined for secrecy. Bill's gaze darted from me to Nathan and back as he helped to maneuver Ziggy into a sleeping bag. "I don't feed from the vein, okay? So you guys need a plan in place."

"We're going back to Chicago as soon as the sun goes down," Nathan answered tersely. "That's the plan."

He settled on the floor, his back propped against the rough stone and crumbling cement of the wall. Bill retreated to the other side of the shelter and I sat beside Nathan.

"Do you really think that's smart?" I asked, my voice low not to keep our conversation private—that would have been impossible—but to indicate that Bill should try to politely ignore us. "I mean, with the Soul Eater having his heart and every—"

"I know what the Soul Eater has!" Nathan exploded. He banged the back of his head against the stone, just once, and dropped his forehead to rest on his hands. His next words were softer, full of heartrending dismay. "What a mess this is."

I leaned against him, my head on his shoulder, one hand on his back. Comforting with words isn't something I'm good at.

"We can't go back to Chicago," I said, quieter. "At least, not now. The Soul Eater will be looking for us, and he'll follow us there. At least here we have the resources to protect ourselves."

"And there we have security," Nathan argued, but I cut him off.

"What about those creatures? Who do you think will stop them? The doorman? The janitor? The head of the building association?" My voice had grown louder, and I lowered it. "Have you thought of how many people will die when he lets those things loose in Chicago?"

"But the book, Dahlia's spell book—"

"Is in the car. I'm not an idiot, Nathan. I wouldn't leave something like that behind. We have to stay here, where we can keep a closer eye on what the Soul Eater is up to." I watched as he tried to form another protest, and then as defeat finally registered on his features.

He looked up, acknowledging Bill for the first time. "Thank you. For your help. You've done more than I ever would have asked you to."

Bill held up one hand, letting it fall in obvious exhaustion. "It's nothing. I mean, it's something. If it were my kid, I'd want someone to help me."

"Do you have kids?" It was something I hadn't thought of. Had I dragged him away from his family, possibly to get him killed?

"No. But if I did." He shook his head. "You're right. If we head back to Max's place, they're going to follow you guys. And if this Soul Eater guy is going to track you down wherever you go, well, why not stay where you can keep a closer eye on him, rather than be surprised when you wake up dead?"

Nathan snorted. "Well, when you—a human who has little knowledge of the situation aside from vague rumblings in the Chicago underground—frame it that way, in the context of the knowledge you don't have, I really can't argue."

When he tries to, Nathan can be an incredible ass. "I filled him in on the details on the drive up here. To save you. Which he helped with. You'd be in your sire's living room sipping tea right now, if he hadn't. So, can you at least pretend he's a human being, worthy of respect?"

We sat in silence for a minute. I studied Nathan's face, amazed as ever to watch it visibly healing. My head still throbbed. I probably had—and would have—a fractured skull for a few days. The pressure behind my eyes forced my eyelids closed, sleep making my thoughts heavy. Just as I dropped off, I roused myself. "I'm sorry, I'm falling asleep," I mumbled, rubbing my eyes.

Nathan patted my shoulder, urging me to lean against him. "Go ahead, get some rest."

"No," I protested. "We've got to keep an eye out, in case—"

With a beleaguered sigh, he wrapped his arm around me. Not around my shoulders, but around my head, bringing his hand to neatly cover my mouth as he pulled me close to him.

Bill chuckled, and Nathan dropped his arm to my shoulders. My eyes eased open for a moment and I saw Ziggy, still unconscious, like something out of a dream. He was alive. And he was back home.

Morning came too soon.

Lately, it always seemed to come too soon, Max realized. When night was the time for him to be up and moving around, cleaning, doing laundry, going to the bar, hanging out, the night seemed to be plenty of time to get everything done. He'd even found himself bored on occasion. But now, when he had to tear himself away from Bella's warm, soft body, the night seemed unfairly short.

Now, the dawn loomed on the horizon, and with it inevitable separation. He was trying hard not to be morose, but it was more difficult than he'd expected. A few months ago, he would have been aching for a fight, any kind of danger to break up the monotony of the everyday. And it never occurred to him then to worry about what would happen if he didn't survive. Bella was his everyday now, and it terrified him to think he might not get back to her.

He supposed he was the perfect example of "be careful what you wish for."

Rising from the bed as gently as he could, trying not to wake Bella until absolutely necessary, he reached for the jeans wadded up on the floor. He pulled them on, set a teakettle of blood on the hot plate by the bathroom sink and went out to the balcony while he waited for it to warm.

The sky over the lake was a black-tinged blue, turning slowly golden near the eastern horizon. Some mornings he saw pink reflected on the clouds. Some mornings, the sun seemed to just appear; one moment it was night, the next, day, without him even noticing. It wasn't something he'd ever experienced in his human life, definitely nothing he'd purposely hung around to watch in his vampire days. Usually, it put him in a great mood. Now, as the sun rose in the east, his gaze was drawn to the runway at the cliff's edge. The jet parked there had its lights on, a small truck was stopped next to it.

"Great, don't rush me along or anything."

"Max?" Bella's sleepy voice called. "You are already awake?"

He strolled into the bedroom, his heart catching in his throat a little bit at the sight of her, struggling to sit up, reaching for her robe that was impossibly far away. How would she fare when he was gone? Sure, one of her surly relations would probably help her, but how could they be there for everything she needed? How could anyone take better care of her than him? It was another reason that he would have to make damn sure to stay alive and get back to her.

As if she'd read his thoughts, Bella's expression turned dark. "Do not look at me with such pity. I am capable on my own."

"I know you are," he said, trying not to sound patronizing but handing her the robe all the same. "I'm just worried that you won't have everything you need here. That you'll be…neglected."

She arched a sardonic brow. "You think I would tolerate being neglected?"

"I think your family will take better care of you than they would me, were the situation reversed." Max helped her ease her arms into the robe, lamenting the loss of all that tight, tanned skin from his view. He didn't want to be so shallow as to add "see my girlfriend naked again" to his list of reasons to survive.

"That is probably true," Bella agreed, then, slowly, she said, "I…have been thinking. About you leaving."

The smell of the blood alerted him to the imminent prospect of overwarming, and he went to the bathroom to retrieve the kettle. "I'm listening."

"I thought perhaps…" She hesitated, as though it was difficult for her to speak. Max supposed he should worry that she would say she thought the separation was a good idea, that they should make it permanent, but he couldn't quite get to that state of hysteria. He knew Bella too well, and he was secure enough in their relationship to know that whatever she would say next would be something along the lines of "I want to do something incredibly stupid and dangerous to protect you that I know you will reject outright."

"I want to gather a few of the women, the other magic workers, and maintain our contact with you while you are gone. Perhaps we will be of use—"

"Until your father finds out, hates me more, banishes you and the other women—" Max interrupted, only to be cut off again by Bella.

"My father will not banish me. Sometimes I fear he cannot make the best decisions for the pack when acting as both my father and the pack leader." She closed her eyes and rubbed the bridge of her nose with the back of her hand. "I worry what will happen when werewolves become involved in this fight. My father only sees himself as potentially being rid of a nuisance."

"Thanks," Max interjected.

"He has no concept of how enraged the Soul Eater will be, and what repercussions might affect the pack as a whole." She looked to Max, golden eyes pleading. "Please, just keep in contact with me. I will rally support quietly, and when the time is right, if the time comes, I will be able to do my part."

One thing Bella wasn't good at—the only thing Bella wasn't good at, actually, if Max didn't count being humble or ugly—was being helpless. And he sympathized with her. There were times in the past when he'd gone about crazy waiting for orders from the Movement to go ahead and do what he already knew would have to be done. But he didn't trust her father not to banish her or, God, hurt her, even. Julian was, after all, the man who'd tattooed multiple lines of ancient prophecy into Bella's skin when she was a teenager. It might be a cultural difference that kept Max from understanding Julian's motives, but culture be damned, he wasn't about to let Bella's father's weird vendetta against him harm her.

But then again, Bella had been a teenager once. She'd probably defied her father's orders hundreds of times then without being caught. And pack pecking order or no, Bella's aunts were frightening creatures who would bristle like porcupines if anyone, Julian included, tried any funny business.

"Fine," he conceded wearily. "Do what you have to do. But I want no part of it. Plausible denial is the best tool one can possess in some situations."

"Come," she said, putting her arms out to him. "Help me into the chair. Then get yourself some blood and we will watch the sun rise together."

It was as much of a goodbye as he knew he would get from her.

I woke, disoriented, to the sound of Nathan cursing and shoes scuffing on the dirt floor. My brain became aware reluctantly, an inconvenience at a time when clearly all hell was breaking loose around me. I staggered to my feet and promptly struck my aching head on one of the overhead beams. When I was finished swearing and rubbing my head, I finally saw what was going on.

Ziggy had woken up. He'd made it halfway up the steps, from what I could tell, and now Nathan had one of his legs in a death grip, trying to pull him away from the trapdoor. Bill leaned against the wall, hands to his throat, a look of shock—the clinical kind—on his face.

"Carrie!" Nathan shouted, and I realized that was what had woken me in the first place. "Help Bill before he bleeds to death!"

I walked awkwardly on my knees to Bill's side. Blood cascaded from between his fingers to stain the front of his T-shirt. "He bit me," he mumbled. "He bit me."

"I take it you've never been bitten by a vampire before," I started, completely calm, completely oblivious to the struggle behind me. If I got him talking, diverted his focus, I might be able to save him. "It hurts like hell, doesn't it?"

His forehead shone with perspiration, and he looked not at me, but through me. "He bit me."

"I know. Let me just…" I gently pried his hands away from his wounded throat. I'd braced myself for the blood to spray, and thankfully, it didn't. I replaced his hand with my own, pulling the bottom of his shirt up to press against the wound.

Behind me, Nathan growled to Ziggy, "Sit down and we'll talk about this!"

"Talk, my ass!" There was a thud, and I imagined Ziggy's foot connecting with Nathan's chest. There was a scrabbling sound against the wood, and the trapdoor banged open. "If I don't get back there, he's going to fucking kill me!"

I grabbed Bill's hand and held it over the wound. "He

didn't hit anything critical, but you need to hold this here until the bleeding stops. Not too tight." I felt behind me for the sleeping bag and pulled it around his shoulders. Somehow, I resisted licking his blood off my fingers. "Are you all right?"

He nodded toward the sound of the struggle, wetting his lips. "Help him."

Ziggy broke free of Nathan and made it up the few steps into the bookshop. Nathan and I raced after him in time to see the door fling open, admitting scorching sunlight. Ziggy managed to close it before he burst into flame, but when he sank, panting, with his back to the thick, scarred wood, his face was orange with sunburn.

"Fuck daylight," he rasped, closing his eyes, his head falling back in defeat. "I'm going to die."

"You're not going to die," I reassured him, knowing he wasn't talking about his burn.

Ziggy shook his head and yanked up his shirt, displaying for us the scar we'd already seen. "Jacob has my heart. He'll kill me."

"Jacob," Nathan muttered behind me, disgust plain in his voice. I knew what bothered him, without feeling it through the blood tie. I'd heard that same reverence in Nathan's voice, when he'd willingly let me into his memories. The Soul Eater's power over his fledglings ran deeper than the blood between them. Jacob Seymour was a powerful, ruthless, charismatic man. If a person didn't fall for his promises of power, they were frightened by his cruelty. But always, always they were impressed by his way of making them feel as though they were the only person who mattered to him.

I knew I almost had been.

"Ziggy, he won't kill you," I began, steamrollering past whatever Nathan had opened his mouth to say. I had the distinct feeling that whatever words he chose, they wouldn't be constructive. "He has your heart, but he had Cyrus's heart for years. He never did anything with it. And eventually, he gave it back."

"Cyrus never ran off on him, either." Ziggy practically spat the words. "He's going to think I've betrayed him. He's going to think I don't l—"

"He's going to think what you make him think," Nathan interrupted. His face was a mask of pain. He didn't want to hear that his son loved a monster. "You haven't been blocking him from the blood tie. He knows you've been kidnapped."

"He does." Ziggy nodded vigorously. "He does. He'll come back and get me."

"Is that what you really want?" My heart ached for him. I knew what it was like to feel so strongly for someone who was so destructive. Of course, it also terrified me to think that Ziggy might send out a homing beacon, leading the Soul Eater straight to us. "You don't have to go back to him—"

"No," Nathan said quickly. "No, don't make him think about that." I opened my mouth to protest, but he shook his head so vehemently I closed it again. He never took his eyes from Ziggy. "If he doesn't think about it, he doesn't have to give anything away to Jacob. And he hasn't had the practice disguising his thoughts that I've had. The Soul Eater will see through him in a minute."

"Well, he'd better start practicing," I said, sounding

more harsh, I'm sure, than I intended. "We can't afford to have him broadcasting all our plans to the enemy."

"Your enemy," Ziggy snapped, rising to his feet.

"Do I need to tie you to something?" Nathan stalked toward his son with a decidedly unfatherly glare.

To his credit, Ziggy didn't flinch in the face of Nathan's stare down. "Jacob is my sire. Some of us stay loyal."

"He might be your sire, but you're still my son," Nathan snapped, hands clenching at his sides. "And I'm not losing you again."

When he grabbed for him, Ziggy moved out of the way. But it wasn't murderous intent that made Nathan reach for his son. His arms swooped around his shoulders and pulled him away from the door. And while I stood there, watching as Ziggy remained passive, stoic, Nathan embraced him.

I didn't know what had happened to turn Ziggy from the unnervingly self-possessed, friendly youth he'd been to the jaded drone he seemed to be now. I didn't want to know—I'd heard enough about the Soul Eater's cruelty to last a lifetime. But it rent my heart to imagine it.

While Nathan buried his face in his son's shoulder, I saw Ziggy's hand raise to lie, comforting, on his father's dark hair. The gesture was so private, I turned away, ducking back into the shelter to check on Bill. I had no qualms about leaving Ziggy alone with Nathan. He wouldn't hurt him. He'd had a chance to kill him once, and he hadn't. In fact, if Ziggy was to be believed, he thought returning Nathan to the Soul Eater would save him, not damn him. I wondered how long it would take to deprogram him from that way of thinking, and whether or not it would be worth it.

Bill's neck stopped bleeding without further intervention—thank God for small mercies—but the bite was still puffy and nasty-looking. "Do you want something for the pain?"

He grimaced and shook his head. "No. I'm tough."

"You don't have to impress me." I arched an eyebrow and subtly nudged the tool kit containing our amped-up first aid kit. "I won't tell them."

"You're an all right lady, for a vampire," he said with a forced smile. "Now, the other two…"

"Don't get started on the other two," I admonished playfully.

His smile became more relaxed and natural. "How can I not? He bit me, remember?"

"Yeah. And bites hurt worse than everyone seems to think." I pressed a clean gauze pad over the wound and set to sticking it down with tape.

"They never get it right in the movies," he mused, his eyes rapidly taking on the glassy look of someone who'd just mainlined an opiate. "They always make it look erotic. Like sex, you know?"

"I know." A distinctly uncomfortable memory of sitting in my apartment on a Friday night, watching Gary Oldman's Dracula seduce and turn Winona Ryder as Mina, flashed through my mind. If I'd known how much more complicated being a vampire would be, I might not have found it so romantic then. "Of course, I don't have to wear a corset, so I suppose it's a trade-off."

"Excuse me?" Bill asked with a loopy laugh. "I don't think I'm so far gone that I could have possibly misheard that."

"Nothing." I waved a hand to dismiss the conversation. Ziggy marched down the stairs, Nathan behind him, surreptitiously wiping his eyes.

"It's nearly sundown," Ziggy said, touching his quickly healed face. "They're going to be after us soon."

"We need a better hideout than this," Bill said, reaching over his head to knock on the low ceiling. "It's not as secure as I'd like when it's my neck that's concerned."

"We've got a plan already," Nathan said, wearily defensive. "But we're all still dog tired. Let's get some more rest. We'll check out the apartment later and get everything secured."

"Personally, I don't care what you do," Bill interjected. "Just so long as you can find food that doesn't have pain receptors."

Ziggy looked a bit sheepish as he brushed off a spot on the dirt floor. Finally, he looked up, extending a hand toward Bill. "Sorry, man. I don't know what I was doing."

"You knew," Bill responded, but it wasn't the sound of a grudge being formed, just a simple statement of fact. "You had a hell of a disorienting day."

"You're telling me." A faint smile played across Ziggy's mouth, a ghost of the boy he used to be. It hurt to see it, hurt more to see it vanish a moment later. "Maybe I should go back to Jacob. Not because I want to," he corrected hastily. Then, he folded his legs up and crossed his ankles, leaning his chin on his knees. "Maybe I do. I don't know. But if I'm here, I feel like I'm going to give you guys away. I don't want to, but he'll make me do it. He's good at that."

"It will take time." Nathan motioned for me to come

sit beside him, as if he needed the moral support to speak to his son. "But it can be done. I've blocked the Soul Eater out of my head for almost a century. Carrie managed to block out Cyrus when she was living under his roof. It's not impossible to close off the blood tie."

"No." Ziggy smiled sadly. "But it's impossible to want to do it."

That, I could definitely sympathize with. An orphan in the true sense of the word, I'd felt that unique pain all over again when I'd killed my sire. If I were honest with myself, I had to say that I'd felt it with each small betrayal, felt it snowball larger and larger until the moment I'd plunged the knife through his heart. For someone like Ziggy—someone with few familial ties on this earth—the bond of the blood tie was a powerful aphrodisiac. It had certainly led me to do things I wouldn't have otherwise.

Reluctantly, I gave in to the idea that Ziggy might still end up our enemy. He honestly believed he would never betray us on purpose, but that hunger for his sire might tempt him to do things he wouldn't have normally. But it didn't seem realistic that we could keep him ignorant of our whereabouts for long. All he would have to do is slip out for a pack of cigarettes and he could turn us all in.

Nathan scooted his back against the hard wall of the cellar and leaned his head back settling in for more uncomfortable rest, his long legs almost touching Bill across the small space. The human mimicked Nathan's posture, falling into obviously unwilling sleep. I didn't have any hard feelings toward him for not trusting us. After all, the vampire who'd just taken a chunk out of him was curled into a seemingly harmless ball on the ground beside him.

I got closer to Nathan, pulling my legs under me and leaning my head against his chest. *How are you doing?* I whispered through the blood tie.

Scared to death. But I'll survive. He hooked a finger under my chin and lifted my face up to his. His lips brushed mine softly, barely a touch but enough that I could feel his cold breath on me, and my toes curled. *I'm sorry we fought.*

No, I'm sorry. The distance between us, first emotional, then physical, was more acutely painful now that it was resolved. Touching him was torture, because I couldn't have him the way I wanted him. *I haven't been right since—*

He cut me off gently with a finger to my lips, even though I hadn't spoken out loud. *I know. Let's not do this right now.*

I smiled. *I doubt we'll get a better time. Seems like things are going to be a bit hairy for a while.*

I don't want to wait for a better time. I want to just…go back to things like nothing ever happened. His gaze flickered to the two other inhabitants of our shelter. *This doesn't seem like the right place.*

I sighed and closed my eyes, laying one palm over his chest. His big hand covered mine, held it over his dead heartbeat. *I could try a thousand different ways, and no matter what I tried, I still couldn't say it properly. But I want what I imagined that first night I met you.*

And what was that? I turned my palm upward and let him lace our fingers together. The feeling of being pulled from my own body into his memory surprised me, even after all the times I'd felt it. When Cyrus had been my sire, I'd seen into his memory often, but that time seemed years away, and Nathan rarely let me glimpse what was in his mind this way. Now, as the rushing in my ears stopped and I adjusted to the feeling of being slotted into someone else's world, the colors in my vision began to form into objects, and I saw myself, all those long months ago, standing in the bookshop in my black wool coat, a baseball cap pulled over my lank, blond hair. I looked furious as I ground out, "Yeah, I have questions. Who the hell are you? Why did I get attacked when I walked through that door? And what the hell makes you think I'm a vampire?"

I'd thought that he'd been annoyed with me barging into his shop with hostile questions, but the feeling I got from his memory was amusement. He'd actually thought I was funny and…cute? The memory jerked forward, to the two of us standing in the living room of the apartment, that same night. Right after he'd told me he would kill me if I didn't join the Movement, if I remember correctly.

Of course, I also remember being attracted to him, however inappropriate an instinct it had been at the time. I saw myself wet my lips, trying to look braver than I'd felt, saying, "Do I look like the kind of girl who runs away from trouble?"

I wasn't the only one who'd felt sparks. Nathan's memory stayed focused, but his brain fired off a series of random, scattered images. Me, beneath him in his bed. Walking through falling leaves in a park on a sunny day. My face, flushed with wine and candlelight. Cradling a child in his arms. And then, his wife's face. *God, she reminds me so much of her.*

I pulled back from the memory willingly, and when my

vision cleared and I was safely back in my body, I frowned at him and whispered out loud, "I thought I was nothing like your wife."

He smiled. "You're not. Not since I've gotten to know you. But then…ah, well, I just wanted to get you into bed."

I slapped his arm and leaned my head on his shoulder. *Well done then. But seriously, all of that other stuff? Having babies and romantic walks and all of that? Guys really think about that kind of thing?*

Sure they do. I hope. He gave a tired laugh. *And it was stupid to be thinking of those kinds of things…having children, being exposed to daylight. I don't even know if you like children.*

The familiar, sharp pain in my heart was getting easier to ignore. *Too late to think about that now.*

He sighed, and the pain in it cut my heart to ribbons. Then, with forced cheerfulness, he pointed out, *Actually, it might be a blessing. Having no reason to question it. If we were human, we might not agree and then where would we be? Not together.*

Did that ever bother you with your human girlfriends? I felt a little curl of jealousy, ridiculous as it sounds. He'd mentioned having a girlfriend before, but I'd never questioned him further. *I mean, did it ever create a problem?*

The only woman after Marianne—besides you—was Linda. And she…ugh, what a mess that was. Under my cheek I felt his laughter, a low, dismayed sound deep in his chest.

Still, I wondered if he was right, if we would still be together even without the bond that held us. Nathan and I might have been through a lifetime's worth of emotional woes, but our relationship stood the chance of lasting far longer than a single lifetime.

The thought struck me like a hammer. Nathan was my sire…as long as he lived and I lived, we were stuck with each other. And if our romantic relationship didn't last that long—and so far things looked bleak—what then? But if it *did* last that long, what *then?* For the first time, I very seriously considered what was involved in vampire relationships, and it scared me more than any monster I'd faced thus far. Nathan and I could, for all intents and purposes, end up together forever, literally. And would it be because we truly wanted to be, or because some mystical force made it that way?

Clearly picking up on my freaked-out vibe, he cupped my jaw in his palm, stroking my face with his index finger. *That relationship ended because she was ready for something I wasn't. Bad timing. That, and it was a hardship trying to pretend that I wasn't a vampire. Neither of those reasons apply to us.*

My face scrunched up in embarrassment as I laughed at myself. "I know that."

"And you love me?" he asked, running his thumb over my bottom lip as he leaned forward to kiss me.

Those momentary fears—and the ones that had stacked up on me for months—seemed so ridiculous now in the face of nearly losing him. I smiled against his mouth. "Yes. I love you."

He kissed me, so long and gentle and thorough that I lost track of time before it ended and yet it seemed torturously short when it actually did.

Ziggy stirred. "You guys aren't making out, are you?"

Nathan reached over and smacked the back of his head, playful in that rough way men have. "Go back to sleep. This is grown-up time."

Ziggy's back shook with laughter we couldn't hear. "Yeah. Just don't let it get too adult. I'm a kid, remember."

"You're a pain in the ass, is what you are," Nathan said, his voice full of relief and love and happiness despite the fact that so much still lay ahead of us. "I'm glad you're back."

I heard Ziggy's rustling movements, then a small noise of approval. "I knew it."

"Knew what?" Nathan asked.

Ziggy yawned. "You two. I knew you'd hook up."

"Ah, well, I knew that, too," Nathan said offhandedly. "Just wasn't sure how it would happen."

"I'm glad somebody let me in on it," I said sleepily, my eyes drifting closed. "But you're forgetting, there's a very large piece of information Ziggy doesn't know."

"What's that?" he asked, suddenly alarmed and eager all at once.

"Nathan's my sire," I responded on a yawn.

Before Ziggy could respond, Nathan interjected, "It's a very long story. Best saved for another time."

"Whatever," he replied amid more rustling of his coat. "Wake me when the sun is down."

Try to get some sleep, yourself, I mentally nagged Nathan, and he pressed a kiss to the top of my head. If he responded, I didn't hear it.

Six: Reconnection, cont.

Our first order of business when we emerged from the shelter was to make things more livable in the apartment. It didn't take as long as I had expected, though Nathan was dismayed every time we turned up another ruined notepad or book that was too damaged to be salvaged.

Something about the apartment had changed in our absence. Nothing physical, but the atmosphere had shifted. After I'd first been changed, I'd seen Nathan's home as a fortress, a refuge. Sanctuary. And then, after I'd become a permanent resident, as home. Now it was cold and unfeeling, as if the walls were living things who would just as soon give us all up to our enemies and be done with us as abide us living within them.

"I hate to point this out, but you guys kind of destroyed my car and put a giant kink in my livelihood," Bill said, sliding a stack of mutilated notebooks onto a shelf. "The least you can do is give me a ride back to Chicago."

"Not right now." Nathan's reply came out as if it had been at the ready for most of the night. "I'm sorry, but you're too much of a liability to us. We don't know you that well, and we don't know what kind of people you work for."

"So, he's a hostage, then?" Ziggy asked, something bloodthirsty and eager in his voice that strangely suited him.

Nathan shrugged. "For all intents and purposes. But we'll find a way to compensate you for the time and income you'll lose. I just can't think of a way now."

Bill considered, plainly unhappy. "I guess I can think of worse places to be stuck. But I can't say I've ever been a hostage before, and I'm not entirely cool with this idea. I'm not here to help you with some grand, world-saving plan."

He had a very valid point, and every right to be angry with us. We'd never asked him to help us this far, and we'd definitely taken advantage of the little assistance he'd offered us. Now, he was our hostage. I wondered again if there was a family waiting for him at home that we were keeping him from.

"Thank you so much, Bill, for all your help." Of course, my thanks seemed too little too late, considering he'd just been told he was a prisoner, but I wanted him to know he was at least appreciated. "Really, you've done more than necessary."

"And will continue to do," Nathan said cheerfully. "He's a good man."

Ziggy wandered to the bottom of the stairs that led to the street. "So, how are we going to secure this place? It's not exactly the Reichstag here."

"Two men awake, two men asleep, take turns on four-hour watch," Bill answered quickly. "One up here, one down in the bookstore seems reasonable. Do you guys have walkie-talkies?"

"You used to be in the A-Team or something?" Ziggy quipped, and I smiled to myself. He was beginning to sound like the kid I remembered.

"Bill used to be in the Marines," Nathan said in the same patient tone someone would use to explain the bizarre behavior of a mentally handicapped relative.

I picked up the spell book, which I had snagged from the car on the way up to the apartment. "What about something out of here? She has all sorts of protection spells. There has to be something that will work on the building."

Nathan took the book from me with a frown. "Probably nothing useful. Dahlia seemed to be more concerned with destructive magic than anything that would do anyone any good. There might be some lesser wards worth checking into, though."

"Good. We'll do that, and Bill and Ziggy can go look for blood." I turned to the door and wrenched it open. "We'll do it in the bookstore."

"Kinky."

The voice came from the bottom of the stairs. My mouth went dry and my throat closed up. Which was unfortunate, because my heart had just leaped into it.

"Aren't you even going to say hi?"

"Max!" My voice came back before he reached the top of the stairs, and once he stood in the doorway, my reflexes returned, as well. He stiffened, bracing for the impact as I lunged to embrace him, but relaxed as my arms closed around him.

"I'm glad to see you, too." He laughed, giving me a gentle squeeze. "I would have been even happier to see you in Chicago. It would have saved me five hours in the car."

Nathan was right behind me, and, to my surprise and Max's, I'm sure, hugged Max as soon as I stepped back. "We've been worried about you, friend."

Slapping Nathan on the back, Max stepped away. "I should disappear without saying goodbye more often. You guys are in a better mood when I turn up."

"Don't you dare ever do that again," I admonished, aching to hug him again. "We were so worried."

"I called. I left a message. If you would ever check your voice mail—" He paused and looked into the living room. "Bill?"

"And Ziggy. He's alive," Nathan said, his brow furrowing. "You don't seem surprised to see him."

The friendly vibe fled the scene, replaced by something electric and cold. Something ready to escalate, like the feeling of doom right before you grab the doorknob that gives you a wicked electric shock.

"Like I said, you should check your voice mail." Max shrugged, then half smiled, but I could tell from the nervous glint in his eyes that he knew he'd said the disastrously wrong thing.

Nathan grabbed him by the front of the shirt and pushed him against the wall. Some plaster fell from the ceiling, and the wall creaked ominously. "You called me to tell me that my son was still alive and instead of talking to you you left it in a voice mail?"

We all stood silent in the dying echo of Nathan's shouted accusation. If everyone was on the same page as I was, they were trying to figure out a way to end this confrontation without Nathan hurling Max down the stairs.

"Nate," Ziggy said cautiously. "It's not like he had another option."

"He had another option. He could have gotten you out of there and brought you home!" He shoved Max again, and something fell somewhere in the other half of the apartment.

"He didn't want to come with me," Max said. He wasn't angry, and that only infuriated Nathan more.

I felt his rage spike through the blood tie, and scolded him mentally, *Not quite as fun when the person you're beating up just sits there and takes it.*

Stay out of it, Carrie, he warned, turning his head to glare at me. "Of course he wanted to come with you. He was scared out of his mind when he called me!"

"When I called you, it was a trap." Ziggy stood and shrugged his jacket on, not making eye contact with any of us. "Don't blame him. I'm the fuckup."

Nathan tried to hold on to his anger at Max, but it was a losing fight. He let go, and Max dropped a few inches—I hadn't realized that Nathan had managed to lift him off the ground—but he quickly recovered, brushing himself off. There was a sizable dent in the wall behind him. "I tried to get him to come along, really, I did. But I had Bella with me—"

"Bella!" I couldn't believe I'd forgotten to ask about her, regardless of the dustup I'd just witnessed. "Is she with you?"

"No, she had to stay behind," Max said, his gaze flitting distractedly from me to Nathan, keeping alert to another possible attack. "She's not able to walk yet."

"My God, what happened?" I asked, but I didn't get an answer. Ziggy pushed past us without a word and charged down the stairs. A person would have to be blind to miss the anger in his posture. I can't say I wouldn't have reacted similarly to see Nathan behave the way he was on my behalf. As if I were helpless or something.

"Ziggy!" Nathan moved to go after him, and I stopped him, gripping his arm.

Let him go. His moodiness would pass. He'd been through a lot and needed time on his own. And Nathan must have agreed with me, because he let him go.

He turned to Max and held out his hand, unable to meet his gaze. "I'm sorry."

"Yeah, I don't have tact." Max took Nathan's hand and shook it, then gestured to the sofa. "Maybe we should catch up a little. I'm here for a reason, and I'm betting it's a little project you're going to want to help work on."

"Listen, guys," Bill said, his words swallowed by a yawn. "I need to go to bed. Your schedule is killing me. Is there someplace semiprivate I can sleep?"

Nathan eyed him suspiciously, looking for a split second in the direction where Ziggy had just departed. "You know, the best way to adapt to it is to just tough it out."

I sent Nathan a warning vibe to go with my arched eyebrow. When I managed to catch his eye, he looked away. *Do you know how old he is, Carrie?*

Do you know how old "Jacob" is? It was a low blow, but we didn't have time for Nathan to play protective father. I smiled at Bill and said, "You can crash in the back room of the bookshop. We'll leave you alone there. Just don't let the bedbugs bite."

"Or anything else," Max said with a snort, which he immediately squelched at Nathan's angry glare.

"Before we start discussing battle plans—" Max knew Nathan almost as well as I did "—there's something I need to tell you guys."

As he gestured, I noticed something strange about his hand, out of the corner of my eye. I reached for his wrist and brought his hand up easily. He was missing two fingers.

"And a toe," he said, before I could say anything. "It was a torture thing. That's not important."

On that grim note, we settled into the living room—Max on the couch, Nathan in his chair and I on the arm of it—and listened, trying not to ask too many questions as he told us what had happened with the Oracle.

I was able to accept that he'd gotten Bella pregnant under the influence of one of Dahlia's potions. We'd figured that much out on our own. I was able to accept that Bella had been maimed in a horrific car accident and that she'd turned Max into a lupin. But I was a little stuck on the part where Max could walk around in broad daylight.

"I know, I'm as mystified as you are." He shrugged helplessly and stood, prowling around the living room like, well, a caged animal. "You have no idea how much it changes you, after all those years of not seeing a sunrise or, hell, even being awake at the same time everyone else is."

There was something sad in Nathan's eyes as he nodded, even though he smiled. "Congratulations on the baby. There's something that will change you."

Max turned serious then. "If I can get back to her. That's kind of why I came to find you. My father-in-law has more or less banished me from the pack until this unseemly business with the Soul Eater is taken care of." He made a noise of disgust. "Because I'm going to be held personally accountable for the actions of every vampire on the planet until the day I die, apparently. Probably beyond that."

"Well, we're not going to be much help." Nathan looked at me as if to reassure me he was okay, but I felt his sadness and even a little bit of envy through the blood tie. The thing he'd wanted most in life was a family, and if the Soul Eater hadn't taken it from him, his wife's fragile condition already would have. I knew how much it must have stung to find out that Max was going to be a father. "We haven't gotten very far, ourselves. But Carrie has some experience in working magic that could prove handy."

"If I don't die of starvation first." My stomach grumbled loudly to illustrate my point.

Max laughed. "I have some blood downstairs. It won't keep us going for long, but we've got enough that we won't starve for a couple of days."

Max and Nathan went downstairs together to grab the blood, which I warmed up for us and managed not to guzzle down on my own. Before Max fell victim to our "weird" schedule—though from his drooping eyelids and the six-hour time change he'd endured, I believed he was actually tired—we filled him in on the Soul Eater's new minions and all that had occurred with Ziggy.

"I know he's your kid," Max said, his voice full of genuine sympathy. "But we need to keep an eye on him."

Nathan agreed easily. "I hate to say it, but it hasn't been far from my thoughts."

"Well, I think I need to find a place to sleep, myself." Max stood and stretched, and I found my gaze following his maimed hand.

"Max," I said, meaning to tell him thank you for helping us, thank you for being horribly tortured in the line of duty, but that wasn't the kind of thing he would have wanted to hear. "You could take Ziggy's old room."

He cracked a reluctant smile. "No, I think the kid will need it. I'm a dog now. Just dig me a hole out back and throw some straw in it and I should be good to go."

"Well, there is the emergency shelter under the counter," Nathan said, and I elbowed him. "What?" he protested loudly, cradling his bruised ribs. "He said all he needed was a hole."

"Hey, at least that one has a sleeping bag in it. It's one up from straw." Max slung his duffel bag over his shoulder and started down the stairs. "If I see the kid, I'll tell him to get up here and grab some chow."

When Max was gone, and we were left alone in the apartment, Nathan opened a book and settled into the chair, but I could tell from the look on his face that he wasn't reading a word.

"Strategizing?" I guessed, sitting on the arm of the chair he occupied. I ruffled his hair and kissed his forehead.

"No. I was actually thinking of which of my rebellious children to discipline first." He closed the book and looked up at me, dismay giving his face a tired expression.

"Don't do that, it's gross. Calling me your kid," I added for clarity.

He closed his eyes and inhaled deeply, as if the oxygen would clear his head. "I suppose you're going to tell me to go talk to him?"

I shook my head. "No. Give him time to cool down."

"Am I a bad father if I say that I'm very glad you suggested that?" He leaned his head back, eyes closed. "Where did this go all wrong?"

"Six months ago. Six hellish months ago." I laughed. "And it's getting better every moment."

His hand slid up my arm, under the sleeve of my T-shirt to my shoulder, where he slipped his fingers under my bra strap. "It hasn't all been bad."

He pulled me into his lap, and I didn't resist him. The spells and protection wards could wait twenty minutes, and I refused to feel guilty or wary about ignoring them for the moment.

I pulled my shirt over my head, grateful that I'd worn one of my form-over-function bras today and not some cotton comfort thing. Not that I'd planned on having sex. It wasn't something we'd done in quite a while.

Nathan murmured his appreciation for the pink lace against the pale tops of my breasts—I'd lost a lot of skin color in the past six months, I noted with dismay—and kissed a path up to my neck.

Briefly, I worried. "What if Ziggy comes back? Or Bill or Max?"

Nathan shook his head, breathing faster as I reached between us to slide his shirt up. As he pulled it over his head, he mumbled, "They won't."

It was a good enough answer for me, after nearly a month of self-imposed celibacy. I stood just for a moment, to pull down my jeans, and Nathan assisted with trembling hands.

"What's the matter?" I laughed as he fumbled with the zipper. "Nervous?"

"Actually, a little." He looked embarrassed to admit it. "I can't help it, it feels like it's been forever."

We laughed, and he yanked the jeans down over my hips, my panties with them. He unzipped his own fly, and I climbed onto the chair to straddle him. When he slipped inside me, he groaned and a little thrill shot through me at the sound.

It might have been a while since the last time, but that proved no real hurdle for us that I could determine. I gripped the back of the chair to gain leverage, whimpering in frustration when it finally proved too difficult to raise and lower myself on him.

"Hang on, sweetheart," he rasped against my ear, and he lifted me in his arms as he rose. He carried me the few steps to the small kitchen table and swept our dirty mugs from it with one arm. I gasped in protest at the sight of the mugs cracking to pieces as they hit the linoleum, but all thoughts of collateral damage fled when the cold, hard plastic tabletop met my back, and Nathan thrust into me, deeper and harder than he'd been able to in the chair.

I opened my eyes to take in the sight of him, naked and hard, white skin gleaming like marble in the weird yellow glow of the ceiling lamp. My gaze slid over the scars from the Soul Eater's possession, which still hadn't healed, probably never would, that marred his arms, down to where his hands flexed as they gripped my hips and pulled me tighter against him as he drove deeper inside of me. I watched the way the muscles of his stomach bunched as he moved, the dark line of hair that fanned out over his chest, noted with strange fascination that I could see his pulse leap at the base of his throat.

As I raised myself up he slipped his arms around my back to support me. "Can I bite you?" I whispered against the hollow of his elbow. Though he didn't answer in words, I took his noise of strained self-control as an affirmative. I let my face change, just long enough to puncture his skin with my fangs, then let it ease back to normal, fastening my lips to the wound I'd made.

He'd hissed in pain when I'd first bit him, but now he only groaned and took great, gasping breaths. All sense of rhythm abandoned, he shoved inside me so hard the table rocked on its pedestal. He captured one of my hands and brought it to his mouth, twisted into his feeding face, and bit down on my palm at the base of my thumb. It hurt. I hissed at the pain, and then again at the pleasure that shot through me.

I closed my mouth over the wound I'd made on him and sucked hard. I felt everything. Him inside me and what it was for him to be inside of me. What it was for him to feel what I felt. The taste of my blood in his blood, his blood in my blood. It was a never-ending loop, a whirlpool of sensation that dragged me under, left me gasping, shaking as my body tightened around him, my legs locking around his back as he surged into me.

After a moment, he withdrew, kissed the spot on my palm and slumped to the floor. I opened my eyes and saw him wince as he flexed his arm. I could only lie sprawled on the little table, my feet brushing the floor as my legs dangled over the side.

I heard a dull rip, the rending of fabric, and Nathan pressed something into my hand. Half of his T-shirt, I noted with a giggle.

"What's that about?" he asked, out of breath.

I smiled, sitting up and winding the shirt around my bleeding palm. "Nothing. I just feel good."

"I'm glad you feel good," he said, eyeing me warily. "I didn't take too much, did I?"

"No." I giggled again. I couldn't help it. "Did I?"

He bent his arm with a grimace. "No, but it hurt like hell. It's been a long time since I've been bitten."

"Me, too." I reached for my jeans and pulled them on. "But it was nice."

He grinned, a little embarrassed, if I guessed correctly from his expression. "It was. I don't know why you asked to do it, though."

And I realized then that I didn't know, either. Biting had seemed so…bad. So dirty in the past. But it hadn't this time. It had been as erotic as hell. "I don't know. It just felt right."

In fact, it had felt more than right. It had felt like something a vampire would just *do*.

And I felt more like myself than I had in a long time.

Seven: Spirited Away

❧❧❧

Grand Rapids was no kind of city for a vampire.

Ziggy lit another cigarette and peered at the clock behind the bar. They kept it dark enough in the place, they should have at least invested in a clock that lit up or glowed in the dark or something.

He wished he hadn't stormed out the way he had. Nate probably thought he was mad at him. Maybe he was. But he couldn't tell. Jacob could be sneaky like that, putting thoughts in when you weren't looking and just leaving them there for you to stumble over. Half the time, Ziggy wasn't sure he had an original idea about anything anymore. Maybe it was all Jacob, filling up his head, making him crazy as shit when all he wanted was to just fix things with Nate and get back to life as normal.

But who decided what was normal? Coming back from the dead, was that normal? And how did you fix things with someone when you knew they'd be happier if you were dead? When they'd even left you for dead in the past?

He swore and gulped down the last of his beer. It

wasn't good, but it was tricking his stomach out of its hunger for now. The bartender gave him the fish eye when he picked up the empty glass and refilled it. Ziggy's fake ID hadn't fooled him, but he didn't look like the type who'd take an argument over a tip, especially when the bar was as empty as it was.

The heavy door scraped open on its sticky hinges. It was a terrible sound. Worse, because it could mean that one of Jacob's hired goons was sneaking up right that very second. Ziggy put his hand casually on the hunting knife concealed beneath his jacket, then relaxed when the guy behind him let out a mock-impressed whistle.

"Wow. Flashy." Bill sat down on the stool beside him and motioned to the bartender. "Seven and seven, and another one of whatever my friend here is having, for him."

The bartender, who would have looked like Santa Claus but for the stained polo shirt he wore and the toothpick hanging out of the corner of his mouth, gave Bill the same suspicious look he'd given Ziggy. Maybe he was just a naturally suspicious person. It wasn't the best part of town, and the town was infested with vampires, after all.

"Unless you'd rather go grab a bite," Bill said, the corner of his mouth twitching. "In which case I'd just as soon stay here."

Ziggy didn't respond. It was kind of fun to watch the guy scramble mentally while his joke fell flat as a pancake.

Bill's throat moved as he swallowed. "See, it was a joke. Because you bit me."

"Yeah, I got it," Ziggy assured him, still not cracking a smile.

Running away from the conversation as if it were on

fire, Bill turned his head and nodded to the small television attached to the wall above the corner booth. The screen showed some sports channel. Guys in suits, talking about statistics that didn't mean anything important except to guys like Bill. "Tigers are doing good this year, huh? They've actually got a shot at the postseason again."

"I don't like baseball." Ziggy took a slow drink.

"I'm a Sox fan, anyway. White, not red. But neither of them are doing so hot this year."

"What the hell are you doing here?" Ziggy turned on the stool and let his coat fall open, so the guy could get a glimpse of the knife strapped inside. "Nate send you after me?"

The guy didn't flinch. Ziggy had to admit, he was tough. He'd even tried to fight him off when he'd bitten him. Somebody like that, you could respect.

He took a swallow of his drink before he answered. "No, he did not. And I did not come here to look for you. It's the only place open within walking distance."

"You didn't walk far enough," Ziggy muttered. You could practically see the bar from Nate's bedroom window. There was no way Bill wasn't there on a spy mission.

They sat in silence for a while. Ziggy turned back to the bar and stared into the bottom of his glass, waiting for Bill to leave. No dice. The guy took another drink and said, "So, you got a girlfriend, Ziggy?"

Nice. The guy was as transparent as a piece of glass. Real easy to read. After a while with people like Dahlia and Jacob, it was a refreshing change. "Not so much with the girls. But I'm betting that's why you asked."

"I had a hunch. I'm good like that." He didn't look embarrassed at being caught or anything. Just like…

whatever. Again, a nice change from people who freaked if you guessed their little mind games. He didn't even look away when he asked, "So, any other…friends?"

Ziggy didn't want to laugh, but he let himself smile a little bit. "You're pretty direct."

"As a nonstop commuter flight." Bill laughed, then nervously added, "Yeah, that's another joke. Because they're nonstop, so you don't have to get a connection—"

"Yeah, got that one, too. And I might even laugh if you manage to be funny." Ziggy stubbed out his cigarette and reached for another one. "So, you're a groupie, huh?"

That question actually managed to rattle Bill a little. Good. Showed he was healthy. He stuttered a little as he started to answer. "No, uh…just a blood donor. And I organize a couple other blood donors, take part of their profits."

Ziggy nodded. "So, you're not a groupie, you're a vampire profiteer?"

"I prefer 'donor pimp,' but yeah," he said with a shrug.

Now Ziggy let himself laugh. "Donor pimp. *That's* funny."

"Wasn't meant to be." Bill grabbed Ziggy's lighter and flicked it open against his thigh, lighting it in the process before he held it out for him.

Okay, that was pretty smooth, Ziggy conceded to himself as he leaned toward Bill to light up.

"So, how long have you been doing that?" he asked as he straightened back up. "The donor pimping, not the lighter trick."

Bill made a sort of humming noise while he thought, finally answering, "I started when I was thirty-two, so eight years now? Something like that."

"Took a while to get established, huh?" Ziggy did a quick mental calculation. "You look good for your age. You sure you're not drinking some of your clients' blood on the side?"

"Hey, thanks." He looked genuinely pleased at that. "You don't look a day over eighteen. How old are you?"

"Don't tell Papa Smurf over there, but I'm only twenty." Ziggy was less pleased to hear he looked like a kid. It was going to make eternity pretty unbearable if he was going to have to start with a new identity every five years.

Bill chuckled and slid the lighter across the bar to Ziggy. "No, what I meant was, total. How old are you in total?"

"Twenty." Ziggy met his confused stare head-on. "Really. I got turned a little bit before my last birthday."

"Wow." Bill seemed to contemplate that a moment.

A little flame of disappointment flickered in Ziggy. Now he would be just a kid in this guy's eyes, which was a damned shame. He was fun to relate to as an adult, and not many adults seemed to be taking Ziggy seriously these days. Steering the conversation away from the weirdness of the moment, he said, "So, what did you do before you started donor pimping? The army or something, right?"

Bill smiled before taking another gulp of his drink, and it wasn't the kind of indulgent smile you'd give a kid. Bonus. "I was in the Marines."

"So, you're a big, tough fighting guy?" Ziggy didn't really care for military types. Jacob's place was always surrounded with them. Ziggy had started thinking of them as servants, and it lowered Bill's status a little bit in his mind. That was a good thing. Meant he'd still have the upper hand or whatever if anything started. Not that he wanted anything to start. *Humans are food, not our friends*, Jacob admonished from his memory.

Bill looked nervously back at the television, then at the bartender, then back to his drink. His body language spoke volumes. He didn't want to talk about whatever it was he used to do. "Yeah. I mean, no. I never saw any combat or anything. But I didn't like it. The whole scene was a little too structured for me."

"Is that why you quit?" He took a pull off his cigarette and tapped the end against the ashtray. "Too much structure?"

"Quit isn't really the word for it." Bill looked down at the bar and rubbed his neck. "I was… Let's just say I was politely asked to leave. My services were no longer required."

"Ah." Ziggy had heard the correct terminology for that somewhere. Probably from one of Jacob's guards. But he didn't really care, one way or the other. "I don't think I could do the whole army thing. I'm not big on taking orders."

Bill snorted. "It wasn't the army. It was the Marines. And yeah, I can see where you'd have a problem. I got axed because I have a hard time keeping my mouth shut when I think I have something useful to contribute. For instance, if I thought up a more efficient way to do something, I would tell my commanding officer—whether he asked me or not. And that wasn't exactly what they wanted."

"They wanted a cog in a machine." Ziggy knew how that felt. He got that feeling from Jacob sometimes. As if he was just another employee, no matter what his sire said or did to him. He cleared his throat. "Listen, you don't have to stay here with me. I'm not going to escape."

"Hey, I'm as much a hostage as you are. In fact, maybe I should be tied to a radiator or something." From the tone of Bill's voice, Ziggy knew he was telling the truth. "But I didn't come over here because I thought you were going to escape."

And fuck, wasn't that weird? Having some guy—some actually pretty good-looking guy—sitting there, saying he wasn't there for an ulterior purpose.

Of course, he'd never said that, Ziggy realized. He'd said he wasn't there because he was worried about him escaping. Maybe he was there because Nate *had* sent him. Maybe he was just bored, or an alcoholic. Maybe he was a vampire groupie, after all, and he was just better at covering it up. Maybe he'd come here looking for Ziggy, but for an entirely different reason.

"I'm not trying to pick you up," Bill said quietly.

Ziggy stared back at him. "Did you read my mind?"

"No." Bill laughed, but his smile didn't show in his eyes. "But I read your facial expression. Jesus, have you had some rough relationships in the past or something?"

"Or something. Let's change the subject." Ziggy stood and stubbed out the cigarette, threw some money down on the bar. He started for the door, half wanting Bill to go the fuck away and half wanting him to follow. Weird.

But he didn't do either. He just sat where he was. "You don't have to be a hard-ass with me. I mean, I know I'm supposed to be wicked impressed here, but the unapproachable act gets stale fast."

Funny. Ziggy smiled, but he wiped it off when he turned to face Bill. "I don't get what you're saying."

From the way he laughed, it was hard to tell if Bill was annoyed or not. "I'm saying drop the rebellious teenager who doesn't give a fuck act and be real with me for a few minutes. We might find that if we're not trying to top each other's carefully crafted banter, we'd actually get along."

This time, Ziggy let Bill see the smile. "I thought we *were* getting along."

"And here I thought we were just rehearsing for a bad romantic comedy." Bill gestured to the chair. "Have a seat. We've got time before last call."

So, they talked. And talked. And every time the urge to be himself came along, Ziggy followed the instinct. And every time Jacob—no, the Soul Eater, it hurt less to think of him that way—tried to push into his head and fill his mind with strange insecurities and assurances that he would never be loved or even respected by a person other than his sire, he shoved those away, too.

Bill was actually a cool guy. He had funny stories about vampires, soldiers, just about anything. Even his stories that weren't funny were funny, because something about him was just…well, he was a funny guy.

Yeah, he was great. So great that last call came too soon, which really sucked.

And when they got back to the apartment, the upstairs door was locked, and that really sucked.

"I have a feeling that it's locked for privacy reasons, rather than safety," Bill said with a snicker, and Ziggy glared at him. He cleared his throat then and at least pretended to look remorseful. "I'm sorry. No one likes to think about their dad having sex."

At least the bookstore was unlocked. Ziggy ushered Bill in and pointed to the farthest corner of the shop, behind the toppled bookshelves. "My old bed might be in the back room of the bookstore. You can sleep there and be comfortable."

"Where are you going?" Bill asked as they picked their way through the wreckage. "Back out on the street to be a brooding vampire?"

He bristled at that. "I'm not going to run away, if that's what you think."

"I already told you I don't. But it seems kind of lonely, just wandering around a town that seems to close up shop at 9:00 p.m. when you've got perfectly good company here."

"I like to be alone." Ziggy turned and headed for the door.

"Okay, I get it. You go roam the streets, and I'll somehow pick this padlock and then you can lock me in so I don't get away." He gestured to Ziggy. "Give me one of those safety pins off your boots."

Nate had never padlocked the storage room before. But then, judging from the rest of the place, it was probably good that he had. Ziggy forced down his growing irritation and made his way to Bill's side.

"I've got a better idea." Ziggy gripped the lock and jerked it down sharply. It held together a hinged metal rectangle that slotted over a U-shaped loop attached to the door. The whole thing snapped free from the bolts, bending the door a little where the closure was attached. The whole destruction took less than a second, and Ziggy felt pretty pleased with himself, until he saw the look on Bill's face. He appeared to be torn between being impressed and just plain being scared shitless.

"My sire is pretty strong, and I drink his blood, so…" That was the worst thing to say. He just shut his mouth and went inside.

"Why didn't he have the rest of the place this secure?" Bill asked as Ziggy found the pull cord for the dusty lightbulb overhead.

"I don't know. It used to be. Stuff changed." Stuff like Carrie. Stuff like dying. Stuff like dying because Carrie let Cyrus nearly rip his head off.

Bill pulled the door closed. As closed as he could now that it was bent, anyway. "Well, I'll just have to improvise. You don't have to stay."

"Nah, it's all right. Not like I have anything better to do." And wasn't that the truth. Vampires in New York, Chicago, those were lucky vampires. Stuff stayed open late.

But he supposed it could have been worse. He could live in Alaska.

Bill ran his hand across one of the dusty shelves as if he was testing it for stability. "You fed already, right?"

"Jesus." Ziggy leaned against the wall and closed his eyes. That was officially the very last thing he needed, for Bill to be afraid that he was looking at him like some all-you-can-eat buffet.

"You know, you bit me once already. I'm just playing it safe." Bill sounded defensive.

Ziggy laughed, and he could taste the bitterness of it in his throat. Of course this guy wouldn't trust him. Why should he? Why should any human trust him?

They're not the same as us, Jacob whispered in his mind. *You deserve someone to match your power.*

It was a huge struggle not to respond to him. In fact,

it made him feel a little bit like crying, and that was the last thing he wanted to do in front of Bill.

"Hey, are you okay?" Bill was right beside him in the next second, looking worried as hell.

"Yeah, I'm fine." He wiped his forehead with the palm of his hand and started for the door. When he glanced down at his hand, he saw red. Great. Sweating blood. That was probably really healthy.

"I don't know if I've made it clear or not," Bill said, quiet enough that it wasn't normal volume, but too strong and self-confident to be a whisper. "But I like you. Despite the fact you bit me. That doesn't mean I expect anything. But just so you have that information handy."

Ziggy swallowed hard as Bill's footsteps came up close behind him. A big, warm, human hand touched his shoulder. And then, without asking permission or giving any sort of warning that he was going to do so, Bill spun him to face him, and kissed him.

And Ziggy realized that he hadn't been kissed since… well, since before he died.

It wasn't a timid, gentle kind of kiss, either. It reminded him of one of those movie kisses that he used to think looked painful. Now he knew better. They felt damned good.

True, the only guy he'd ever kissed before was Jeremy and look how well *that* had turned out. But Jeremy had been a fling, a sort of test to see if he was really, really gay. He definitely hadn't been into Ziggy as much as Ziggy had been into him. And Bill sure seemed to be into him.

That was the best part. Oh yeah, Bill's hands in his hair and his tongue in his mouth, those were good parts, too. But knowing that the other guy had an interest in him besides getting laid—hell, at least *suspecting* the guy had an interest besides getting laid—that made it more than a kiss. It made it a validation somehow.

It was a shame that it ended too soon. Suddenly, Bill jerked back, leaving Ziggy dazed and disappointed.

"Did you hear that?" Bill looked at the door of the shed as if he could see through it. "I thought I heard…"

And then Ziggy heard it, too. It was Carrie, screaming.

We were on the way down to the bookshop when it happened. Maybe we were too sex-drugged to be observant, and that was our big mistake. When we stepped onto the sidewalk, Nathan's arm around my waist, hips bumping as we walked, loose limbed and giggling, headed just a few feet to the steps down to the shop, we caught their scent on the air.

A dozen of the Soul Eater's foul humans shuffled out of the alley, like deceptively slow monsters in a horror film. Nathan looked up, and my gaze followed his, to the rooftop, where more stood.

"Carrie, grab me," he said, sounding oddly calm as he locked his arms around me. I had no choice but to grab his shoulders and squeeze my eyes shut tight as he vaulted us both over the iron railing and down the stairwell.

He hit first, landing on his feet on the lip of one step. We both tumbled, rolling down, every other stair finding a new part of me to bite into. We crashed through the door at the bottom and I was on my feet first, pushing it closed and locking it while Nathan wheezed and groaned on the floor.

Of course, the door wasn't as secure as it had been in

the past. The window, smashed out months ago, was still covered only in flattened cardboard boxes. The tape keeping them up had lost much of its hold, so all that really separated me from the monsters was a bit of cardboard now pinned over the opening only by my shoulder.

"Help!" I screamed, not knowing who would come to our aid. Max was asleep in the shelter, so I pounded on the floor with my foot as hard as I could while Nathan got to his feet and ran to the trapdoor.

The door to the storage room scraped open and Ziggy and Bill rushed out, Bill with his gun drawn. I'd never been more happy to see a firearm pointed at me in my entire life.

Then, two skinny but ruthlessly strong arms crumpled the cardboard on either side of me and clutched my shirt, pulling me into the hole where the window had been.

Nathan shot forward and grabbed my arms, but I pushed him back. "My shirt," I wheezed as the collar cut into my throat. He grabbed the fabric and ripped, and the whole thing tore away, sucking out of the hole with the arms and the cardboard.

Max rushed up the stairs, bare chested and jeans unzipped, a stake in his hand. He looked from my near-topless state to the clutching, blood-crazed humans outside the door and shouted, "Cover the window!"

It didn't matter. Before I could move out of the way, the door creaked under their weight and fell in, almost in slow motion, and the creatures rushed in after the four of us.

I didn't have time to think things through. I just started fighting. The first one I came up against wasn't armed. It was a good thing, too, because I couldn't get to any kind of weapon before the first one struck. It was a short, middle-aged woman with a grown-out bleach job and sagging skin. Her dirty, broken fingernails dug into my shoulders as she pulled me against her. She was going to bite me.

The hell she was. Despite the enormous pressure on my shoulders, I raised my arms and grabbed at her head, her ears, anything to distract her, and I pulled. I held two handfuls of bloody hair before she realized what had happened and let me go. She staggered back, but her eyes were empty as she charged at me again. Without full comprehension of why I did it, I grabbed one of the overturned wooden tables that used to hold metaphysical merchandise and held it up in front of me. She twisted to make another grab at me and managed to get my wrist, forcing me to drop the table, but her listless legs tangled and fell backward onto the upturned legs. *Oh, for fuck's sake,* I thought, falling on top of her and ramming her as hard as I could onto the table. Her hold released immediately and I staggered to my feet before another one could fall on us and inadvertently stake me. The blonde didn't get up, her mouth opening and closing, body jerking. One square table leg protruded through her forehead and the bridge of her nose, another through her abdomen. The end of the leg jammed through her head was smeared wet and sticky with harsh gray bits of bone and chunks of flesh.

I felt the vomit rising in my throat. I turned away from the scene when another set of hands grabbed me. There was nothing elegant about this attack. Whoever had me lifted me over their head and hurled me into the counter.

I saw the cracked top of the display case before I hit it, but it was too late. I crashed through, feeling the bite of a thousand shards of glass as they exploded around me.

Still, it was advantageous in that when I got to my feet, I had a weapon. A weapon that scored my palms and coursed blood down my arms, but still, a weapon. And when the creature who'd thrown me, a thin, young-looking guy with greasy black hair slashing across his eyes, came at me to finish the job, I sank a huge piece of glass into his body just under his rib cage and ripped up with all my might, praying my fingers wouldn't get severed in the process. But you know that old saying about an object in motion—what holds true for rear-ending car accidents also holds true for eviscerating a human with a jagged piece of broken glass. The thing moving fastest causes the most damage. The man dropped, spewing a huge arterial spray, and my hand came away just a little bit worse for wear.

I turned and caught sight of Bill, who was holding his own, shooting anything that moved. He had a worrisome gash across his forehead and a fresh bite on his forearm, but he moved like a total killing machine. I revised my battle plan against the Soul Eater. We didn't need an army. We needed the Marines.

Max wasn't doing too bad himself. He wasn't, to my disappointment, in werewolf mode, but he battled the guy who'd had him in a headlock previously with just his fists, and though the guy was a bull, he didn't appear to be winning.

I was about to jump back into the fray when I saw Ziggy, and horror made my blood run colder than it already was.

Ziggy didn't have a weapon. He didn't need one. In the

space of time it takes to blink, he grabbed a woman, twisted her head to the side, and ripped her throat out with his teeth, spitting a huge wad of flesh to the ground as she fell, almost instantly dead. Another rushed at him, and he punched straight through the man's chest, jerking his bloody fist back as the man fell. There was a broken neck. Then a head torn off, spine dangling from the skull like the fuse of a bomb. Ziggy threw it aside nonchalantly and moved on to the next one.

If he'd been in some primal rage, if he'd shown some sort of emotion while killing, I wouldn't have been so bothered. And I wouldn't have been bothered enough to be distracted. And that distraction wouldn't have cost me Nathan.

I've never been staked before. And I suppose, technically, since my heart wasn't in my chest but in a little metal box under the guest bathroom sink back at the penthouse, it wouldn't kill me. But when the creature sank the sharpened wood into my chest—how could anyone move so fast, so quietly?—I thought I would die. Prayed I would. I looked down, horrified, at the thick wood protruding from my chest, and my vision went hazy. The pain intensified tenfold, the way skinned knees always did as a child when I would look at them. I tumbled backward, little black spots of agony forming in my vision.

"Carrie!" Nathan shouted, and I heard a scuffle. He rushed at the creature who'd grabbed me, but the man knocked him aside as if he were a fly. Nathan tumbled onto his back, and two of the other creatures spotted him. They advanced, but they threw their makeshift weapons aside.

I watched in horror as one of them hit Nathan with a punch that sent him flying across the room. He landed with a sick crunch against one of the broken bookcases and went limp, though he tried for a moment to raise one of his hands. He slid to the floor, eyes rolling to the back of his head. Blood pooled on the wooden planks beneath him, a bright red streak behind him showing the path of his fall.

I got to my feet and started to run for him, but the one who'd staked me held me back. The awful smell of him, whether from his filthy, tattered clothing or his grimy body, made me gag.

Max headed for the two who closed in on Nathan, only to be tossed aside like a broken toy. Bill shot one of the pair, but, like the others that he'd shot, they were only slowed down. A dark-complected creature with a bullet wound in his neck gurgled, blood pouring from his mouth, but he still managed to get behind Bill and restrain him.

Ziggy had better luck. One of them took a swing he easily dodged. The other made a clumsy grab for him.

Immediately, alarms went off in my head. Either the Soul Eater had sent out his B squad, which I found doubtful, or they weren't here to kill us. They were here for Nathan.

I struggled against my captor and did the only thing I could think of: I screamed for help, as loudly and shrilly as I could.

"Poor baby, does she need some help?" The voice behind me sent a fresh wave of anger and despair through me.

Dahlia strolled into the room, clicking her long, black fingernails against a length of black vinyl tarp. She unrolled it to reveal a zipper. It was a body bag.

She actually had the nerve to step close to me and pat me on the head. I spit in her smug face.

All the humor went out of her expression. She produced a black handkerchief—she was nothing if not a perfectly color-coordinated cliché—and daintily wiped her cheek. A streak of white pancake makeup stained the cloth when she pulled it away. "Break her arm."

The monster jerked sharply where he hung on to one of my wrists and bone instantly splintered under his hand. I stared, too stunned to feel pain, at the jagged end of my ulna emerging from a split in my skin.

She unrolled the bag beside Nathan and lifted one of his arms, letting it drop back to the ground.

"Is he alive?" I screamed, stamping my foot in a futile effort to get their attention. "I want to know that he's alive!"

With a giggle, she raised one bloodied palm to her mouth and darted her tongue out to taste Nathan's blood.

I howled in rage and lunged forward, but the shock of the broken bone had worn off and my knees buckled. I hung helpless in my captor's grasp, only able to watch as Dahlia rolled Nathan into the bag and zipped him in.

"You two, carry him," she ordered, and one of the humans holding Max clubbed him over the back of the head. He fell with a curse and tried to stand, but the creature hit him again, and he wisely stayed down. They moved forward and grabbed the body bag containing Nathan.

"Please, just tell me if he's alive!" I screamed at them as they disappeared through the door.

Dahlia sniffed delicately as she passed me on her way out. "Kill them," she ordered.

As the creatures moved to do her bidding, Ziggy shouted, "Jacob is going to kill you when he finds out what you did."

"Who do you think sent me?" she asked, then stopped in her tracks and turned, a sick smile on her face. "Besides, I don't recall seeing you here. Alive. They must have killed you before I got here. What a tragic, tragic accident."

"What about me, baby?" Max wheezed from the floor. "We got along, didn't we?"

A laugh exploded from her, a burst of pure evil. "You weren't that good."

And then, she was gone. There wouldn't be any further bargaining. Once, she'd told me that not everything was as black-and-white as I painted it, that evil was more a force of nature. Just the way you couldn't reason with a tornado ripping your town apart, you couldn't reason with Dahlia when she was ripping a life apart.

My only consolation was that the awful feeling I'd gotten when Cyrus had died—the rending of the blood tie that had bound us—hadn't happened when they took Nathan away. And because of that, I knew I had to fight.

I couldn't just let these creatures kill us. I didn't need a weapon. Dahlia being so close, her power so close to me I could taste it, made me realize I already had a weapon. I closed my eyes. I'm sure the others saw it as anticipation of the death blow. I remembered Dahlia using *illuminate* to turn on lights, how easily it had come to her. I remembered the way Nathan had taught me to visualize what I wanted to achieve when we'd used Dahlia's invisibility spell. The word *flame* came to me as easily as if it were printed on the backs of my eyelids. I knew the difference between what I wanted to do and now, and the difference between what I'd seen Dahlia do and what I wanted to happen. I didn't want to light something up. I wanted to burn it down.

In my mind, the word unfurled in fury, with a roar like an explosion that rang off the inside of my skull. I opened my eyes, and the word burned from my lips, so hot I thought they would blister. And with the word, came the flames. They coiled out of my mouth like grasping hands, lighting the creatures' clothes and skin instantly. They screamed and fell back, consumed before they hit the ground, and Max, Ziggy and Bill ducked away from the flames.

Something in Dahlia's blood responded to fire, I realized as the flames died around us. When I'd consumed her blood and taken in her power that night in the mansion, the power hadn't changed its shape. A burst of energy, as hot as any flame, shot through me and I stumbled over a smoldering corpse and toward the door. Bill, Ziggy and Max were right behind me, but by the time we reached the top of the stairs, it was too late.

A black limo careened down the street, bearing Nathan away from us, to the arms of his sire.

Eight: Creation

The evening went by in a weird, dreamlike way. I let Max pull the stake from my chest. It hurt almost as much as when it had first gone in. Bill's limited experience with field medicine was enough to help mend my arm, and with some direction from me he set my wrist with a makeshift splint and an Ace bandage after he picked out the bone shards that protruded through my skin. Inwardly, I was a sea of freakish, calculating calm. Outwardly, I must have been a wreck. I saw Ziggy and Bill give each other "looks" indicating they were extremely concerned for my mental well-being. I wondered what had happened in that storage room and when, exactly, they'd started to use "looks."

I let the guys think I was crazy, or grieving. They didn't bother me, and it gave me time to think.

I'd used Dahlia's magic before. It wasn't all that difficult to do. Nathan believed that everyone had the capacity to perform magic on a small scale. It stood to reason that after I'd imbibed Dahlia's blood and some of her power in the process, my own magical capabilities had amped up considerably. All I had to do was learn to use it. Not in the heat of the moment, fueled by extreme emotion. I'd seen enough movies to know that kind of talent was unreliable. I needed to learn how to get control of the power I had, and find out how it could work for us, against the Soul Eater.

The problem was that I didn't know where to start finding answers. That was usually Nathan's job. I just tagged along.

"Carrie, you okay?" Max looked at me with concern etched into every line of his face, but I could tell he thought he was covering it up.

"I'm thinking." I bit the thumbnail on my uninjured hand. "About what happened downstairs."

"Oh, you mean when you opened your mouth and fire poured out like a dragon in a bad fantasy movie?" Ziggy slowly rubbed his palms up and down his face, the way Nathan always did when he was stressed-out and tired.

"Yeah, what was up with that?" Max grabbed Dahlia's spell book from the coffee table where we'd left it. "Was that in here?"

"No." How could I explain it to them, in a way that would make sense and also not make me feel like a total flake saying it out loud? "It was just heat-of-the-moment. An improvisation based off of things Nathan had told me and things that I'd seen Dahlia do. But that's not the point. I obviously have an advantage here, and we're not exploiting it."

"Why would you want to?" Ziggy finished cleaning the blood off his hands with a towel that had once been white and now sported several mottled shades of pink.

"Because that was badass," Max said, his eyes practically boggling out of his head. "We were sucking against those things, whatever they were, and she unleashed hell and fried them where they stood. Why wouldn't we want her to do it again?"

Ziggy shrugged, but though his body language was casual, his voice was cold as stone. "I've watched Dahlia use her 'talents'—" he made air quotes around the word "—and yeah, she can do some really awesome tricks. But she's insane, and there is no way she's been that way her whole life without someone noticing."

"You think Dahlia's power drove her mad?" That was an intense thought. One I didn't want to entertain. If she'd had the kind of limitless power she wielded now at a young age, someone would have noticed her playmates getting immolated. Maybe the more she'd used her power, the more it had chipped away at her sanity. I certainly didn't need anything else to chip away at mine.

I already had the fact I was a vampire working against me. It seemed that the younger a vampire was, the less evil it was. I wondered if evil was a product of age, like crow's feet or cholesterol for humans. Did the years stack the decks against vampires? I'd been changed for less than a year now, and I could easily see how several centuries of the kind of crap we'd been going through would push me to the dark side. It just seemed easier to be evil, because for as long as I'd known there *was* evil out there, things always seemed to go in its favor.

I blew out a breath and dropped my head to my hands, my elbows resting on my knees. "You're right, Ziggy. It could be dangerous. Nathan believes magic is very dangerous, and he would know better than I would. But we still need to get more help than we've got. Maybe this is the best place to start."

"And we have to save Nathan. We all want to get him back as quickly as possible, before the Soul Eater can do anything to him," Max put in quietly, his gaze leveled dead on Ziggy's face. "But I'm not sure you do."

Ziggy's back straightened at that. "What the hell do you mean?"

I wanted to stop this line of conversation, and at the same time let it crash to its inevitable conclusion. I needed to know—I think Max and I both did—that Ziggy wasn't going to give in to the will of his sire at the last minute and, if not double-cross us, at least back down from the conflict to protect his sire.

"I mean," Max said, as though he was picking up my mental broadcast signal, "I want to know if you're going to stab us in the back to help your sire."

Ziggy turned to me. "Carrie, come on. You gotta have my back here. You know I wouldn't fuck you guys over."

"No, I don't." I didn't let myself back down, not an inch, not even when I could feel Ziggy's hate radiating off him in waves. "I know you're torn. I know you would never hurt Nathan, but you admitted that you find it hard to resist the blood tie to him. How do we know you didn't lead him to us? You haven't been completely honest so far. You know things about these creatures, but you've never volunteered that information."

I hadn't expected Bill to back me up. I thought he would stay quiet, waiting for a safe time to speak. But he surprised me by putting his hand on Ziggy's shoulder in a supportive gesture. "Tell us what you know."

I watched the conflict inside Ziggy bubble to the surface. He was so angry—nothing at all like the boy I remembered. It didn't take a blood tie to tell what he was feeling. He blamed himself for so much. For his sire's anger, for his father's capture. For becoming a vampire in the first place.

He reminded me of me, right after I'd been turned. I'd been mad at myself, mad at Cyrus, even mad at Nathan, who I'd barely known then, because my life had spun out of control. In Ziggy's case, I was betting it was ten times worse, because it was a delayed reaction. He'd blithely accepted the horrific changes in his life in characteristic Ziggy style. I wondered if it had ever occurred to him to be angry before we'd entered his life again. That anger could definitely be misdirected, and I didn't want us to bear the brunt of it. Ziggy had a blood tie to the Soul Eater. He could pretend to go along with our plans and spill them to the Soul Eater the whole time, either giving away our position or hiding important information about his sire. If he wasn't letting us in on the things happening in his head, was he maintaining that same radio silence on the other end of the blood tie?

Even though I didn't want to, I had to know. "Did you tell the Soul Eater to send them tonight? Are you working with him, listening to him through the blood tie?"

"Do you wanna know what he's telling me?" Ziggy cracked his knuckles, glaring at all of us. I'm sure he thought he looked tough, but my heart ached for him.

"I'm being urged every second to kill you and return to him. I'm seeing really vivid fucking images of him just handing over my heart to Dahlia—and it's not like there's any love from her, so I know what she'll do with it. And he knows I'm not dead, and I'm trying not to tell him that you're still alive, and at the same time I kind of want to kill you and get back to where I was a week ago."

Ziggy stood and approached Max, every fall of his heavy boots sounding like ominous drumbeats on a movie soundtrack. "Right now, I don't know what to do. Do I tell you guys these things? No, because what good does it do? Especially when I'm not sure if I want to be here, or back with him. Do you really want that kind of running commentary from me? Because I can tell you every time I think of killing you. Every time I think of how easy it would be to get my life back and never see you again."

He was halfway to the door when Max called after him, "If your life was so great, if you don't want anything else, why did he need to take your heart?"

Ziggy's back went rigid. So softly I could barely hear it, he said, "Shut up."

Max shook his head. "No, I want to know. Really. If you're so important to him, why does he keep you on a leash? If you're so content in your 'life,' why does he need that insurance?"

Ziggy turned, looking more enraged than I'd ever seen him. When he reached Max, his fists clenched and unclenched, but he didn't strike him. Then, the anger left his expression, and he did something I'd never have expected Ziggy to do. He cried.

It was as though his tears deflated him. He slumped onto the couch and, at first, he covered his eyes with his hand. When his back began to shake, Bill slid an arm around his shoulders, and Ziggy turned into the embrace, sobbing openly.

I itched to do something. I always feel that way when someone cries. But I could never think of a productive way to make them feel better, even now, when faced with Ziggy's tears. So, I did nothing.

Bill looked at me over the top of Ziggy's head, and though I hadn't known him long, I could read the look. He didn't want me to go easy on Ziggy. He liked that we were getting results.

"Ziggy, tell me what you know about these creatures he has. Anything you've done to betray us—" the ugly word slipped from my lips before I could stop it "—or anything you think you've done…. It doesn't mean anything if you tell us what those creatures are."

He sat up a little, as if reluctant to break contact with Bill. "Dahlia says they're ghouls. But Ja—the Soul Eater doesn't call them that. He said his are better. Different, because they started with his blood, but we fed them. They got something from both of us."

"What did they get?" Bill's voice was soft, soothing. I don't know what it did for Ziggy, but it sure put me at ease.

"From Dahlia, they got her…power." Ziggy sniffed manfully and straightened. "I don't know what they could have gotten from me. My physical strength, maybe? He said I had more than any fledgling he'd ever sired. I guess it was supposed to be a compliment."

My fingers twisted the hem of my T-shirt of their own

volition. "Forget about that for now. Do you think Nathan is still alive? Do you think we have time?"

Ziggy shrugged. "I know that he wants Nathan for something. But I don't think it's to kill him. Wherever Nathan is, he's with the Soul Eater."

I stood and paced to the door and back. "We're going to get him back. Tomorrow night."

"Why not now?" The restlessness had returned to Bill's voice. "We're sure where he is. Let's go get him."

"And get killed." Ziggy laughed hopelessly. "He's got dozens of those things. I mean, at least a hundred."

"A hundred dozen?" My knees went out from under me.

Ziggy waved his hands in front of him. "No, no. Total. A hundred total, maybe more. I've never bothered to count."

"What can kill them?" Max asked, and I was glad he could focus all of our ready-to-go energy on something constructive.

Ziggy shrugged. "I don't know. Maybe nothing. We've never tried before."

"They were strong," I noted, hearing a little of my old, stupid confidence creeping into my words. "But still human. I'm willing to bet they're like anything else—destroy the heart, burn it up, cut off the head and they're no more problem to us."

"Heads off, check." Max stood and rubbed his hand across his jaw. "This is going to be dangerous."

"It's not the first time," I said, suddenly feeling the weight of the last year full on my shoulders. "It probably won't be the last."

"Well, it should be!" Max stomped a few paces away, then stopped, covering his face with his hands. "This is ridiculous. I was right there. Right there! And I let them get by me."

"It wasn't your fault—" I began.

Bill interrupted. "I was right there, too. Are you blaming me?"

"Of course I'm not!"

"And I'm not blaming you," I interjected. "Or Bill or Ziggy. No one is to blame. But Nathan was taken and we have to get him back."

In the moment that Bill didn't look as though he believed either of us, I realized something. Something that was a little bit silly, something that completely detracted from the seriousness of the situation. But it seemed to be needed, so I said it. "Bill, I think you're officially one of us."

"Fantastic," he grumbled, then smiled grudgingly. "Listen, I'm not used to this sort of thing."

"Neither am I," Ziggy said with a sympathetic nod. "But she is. And so is Max. So I say we listen to them."

"Okay, guys, you stockpile weapons, whatever you need to get this done." I looked nervously at my watch, cursing the shortened summer nights. "I'm going to see what I can learn from Dahlia's book."

While everyone went to prepare, I locked myself in the bedroom. Past situations of dire peril would have found me weeping at my powerlessness, or at least worrying over the horrible fate Nathan might have met. But not tonight. Tonight, I wanted to arm myself with more than a wooden stake. I wanted to wield the horrible power Dahlia had shown me.

I opened the book, and the moment my fingertips

skimmed the pages, I felt calm. In control. More like myself.

Imagine how good you would feel if you set that evil thing on fire.

I blinked, twitching my head and shoulders. Why would I have such a crazy thought?

There's nothing useful in it. All the spells you've been able to do, you've figured out on your own.

That seemed reasonable. I lifted the book and saw the word *flame* coiling like a snake in my mind, gathering power and pulsing with an evil energy. The image had come far too easily, and it looked so different from how I would have imagined it.

You must be getting more powerful. Don't worry about that now. Burn the book.

I was poised to do so when my common sense broke through. The book was the only solid piece of enemy intelligence that we had. What was I doing?

Anger burned through me as I remembered the casual way she'd ordered our deaths. And it had all been a game. She knew we weren't dead.

"Dahlia!" I shouted, knowing that she would hear me, even though a physical distance separated us. "Dahlia, I know it's you!"

You'll know better next time you steal someone's blood, my inner monologue taunted, and then, to my horror, the voice of my thoughts laughed Dahlia's unmistakable, crazy laugh.

The bitch. The consequences of drinking her blood hadn't occurred to me at the time I'd done it. But I'd done what I'd thought I'd had to to stop the Oracle. Now, the ramifications of my actions hit me full force. I'd drunk the blood of a vampire, sired by one of the most powerful vampires I'd ever seen, who'd been a force to reckon with while still a human witch. Nathan had warned me of her power before she'd ever been turned.

"*A vampire's blood is very powerful. Combine that with a witch's abilities and you've got spells to raise the dead, summon armies from hell…*"

Dahlia's powers had been dangerous before she'd become a vampire. It was the addition of vampire blood that had turned her into a supersorceress.

And I had that blood. A very little bit, but it seemed to work.

I threw the spell book away from me before I could do anything rash. I didn't want to raise the dead. Did I?

No, zombies—if they existed—were definitely a last-resort kind of option. And armies from hell? I was officially putting that on the "not an option" list. I'd gotten my ass kicked by enough supernatural creatures already.

So, Dahlia could get inside my head. Fantastic. I wondered how many of my thoughts had been my original thoughts, and how many had been hers. Had I really fought my attackers earlier? Or had her thoughts held me back? Had my decision to go after Nathan been my own, or a trap planted by Dahlia?

I could second-guess myself all day, and it wouldn't make a difference. We had to rescue Nathan. There was no other option. And I couldn't worry about Dahlia messing around with my head. Worrying about it would just mean she'd succeeded in doing it.

I was done waiting, done trying to find someone to rely

on. I was going to do something, even if it seemed totally crazy. If the Soul Eater had raised an army, then so would we. He had used Dahlia's power to do it. So would I.

The book lay where I had tossed it in my panic. The pages that had been bent in its fall flipped back of their own accord, free from the resistance of the floor, and settled open on a page titled "Golem."

I chewed my lip. The name seemed so familiar. Instantly, I recalled my father sitting in his study and me, playing on the floor in front of his desk. The place was decorated with relics of psychiatry. Busts of the human head marked off with dashed lines for phrenology references, bottles of curatives from the Victorian era, even a leukotome and mallet kept under glass. I remembered asking what they were for, and the nightmares I had when I got my answer.

"It was a very old school of thought that if you damaged the brain of an unhealthy patient, you would restore their health."

"You mean, they made the bad brain part go away?"

"That was their intention. But they didn't know enough about the brain and how it works to isolate the bits that were unhealthy. They ended up doing much more harm than good."

"But I thought doctors weren't supposed to harm people. It's in the hippopotamus oats."

He'd laughed then and hugged me. He was never a very affectionate man, but I remember, at least that time, that he hugged me.

"They don't do that to people anymore, do they? They don't do it to kids?"

"No, they don't do it anymore. But sometimes I wonder if we should do it to you. Stick you in the eye with an ice pick and make you as docile and obedient as the Golem of Prague."

It hadn't sounded horrific to me, because all the while he'd tickled me and blown raspberries on my cheek, making me squirm and wriggle and scrunch up my neck. Then, the phone had rung and he'd had to take the call from a patient in the middle of an episode and I'd been shooed away. I'd asked my mother what a golem was and she hadn't known. Or, she had and didn't have time to explain it. There were so many instances where my questions had gone unanswered because of this patient on the phone, or that newspaper reporter calling to talk to an "expert."

I set the spell book aside and went to the darkened living room to find a dictionary. I found one—a miracle, considering how very few non–New Age books Nathan owned—and flipped to the correct page. "'A man artificially created by kabbalistic rites; robot,'" I read aloud. The robots part certainly sounded like the humans the Soul Eater had sent after us. Could the Golem spell be the one Dahlia had used?

Her handwriting was abnormally small and cramped. Through most of the book, she wrote with big, round loops, but here the writing scrunched in on itself, almost as though she were trying to hide the words from each other. The ingredients list, unlike those of her other spells, was very simple. A ball of clay, a drop of blood.

Looking around the room, which I was sure lacked clay, I despaired a little. Then, I realized I actually planned to do the spell, and chills ran down my arms.

What was I doing? Would I really be able to create some monster to fight on our side? What if I couldn't control it? What if the spell didn't work, or something horrible, *Monkey's Paw* caliber horrible, happened?

You'd never know until you try, that reasonable voice in my head nudged, and I wondered if it was really me or Dahlia planting a trick there. The book seemed to pulse with energy under my hands. I opened it and stared down at a page containing what appeared to be a love spell. It was ridiculous, and I laughed as I ripped it out. Without any conscious effort on my part, the page burst into flame and the ashes rained to the floor in a neat little pile.

Use the ashes.

I knew that was Dahlia's blood in me, feeding my excitement, calling me to go ahead with the spell before I could think rationally. But there was no malice in the message that I could feel. Maybe that was her trick, but somehow I couldn't believe it. She was as curious and excited as I was. Ever the opportunist, Dahlia wouldn't resist the chance to see if her spell worked, even if it was to the detriment of her own cause.

I knelt on the floor and scooped the ashes into my cupped hands, then let them fall again, watching with fascination as the dust settled into serpentine patterns on the wood. I thought of my parents, their earthly remains reduced to ash, their urns resting in expensive marble vaults miles and miles away. I imagined touching the carbon that used to be my father, used to be my mother. I changed my face and used one fang to puncture the tips of two fingers. The blood welled there, red, violent, immediate. I thought in a far-off way of mixing my two parents together and giving them life, the way I would give these ashes life. Could I make them whole again, like before the accident? I saw the blood fall from my fingertips, as if in a dream, to strike the gray ash that filled my vision. Could I mix it all together—my father, my mother, my blood, my dead fledgling, his ashes scattered in places I couldn't find? Could I mix them all up and come out with something whole?

I imagined the end product would be me, but made of ash. A creature of various grays, moving brittle limbs that would flutter away in a draft. I saw lips that looked like mine, eyes that looked like mine, but liquid and bloody, running into the spaces between the ash, abnormal cracks in the gray, like a grim artistic parody of a harlequin fetus.

The creature I imagined reached toward me, began to speak, but it had no words. I had no words. For the spell to work, to create my golem, I needed words. I'd used words to create fire and to put it out again. Those elements seemed so trivial in the face of this power of creation I worked now. As the creature's mouth moved, so did mine, and I saw, from the space between my heart and my stomach, a word form. It coiled and writhed like the serpent of fire I'd seen in my mind, then burst forward, as if to strike the creature. I couldn't understand what I said, or even begin to guess at the meaning. But when the voice of scales and fury poured from me, I was left an empty vessel. I collapsed, the sound of the strange words in my voice ringing in my ears: *"Shem. Shem gal'mi. Gal'mi emet. Azel Balemacho!"*

I opened my eyes and saw a man. He didn't resemble

the creature I'd imagined. His skin, while gray, was solid and very definitely real, not some figment of ashes bound together with blood. His lips and eyes weren't the bloody things I'd seen, either, but gray as the rest of him. His head was bald, his appearance generic. Nothing was unique about him but his grayness. That, and the fact he hadn't been standing there before.

He stared down at me, not confused, not intelligent, not pitying me or even curious as to my presence. He was tabula rasa, a completely blank slate, waiting for my instruction.

"I have to sleep now," I told him, my voice scraping from a throat coated in razors. "Stay right there."

He nodded, once, and I fell into an uneasy, but inescapable, sleep.

Nine: Falling

The water was getting cold.

Ziggy opened his eyes and stared up at the shower-head. It felt good to get the blood off him. Made him feel more human than animal.

He dunked his head under the frigid spray one last time. He hated getting out of the shower with half-dry hair, and he wanted to make sure he'd gotten all of the blood out of it anyway. His mouth opened in an involuntary O of surprise at the sting of the cold against his scalp and he decided he'd had enough. He stepped out of the shower, wrapping a towel around his waist.

This has to stop. Jacob's voice, smooth as silk, wound through Ziggy's brain, taking away all the conflict and confusion. *You did what you thought was right. I can't fault you that. You are impetuous and you never believe that which you cannot see with your own eyes. I wouldn't have you any other way.*

"Get out of my head, old man," Ziggy whispered, staring hard at his reflection in the mirror over the sink. The fog on the glass had begun to recede, framing him in mist. He concentrated on the drops falling from his hair, down his face. One slithered down the bridge of his nose to hang, trembling, at the tip, and he focused on that as he forced his sire's mind from his own.

Now you've seen what it is, to be on their side. What it makes you.

He scrubbed his hands over his face. "I'm fine, I'm fine," he chanted. The smell of blood, emanating from the clothes he'd discarded in a damp, crusting heap on the floor, made his stomach alternately sour and growl. It would be better when he got something to eat.

Emerging from the bathroom, he rummaged through the box of clothes Max had hauled up from storage for him. For a minute he worried that all it contained were jeans with the crotch worn out and ripped-up poet shirts he'd worn in his "I want to be Robert Smith" phase, but there was a pair of plaid flannel sleep pants that fit, and some T-shirts that had been washed so many times they were as soft as butter. He used to make fun of Nathan for saving everything, but if they managed to get him back, he never would again.

He got himself dressed and headed for the kitchen. He could leave the laundry until later. Right now, he needed some time on his own to think, and something in his stomach to keep him from thinking too deeply.

The light in the kitchen was on. Sitting at the cracked Formica dinette table, hunched over a glass of something clear that was sure as hell not water, Bill looked up as Ziggy entered. "Hey."

"Hey, yourself." Ziggy watched him from the corner

of his eye as he went to the refrigerator. There was a bottle next to Bill's left hand, and it was half-empty. "You're up late. Or early. Whatever it is for you."

"Couldn't sleep." Bill raised the glass, hesitated for a moment, then gulped it down. He reached for the bottle. "You want some of this? Or wait, no...you're underage, aren't you?"

"Never stopped me before." Ziggy grabbed a mug from the dishwasher and held it out to Bill. "What is it?"

Bill waited until the cup was safely filled and back on the countertop before answering. "Gin."

Ziggy set the mug aside while he poured a bag of blood into the teakettle on the stove. He wondered what the hell had happened to the microwave while he'd been gone. All the while, he felt Bill's stare boring holes into his back. The air crackled with the kind of high-alert energy most humans gave off when they knew they were dealing with a monster. "You don't have to be afraid of me. I'm not going to do anything to you."

A picture of what he must have looked like, tearing those creatures apart with his hands and teeth, flashed into his brain and his sire's voice murmured, *It must have been beautiful.*

"Stop," Ziggy said before he could help it, and then he knew he looked like a crazy person *and* a murderer, and things were just not going his way.

"Are you okay?" Bill's voice was dry and scared sounding, miles away from the guy who'd hugged him and comforted him earlier. "Do I need to go get Carrie?"

"No." Ziggy turned and pasted on a fake smile that he hoped didn't look sinister. A kid in elementary school had told him once that his smile looked like an evil jack-o'-lantern's, and even though he was pretty sure it was because of the snaggly state of his baby teeth at the time, the last thing he wanted to project to Bill was evil. "Let her sleep. I'm just keyed up, is all."

"Me and you both." Bill seemed to relax a little, or at least, he seemed to want to relax. He took another swallow from his glass. "I don't know if I can take much more of that kind of thing."

"I thought you were a big, tough army guy." He leaned against the counter. "You afraid of a few little creatures of the night?"

"First of all, I was a Marine, smart-ass. Second, no. No, I'm not afraid of those things. I'm afraid of you." The look he gave Ziggy was so pointed, it could have been a sword. He turned back to his glass, staring straight ahead as he gulped it down.

"Damn. That's harsh." Ziggy took a swig of the foul stuff and forced himself to maintain a straight face. He'd covertly snuck booze from Nathan's personal stock since he was fourteen years old, but he'd never gotten used to the taste of it solo. Gin, if he remembered correctly, tasted best mixed with Kool-Aid. "I mean, especially after you were all strong, silent, supportive type just a couple of hours ago."

"A couple of hours ago I wasn't dumping bodies with their heads nearly chewed off into a lake with my new vampire-werewolf buddy." At least he had the decency to look a little ashamed. "I'm sorry. I'm just trying to get my head around the transition from sweet kid to…"

"To monster?" The feel of flesh crushed to pulp zinged

along the nerves in his fingers, and he wiped his hands against the flannel pajama pants.

Part of him was ashamed of what he was. He wanted to apologize to Bill, to do anything to take away that fear he said he felt. Because he *did* like Bill, and he did want something to happen. He didn't know when, but he did want it.

But another part of him—the selfish, childish part—wanted to tell him off. Who the hell did he think he was, telling a vampire how he should act or feel or whatever? He was just a human. A cute human, but still…

Bill shook his head, but his expression was still grim. "I'm not making judgments. I'm just saying, I'm not used to the guys I'm interested in tearing people's throats out with their teeth."

"I did that?" Ziggy searched his memory, but the teakettle whistled, bringing him back to the conversation at hand. "Hey, I did what I had to do. Don't fault me for it. I'm not a human. You knew that when you followed me to the bar."

"Yeah. I knew it." Bill turned back to his drink, and Ziggy poured the warm blood into his own mug, mixing it with what remained of the gin. He would need it, to put up with this bs.

Bill reached for the bottle again, and Ziggy's conscience forced him to intervene. "Hey, take it easy there, cowboy," he said, trying to sound friendly as he put his hand on Bill's arm to keep him from pouring more booze that he didn't need down his throat.

The way he moved, Ziggy was almost a hundred percent sure Bill was going to slug him. He even let go of his arm and stepped back defensively, because the last thing he needed was a broken nose and to have to fight a drunk human. Not to mention the fact it would make him seem more monstrous in Bill's eyes.

But he didn't hit him. He grabbed him, a hand on each shoulder, and pulled up hard against him. Bill's mouth touched his, just a little touch, and it was like electricity running through his entire body. And then he had no willpower. He should have. He wasn't the one who was drunk and had some weird prejudice against vampires. If this went too far, Bill would probably regret it, and that would make Ziggy regret it, but he just couldn't make himself care.

Bill's hands slid under Ziggy's shirt, the warmth of human skin a shock to his chilled flesh. "You're freezing," Bill said, his voice half-muffled by the proximity of his lips to Ziggy's, and Ziggy couldn't help but laugh.

"I'm dead," he whispered back, and then he wished he hadn't said that. Bill didn't like that he was a vampire, that much was clear. No need to remind him, when he was so close and it felt so good to be pressed against him.

I'm just not going to think anymore, Ziggy decided, smothered under another of Bill's kisses. He ached to be touched, not in a way that only seemed gentle, but in a way that *was* gentle, with no threat of pain to follow. Or, if it was rough, roughness for its own sake, not because he was a plaything to be dominated or tortured for someone else's amusement.

He wanted to be treated like a person. It had been a while since he had been.

Bill's hands slid under his T-shirt again, lifting the fabric up. Ziggy broke the connection of their mouths and put his hand out to stop him. "What if Carrie or Max comes in here?"

"What if?" Bill retorted drunkenly, and when his mouth descended again, sliding from lips to jaw to neck, Ziggy really couldn't argue with his logic. Hell, if the Pope walked in right now, Ziggy wouldn't care. He leaned back, feeling the bite of the counter in the small of his back, and pulled his T-shirt off. Bill mercifully skipped past the physical inspection, that moment that always left Ziggy to mentally narrate all the flaws the other guy was finding with him, like the fact he didn't have washboard abs—hell, any visible abs—and he'd never grown more than a few chest hairs. Whether Bill was too drunk to care or he really just didn't care, either way, Ziggy was glad when, once he'd whipped his own shirt over his head, Bill reached for him again, pushing him a little awkwardly to lean against the refrigerator door. The cold, smooth surface hitting his back coincided with the hot skin of Bill's chest meeting his, and Ziggy shuddered at the contrast.

Bill dipped his head to kiss Ziggy's left collarbone, hands locked firmly on his hips through the flannel sleep pants. He gave the fabric a short, experimental tug as he stooped to spread more kisses over his chest, then paused, looking up with such a serious expression that Ziggy was sure rejection was about to follow. Instead, Bill said, a little nervously, "You've done this before, right?"

Ziggy smiled down at him, unable to work up even a little sarcasm for a guy as nice as Bill. "Yeah. You're not being a creepy old man, if that's what you're wondering."

"No, it's not that, it's just…" Bill laughed and bent his head, nibbling and sucking a little trail to the waistband of the pants before he finally pulled them down. Ziggy's cock, hard to bursting, leaped at the first touch of Bill's hand and his warm, hesitant breath. "You got a condom on you?"

Oh, shit, Ziggy thought, then remembered with a mental palm to his forehead that he wasn't some human teenager anymore. He cleared his throat and tried not to sound like "that guy" when he said, "No, it's cool. I'm dead. No diseases."

Bill didn't respond. Ziggy saw the muscles of his back tighten up a little, as though he would push away and call the whole thing off, and then, in a moment like an electric shock, Bill slid his mouth over Ziggy's cock and sucked him in, as far as he would go.

The proper response was probably something like, "Jesus" or "God yes," but all that came out was a strangled noise. Ziggy's hands curled into fists and one of them pounded backward against the gleaming steel face of the refrigerator as white-hot neurons fired jolts of pleasure through his brain. The hot wet of Bill's mouth, the fingers digging into his thighs and the palm cupping his balls, every pleasure-feeling nerve in his body seemed right there, right wherever Bill touched him. And there was no fear of pain, no thought that now he would draw back and sink fangs into his thigh or more sensitive places. Everything felt good. Beyond good. Fucking incredible.

Too fucking incredible, after a few short minutes. "Hey, stop, stop," Ziggy gasped, planting his hands on top of Bill's sandy-blond hair to push him away. "I'm sorry, I was just really close there for a second."

"That's kind of the point," Bill said, standing to kiss him. To clear his head—and to get his mind off his hyperaroused dick pressed between them—Ziggy reached for the fly of Bill's jeans and tugged the button open. He slid a hand inside and found his cock, hard and eager and weeping a drop of silky fluid.

"Commando, huh?" Ziggy mumbled against Bill's neck, sliding his fist up and down. Bill trembled against him, and Ziggy smiled against the shell of his ear, flicking his tongue out to trace it.

"I want to fuck you," Bill groaned, thrusting against his hand. "Can I?"

His hand stilling on the thick, hot flesh under his palm, Ziggy considered. It didn't take much to sway his decision, just the steady pulse beneath his fingers. "Yeah." His breath caught in his throat as Bill traced his lower lip with his thumb. "Oh, definitely."

"Turn around," Bill said, his voice as low and rough as the gin they'd drunk. Ziggy complied, kicking the pajamas aside. He braced his hands on the counter, his sudden vulnerability a little frightening. Bill's hands came to rest on his shoulders, then stroked down over the plane of his back, returning to repeat the motion again and again, pulling shivers from his spine.

He'd felt secure before now, but it went against every fiber in his body that he would turn his back—his naked back, at that—to a stranger. Jacob had done it to him before, to test him. He'd stripped him, made him kneel, made him wait. And then, when he'd just begun to let down his guard, the lash had fallen over his back.

The memory made his knees buckle, and he hoped Bill thought it was a reaction to what he was doing, not an emotional scar. That was the last thing Ziggy needed, to miss out on some really hot sex in order to explain his mental dysfunction.

To take his own mind off things, he reached for one of Bill's hands, pulled it to his mouth and sucked the thumb in. Bill groaned and pressed against him, full body contact, and Ziggy wondered when exactly he'd gotten rid of his jeans. He pushed back against him, just to be antagonistic, and Bill pulled his hand back, tracing his fingers down Ziggy's spine, to the small of his back, the line of his tailbone and farther.

"You get right to the point, huh?" Ziggy gasped as Bill's thumb, still wet with saliva, pressed inside. Had anything ever felt this good with someone else? A pang seized him at the thought that, when all was said and done, he would still be a monster and Bill would still be afraid of him. And then it would be over. And this would be the big mistake that hung between them for the rest of the time they had to be around each other, until one of them found a tactful way to get the fuck out of Dodge.

Bill's lips were against his neck, his cock nudging him from behind, and he whispered, "We might have a little problem."

Ziggy tensed. This was the moment he could be the sober, responsible party. This was the moment he could easily save them both from the consequences of an ill-advised hookup.

Leaning forward, bringing his whole body into clumsy contact with Ziggy's, Bill reached for something on the counter. He sounded much more cheerful, proud of himself, even, when he said, "Wait…never mind, we're back in business."

Ziggy half turned. "Back in—" His words were cut off by the shock of something cool and wet spilling onto the small of his back. After a split second of confusion he recognized the scent with a perverse thrill. "Is that…is that olive oil?"

"What, you wanted to do this the real rough, manly way?" Bill asked with a quiet laugh. Ziggy laughed with him, until Bill's fingers, slippery with oil, slid down to press inside of him. First two, then a third that took all the breath from him and buckled his knees with a jolt of pleasure that shot straight to his groin.

Pleasure that mixed with nervousness as Bill's hand withdrew, replaced by the wide, firm tip of him.

"Is this okay?" he asked in a strained voice, and Ziggy had to admire his restraint. He took a deep breath and nodded, held that breath as the pressure increased, then gave over to stinging release when the head of Bill's cock was finally inside of him.

There was pain. A dull burn that reminded him that Bill wasn't a small guy, and all the benefits of that were soon to come. Bill asked if he was still okay with it, still wanted to take all of him, and Ziggy could only mumble something incoherent and impatient in response. Something half-begging, half-demanding, that made Bill chuckle hoarsely and push forward, and Ziggy squirmed back until he was more filled than he'd ever been before.

Then Bill began to move, and Ziggy wasn't sure when he'd stopped supporting himself and started to just rely on Bill's weight pinning him to the cabinets to keep him from falling. He reached down to touch himself and Bill's oil-slick hand snaked around to get there first, grasping the base of Ziggy's cock, jerking him off with firm tugs timed so that Ziggy didn't know what he wanted more—to thrust into his fist or push back and hinder Bill's withdrawal. He turned his head, mouth open, breathless, and Bill kissed him, his tongue moving in time with his hips.

When he broke away, it was to apologize. "I'm sorry, I can't…" and a deep, throaty groan rolled over whatever else he was going to say as his body stiffened. His hand tightened, almost too hard, but he didn't stop stroking as he came. Ziggy almost shouted at the feeling of Bill inside of him, the way his cock twitched as the warmth of his come spilled from him. And then he was coming, too, making a strangled half sob as his dick jerked in Bill's hand.

Even if he was supposed to be the stronger creature, Ziggy's legs were weak, so weak he had to lean on Bill after he'd withdrawn, and they both slid to the floor to get their breath.

Bill leaned back against the base cabinets, his eyes closed. A single bead of sweat rolled down his temple and Ziggy had the weirdest urge to lick it away. In the name of not looking like a total psycho, he restrained himself.

"Jesus," Bill said when his breathing returned to normal. "That was…"

"Regrettable?" Ziggy supplied for him, wincing as he shifted on the cold linoleum.

Bill actually looked wounded. "I was going to say great. Obviously we didn't just have the same experience."

Way to say the right thing, dumb-ass. Ziggy closed his eyes and rubbed his forehead with the back of his hand to keep from making eye contact. "No, it was, really great. I was just trying to say that we shouldn't have, before you did."

"Ah. I see." Bill climbed to his feet and found his jeans. After he pulled them up over his hips, he turned to face Ziggy again. "And why do you think we shouldn't have?"

It wasn't fun being the naked, interrogated one. Ziggy grabbed the T-shirt and pajama bottoms and got them on as quickly as he could without falling over on his trembling legs. "You're drunk, for one—"

"I'm not drunk anymore," Bill interrupted with a lopsided smile that made something inside Ziggy's ribs squeeze up.

Still, since one of them had to be the voice of reason, he continued. "Second, you don't like the fact I'm a vampire. You sat there and said, 'Hey, nice of you to kill those people, jackass,' and then just decided you wanted to fuck me. I get being attracted to me, all right? I know I probably come across as some wounded charity case, the abused boy wonder or some shit. But that doesn't hold anybody's fascination forever." He swallowed, and it was like a lump of gravel going down. "Not that I'm saying I want the whole forever thing. I'm not going to be possessive and weird now. It was just a figure of speech."

Bill nodded gravely, his eyebrows slightly raised. "You done now?"

Ziggy nodded in reply.

"Fine. Then let me clear up some misconceptions you seem to have." He stepped close, so close their lips were almost touching, and just before they did he turned his head just slightly to say softly into Ziggy's ear, "I'm not looking to make forever out of this right this minute, either." He stepped back, letting the statement sink in a moment before continuing, a little more pissed-off sounding. "But at least I'm open to the possibility that you're someone I could spend some serious time with. And yes, you're a vampire. I don't like that. I don't like Republicans, either, but I don't cut them out of my social pool. I realize that this, between you and me, is a shock. It has sure shocked the hell out of me. But from the minute I met you—after the bleeding stopped—I was never thinking you were some little lost boy I could save. From the minute I met you I knew I was in some serious trouble, and that I could fall for you hard if I wasn't careful."

"Way to be careful," Ziggy said with a snort.

Bill's serious expression cracked only a little. "I didn't say I'd fallen hard yet. But I'm definitely on the way down. I want to know, is this the point where you want me to bail out? It's only fair to tell me now. But don't throw up a bunch of imagined or perceived roadblocks on my behalf."

Ziggy had to be careful when he spoke. The squeezing pressure in his chest was almost unbearable, and he didn't know what sound would come out when he tried to talk. He took a deep breath and blinked, surprised to find there were actually tears waiting to be shed. "No. I think I can safely say I don't want you to bail."

Stupid boy, Jacob raged inside his head. *No one will care for you, protect you as I have.*

Yeah, I know. Ziggy kept the thought to himself. He'd given enough to his sire already. *But let's give him a chance.*

Ten: Here's...Henry

I woke with a searing pain in my head, centered right behind my eyes. When I opened them, I panicked, thinking that I might have gone blind. Then I remembered I'd fallen asleep on the bedroom floor. I sat up and looked around. Sunlight showed through around the edges of the blinds. How long had I slept? Why hadn't anyone woken me up? My back ached as I slowly sat up, feeling every crack and pop in my spine.

Maybe they had tried to wake me up, but just hadn't been able to rouse me. My dreams had been strange, a jumble of weird birth imagery and memories of my parents. I reached a hand out in the semidarkness to touch something. I didn't care what; I just wanted to assure myself I was awake and not in another freaky dream. My fingers skimmed something soft and warm, like human skin, but without the energy of something living.

I scrambled backward, ignoring the pain in my head. "Don't touch me!" I shouted to whoever was in the room with me. "Help! Max, Ziggy!"

When they didn't immediately come, I got to my feet, still calling for them, feeling blindly for obstacles as I made my way to a light switch. I knocked my shins painfully on the dresser, swore, and only then remembered I could use a spell to get some light going. "Illuminate," I commanded. The lightbulbs in the wall fixture and the bedside lamp popped on and my gaze immediately flew to the man standing in front of me.

There was no concrete way to describe him. Actually, concrete would be a good way. He was completely gray from hairless head to toe. In fact, his whole body was hairless. No eyebrows, no body hair. Just a plastic-looking expanse of gray stretched over a generic male form. If not for the distinct genitalia, he could have been a Ken doll. He looked at me with gray eyes, but said nothing and made no move to come near me.

I remembered more clearly what had transpired the night before. Using the ash to cast Dahlia's spell, feeling all the power and all my memories rush out of me to form this thing. I could only stare at him, mute, as one thought ran through my mind: *I did it.*

I approached him cautiously, though I was pretty sure I remembered something from mythology that said a golem couldn't do anything unless commanded. I decided to try it out. "Put your finger on your nose."

He didn't even give me a funny look as he did it. Just unquestioning obedience.

"Turn around," I ordered, and noticed that he did literally what I said. He didn't just turn three hundred and sixty degrees. He kept going until I told him to stop.

"Okay." I tapped my lips with my forefinger as I

watched him. What were the limitations on golem actions? If I told him to prepare a soufflé, could he do it?

"Do the Hokey Pokey," I ordered, as a test.

"You put your left foot in, you take your left foot out," he sang in a dull monotone as he performed the actions he described.

"Put some pep into it," I barked, but I couldn't hold back my laughter to make it sound serious. Even so, he continued his song with more enthusiasm. "Stop," I called out, and he stopped immediately, his overdrawn expression of happiness fading immediately to the blankslate look he'd been wearing before. "Well, you know the Hokey Pokey, at least. What else do you know?"

He simply stared at me.

"Tell me what else you know," I prompted.

Immediately, he began to speak. "I know anything that you can command me to do. I know exactly as much as you know."

I thought about that for a minute. "So, if I told you to sing the entire score of *Rigoletto*..."

"You do not know the entire score of *Rigoletto*," he replied in his flat voice.

"Right." I was still wondering just what I had created when the bedroom door burst open. Bill and Ziggy ran in, looking haggard and sleep-disturbed.

"Carrie, are you all right?" Bill asked, but Ziggy immediately caught sight of the golem and charged it. The creature made no move to defend itself. It stood, rooted in place, as Ziggy tackled it to the floor.

"Ziggy, no," I shouted, pulling him off the golem. "He's mine. I made him."

There was a moment of confused silence. Then, very cautiously, Bill asked, "Made him?"

The floor in the hallway creaked and Max appeared at the door. His gaze went directly to the golem, and then met mine, full of confusion. At least he didn't rush him with the intent to kill, the way Ziggy had. "What the hell is going on?"

The golem lay on the floor were he'd landed. "Get up," I said softly to him, offering my hand for help. He wouldn't take it. *Of course,* I realized, feeling like an idiot. *You told him not to touch you.*

I turned back to Bill and Ziggy, who were staring at me as if I were a crazy person. "I used a spell from Dahlia's book. We needed help. I mean, we're going to need help to get Nathan back. More manpower. And this seemed like a logical solution."

"So, what, he's like, a zombie?" Ziggy cautiously approached the creature, reached out to touch him as if he hadn't just full body tackled the thing to the floor. "He feels like rubber or something."

"He's made out of ash. And blood. I don't know why he feels the way he does. To be honest, I only touched him by accident, just the once." I shrugged. "He's a golem."

"Like the fairy tale?" Max asked incredulously. "The guy who has to do everything you tell it?"

I nodded. Bill considered for a moment, then motioned with his head to the golem. "Hey, you. Do the Hokey Pokey."

The creature didn't move. "I think I might be the only one who can do it," I suggested. "Since I'm the one who did the spell. Golem, do whatever Bill tells you."

"Now do the Hokey Pokey," Bill said, but as the golem began to comply, I stopped him.

"I don't think that's going to get us anywhere right now," Ziggy said, his voice full of amusement. "Can it fight? Will it be any good to us?"

"I don't see why it couldn't fight. It can do anything I can do." I hoped they wouldn't point out my lack of grace and ability in the combat arena. "That's the catch. He can't do something if I don't know how to do it."

"So, welding is right out, hot-wiring a car, that kind of stuff?" Ziggy gave the golem a little push. "What if you learn how to do it?"

"Yeah, what if I learn it?" I asked the golem. When he didn't answer, I rolled my eyes and said, "Answer my question."

"You would have to create another one of me," he said, staring straight ahead.

"So, you can't upgrade him, you just have to get a whole new model. That's a drawback." Max came forward to join Bill and Ziggy in examining the creature.

Ziggy shook his head. "No, man, think about it. Carrie is a doctor. This could be really useful. Not to us, but think about it on a global scale. She could drop him off at a hospital and he could help out with organ transplants and stuff."

"I was an emergency room doctor," I pointed out. "Didn't do a lot of complicated surgeries."

"Yeah, but think about how helpful he'll be to us. Especially if she can create more." Bill stepped away from the golem, clearly weirded out by it.

I thought of the agony of the process, the splitting pain

in my head that hadn't faded yet. "Let's hold off on it for now, if you don't mind. I don't think I'm quite experienced enough to do it again right away."

"So, we're it then?" Ziggy asked, his expression dark. "I mean, when we go get Nathan. We're it?"

I swallowed the lump of trepidation in my throat. "We're it. We didn't do so good against those creatures, did we?"

Bill's jaw tightened as he stared at me. He didn't say anything, and I wondered if he was waiting for me to think up something. Then, like a man coming out of a trance, he rubbed his hands together and looked from Ziggy to me, his gaze sliding over the golem as if he wasn't any more than a piece of furniture. "Okay, you can do this, and you can do the fire thing. What else can you do?"

Ziggy cut him off, shaking his head. "Bad idea. She looks like hell right now. And Nate has always said magic has a way of draining people. Like, you might get something, but it's going to take something in return."

"Well, thanks, I'm glad I achieved the look I was going for." I was too tired to be truly offended. "But you're right. I don't think we can rely just on me for this."

"We can run in blind, hacking and slashing our way through the place," Ziggy said, without a trace of sarcasm. "I know my way around, and I actually think we have a pretty good chance of taking them out. At least, long enough to get Nate out."

"I'm up for anything at this point," Bill agreed. "We've wasted enough time."

We sat in silence for a minute, then Max asked, "But just in case…Carrie, what else can you do?"

I knelt down and picked up the spell book from where I'd left it on the floor. "There are a couple of spells in here that I think I recognize. For instance, one says it will knock out your intended target. It must be the same thing she used on Bill. And one will shove them backward, so they can't reach you. But I think I make things up on my own, as well."

"Things like?" Max asked, and instead of answering, I went to the living room. I knew they would follow me, but I wasn't being intentionally mysterious. I was thinking.

Aside from the potions and amulets listed in the book, most of Dahlia's spells required nothing more than a word and a focused intention. As written, they should have required all kinds of occult materials, but those were only listed as distractions, a lot of flash and stage dressing that would have little impact on the final outcome. In some cases it would discourage someone from trying altogether. But now that I knew her secret, that her power came from within and not from toads' eyes and graveyard dirt, I could, in theory, create any effect I wanted.

In the living room, I went to the bookshelf and trained my eye on the spine of one of the books with a crescent moon as the publisher's logo. I knew Nathan wouldn't mind losing it—"Another Wicca 101 book," he would scoff after a customer left with such a volume— so I figured it would be of more use to us if it was sacrificed for the cause. I held out my hand, directing my concentration at the book, and it slid off the shelf, suspended in midair. I imagined what would happen next. The covers would open, the pages would rip out one by one, then the whole thing would dissolve into sand. I visualized the word "apart" as it came from my lips, each letter tipped with acid, the whole word sharp as a razor blade. It sliced into the book, and, when I opened my eyes, I saw exactly what I'd imagined happening, and the guys' horrified expressions as they witnessed it all.

"Can you do that to…to people?" Bill asked in quiet awe. He seemed to remember himself, held up his hands and said quickly, "I mean, I don't want a demonstration or anything, but…can you teach us that?"

"I don't know. I mean, I can do it. I suppose if I can, anyone can." I sat down and noticed that the three of them flinched as I did so. Ignoring it, I explained to them my thoughts on how magic worked. Namely, that I didn't know how, just that it did, and how I managed it.

After I brought down a pile of books from the same publishing company—glossy covered books with titles like *To Sip From A Goddess's Chalice* and written by authors with names like "Golden Crowfox"—Max and Ziggy set to merrily tearing them to shreds with their new knowledge.

Ziggy did far more damage than Max did. In a battle situation, being able to rip the limbs off someone was handy, but considering what we were potentially up against, I really wished he could do it a little faster, and with less muttering under his breath.

Max, though…I remembered learning about werewolves and their abilities. Most notably, that they practice magic. Max must have gotten a lot of practice. He obliterated his first book almost faster than I could see it fall apart, and he didn't have to actually say anything.

"Wow." I knew I was staring at him as though he were a circus freak, but I couldn't help it. He seemed almost more powerful than Dahlia.

He just shrugged. "I suppose it comes with the hairy palms."

"I might not be cut out for this kind of thing." Bill sounded a little embarrassed, still holding an undamaged copy of *Merlin's Majikal Almanac*.

Ziggy finished destroying a copy of *Wiccan Sex Magic For One,* which I made a mental note to tease Nathan about later, and turned to me. "Why is that? Why wouldn't he be as good at it as we are? Is it a vampire thing?"

"It can't be just a vampire thing. Dahlia could do it before she was a vampire." I wondered if witches were born, not made. Maybe Nathan was right when he said that the dangerous witches were the ones with talent. The kind of power Dahlia had would have been venomous even without a knowledge of spells and potions.

Of course, I didn't think I had any inborn talent toward the occult. If I did, I would feel awfully gypped that I didn't use it to do better in medical school. No, it probably had more to do with Dahlia's blood.

Max, I could understand. He was some strange monster hybrid, and to my mind that explained all sorts of weirdness. But then, why was Ziggy so good at magic? Could it be the Soul Eater's blood, or—

"Did you drink Dahlia's blood?" I asked, the question out before I could cushion it with tact.

Ziggy didn't—maybe couldn't—look me in the eye.

"It's not a big deal. I've had Dahlia's blood before." But it was a big deal, and it was a little uncomfortable trying to compare my experiences, which were probably tame next to what he'd been through, to his. "You don't have to tell us how or why. I'm just wondering if it has anything to do with why you're able to do magic."

He nodded, not at anything I said, though. More like he was psyching himself up to answer me. He looked up, and the expression on his face spoke of things I would never want to hear out loud. "Yeah. I've had her blood."

"So, if I drank this Dahlia's blood, I'd get magical powers, too?" Bill's expression changed to one of utter disgust. "I can't believe I just said 'magical powers' in a serious way."

"It's okay, you'll get used to it," Max reassured him.

I cleared my throat, a little amazed myself at the way the conversation was spinning. "If you drank Dahlia's blood, you'd become a vampire. Or, maybe you would when you died. I don't know what would happen."

"If you drank a vampire's blood and they didn't exchange with you, you'd become like the humans the Soul Eater keeps." A visible shudder went through Ziggy as he spoke. "That is seriously bad news."

"Okay, so, I'll rely on the little bit I've managed to do here, and this." Bill pulled his gun from behind his back and put it back just as quickly. "You can shoot these things, right?"

"Absolutely," Ziggy said, looking a little disappointed at not having a firearm himself. "It might not stop them entirely, but it will definitely knock them down. They aren't immortal, just really, really strong."

"Okay, I think we have a plan of attack." I couldn't believe how close we were getting, how soon we would be doing all the dangerous things we'd talked about. "When do you want to do this?"

"Right now," Max answered, but his words were covered up by Ziggy's.

"The humans usually get fed at one. They lose strength between feedings, so if we hit them at like, twelve, twelve-thirty, we have a really good chance of getting them at their weakest."

I considered that bit of information. "What about the Soul Eater? Will he be there? Or Dahlia? What are their schedules like?"

"Ten kinds of crazy," Ziggy answered without hesitation. "They'll either be there, or they won't. We need to be prepared."

"I'm prepared. They have Nathan. There could be ten Soul Eaters in there, and I would take on every one of them." And I meant it. I leaned so I could see the clock in the kitchen. "Okay, midnight gives us two hours to get our heads together and get things ready to go. Is that enough time for you guys?"

Ziggy nodded, and Bill affirmed with a loud "hell yes."

"Good. Get what weapons you need. And…" Struggling for some other good, inspiring advice, I finished with, "Wear comfortable shoes."

"What are you going to do?" Max called after me as I walked down the hall.

"I'm going to worry, and pace," I said, but as I closed the bedroom door behind me, I admitted to myself that what I was actually going to do was pray.

* * *

Bill wanted to ask him something. It wasn't as if Ziggy was psychic or anything. He could just tell that when someone kept giving you sideways looks, they were probably working up the courage to ask you something.

With their arsenal collected and safely stored in the van, Max had excused himself to call home. Left alone, Ziggy and Bill sat on the couch, drinking coffee because beer seemed like a bad idea, and besides, they probably didn't have time to run to the liquor store. Drunk might be more comfortable than sober when facing a life-or-death situation, but it probably cut your chances of living through it in half.

"So, what do you think about this?" Bill asked, but Ziggy could tell that wasn't the question that was bothering him.

He could wait him out. "I think it might be suicide. But we don't have anything else we can do. You?"

Bill shrugged. "Never know. We might have a chance. You're pretty good with that spell thing. And I'm an okay fighter. And Max is pretty good, even though he seems pretty distracted by stuff at home. But if it really came down to it…would you go out fighting?"

"What, to bring Nate back?" That was a kind of hard question. In the past, it wouldn't have been an issue. He would have done anything for Nate then. But after the last couple of months…

"What the hell happened to you?" Bill asked suddenly. "With your sire or whoever he is? What did he do to make you so…cold?"

"I'm not cold." It came out more defensive than he'd meant it to. "I mean, there's just other things to consider right now. Nate has definitely put his butt on the line for me, tons of times. But I did not survive the last couple of months through self-sacrifice, okay?"

"I get that." Bill put his arm across the back of the couch, trying to appear casual and relaxed. "But this is the guy you consider your father. How can you be in self-preservation mode when it's him you're talking about?"

"Because I'm always in self-preservation mode." Ziggy startled himself with his easy answer.

"And that's why, when you were with your sire, you did whatever he wanted you to. And the things he wanted you to do just made you feel worse," Bill said, and it was as if he'd read Ziggy's mind. "I was in kind of the same situation, when I was younger. With my father, actually."

Ziggy felt something tug in his chest, but that self-preservation forced him to ignore it. "Really? You think your dad did anywhere near the damage my sire has done to me?"

"Yes." Bill didn't hesitate. "Not the same kind of damage, but he certainly did damage me."

Ziggy leaned back, letting his head rest on Bill's arm. What he really wanted to do was hug him, but that would breach both of their defenses.

Bill shook his head. "I won't go into all of it now, but…if you get to the point where you start adapting, trying to become what other people want you to be, no one will ever know you. The real you."

Sighing, Ziggy closed his eyes. "You want to know who I really am? I'm a condemned fucking building. There are so many things wrong with me that I know I'm not going to get over."

"You're not a condemned building. And you don't have to get over anything. You have to move on from them, and you have to get beyond thinking because someone degraded you, that's what you're worth." Bill looked at him, not with pity, but understanding, and it had the same effect as if he'd stripped the skin and muscle from Ziggy's bones. It sucked to be the one who gets their defensive wall blown all to hell.

"How do I know that's not all that I'm worth, though?" Ziggy leaned forward, not wanting to touch any part of Bill, afraid his bruised feelings would seep through his skin and translate into a clear picture of how damaged he was in Bill's brain. "You don't know what he did to me. How could he do those things to me if I was really worth anything at all?"

"Because he's a sick bastard, apparently." Bill's jaw clenched, like he wanted to punch something. It was a good feeling, to know someone wanted to hurt someone else for hurting you. "Ziggy, you are amazing. And I don't mean amazing in a sexual sense. You are, but that's not the point I'm trying to get across right now. You're amazing because you've lived through all that you have, and it's torn you down and you've made your own armor to protect yourself. But I don't want you to feel like you have to do that anymore."

"Why, what are you going to do about it?" Oh God, did that sound desperate? Did it sound as though he was pushing for some kind of big declaration?

He opened his mouth to take back his question, but Bill seemed to shrug off the words anyway. He took a sip of coffee before he spoke. "Nothing, really. What the hell can I do? But, as I've said before, I like you. I don't want you to suffer."

"Thanks."

"And I think you would suffer if you didn't do everything you possibly could for Nathan."

Ziggy had never cared for people who had that kind of common sense. "Doesn't matter. We'll probably be dead before we get the chance to do anything truly heroic."

Bill laughed quietly at that. "You're probably right. Just promise that if something really horrendous happens to me, you'll put me out of my misery."

"Like, I should eat you or something?" Ziggy was relieved when the joke actually made Bill smile, not recoil in terror.

Bill leaned forward, so their lips were almost touching, his breath teasing Ziggy's mouth as he said, "I can think of worse ways to go."

And then he took Ziggy's hand and pulled it to his neck, where the scar from that first bite was, and Ziggy shuddered. "I'm really sor—" he started to say, only to have his words cut off by Bill's mouth on his.

And then he didn't feel like apologizing for anything anymore.

Before we left, I dressed Henry—I had decided the golem needed a proper name—in some clothes Max loaned me. Henry had the same lean-muscled build that Max had, and I wondered if subconsciously I'd chosen that form for him. The clothes didn't quite disguise the gray skin completely, but I figured if anyone noticed him in the short walk to the van we could say it was a rare side effect of iron supplements.

"He is not sitting in the back with me," Ziggy said, shaking his head when we met him and Bill on the sidewalk. "Too creepy."

"He can sit in the passenger seat." I opened the passenger side door for him and commanded, "Get in. And buckle your seat belt, too."

I watched as Henry did what I'd asked, that same blank expression on his face the entire time. Bill pulled the back doors open and motioned us in, giving Ziggy a playful shove. It was as if we all felt lighter, somehow, despite the ugly circumstances. Taking action seemed to spark hope I hadn't realized was gone.

Bill closed the doors, and I winced at the loud creak of the hinges. Ziggy settled against the side wall and leaned his head back, closing his eyes, while Max stationed himself against the opposite wheel well.

"I can't wait to get this thing done and get back home," Ziggy said, as if we were headed to the Secretary of State's office to get our license plates renewed, and I wished I had some of his bravado, even if it was mostly put on. He rolled his head, popping his spine loudly. When he straightened, I saw a fading bruise peeking out above the neck of his T-shirt.

"Oh my gosh, is that still there from the fight?" I leaned toward him to touch it, and he jerked his collar over it.

The mark faded with the red that crept up his neck. "No. Not from the fight."

Oh. Right. I looked away from him so I wouldn't stare at the hickey. "So, you and Bill are—"

The driver's side door opened with a screech and Bill climbed inside. "Getting along well," he supplied from the other side of the canvas drape, and the door closed.

Ziggy's flush deepened, but a pleased smile tugged the corners of his mouth.

As obvious as it all seemed—now that it had been pointed out to me—I couldn't quite get my head around their hookup. It was none of my business, but I couldn't help it. The situation was exactly like when my best friend got a boyfriend during junior year and the rest of our clique wondered obsessively over whether or not they'd "done it" yet.

In a more maternal way, I worried that Bill didn't appreciate what Ziggy had gone through with Cyrus and Jacob, if Ziggy had even mentioned it at all. Ziggy was a very private person, and if he didn't warn Bill to tread carefully, he could wind up getting very hurt by his own omission. If Bill thought they were just having fun with no strings attached, would Ziggy even bother telling him if he felt different? Or, would he just hold all that hurt inside and go along with whatever Bill wanted?

And would I ever stop projecting my own relationship crap on others? I shook my head and grimaced at my own idiocy. Ziggy had done a lot of growing—had been forced to do it, actually—and Bill wasn't a teenager. I was worried about things that not only were beyond my control, but also probably not worth worrying about in the first place.

You know why you're doing it, right? I asked myself, and I had to agree that I did. I hadn't heard anything through the blood tie from Nathan. It didn't mean he was dead—I carried the broken connection between sire and fledgling around in my heart every day; I would know if he'd died. It did mean that he was experiencing things he didn't want me privy to. A sick part of me worried he'd been seduced into following his sire's whim, the way Cyrus had always fallen to the machinations of his father. But Nathan had made that mistake before, and it had cost him dearly. He wouldn't do it again.

The most likely—and horrific—explanation was that whatever they were doing to him was so terrible, he didn't want me to know about it. I tried to imagine the most vile, cruel thing the Soul Eater could be capable of. I had to stop myself to keep from bursting into tears.

"Next stop, certain death." I tried to make it a joke, but the sick fear wound tighter and tighter through me as we pulled away from the sidewalk.

"I hope we make it back here," Ziggy said, as if he'd read my thoughts.

I nodded. "I know how you feel."

Eleven: Skin

The Soul Eater's new residence was a far cry from the mansion I'd met him in. That had been pristine brick-and-marble columns with a fine manicured lawn and lots of clean-cut henchmen. The building I surveyed through my binoculars was all peeling paint and dangling gutters, and I was pretty sure the grass hadn't been mowed so much as worn off the ground by feet and cars.

"The Soul Eater lives there?" I hissed from the back of the van. I don't know why I whispered. We had parked the van a safe distance down the road from the house, where Ziggy had assured us we could see the house but no one on the property would think to look our way.

Ziggy made a noncommittal noise, his body rigid in the passenger's seat he'd evicted Henry from. "Yeah. Well, he needed to go somewhere no one would try to find him while he healed."

The last time I'd seen the Soul Eater, he'd just killed my fledgling. But he'd also made the mistake of replacing his own heart with the Oracle's heart. It may not have killed the Soul Eater when Cyrus sank the stake into his chest, but it had killed the Oracle, and the heart had combusted inside the Soul Eater. It had done plenty of damage, and Jacob Seymour had already all but destroyed his ability to function as a normal vampire by constantly cannibalizing others. It wasn't a long shot to think he was still healing. Unless…

"How is he doing? I mean, after what we did to him before?" I hoped the answer was that he was still twisted and crippled by the attack, and I'd be able to single-handedly take him out, thus ending our problem forever.

I knew that wasn't to be when Ziggy shrugged. "He's dangerous now. He's been feeding on his fledglings. The last one was some woman from Nevada who came up here thinking he just wanted to talk. I don't get how these people can be so dumb."

It must have been March, the madam of the vampire brothel I'd met on my travel to rescue Cyrus. I couldn't feel too bad about her. There were just some people who made my life easier by dying.

"So we should steer clear of the guy?" Bill asked.

I answered for Ziggy. "Yes. I think our plan should be simple. We fight our way in, or as far in as we can. I'll get myself into the house and look for Nathan. There's nowhere else they would be keeping him, right?"

Ziggy shook his head. "No place I can think of."

"Then I'll go in and find him. If I run into Dahlia or the Soul Eater, I'll try to make it back out." A spark of hope ignited in my chest. "Unless you think they're not here."

"No, they're here." Ziggy took the binoculars, scanned the area quickly and handed them back. "Look, the humans are out and about. When he's not home, the humans are locked in the barn. Just in case one of them comes to their senses and tries to get away. If the Soul Eater and Dahlia and me—when I lived here—were home and somebody tried to take off, we just…"

"I get it," I said, not wanting to hear the rest. "Fine. So, the humans are out, the Soul Eater is in, and we're going after Nathan. There's no time like the present."

Ziggy and Bill got out, then opened the back doors for Max and Henry and I. We gathered our weapons quickly, as if attack could come at any moment. And it could.

I'd planned my weapons for speed. A stake in each back pocket, a few vials of holy water in a passport holder hanging around my neck. I'd lined the pouch with a plastic bag, just in case the vials broke, and tucked the whole thing inside my shirt. A knife was concealed by my pant leg. I didn't have a neat holster or anything to hold it there, so it stayed in place with a strip of duct tape. I hoped I wouldn't have to use it, not because it was my last line of defense, but because it would hurt like hell to rip it off.

Ziggy and Bill were more heavily armed. Ziggy had Nathan's big, scary ax in one hand, his crossbow strapped across his back. I couldn't help but remember the first night I'd met Ziggy, when he'd shouted, "Die, vampire scum!" and charged at me with the very ax he held now. It seemed years away. It was hard to believe it had only been a matter of months. Bill, on the other hand, was content to take his gun and a couple of knives I was pretty sure he'd taken from the kitchen drawer. Still, both of them had stakes in every available pocket, and a few, I'm sure, duct-taped the way my knife was. Max had stakes, but when I had offered him other weapons, he'd just shrugged them off and said, "I won't need them."

"They'll see us coming up the driveway," Ziggy said, handing Henry a stake and a knife. We figured he would know what to do with them.

"Well, if they're going to see us anyway, might as well make an entrance," Bill reasoned. "Get back in the van. I'm driving us down there."

"Try to take out a few of them on the way in," I said, silently praying we wouldn't get ourselves killed in a car accident before we could get ourselves killed in the assault on the house.

"Will do," Bill assured me cheerfully as we piled into the vehicle. The engine roared to life and Bill did indeed make an entrance. He ignored the gravel driveway, charging the van instead through the low-lying brush that lined the road. "Element of surprise," he shouted over the noise of branches clanging against the underside of the van. He was enjoying himself way, way too much.

"We do need this to get back, you know," Max yelled as I braced myself against the backs of the seats. I squeezed my eyes shut as we passed between two trees. When I opened them, the driver's side-view mirror was gone.

The house was surrounded by a huge lawn, and on either side abandoned fields. Bill plowed through the field, toward the house, where a few startled human servants clustered. They didn't have time to get out of the way, and I heard body parts hitting the undercarriage of the vehicle. It reminded me of the way dandelion heads sounded smacking against the bottom of my little red wagon as I'd pulled it through the backyard as a child.

"Here's good," Ziggy yelled, pushing the door open. He jumped out, ax swinging.

Bill took advantage of the cover of the car to shoot a few of them from where we sat. I hadn't even seen him open the window. I clapped my hands over my ears, thinking I would never be able to hear again. Soon, a ring of dead and critically wounded humans surrounded the van.

Ziggy let us out of the back. "More coming. From the barn," he said, helping me down. Bill joined us at the back, reloading.

I looked toward the house, my goal. We were about a hundred feet away, and the distance seemed impossible. More humans came from that direction, and some vampires. I could tell that was what they were from the fact they weren't wearing heavily soiled clothes like the humans. "Great. Bill, keep clear of the clean ones, they're probably vampires."

"Will do." He tried to pick off a few of the approaching humans in the direction of the barn, but they were too far out of range. All we could do was wait for them to get to us.

Henry stood beside me, holding his stake in one hand, the knife in the other. "Henry, follow me and…Max."

"I'll kill anyone who tries to get in your way," Max vowed.

Bill looked at me for a minute as though he might be one of those people, his hand flexing around his gun. Instead, he said in a tight voice, "We'll back you up. You just worry about getting inside."

"What about the ones coming that way?" Ziggy jerked his head toward the creatures nearing from the direction of the barn.

Bill shrugged. "I guess we end up in the middle and go down in a blaze of glory."

I guess that must have seemed reasonable to all of us, because it only took a briefly shared look and we were off, running headlong into the mass of humans—it seemed, frighteningly, as though their number had grown. Over my left shoulder, Ziggy's ax flashed, and a stream of blood sprayed the side of my face.

"Sorry," I heard him shout from somewhere, though the volume wasn't necessary. The only noise was our own exertion. The creatures didn't make much sound. No screams, no wisecracks, just an occasional grunt as one of them fell. It was an eerie kind of quiet, because you expect a battle to have more sounds, like in the movies. All I heard was the rhythmic slash of Ziggy's ax and the crack of Bill's gun.

The first one to try and hit me, a rail-thin man with eyes that seemed to bug out of his dirty face, missed. I grabbed his arm as it swung past and forced it down, feeling the pop as the joint of his shoulder separated.

"They haven't been fed yet," Ziggy called, and I turned in time to see him twist a woman's head completely off her body. I shuddered at that and turned back to my goal: the house.

Another of the humans grasped my leg. I looked down to see a scrawny girl, her hair thinning in patches over the mottled skin of her scalp. I wondered if she clutched me for help or to harm me, but I didn't need to wonder further when she sank her teeth into my leg. I kicked her free and fended off another set of snapping teeth at my right arm.

"You're right, they haven't been fed!" I elbowed a

shockingly elderly woman in her throat, praying she wasn't someone's beloved grandmother.

"Watch your blood, everybody!" Max warned, and I saw him hit one of the creatures in the side of the face so hard its jaw completely detached and flew into the melee. He really didn't need weapons, after all, as it appeared werewolves were a lot stronger than vampires.

Bill screamed, and I turned to see him press the barrel of the gun into the top of a sandy-blond head that had latched on to his forearm. He squeezed the trigger, sending a spectacular stew of brain, blood and bone over the front of his shirt before the body dropped, teeth still embedded in his flesh.

"Careful you don't shoot yourself, for fuck's sake!" Ziggy yelled, bringing his ax down on the back of a creature he'd kneed in the groin. "Carrie, get to the house!"

I turned to Henry, who waited patiently at my side. "Why the hell are you just standing there?"

A creature grabbed him, dragged him back and released him when it realized he had no blood in him... something I hadn't realized until that moment, either. But even under attack, Henry waited to act. "Henry," I called as we became separated in the action, "kill all these humans!"

That was all it took. Suddenly Henry, a weapon in each hand, began to plow through the humans like a killing machine. It was a bizarre dance; Henry grabbed a human, pulled them close, jammed the knife low in their abdomen and slit them upward, as though he was opening an envelope. The hot, foul smell of open bowel filled the air by the time he gutted his second creature.

"Carrie, watch out!" Bill shouted, bringing me back to the reality at hand. Another human reached for me. I got a sick feeling in my gut when I saw how young she was— probably sixteen and, under normal circumstances, scared for her life. But this wasn't a normal circumstance, and she was definitely not a normal girl. Her eyes registered nothing but feral hunger and a desire for destruction. She gripped both my arms and pulled, and I thanked God she hadn't been fed tonight, or I might have had no further need for sleeves. I tried not to think of Cyrus—the first time I'd known him—and the perverse joy he would have had watching me destroy this poor girl. But she was beyond help, there was no doubt in my mind. I lifted one foot and kicked at her, not caring where my foot connected, and then, because I couldn't reach my knife, I found a stake with the hand I'd freed and jammed it hard into her chest. In my mind I saw the view from the inside, skin, sinew, cartilage splitting and splintering under the force and point of the wood. I saw the pumping core of her and kept forcing, until my hand followed the hole the stake had made and buried with a wet sucking sound into her chest. Her eyes rolled up, displaying only white, and blood gushed from her mouth and nose. I yanked my hand back, horrified and ashamed at my actions, and let her drop.

Through a heady rush of bloodlust, I viewed the house ahead of me. I needed to get there, fast, before I did some-thing else. Something I would regret more than jamming my fist through a teenager's rib cage, if I could ever pos-sibly top that. I started just throwing the humans aside for Max and Henry to deal with, buying myself time and for-ward momentum. For a split second, I felt guilty at leaving the guys to fight all of the creatures on their own. But some weird elation at being closer to my goal filled me, made me feel more powerful, ready for anything.

That was Dahlia, and I knew it in a second.

I don't know if she thought she was driving me closer to my doom. Maybe she and the Soul Eater were waiting just inside the weathered front door, and they would kill me instantly when I stepped inside. But whatever reason she had for messing with my mind now, she reminded me of one crucial detail.

Using a spell I'd improvised, I imaged the word *back* shooting from my mouth like a gale-force wind. The creatures were knocked back long enough for me to scream, "Remember to use that spell!" I saw Ziggy's face brighten under a mask of blood. I turned back to the house, but I heard one of the creatures scream—finally scream—and the sound of flesh tearing like the pages of a book.

As soon as I got free of the battle, I ran to the house as fast as I could. My lungs burned and my legs ached as I pushed myself up those final steps, but I didn't let myself stop. The door was unlocked, so I abandoned all pretense of stealth. Dahlia knew I was there. If she was in the house, she would hear me.

"Nathan!" I screamed, and I was impressed in some detached corner of my mind at how desperate and horror-movie damsel-ish I sounded. "Nathan, where are you!"

Carrie, get out!

For the first time in far too long, I heard Nathan's thoughts through the blood tie, soaked in fear and pain. And weak. More weak than I'd ever heard him.

"I'm not leaving here without you!" I shouted, scanning the wide hallway for any of the creatures, or other vampires. "Tell me where you are!"

The house was built like an old Southern farmhouse, though how it got to the middle of Michigan I had no clue. The entrance hall was long, with a staircase leading to the second story. Beyond the staircase I could see the back door. On a hot summer day, when the doors were both open to let in the breeze, you would be able to see all the way through the house.

Unluckily for me, it wasn't a hot summer day. It was night, and though I could make out the general layout of the house, I wouldn't be able to see if something was shuffling around in the darkness.

Come on, baby, you've got to tell me where you are, I thought, partly for him and partly to urge myself on the search. There was no answer. Maybe they had him drugged, and he couldn't remain conscious.

Of course, it could be much worse. I prayed he was just drugged.

I ducked through a doorway to my right. It was a large dining room, with remnants of the last meal still on the table. The overwhelming stench of the corpse made my eyes water and my throat flex closed. There was a large kitchen knife buried in the body's face. The whole thing was hacked to pieces and in some places partially skinned. I couldn't tell if the poor soul was a man or a woman, but it had certainly been fed better than the mindless zombies they'd made the humans outside into. Sticky globs of jelled fat gleamed on the table in the moonlight from the windows, and the beefier parts left on the corpse wobbled as I disturbed the floorboards by walking on them. I pulled the collar of my T-shirt over my nose and moved to the door I assumed led to the kitchen. No leftovers there. In fact, nothing at all, except for a few blood-crusted cups in the sink. I moved on.

Back in the hall, I considered my chances of finding anyone in the rooms to the left side of the house, and weighed them against getting trapped upstairs if the humans from outside came in after me.

They won't. They're not allowed. Nathan was conscious again.

Where are you? I tried to keep my mental voice even, despite the panic I truly felt. *Please, Nathan, I can't do this alone.*

Get out of here, he insisted, and then the connection broke again. I wanted to scream my frustration. Instead, I ran through the door near the foot of the stairs, which led to a small living room scattered with broken furniture and then, guided by the miraculous appearance of a sliver of light under another doorway, to a back bedroom lit by candles and, tied to a narrow bed, Nathan.

It was a strange sort of relief, finding him. I would have preferred to find him in a much different state. He lay on his stomach, arms stretched above his head, wrists tied apart to the white-painted iron spindles of the headboard. His feet weren't tied, but he didn't try to move. There were marks on his back, long slashes indicative of a whip or a scourge. My gaze darted—guided by Dahlia's urging in my head, no doubt—to the old-fashioned washstand at the end of the bed. It was a scourge, all right, a wicked weapon with a surfeit of leather straps, all ending in some terrible, sharp object that appeared to have been added as a homemade afterthought. I saw at least two broken razor blades tied to it before I tore my tear-filled eyes away.

"Nathan," I said quietly, approaching the bed. The blood on his back was still sticky; the wounds hadn't healed. Either Dahlia had just been here, or he was wounded beyond healing. *It doesn't look that bad,* I argued with myself.

I knelt beside the bed, gagging a little at the smell of his blood. Usually, it would have been a comfort, but not when there was so much of it soaked into the sheets and mattress below him.

"Oh," I whispered, reaching to touch what little skin on his back remained unmarked. I couldn't help the pity in my voice, or the half sob.

He turned his head to me, his eyes black and swollen shut. The lids flickered as if he would try to open them, and they did open, just a little. "You're really here?"

"I'm really here." I touched his hair, matted and sticky with blood. Underneath it I felt hard, scabbed over wounds. "You're going to be okay, we're getting you out."

"No!" He tried to shake his head, but it was a pathetic half movement that caused him to whimper in pain. "No," he began again, more subdued. "You can't move me."

"Bill is here, Ziggy is here. They'll help me carry you." I didn't mention Henry. There was no time to explain, and he had no energy to be pissed at me.

The ropes binding his arms weren't tied in any sort of complicated knot. If he had wanted to get free, he would have. I wondered why he hadn't tried, then chastised myself inwardly. He was wounded and weak, though a sick part of me couldn't pity him too much, as I'd seen much, much worse.

I pulled the binding free and his arms, hands purple from lack of circulation, dropped to the bed. He screamed when the movement jostled him.

"What's the matter?" I asked, feeling suddenly that something was definitely far worse than I had anticipated, but not knowing exactly what.

"Don't move me," he pleaded, but I couldn't heed him. If he was severely injured, I had to know the extent.

"I'm sorry, I have to." I eased one hand under him and he screamed again. I'd never seen him like this, so completely delirious with pain. "Roll over, please. I can't lift you."

"No," he sobbed, but he did help me a little as I slid my other hand beneath his torso and tried, gently as I could, to ease him onto his back. The sheet stuck to his chest and stomach the way a wet washcloth sticks to skin. It pulled away with a sloppy, sucking sound, revealing flesh so bloody I couldn't tell where the injury originated from. Once he was completely on his back, and unconscious as a result, I lifted one of the tall pillar candles from the bedside table for more light. I looked around the room for a light switch, but saw nothing. I wondered if the place even had electricity.

Hesitantly, I raised the candle, widening the circle of light it cast over the bed. And at what I saw, I dropped it.

Nathan had been skinned. There was no other word for it. From his collarbones to the tops of his knees, nothing but muscle and in some places, bone showed through. I tried to choke back the bile that rose in my throat, but I couldn't hold it. I doubled over and vomited on the floor, on my shoes, wishing I never had to look at my sire again and see him this way. But I had to look. I had to figure out a way to get him out, to save his life.

Tears streamed down my face as I finally got the courage to examine him again. In Gross Anatomy, you start with your cadaver from the outside and go in. The feeling of my scalpel slicing into skin to make a button-hole incision, dividing the flesh into large strips that could be peeled away, came back to me, and I almost threw up again. How long had this taken? How long had he suffered like this? The pain was unimaginable.

The worst was, she hadn't stopped at skinning. It appeared she'd gone as low as his knees and then grown bored, only to return to the top of his chest and begin on the muscle. His ribs were exposed. His two, pulsing hearts were visible behind the bloodstained bones. His lungs, his liver, all of it hung there unprotected.

I don't know when or why in the course of all of this that I decided Dahlia was the culprit, but I'd never been more recklessly sure of anything in my life.

"Like my work?"

When I heard her voice behind me, smug and superior, confirming all my suspicions, I lunged for her.

Twelve: Soul Eater

Dahlia paled and stepped back as I ran at her. I wished I had whatever implements she'd used to torture Nathan. I would have jammed them into her throat. I would have carved her into pieces that didn't die, just wriggled in agony on the floor. I would have smashed those pieces one by one under my shoes.

I didn't reach her. She held up her hand and knocked me back, the way I had knocked back the humans outside. I felt as weak and inconsequential as a human in the face of her power. She'd done things to me before, but I'd never sensed how incredibly dangerous she was until now.

"I suppose I could have done that with magic," she purred, nodding toward Nathan. "But I like getting my hands dirty."

I struggled to my feet, spat, "Apart," imagined it like a razor blade, but she held it off and knocked me down again.

She stalked toward me. "Well, for some things. I like to get my hands dirty when it's fun."

I was the only thing between her and Nathan. If I died

doing it, I was going to at least try to protect him. "Apart," I tried again, and again she shook it off.

"Please, bitch. You think you can hurt me? I bet you think you know everything, just because you have that little book of mine." She raised her hand again and conjured a ball of crackling purple energy. She released it at me and it was as if every inch of my skin had become fiberglass, splintering and prickling with the slightest movement, even breath.

"That's amateur stuff," she continued, looking down at me the way someone would look at a mouse smashed by a trap, dispassionate, just waiting for the death throes to end so they can throw the disgusting vermin in the trash.

I drew a deep breath, despite the pain it caused in my ribs, my lungs. "Apart."

This time, it worked a little. She didn't rip apart and she definitely didn't turn to sand, but a long slash opened on her cheek. Some of my magic had gotten through. And hers faltered.

She looked as surprised as I did.

"I drank your blood, *bitch*." I put as much emphasis as I could on the word, hurling it back at her with as much venom as she'd wielded against me. "I've got your power."

"Not all of it." She sounded confident, but she took a step back.

"Yet." I don't know why I said it. Maybe to scare her. But the fact that I meant it, that scared me.

"You wouldn't dare!" she shrieked. It did scare her. She took another step backward, and another.

"I would do more than you could imagine to protect him." I advanced on her. "Apart!"

She gasped and tried to protect herself, but a little too late. Another long slash opened across her neck, red weeping from it like wax dripping from a candle.

I reached into my shirt for a vial of holy water. I pulled one out, hurled it at her. It missed and exploded against the wall. She ducked, and only a few drops splashed across her face.

Dahlia smiled and licked one of the drops away, a little wisp of smoke curling up from her pointed tongue.

I looked at Nathan, all torn apart on the bed. I thought of Cyrus, feeding me information and then going back to laugh at me with Dahlia. And I got angry. Angry at being defeated over and over, at gaining ground only to have it ripped from under me, at watching the people I loved being hurt over and over.

"Dahlia?" I asked, hearing the feigned weariness in my own voice, evilly anticipating the shock she would receive.

She snorted again, a look of pure joy on her face at having won so easily. "What? Going to beg me for mercy now?"

I was on her before she could even think to run. She tried to form the words to create a spell. I crushed her windpipe. She raised her hand to zap me with another ball of energy. I slammed her hand down and pulled her fingers back, toward her wrist, until I heard them snap and splintered white bone erupted from her skin. She tried to scream, but without the air to do it, it came out like a death rattle. I looked into her eyes and saw fear. She knew she was going to die.

Maybe, if I had been in my right mind, I would have just killed her outright. I would have had pity. But the smell of her blood leaking from her neck and the intoxicating feeling of power at finally, finally being able to do something I'd wanted to do for a long time—to hurt her as much as she'd tried to hurt me, a fraction of what she deserved for what she'd done to Nathan—clouded my senses. She communicated with me frantically through the hold she thought she had on my mind, trying to impress me with visions of the consequences of my actions, but I ignored her.

When I bent my head to her throat and bit, tearing away all the flesh at the front of her neck, I knew I could kill her now and stop. But I wouldn't. I gulped down Dahlia's blood, felt her cease struggling by degrees, and I still didn't stop. I drank until I knew she was dead, and when the blood no longer moved, I sucked it from the wounds. And then, suddenly, the taste of her blood became the taste of something else, something liquid blue and resistant, fighting against me so that I wanted whatever it was even more.

"Carrie," I heard Nathan say, weakly, behind me. "Carrie, stop now. Please."

I ignored him, ignored the impassioned pleas in my head from both him and Dahlia. Hers became increasingly incoherent, until all I heard was senseless, terrified babbling. But still, I drew the blue essence into myself, felt it fill my veins and imagined them burning white-hot under my skin.

A rushing started in my ears. I saw through Dahlia's eyes. It was a sight without sight, moving backward through a reality I'd never seen before. From the moment I bit her, to her glee as she carved into Nathan—she had laughed at his screams, and for that I wanted to kill her all over again—to her days as Cyrus's pet, the images flashing through my brain faster and faster, more time elapsing backward as it was lost to the speed of her thoughts.

It was Dahlia's life flashing before her eyes, I realized, and when I did, everything slowed. I saw a man, a priest, in white-and-gold vestments, and he seemed so tall, like God himself, as he leaned down to the prayer rail and placed the wafer on Dahlia's tongue. The taste was sharp, sharp like the sudden pain in her tiny, gloved hands. And before she looked down, the priest's face went pale, the girl next to her shrieked. She couldn't swallow the host, her first Holy Communion, as she gazed down, transfixed, at the sudden wounds in her wrists. Rivulets of blood poured onto her crisp, white communion dress.

The white of her dress blazed with blinding intensity, overlapping the bloody spots until all that filled my vision was light. Then, the white burst through me and my vision cleared. I looked around the room—it took me a moment to remember where I was, and why—and everything seemed to be in sharper focus. It seemed as though the pattern on the peeling wallpaper could cut me if I touched it.

Dahlia still begged and pleaded, but I found it easy to ignore. Probably because she lay dead in my arms. Really, truly dead. I wasn't sure where the crying came from, but it didn't really matter. I found that if I made a concentrated effort, I could block it out.

Carrie, what have you done? Disgust, fear and a sliver of admiration—which gave way to more disgust—flowed across the blood tie from Nathan.

"I don't know," I said out loud. "I killed her."

"You didn't just kill her." Another voice, this one from the doorway, snapped my head up. Jacob Seymour loomed over me, but he didn't appear as godlike and impressive as he'd seemed in the past. In fact, he seemed angry, and perhaps a little sad.

Letting Dahlia's body flop unceremoniously to the floor, I stood to face him. "Are you going to kill me?"

A sinister smile formed on his weathered face. The sadness faded from his countenance, leaving behind only rage. "I'm not *just* going to kill you."

I shook my head. "I won't let you take my soul."

"You don't have a choice!" he roared, and he grabbed me by the throat, lifting me from the ground. He hurled me through the door, into the ruined parlor. I landed on an overturned chair, and the graceful arch of the padded wooden arm embedded in my back. If I'd been human, it probably would have broken my spine.

"You are a fool!" he raged, storming after me. I couldn't stand fast enough, and he got hold of me again, this time grasping one wrist and one ankle. When he threw me this time, I spun. I couldn't get my bearings before I fell, and I crashed through a marble-topped end table. This time, I felt blood pour down my back. If I let him toss me around like a doll caught in the middle of a child's temper tantrum, I wasn't going to last long.

"Did you think you could become my equal?" He knocked aside the sofa as if it were made of nothing. "From one puny soul?"

Still dazed from my injuries and the heady feeling of Dahlia's soul running like a drug through my brain, I didn't fully process his words. In my fight with Dahlia, my hatred had spurred me on. But strangely, I didn't hate the Soul Eater as much as I'd hated his fledgling. I had nothing to fuel me, and my body ached, not just from the blows Jacob had dealt me, but from all the stresses and pains of the last week.

If you die, he will *kill Nathan.* I couldn't argue with myself on that point. It was only for Nathan's sake that I managed to stagger to my feet, put up my hands and shout, "Back!"

The priceless, gratifying look of surprise on the Soul Eater's face as he flew backward was an expression I would remember forever. It probably mirrored my own, as the power came to me as effortlessly as it ever had to Dahlia. He hit the wall and it crumbled, the cloth wall covering split over the splintered boards and a fine mist of plaster dust surrounded him.

Dahlia's blood must have been more powerful in large quantities.

He realized it, as well. When he staggered to his feet, he headed straight for Nathan.

"No!" I ran after him, pure fear pumping through my veins. I felt all of it rush straight to the word "Apart!" as I screamed it at Jacob Seymour. He'd nearly reached the door to the room where Nathan lay, but he fell backward, his body jerking like a marionette whose strings had been cut. I hadn't managed to completely kill him, but he was out for the moment, at least.

Kill him, Nathan ordered. The strength of his mental signal had faded considerably. I had to get him out, fast.

Pulling my last stake from my back pocket, I moved

cautiously to the Soul Eater's side. My hands trembling, anticipating the moment that would come next, when everything I'd been fighting since the moment I'd become a vampire all vanished in a shower of ash, I adjusted my grip and knelt down beside him, ready to strike.

The Soul Eater's arm shot up, his hand closed over my throat. I dropped the stake and clawed at his hand, noting with satisfaction that it wasn't as attached as it had been before my spell hit him.

"Inconvenient, isn't it?" His fist flexed tighter around my neck, as if he was trying to squeeze my head off. "If you can't speak, you can't cast any more of those nasty spells."

Tears leaked from the corners of my eyes. Jacob's grip on my throat put merciless pressure on my jugular and carotid. My brain, starved of oxygenated blood, began to punch black holes in my peripheral vision.

"Father, stop."

The Soul Eater immediately released me, but I still fell to the floor. I wondered if I'd been mistaken, if he'd actually killed me. Because standing in the doorway was Cyrus.

It was as if he'd never died. His hair was a little longer than the last time I'd seen him; now it brushed the collar of his shirt. He was dressed all in black, from the laced front of his shirt to the tight, black leather of his pants. A long, straight scar slashed down his chest, and I realized with sickening clarity that he'd been sired again, that his father had taken his heart again. He was as unobtainable to me as he'd ever been.

He didn't look at me. He kept his eyes on his father, expression bored and disinterested. "You owe her some gratitude. If it weren't for her, you wouldn't have the final component of your ritual." He gestured to himself as he said it, and I saw blood on his hands.

"Cyrus?" I whispered. All of the air had been forced from my lungs, and I couldn't pull any back in. And I couldn't look away from him. "Cyrus?"

He didn't acknowledge me at all. But the Soul Eater did. He glowered down at me, then turned back to his son with the movements of a vulture circling the most likely prey. "Gratitude? It was not her, but my money that brought you back. And more than once. Who let you out?"

"Dahlia." Cyrus examined his nails, which I noticed matched his clothes. "She wanted me."

"She doesn't want anything, anymore," Jacob hissed, stalking toward his son. "This sniveling whore killed her."

Cyrus shrugged. "Did she? That *is* disappointing. I suppose I'll just have to go back to my cell without the pleasure of Dahlia's company. Perhaps I can slam my hand in the door over and over again to compensate for that loss."

"This is not the time for jokes!" The Soul Eater moved so fast I barely saw him hit Cyrus, but deep slashes marred his cheek a second later, weeping blood down his neck.

Slowly, deliberately, he touched his face, then licked his own blood from his fingers. "Thank you, Father. I didn't get a chance to feed tonight."

Jacob moved again, and this time it was slower. I saw the motion, and I saw Cyrus's gaze flicker to me, almost imperceptible, and the slightest incline of his head in a nod toward me.

And it didn't take more than that for me to decide that this was the moment to act.

Dahlia hadn't used any words when she'd done her spells. Maybe she was just more powerful. But she was inside of me now. I opened my mouth in a weak pantomime of the word *back,* but in my head I imagined the letters like battering rams slamming into the Soul Eater, one after another. The Soul Eater jerked backward and slammed into the wall again. This time it crumbled away and he fell through the hole, onto the lawn where Max, Ziggy and Bill still fought the human creatures.

I climbed to my feet, awed at what I'd done for only a second before another kind of amazement came over me. I turned, expecting to see Cyrus had evaporated, that he'd been a part of my imagination. But he was there. He didn't take his eyes off me as I staggered, weak-limbed, toward him. "You're alive?"

He didn't answer. As I got closer to him, I saw a muscle in his jaw tense. Though I was within his reach, he made no move to touch me. And when I put up my hands to touch him, he grabbed my wrists and forced them down, then stepped back quickly. He reached into the gaping neck of his loose silk shirt and withdrew a plastic bag with a grayish, blood-smeared object in it and pressed it into my hands.

"Now get Nolen and get the hell out of here, before I kill him myself." His face was hard, and though I thought I saw pain in his eyes, his words cut me to the core.

I turned back to the hole in the wall. Nearly all of the humans were dead. Only about a dozen remained, and the men, aided by Henry, were making short work of them. I glanced down at the Soul Eater's unconscious form on the lawn. Two of the humans had caught his scent and they ran for him, lapping the blood from his wounds.

I definitely wouldn't want to be them when he woke up.

When I turned back, Cyrus had gone. I almost called out to him, then remembered what he'd said. "Max! I need help getting Nathan to the van!" I shouted. At my words, Ziggy broke away from the fighting, leaving Henry to assume his place. He easily held his own against the few remaining humans.

Bill loped off in the direction of the van while Max corralled Henry, and Ziggy mounted the steps to the porch. As he came closer, I saw the faint purple lines of minor wounds that had already begun to heal. "Much easier than I thought it would be," Ziggy said cheerfully, though I could see a glint of grim steel in his expression. "How bad is he?"

I didn't mince words. I wouldn't be able to protect him from what he would see. "She skinned him."

He looked as if he might vomit, but he got it under control. "Fine. Let's go." He moved a few steps ahead of me, then stopped. "Is that my heart?"

I'd almost forgotten about the bag in my hand. I handed it over to Ziggy, then went in and covered the worst of Nathan's injuries. "If we wrap him up in the top sheet, it will give him some protection against dirt and other things getting in the wound," I explained to Ziggy. Diseases and infections wouldn't be able to take hold in a vampire body the way they did in a human body, but cleaning dirt out of someone's skinned torso probably wouldn't be any fun for the person doing the work or the person getting worked on.

Once we had him securely wrapped in the sheet, Ziggy lifted his feet and I very carefully grasped him under the arms, trying not to touch the ragged edges of removed skin. We went as fast as we could through the house, but the broken furniture and general squalor inhibited us greatly.

Outside, the van roared up to the porch. Bill laid on the horn.

"That doesn't sound like a good sign," Ziggy said, nodding toward the door.

We rushed the rest of the way, almost dropping Nathan at the threshold. At the top of the driveway, four sleek black cars pulled in, tires kicking up gravel as they spun out on their way down.

"Guards," Ziggy explained. "The house was too small, so they live in a house off-site, down the road. And there are more. We have to get out of here, now."

My heart leaped into my throat. "You could have mentioned that before, Ziggy!"

Bill left the car running as he hopped down from the driver's seat to open the back doors of the van. He looked from the bloodied sheet covering Nathan to me, and I shook my head, indicating there wasn't time to waste.

Ziggy got in first, and Bill took over for me, helping to load Nathan in the back. All I could do was stand by, wincing every time they jostled him, repeating things like "Be careful" and "Hurry."

I was about to climb into the back with them when Ziggy asked, "What about Henry?"

I'd forgotten about him. "Henry, come on, we've got to go!"

"More specific, Carrie," Bill reminded me tersely, jumping down from the back. "Henry, come and get in the van!"

The cars screeched to a halt and black uniformed men climbed out, running across the lawn toward us.

"Forget him, you can make another," Ziggy shouted as I climbed out.

"Henry," I called, and, over Bill's shoulder, I saw him dart around the front of the van. For a moment I was grateful to see him. Then he raised his knife and, without any change in his blank expression, brought it down.

Bill turned, his face frozen in disbelief, the knife handle jutting out of his chest.

Thirteen: How to Save a Life

―⟳―

"Bill!" Carrie screamed, putting her arms out to grab him as he fell. But Ziggy grabbed him faster than she could and slung him over his shoulder. "Max, get in and drive."

How the hell had he managed to say that without screaming? It was all he felt like doing, dropping to the ground and wailing at the unfairness of what had just happened. But he managed to get Bill's body in the back, beside Nathan's, and Carrie crawled in beside them. That ghoulish gray thing sat in the seat beside Max. Carrie pushed the canvas curtains back and screamed at it. "Why did you do it? Answer me!"

It didn't even turn its head. "'Kill all of these humans.'"

The transmission scraped as Max forced it into Drive and stomped on the gas, and Carrie fell back, nearly crushing Nathan.

"Bill, can you hear me?" Ziggy slapped his face. This was *not* happening. It was not happening. "Bill, come on, you fucker! Wake up!"

If he had paid better attention in Boy Scouts, he would

know first aid beyond a vague idea of CPR. Jesus, he couldn't even tell if Bill had a pulse. "Carrie, what do I do?"

It was a really long time before she said anything. At least, it seemed that way with Bill's blood pumping slower and slower out of the hole in his chest and Carrie staring at him like she was in shock.

"Put pressure on the wound. Not too much. If it's his heart…"

"If it's his heart, what?" He tried really hard to keep the panic out of his voice, to keep from screaming at her for being so stupid. It wouldn't help, and Bill was opening his eyes, kind of moving his head around. "Bill, can you hear me?"

He opened his mouth as if he would talk, but instead a bloody bubble pushed out.

"Oh God." This time, Ziggy couldn't care less the way his voice sounded. And he didn't care all that much about the tears in his eyes, as long as Bill didn't see them.

"Shut up…I'm fine," Bill wheezed, choking on more blood. "I think. I'm lying…on a…" He reached a hand out to touch something in front of him, but nothing was there.

"You're going to be all right, okay?" He pulled back the canvas flap. "Can I move him? He's lying on something."

"No." Carrie shook her head. "He's not lying on anything. Internal bleeding is putting pressure on—"

"Shut up!" Ziggy shouted, and he realized he sounded like Nate had the night he'd been dying in Cyrus's study. It made a horrible chill go up his spine, and he shut his eyes tight.

When he opened them again, there were light droplets of sweat on Bill's skin, but if you didn't look into his eyes, you'd think he was the most stoic motherfucker on the face of the planet. "Not thrilled…about dying."

"Shut up, you're not going to die." Ziggy ignored the thump at the side of the van that made them swerve again.

Max cursed loudly, then shouted, "I think I lost them!"

Somehow, Bill's hand managed to find Ziggy's. "Sorry…we won't—"

"You're not going to die," Ziggy said, but he couldn't be as vehement this time. Because he was starting to believe that Bill might have a very serious problem. "Just rest now, okay?"

"We don't have far to go," Carrie reminded him, but as the minutes passed and they seemed to hit every red light in Grand Rapids, Ziggy started to lose hope.

"Bill?" he said quietly, touching the side of his face. Bill didn't answer.

And that was it. He was gone. Ziggy felt for a pulse. And then Carrie did, holding her hand at his neck for a long time before letting it drop hopelessly to the dirty, bloodstained carpet. There was nothing. Bill was really, truly gone.

A feeling Ziggy despised formed a giant fist in his chest, pushing up, trying to push the air and voice and tears out of him. He tried hard to swallow it down the way he had whenever one of his mom's boyfriends had hit him, whenever he'd found himself sleeping in a doorway in the dark, by himself. Whenever someone or something he loved was taken from him. It should have gotten easier every time. It didn't. And it wasn't now.

I told you, foolish boy. Jacob's voice was cracked and weak, but there was the seductive warmth he always had, hiding beneath the surface.

"I'm not listening to you," Ziggy whispered, barely louder than a breath.

I told you no one would care for you as much as I. Look at him. Mortal. Dead. How stupid of you. There was a sound, almost as though Jacob was trying to laugh, but didn't have the strength. It was absurd, since the blood tie was a mental connection. Carrie must have really messed him up.

No matter. My heart is open to you, as always. You are my fledgling. The moment of silence that followed was either a dramatic pause, or Jacob had lost consciousness. It gave Ziggy some time to regroup. *Come home to me. Come home to me, son.*

I'm not your son! Ziggy shot back, bombarding his sire with images of all the perverse, abusive things he'd done to him. Images of pain and humiliation. *You don't do that kind of sick shit to someone you love!*

Bill's body jerked, just a little. The kind of spasm dead bodies always have, right after.

What did you do for someone you loved? If it was the exact opposite of what Jacob had done, then the thought Ziggy was beginning to have was definitely out. But what if it was a sliver of what Jacob had done to him? Jacob had saved his life, after everyone had already thought he was dead. That was something, wasn't it? Didn't that count for something?

"Ziggy, I'm so sorry." Carrie's voice was a ghost of what it usually sounded like.

"No. He'll be fine. He'll be fine." Ziggy heard the wobble in his voice, felt the tears that had escaped against his will.

But Bill wasn't fine, and wouldn't be fine, unless he did something now. And even then, it could be too late.

He leaned close to Bill's ear, praying his words would penetrate to whatever part of him hadn't left yet. They said that hearing was the last thing to go, and Ziggy knew that firsthand. "Please, forgive me. I have to do this."

Waiting for some sign, some indication to proceed or not to, was the hardest thing Ziggy had ever done. But there was nothing left in Bill to answer.

"We're almost home, Ziggy, hang on," Carrie urged. As if she knew what he was considering. And she might have. He wished she would come out and say it. Say no, say don't, say do it, he didn't care. As long as she took the decision from his hands. But she couldn't and he knew that.

There were two options available to him. Let Bill die. Or not. And he didn't know if he could live with either one.

I suppose I could just kill him if he doesn't like it or it doesn't work out. Right? What if he didn't mind being a vampire but really wasn't big on the whole tied forever to Ziggy thing? What then?

You really don't have time to consider a future broken heart. When it came down to it, he realized it didn't matter. If he could have stopped that knife going into Bill's heart, he would have, whether or not they had any kind of relationship future. He couldn't turn back time and keep him from getting stabbed. But he could help him now, and that should be his only consideration.

So, while the van pulled to a stop, he rolled back his sleeve, spit on his wrist to wash away the blood that had crusted there, and then bit down.

He'd tasted Bill's blood before. That would be enough.

How many times had Jacob warned them never to feed off the humans in the barn, to wait for clean feeders who'd never tasted vampire blood? That had to mean something, or he wouldn't have been so careful about it. So, he held his bleeding wrist over Bill's mouth and pressed down.

A few seconds passed. Nothing.

"It's too late," Carrie whispered, tugging gently on his shoulders.

Ziggy ignored her. "Come on. Come on." He willed Bill to come alive somehow. Maybe coughing and sputtering like drowning victims in the movies. Something to tell him it worked. Just so he didn't have to wait any longer.

He began imposing time limits. Two more seconds. If Bill wasn't alive again in two more seconds, he was giving up. But then two seconds passed, and he couldn't give up. Four, six, he kept extending the deadline.

At a minute, he knew Carrie was right. He'd debated too long, he'd been selfish, and now Bill was dead.

Really dead. The no-coming-back kind.

He was really gone.

"I can't believe that just happened." Ziggy hadn't meant to speak. But then, he hadn't meant to cry, either, and that hadn't stopped the tears. Probably nothing would.

Jesus. It wasn't as if the guy was like, his long-term boyfriend or anything. They'd just met. This was so fucking stupid.

Stupid, and he couldn't stop crying.

"This just can't…" he said, his voice breaking as he leaned down to kiss Bill's forehead. And then he wrapped his arms around Bill's head and pulled him into his lap, curling over him and crying.

Stop. The voice in his head came on a wave of pain so intense he cried out at it. He let go of Bill and clutched at his temples, gritting his teeth. It was like someone was ripping a hole in his brain and pumping something in. Not matter or anything, just something…energy. He cried now for a totally different reason.

"Don't cry. I'm fine." The voice was outside his head now. "I don't know how, but I'm fine."

He looked down, tried to open his eyes against the splitting pressure in his head and saw Bill, his mouth streaked with blood, his face still ashen. "It worked."

"My God," Carrie breathed, and then she fumbled for Bill's wrist, a disbelieving smile spreading over her face. "It worked!"

But then Bill coughed up more blood, and his head fell back. The energy that had flowed into Ziggy's brain stopped, and that hurt almost as much as it had when it started coming in.

"No." Ziggy shook his head, as if denying it—and making the worst headache of his life even more painful—would undo it all. "No!"

The van pulled over. A second after he heard the driver's door open, Max flung open the back doors. "Henry, get Bill," Carrie ordered, and Ziggy put himself between them, pronto.

"That thing has done enough damage to him." Even as Ziggy spoke, Henry reached out for Bill. He kicked him back, hard. "You aren't going to touch him!"

"Fine," Carrie said, nodding to Max. "Get Bill. Henry, you help me with Nathan."

"We have to get inside fast. I don't know if any of them

followed us," Max warned, lifting Bill up in his arms as though he was a huge rag doll.

Once up the stairs, Carrie and Henry took Nate into the bedroom. Ziggy laid Bill on the couch, wishing he had a more stable surface, thinking it would probably do less damage to him, what with the knife sticking out of his chest.

If there *was* any damage to be done. Bill still hadn't moved, and that weird hole in Ziggy's head, while not closed up, wasn't feeling any better.

Carrie came back down the hall carrying Nate's big red box of medical supplies, her face full of worry, and Ziggy felt instantly bad for thinking anything even halfway mean about her.

"Did he turn him?" Max looked from Carrie to Ziggy to Bill on the couch, his hands opening and closing as if he desperately wanted to do something.

Ziggy shrugged, suddenly too tired to be emotive about it. "I thought I did. But he...he woke up and then...nothing."

Carrie spoke quietly. "I hate to say this, but I think it could be because of the knife. Because it's in his heart."

"What do you mean?" Fuck that, he didn't want to know what she meant. Not if she meant what he thought she did.

She reached down and felt for a vital sign. "There's a pulse, but it's weak. I could...I could take a look, but it would be messy."

"I don't care. Just do it. Do whatever." As long as he didn't have to watch. He'd seen enough blood and gore, he didn't need to see it on someone he...well, someone he knew well.

He turned his back, fixed his eyes on one thing as long

as it would hold his attention, then darted off to the next. He started to anticipate things he could concentrate on to keep from looking at Bill. He heard Carrie's soft, "Oh, no," and still he didn't turn around. Not until she put her hand, that smelled like Bill's blood and his own, on his shoulder.

"Ziggy, I'm sorry. But the knife…it's almost like he didn't turn all the way. Half of his organs still appear human, the other half…" She pressed something into his hand and he looked down at the pages of *The Sanguinarius,* open to an anatomy drawing. He pushed it away.

"It's kind of a blessing, maybe?" Max didn't have to sound so halfheartedly positive. "If he had changed, the knife would have instantly staked him. The heart of a vampire stays human. We grow another one, but the one that matters, the one that kills us…that's the one with the knife through it right now."

"How is it a blessing?" Ziggy managed through gritted teeth. "How is it a blessing that he's going to die?"

Max faltered a little when he started to speak. "I don't know. Maybe…you could give him a proper burial. Somehow. You could have closure."

"I don't want closure. I want Bill." Ziggy knew how childish it sounded. He turned back to Carrie. "Listen, I just… Is there anything you can do?"

"Short of give him a new heart?" She sounded defeated. She'd given up.

Heartless. They are all heartless, Jacob pushed into his brain. *Come home to me.*

Heartless. The word fired off a network of lightning-fast memories in him. "Wait. The Oracle sent Jacob her heart, and he put it inside him."

"Yes," Carrie said, as if she already knew what he was going to say and didn't like it at all.

He turned then to look at Bill. He was splayed open like a gutted fish, and the knife really was sticking into him. It was weird. Looking at it head-on, it seemed that maybe there was only a little bit of blade in there, that there wasn't room for more. But it had made room. Six inches deep, all the way through his heart, into the squishy bits behind it. But Carrie was right. There was only one heart.

"Take mine."

It took surprisingly less consideration than he'd given turning Bill in the first place. Shucking his coat, he reached into his shirt and pulled out the slimy plastic bag containing his heart.

"Ziggy, it won't work. The Soul Eater was already a vampire. It's not which heart is in the vampire at the time, but whose. She could stick your heart in him, pull out his, the change might complete and then whoosh, he goes up with your heart in him and kills you, too." Max's face turned red. It was a weird thing to see on a vampire.

Carrie was uncharacteristically quiet, considering how much she usually argued in this kind of situation. It gave Ziggy the will to press on. "If you put my heart into him, do your doctor thing, hook it all up, while he's still human, then it's like a transplant. While he's human. And then we let him change the rest of the way and it's like it's been his heart all along, right?" The more he described it, the more it seemed as though it could probably work.

Finally, Carrie spoke. But she didn't sound as if she believed her own words of denial. "Ziggy, no. It sounds interesting. I might even try it if… But I couldn't endanger you like this. What would Nathan—"

"You and Nate left me for dead at the Vampire New Year party. You put that death sentence on me and told me everything was going to be all right, when you had no clue what was going to happen." His voice rose as he remembered it, and he forced it down. He couldn't let his anger get in the way of proving his point. "You owe me. You didn't protect me, and now you owe me."

"Bullshit, she owes you!" Max raged, his fists curling at his sides. *Let him hit me,* Ziggy thought, his vampire heart beating faster in his chest. *I don't care. I have to do what I have to do.*

He looked into Carrie's eyes. They were hollow and rimmed red. She still felt guilty. Good. She should feel guilty, and it would work to his advantage if he played it like that. "You got Bill killed, too. It was your monster that did this. Carrie, you have to fix him. You owe me. And you owe him."

She sighed, her shoulders sagging. "I'm not a surgeon, Ziggy. I don't know how to do a heart transplant. Besides, it takes a whole team of people to do one of those."

"Right, but they want their patients to live. We just need him to…not die right away. Can you just do a half-assed job?" Half-assed wasn't the best word choice, he supposed, but he stared at her, hard, daring her to meet his eyes. "Please. You could always just tell Nate I was wounded or something."

"Of course. 'Nathan, your son is dead. He was wounded or something. Never mind this vivisected human and all these surgical tools,'" Max grumbled, raking his mutilated hand through his hair. "I can't believe you'd even consider this, Carrie!"

Ziggy couldn't argue anymore, and he didn't have anything to bargain with. It all rested on her now. "Please, Carrie. Please."

She looked at the box of medical supplies, then held up her hands, helpless. "Fine. But we have to do it now."

Ziggy swallowed the lump of stones in his throat. A nagging doubt grew in him, telling him he should be overwhelmed by near-painful relief. That he wasn't might be a sign that he'd made the wrong choice.

"This is crazy," Max exploded, pacing back and forth behind them. "Bill is dead! Nathan is close to it! What the hell are you doing?"

Carrie's expression was grim as she settled beside Bill, the bag with the heart in her hand. "I'm trying to save life instead of taking it for once."

Fourteen: Wounded

Transplanting Ziggy's vampire heart for Bill's human one was, by far, the stupidest thing I've ever done.

It also turned out to be the most brilliant. Even before I completed the sloppy job, a technique I improvised with common sense, a copy of *Gray's Anatomy* and liberal amounts of guessing and prayer, the change started to creep through his other organs. I watched, horrified and dazzled all at once, as the vampire blood began to flow into his heart, mending the places where I'd poorly patched veins to ventricles, occasionally bursting a connection. The left atrium and ventricle split completely away, and I held my breath, wondering if Ziggy was about to die or the transformation was about to complete. The left half of the heart fell back, pressing into the lung, and regenerated its missing right half. However, unlike the right half of the human heart, the right half of the vampire heart was covered in soft, pointed spines, and it beat with its own weird rhythm. A long, purple vein snaked from the left side, slithering past the other organs, out of view. I assumed it must attach to the stomach, as in the diagram from *The Sanguinarius*. Forcing back a shudder at the memory of that horrible illustration, I watched the remaining half of Ziggy's human heart regenerate its left side, free from those nasty, dark spikes, and, for just a moment, cease beating. The veins connecting it to any blood source pulled free, and, with nothing but memory to account for it, the heart started up again, thumping but not processing any blood through it. Just a spectral beating heart, the only human thing that remained in Bill's chest. Before my eyes the pericardium, the sack around the heart and lungs, lashed itself back together. His sternum closed, too, but the skin over it did not. The healing power of Ziggy's blood stopped short right there. I would have to stitch him up.

"When will he wake up?" Ziggy asked as I reached for the needle drivers again.

I shrugged. "I don't know. It took two months for me to change, because I didn't feed. He won't be completely finished until he feeds the first time. You should probably give me some of your blood to transfuse into him to make the healing go faster."

"You should open up a vampire hospital," Max said angrily. He'd stood by and watched as I'd worked, interjecting unhelpful comments and muttering under his breath about how crazy I was. "Not like anyone can stop you. At least, not with rational arguments or common sense."

A vampire hospital. Now there was an idea worth considering. I tucked it away for a time when I was less tired. "I need to go tend to Nathan."

"And I need to wash the van so no one comes asking

about the blood and hair stuck in the grill," Max snapped, heading downstairs and slamming the door behind him.

I let him go. There were already so many sparks flying in my overloaded brain, I didn't feel like adding to the commotion by fighting with Max over something he'd get over on his own.

Nathan lay exactly as we had left him, on top of the blankets on the half-made bed. The pinkish fluid of white blood cells mixed with dried blood from his wounds had seeped through the sheet he was wrapped in. I'd have to get him free from it before it healed to his skinned torso.

I was shocked by the sudden realization that I'd left Nathan alone to help Bill. I guess there was still something of a doctor in me. I'd helped the one who'd needed it most first and trusted that Nathan wouldn't die in the meantime. It was something I'd done on autopilot, because there was no way I'd have taken the chance if I'd been thinking right.

Hell, if I'd been thinking right, I wouldn't have transplanted a vampire heart into a half-changed human.

Pushing aside those thoughts—because I didn't want Nathan to hear them right now—I got a large mixing bowl from the kitchen and filled it with scalding hot water from the tap. Then I grabbed every clean washcloth I could find. By some miracle, the vampires who'd ravaged the apartment hadn't trashed the linen cupboard. Nothing fun to smash there, I guessed.

"Hey," I said softly, gently shaking Nathan's shoulder.

His eyes opened, just a little, and he half smiled at me, but didn't speak.

"I'm going to have to clean all of this out." There was no other way to put it. "Do you want anything for the pain? Maybe something to make you loopy?"

"No." His throat sounded parched, and I cursed myself for not bringing him something to drink. "No, save it. For when...we need it."

"If this isn't when we need it, I shudder to imagine what those circumstances will be." Slowly, I peeled back the sheet covering him. "This might hurt, if it sticks."

"I might cry." If he'd been less tired, less injured, it would have sounded like a joke. But I knew it wasn't when he said, "I thought I should warn you."

I had to struggle to keep from crying, myself, as I viewed again the damage that had been done to him. "I wouldn't blame you if you did."

"I'm so sorry, Carrie." Nathan did start to cry then, and before I could wonder what he meant, something in my mind showed me.

Dahlia. Dahlia showed me. I saw the little room where I'd found Nathan, saw him tied to the bed, not as he'd been when I rescued him. He lay on his back, his pale, nude skin still intact, still stretched smooth over his tightly corded muscles. And Dahlia was there, burning something in a metal dish beside the bed. The smoke was strong and sickly sweet. She climbed onto the bed beside Nathan and kissed him, sliding her hands over his chest. He didn't resist her, though I saw a flash of confusion and regret in his drug-clouded eyes.

I shook away the image, forced Dahlia to the back of my mind. "Don't apologize. It was a spell. You couldn't help yourself."

He looked at me with confusion that slowly faded to horror. And through the blood tie, I saw him make the connection between what I knew of Dahlia and what I'd done to her. His lips moved, but I barely heard the word from his mouth. Instead, I heard it through the blood tie, like a death sentence. *Soul Eater.*

Whether I'd acknowledged it or not, I had known it. I had known what I was doing when I'd gulped down Dahlia's blood. And I had known why I heard her voice in my head, so clear it was a part of me I had to forcibly ignore. I was a Soul Eater. There was no way to deny it.

So, I didn't. I just didn't mention it.

I finished peeling back the sheet and reexamined Nathan's wound. I lifted the edges of his skin, which made him wince, but I had to see how much he'd healed, if at all. The torn flesh tried to mend. There was just too much to regenerate.

I dunked the washcloth into the substantially cooler water and started cleaning the skinless patches as best as I could. Vampires don't get infections the way a human would, but I at least wanted to get the linen fibers and gummed-up blood off of him. It couldn't do any more damage, at least, to be clean.

"Why did you do it?" Nathan asked. For someone who'd been half skinned alive, he was remarkably unconcerned for himself. Maybe it was helping him ignore the pain that made his lips go blue with shock and his whole body tremble.

Since I didn't have an answer right away, I concentrated on washing his wound. When he made a noise of impatience, I sent all the answers I could think of over the blood tie. That I didn't know why I'd done it; that I hadn't known what I was doing; that I had known; that I'm still a flawed human masquerading in a body with far too much power and far too many possibilities and no compass to guide me.

"You did it because you hate her," he said, when the torrent was finished flowing into him. "You can lie to yourself, but not to me. You hated her so much, you wanted to do something to her that you could never undo."

"You're right." I swished the washcloth in the now-pink water and wrung it out. "I did hate her. But this wasn't a planned revenge, okay? I didn't sit around for days formulating how I would do it. And I didn't go there intending to…eat her soul. I went there to get you back."

He reached one arm—oddly half-whole in that the front had been skinned, but not the back—up to touch my face. "You should have left me."

I knocked his hand away, not caring if it hurt him. Hell, I hoped it hurt him. "That's a great thanks, you know? Bill almost died. We all almost died. And you can't even try to be grateful?"

"For nothing?" He wasn't mad, and he wasn't really arguing. Just stating a fact. "I'm going to die."

"No. Maybe not." I couldn't think of a way to heal him or ease his pain, but I knew I couldn't live without him. "I'll figure out a way to fix this. For now, let's just get you bandaged up. And stop talking about dying. I went through too damned much to get you back."

Despite his pain, he laughed. "That's not self-serving at all, is it?"

"My selfishness is what's going to save you," I reminded him. Then I worked in silence, because there was nothing left to say and small talk would only exhaust him.

When the wound was clean, I went to the kitchen and retrieved the plastic wrap. I needed something to cover the wound that wouldn't stick when I needed to change the dressing, and I'd seen how well the sheet had worked. I took the plastic wrap with me to the bedroom, throwing a quick glance at Ziggy, who still sat beside Bill's sleeping form.

I cut the plastic wrap in pieces large enough to reach from one side of Nathan's chest to the other, and secured it around three edges with medical tape. I gently taped the seam between the first piece and the second, and continued down to his hips. From there, I wasn't sure how to proceed. His legs were each skinless from hip to knee. I bandaged those with the plastic wrap, then turned my attention to parts still uncovered.

For whatever reason, Dahlia hadn't done anything to his genitals. *She tried,* Nathan explained through the blood tie. *She didn't have the stomach to do it.*

I almost gagged at the thought myself. "Thank God for small favors, huh?"

He nodded grimly. "She did try, though. Believe me, she did try."

I didn't want to know. "I think what I'll have to do for your hips—" I looked away from the hips in question, where the white of bone actually showed through where she'd cut too deep and stripped away muscle "—is just put on a pair of underwear. It will probably stick, but you won't have much mobility any other way."

"I'm not going to run a marathon," he grumbled, his eyes sliding closed in exhaustion. "Do what you have to."

I went to one of the drawers that had been overturned when the apartment had been ransacked and found a clean pair of briefs. The waistband would put pressure on some of the skinned areas of his lower body, so I used the scissors from the med kit to cut it off. I did the same to the elastic around the legs, and I slit one side to make it easier to put them on him. After I'd carefully rolled him to get the makeshift bandage under him, a lot like the way you roll an injured person to change their bedsheets, I taped the open side together. What he ended up with was a white cotton version of Tarzan's loincloth. At least, the Hollywood version of Tarzan who had to hide his junk from the camera.

"You're too good to me," Nathan said, gripping my wrist as I carefully arranged the fabric so it wouldn't pull on his wound. His words didn't make up for the fact he'd told me he'd rather have been left for dead, but they did soften the blow a little, after the fact.

I rationed a little blood out for him—we'd have to find a way to get more at dusk—and got him to swallow a few Tylenol for the pain, but he refused anything else for his comfort. "Just stay with me while I fall asleep," he asked, and I did, climbing onto the bed beside him and trying to find a place to lay my hand that wouldn't hurt him. I settled for lacing my fingers with his, and he squeezed in acknowledgment before falling unconscious once more.

"What the hell happened?"

Ziggy raised his head and tried to shake some of the sleep out of it. The light in the living room was rosy. It gave the whole place a surreal familiarity. He'd seen the light look exactly like this a hundred times.

But he'd never seen the living room all torn apart and covered in bloody tools, and he'd never seen it with this weird channel in his head. *Hello?* he asked across it.

Bill answered him out loud. "Hey. What happened?"

"Um…" How did you break it to someone that they were—surprise!—a vampire?

"You just did, genius." Bill tried to sit up, groaning as he did, and Ziggy helped him.

"Your chest is going to be sore for a while. I'm guessing. Carrie had to…" He didn't want to go into what Carrie had done. Looking back, it was incredibly stupid to have even tried. "She got the knife out, at least."

"Was that what it was? I couldn't remember. All I knew was I turned around and something hit me. But you'd think that if it was a knife, it would have hurt more. I always imagined I would feel it go in, if I was stabbed." He shrugged, winced and rolled one of his shoulders to ease the ache. "So, I'm guessing that, from the voice I heard in my head when you were thinking, that I'm a vampire?"

Ziggy nodded, unable to think of anything to say.

"Son of a bitch." Bill half laughed, an expression caught between amused and totally, murderously pissed-off on his face. "That would explain why I'm so thirsty."

"I'll get you some blood." Ziggy stood, and stopped when Bill's hand closed over his arm.

"No. Get me water. I don't think I'm ready for the other." When he finished speaking, he released his hold, as if Ziggy was dirty or something.

Great. He went to the kitchen and filled up a glass from the tap and took it silently to Bill.

Bill gulped down the water, and Ziggy had to refrain

from telling him that it wouldn't do any good. No matter how much he drank, even if he swallowed the ocean, nothing would feel right until he'd had some human blood. He wouldn't push it until it was a life-or-death thing, but he really hoped it wouldn't get that far.

"So, I'm blood tied to you now, right?" Bill wiped his mouth and set the glass aside. "Isn't that what you call it?"

"That's it." A hard edge was creeping into Ziggy's tone, a defense against the steel in Bill's words. "Us crazy vampire folk call it that."

"All right, knock it off!" Bill snapped, and the air in the room seemed to crackle with pent-up anger. He cleared his throat and looked away, visibly trying to calm himself. "Why did you do it?"

"Because it didn't feel right to let you die." There was no other explanation. No excuses. No big declaration of love. Sometimes, the cheesiest moments in movies turn out to be the ones you wish for in real life.

Bill sniffed at that, looking around the room as if it was going to be different somehow now that he was a vampire. "So, it didn't feel right to let me die, but it felt just fine to change me into a vampire without knowing what I would have wanted?"

Damn. Put that way, it did seem like a dickweed thing to have done. "Fuck you, you're alive. It's not like you were wearing some MedicAlert bracelet that said, 'Hey, don't turn me into a vampire, okay?'"

"You're right! That's the kind of thing you know about a person after you actually know them!" Bill pounded his chest with his fist and flinched, but he didn't crumple the way someone else would have in that kind of pain. Instead, he put his hand down slowly and glared at Ziggy, as if he could funnel all of that pain into him.

Ziggy stood, slowly, and tried to do his best impression of Nate during an argument over curfew. "Listen, I understand that you're upset, okay? But I was in a situation where I either had to let you die, which is irreversible, or take a chance and try to save you."

"Irreversible? And being a vampire isn't irreversible?" Bill kicked the overturned coffee table and the corner splintered, sending a leg skittering across the debris-covered floor.

"No, it's reversible." Ziggy leaned down and scooped up the table leg. "Let me know when you're ready."

They stood, frozen, glaring at each other. A pulse leaped in the hollow of Bill's throat, but that was the only clue to his fear.

That, and the raging emotions flowing over the blood tie. Ziggy had thought it was a damned powerful connection on the fledgling end. That was nothing compared to what it was like to be a sire. Still, he kept his face completely neutral, even raised his eyebrows in an expression of "come on already" as he juggled the table leg from one hand to the other.

He had no clue what he would do if Bill didn't back down. If he said, "Do it. Stake me," he wouldn't be able to. It would kill him, too, both figuratively and literally. Then what? Bill would still be pissed-off and Ziggy would have lost all kinds of respect and there would be nowhere to go from there.

Great, he loved unfixable situations where everyone ended up unhappy.

Bill's mouth compressed into a tight line, and he took a deep breath before his shoulders sagged in defeat. "I don't want to die."

"Great, then I saved your life. And you can stop being so goddamned judgmental." Ziggy tossed the table leg aside and went to the kitchen, where he took the last of the blood that was left from the freezer. It had gotten freezer burned; he could tell as soon as he opened the bag and dumped the frozen brick of blood into the teapot.

He did everything by muscle memory. Light the burner, put the lid on the kettle, find a mug, all while listening to Bill in the living room. It was difficult, with the stream of garbled emotion that flooded in through the blood tie. Anger was the most heavy, but there was fear underneath it, all sorts of different flavors of fear. Fear of what he might become now that he was one of *them*. Fear that he wouldn't be able to drink human blood to survive. Fear of rejection.

Whoa. Ziggy did a mental backup and probed a little deeper into that one. It wasn't wishful thinking. It was actually there, in Bill's head, available to him courtesy of the blood tie. He was afraid that now the relationship he'd hoped for with Ziggy was way, way too final, and that would freak one or both of them out and the whole thing would be over, in the messiest way possible. He'd wanted to keep flirting, to maintain the casualness for a while, to gradually fall in love with him, to build a bond that would mean something. And now the chance was gone, because there was an artificial bond between them that he didn't want.

Ziggy closed his eyes and pinched the bridge of his

nose, trying to think, but not so Bill could hear him. That would be a disaster and a half. But anything he wanted to hide wouldn't stay hidden for long. He had plenty of practice shutting out a sire, but not a fledgling. That was going to be damn near impossible. It hurt just imagining closing himself off from Bill.

"Listen," he said, not bothering to walk into the living room. He knew Bill would hear him. "As far as I'm concerned, this whole sire-fledgling thing? It's just what happened. I don't expect anything from you. We can keep going the way we were. In fact, I would prefer it. Because I'm freaked out knowing that as long as I live, I'm bound to you." He took a deep breath. "To know that even if this thing doesn't work out, you've got my heart."

Bill's heavy footsteps brought him to the door, and a wave of defensiveness rushed through the blood tie in time with his arrival. "See, that's exactly it. You say something like that, and where does it leave me? What if I say I don't feel the same way? You're all crushed and hurt and I've got to put up with it because you happened to be the one who made me a vampire."

"I wouldn't feel all crushed and hurt. I don't mean my love and romance heart. I mean my actual, physical heart." Ziggy looked down, unable to watch the horror on Bill's face. "Yours was ruined, so Carrie gave you mine."

"You put your…" Bill staggered away, and Ziggy followed him a few steps behind. When Bill sat on the couch, Ziggy stood at the end of it. What he really wanted to do was sit down next to him, put his head on his shoulder, kiss him. Do something so he would feel the way he'd felt a few hours ago, when they'd lain on a pile of blankets in the storage room, not talking, just touching each other and enjoying how new everything was to them. It sucked to think that was all over, and it actually caused a pain in Ziggy's chest where his heart should have been.

Bill looked up, his eyes rimmed red. "I can't believe you would do that for me."

"Well, I didn't. Carrie did it." God, he wanted to find out where the cocky, defensive Ziggy who was snapping at his fledgling hid out and wring his fucking neck. "I mean…I couldn't let you die."

"But your heart…if something happens to me, then you die, too?" He said it as though it was unbelievable that someone would do something like that for him.

He sounded, Ziggy realized, just like himself.

Sitting beside him on the couch, Ziggy tentatively touched his face. "I didn't do it to trap you or anything. But I looked at you, lying there, almost dead. And maybe it was a little selfish, but I couldn't let you die and never know if…" He caught himself before he did something really stupid, like maybe cry. But he had to force his next words out, because they hurt where they were stuck in his throat. "If you were the greatest thing that ever happened to me."

Bill put his arms around him then, and Ziggy heard his own heart beating in his chest. When their lips touched, it didn't feel the way it had the day before. It felt as though they had skipped over a lot of the fun stuff that was a part of being with someone. But maybe, if they gave it enough time, they could get back to that.

It wasn't as if they had anything but time ahead of them.

* * *

The sun had just started rising when Max made it back to the apartment. The cooler at his side was full—someone had to think of the practical necessities while everyone else was busy playing mad scientist—but he didn't feel like going upstairs. The blood would keep, and he needed his space.

And he needed Bella. The longing almost choked him as he made his way down the stairs to the bookstore. Damn, he needed her. Not just in the physical sense, but he needed to be able to talk to her for longer than a few garbled minutes over the cell phone.

Behind the counter he located the trapdoor to Nathan's underground shelter and ducked down the few stairs. It wasn't a bad place, for a werewolf. A vampire would go nuts down there in a couple of days, he was sure, but it was small enough that it calmed the primal need in him to hide.

There was also a small utility sink fed by a hose. Not a proper bath by any means, but he'd do about anything to get the blood and dirt off him. He plugged up the sink, went back up the couple of stairs to find the faucet the hose was attached to, got it running and gave it some time to really fill up before he shut it off and went back down.

He was pleased to find he'd judged it about right when he saw the half-full sink waiting for him. He stripped down and dunked his dirty T-shirt into the water, trying to get the worst of the gunk out before using it to wash himself. When he was clean—cleaner, anyway—he rinsed out his clothes and left them draped over the edges of the sink. He'd worry about the dirty water after he got some rest.

When he lay down, he expected to fall asleep right away. But the sleeping bag under him didn't smell all that great, and his mind wouldn't calm down. He thought about calling Bella, then remembered he'd left his phone upstairs, and he didn't want to deal with the inevitable drama that he would encounter there. He was beginning to wonder if there would ever be a time in his life when he could be around these people and not be tangled up in some crisis.

So much had changed since the last time he'd been here. It was like finally having Bella all to himself made him resent anything that took him away from her. And that wasn't healthy. But neither was constantly fighting to stay alive. There had to be a happy medium.

Just above his head, a phone rang, and he remembered, with the kind of joy he imagined a crack addict felt when they found a rock they'd forgotten, that Nathan's shop had a landline. He wrapped himself in the sleeping bag and climbed out of the hole, then waited for the caller to hang up before he grabbed the receiver. The lengthy process of connecting to an international operator, getting through to the compound, actually getting the call to Bella's room, and then miraculously catching her awake and alone, was a little more bearable this time, as he didn't get cut off three or four times by the crappy reception on his phone. When her voice, breathy and seductive all at once, came over the line, he almost passed out with relief.

Yeah, he definitely had problems.

He filled her in briefly on the way the evening had gone, and she'd taken it in stride, the way only Bella could. Then, with no hesitation whatsoever, she said, "My father brought your replacement by today."

"Excuse me?" She'd better not mean what he thought she meant, or he would be on a plane back to Italy so fast her father wouldn't have time to stop him.

She actually laughed, as if the whole thing was funny. "You are not angry with me, are you? I did not even speak to him. But according to my father, this man is more than willing to accept my bastard child as his own. And I believe he is only a second cousin, so future children would be pure members of the family bloodline."

"That's disgusting." Max couldn't help but laugh. Bella would never leave him for some flea-ridden, banjo-playing country cousin. But his guts still boiled at the thought of his father-in-law being so damned sure of his imminent demise. "Tell him not to count his chickens, okay? Because I'm definitely coming back."

"I will tell him you are of sound mind and body," she giggled over the line.

He sighed. "That's not quite true. I'm not sure whether it's my mind or my body, or a little bit of both, but I'm going crazy without you."

Quietly, she replied, "I understand. I miss you. I do not want to sound as though I do not love all of the time I spend with you, but what I miss the most, at least, at this moment, is—"

"Believe me, I get it." He couldn't hear her say the words, or he would explode. His cock was already hard just talking vaguely about having sex with her. "Let's not dwell on that just now."

It took her a long time to respond. Then, very clearly, she made one of those low, growling moans the way she did when they were— *Oh, sweet Christmas. She wasn't...was she?*

"Bella, that's not funny." He balled up a fistful of sleeping bag and squeezed it, hard. "Really not funny."

"Are you not alone?" she whimpered into the phone, and her words ended on a gasp.

"No, I'm alone. I'm just not in an appropriate place." If he could reach her now, he would be undecided whether to fuck her or kill her. "I'm in the bookshop."

"Why is that an inappropriate place? Do you forget what we did there?" She gave another moan, then purred, "I am touching myself, Max."

"Yeah, I kind of guessed that you were." He tried not to think of what they had done in this room, hell, not even ten feet from where he was standing. He looked at the broken door and the faint sunlight outside. Would someone come down here? Would anyone even bother to be up this early? There was the occasional noise from a car on the street, but beyond that, nothing.

Ugh, come on, man! How can you even be considering this? It's phone sex, for God's sake. If you need a reason not to do it, think of how dated and cliché it is.

Bella moaned again, and he gripped the base of his erection. "I'm right there with you, babe," he groaned, and she breathed a throaty little laugh into the phone.

"Does it feel good?" she asked innocently.

It did. Oh, it did. He flexed his fingers, imagining her wet, tight flesh rippling around him as he tugged up. "It doesn't feel as good as you."

"I wish you were here," she whimpered, echoing his thoughts. "On top of me. Inside of me."

"Baby, if I was inside of you right now, I wouldn't last two seconds." As it was, he was almost ready to blow.

"Neither would I," she gasped. "Oh, Max...I...I..." Her words dissolved into a loud, keening wail, and he pumped his fist harder, almost dropping the phone when he came.

"Max?" she asked a few seconds later, her voice raw from shouting. "Are you still there?"

"In a manner of speaking. Hang on, I've got to find something to clean up with." He grabbed a handful of out-of-date flyers for a tree-planting party and tried carefully to wipe himself off without giving himself the worst paper cut of his life.

"I am becoming very tired," Bella said apologetically. "But I do want to tell you, before we hang up, that there are others here besides you and I who feel my father is not making wise decisions. I cannot tell you any more today, but I sense we will soon be able to help you."

"What do you mean, help me? You're not going to do anything stupid or dangerous, are you?" It was less question, more warning.

It didn't matter, because she ignored him anyway. "I cannot tell you more now. Please trust me. I love you."

"I love you," he replied, but she had already hung up.

Fifteen: Patch Job

I dreamed about making a piñata out of strips of papier-mâché, and when I woke up, I knew how to fix Nathan.

When I told him how I came about my groundbreaking solution, he wasn't entirely thrilled at the comparison.

"So, in this scenario, I'm a piñata?" Just being fed had given him back a lot of his strength, at least enough to make sardonic quips while I tried to make him an informed patient. "Am I to assume that when the treatment is all done you'll string me up and beat me with a stick?"

"I might do it before the treatment is done if you don't shut up." I couldn't help but smile though. He wasn't telling me I should have let him die, and that was enough for me.

I explained to him what I planned to do. To remove a few strips of healthy skin from his back, the way doctors did to perform a skin graft. But I would take narrower strips, so that the hole I made would heal in a day, and I could harvest the fresh skin again the next evening. The skin I took I would graft onto the front of him, wherever it was needed. The edges of the wound would, in theory, heal to the skin the way it does when we get a cut: the two edges come together and just sort of meld. By the next night, the patch of missing skin would be smaller, as it would be every night until he was completely covered again.

"I don't know how well it will actually work. In the worst-case scenario, it doesn't work at all. In the second-worst case, you end up with lots of pink, shiny, patched-together skin like a burn victim. You wouldn't have chest hair. Maybe not nipples. Or a belly button. But you'll be able to function."

"I liked my nipples," he grumbled. Then he sighed. "You're asking me to consent to you skinning the other bits of me. I have to admit, I'm reluctant."

"I'll be doing it under local anesthetic." When he started to protest, I spoke over him. "I'm not going to listen to you sit and tell me that you can take the pain. You're going to get the anesthetic every night like a good boy and shut up. We can always get more somehow." I wasn't sure where, but that wasn't the point. I wasn't going to do to him what Dahlia had done.

He turned his head, looking at the nightstand as if it would lovingly advise him. "I suppose it's a good thing she couldn't go through with…you know. Down there, then."

"Yes. I would say it's a very good thing." Once a nerve was gone, it was gone. No fixing it. Call me a mindless hedonist if you will, but I don't think I could live without ever getting off again.

It just seemed too cruel, Dahlia said in my head, and

I pushed her firmly out. She might be trapped in me, but I didn't have to acknowledge her.

"It's up to you, then. Do you think you could still love me if I looked all pieced together like Frankenstein?" Nathan said it in all seriousness and self-pity.

I laughed at him. "I love you now and you look like The Visible Man. I think I could love you better with some skin on you."

"I'm being an ass, I know." He gave another heavy sigh. "Fine. Do it."

I left Nathan with a firm order to try and get some more sleep while I gathered my supplies and refreshed my skinning skills on some of the frozen chicken breasts in the freezer. Actually, I left off that last part. I didn't think he would appreciate it any more than the piñata comparison.

Ziggy and Bill were still asleep on the couch, half sitting up, leaning on each other. I was glad to see Bill had woken, but less happy to see that the remaining blood was gone. I took the kettle off the stove and put it in the sink to rinse it out. I barely heard Ziggy, wouldn't have if it weren't for the chain on his wallet jingling as he walked into the kitchen behind me.

"I was thinking about hitting Club Cite tonight and looking for a donor. Do you think that's too risky?" He leaned on the door frame, trying too hard to appear casual.

"I don't think it's too risky. I think it's too risky for all of us to sit around starving." I nodded toward the living room. "Are you going to take him with you?"

Ziggy nodded. "Probably. He's better at networking than I am. He did it for a living."

I made a noise in agreement, and let the silence hang

for a minute before I said, "You're taking him with you so you don't have to explain to Nathan."

"That's not it," Ziggy said, his denial coming too quickly. "The last time he found out I had a boyfriend, nothing good came of it. Maybe you could put in a word or two? Like, after we've left?"

I squirted some dish soap into the kettle and reached for the little spongy, macelike thing that we used to clean out glasses. I gave the kettle a few good swishes before I spoke again. "Don't you think you should just speak up and be honest with him?"

"I'm not saying I won't," Ziggy protested. "I just want you to…break the ice. You know?"

I looked up at him, his adorable, boyish face that would always look young, no matter how old he got, and my heart caved in. He wasn't asking me to talk to Nathan because it would be easier for him. He was asking me to protect him from the rejection of his father. "Of course. I'll talk to him."

Of course, I still had to talk to him about Cyrus being alive, as well. I'd just made myself a bearer of unbearable news, twice over.

Max came up the stairs, wearing stiff, dirty clothes from the night before, but looking to be in a better mood than I'd seen him in for a long, long time. He had a cooler with him. "Blood. Not much, but enough for right now."

"You were busy," I noted, nodding to the cooler. "Thanks."

He smiled a smile that told me all was forgotten from the night before. "I live to serve. But we need a donor. There are five of us now, all vampires, and we all need to eat."

"We're on it," Ziggy said, indicating himself and Bill. "We're going to Club Cite in a few hours. Want to come with us?"

"You should," I interrupted, before Max could decline. "I've got to perform a…procedure on Nathan. I don't think you want to be here for that."

Fortunately, they all agreed with me. A few hours and a bag of skinned chicken breasts later, they headed out for Club Cite. I waited until I heard the van chug away from the curb to wake up Nathan.

He gave me a sleepy smile as he woke, and I kissed him. I'd missed him so acutely, even that small contact was irresistible.

"I'd be happier to see you if I didn't know you were here to carve me up," he murmured sleepily. "Are you ready? Should I have faith in your skills now?"

"You should have faith in my skills, always." I laid the scalpel, which I had sterilized in boiling water after using it to carve up the chicken, on the bedside table. I don't care if vampires are impervious to disease, there was no way in hell I would use the instrument on Nathan without purging the salmonella demon from the blade.

At the sight of the gleaming silver, Nathan paled. Which is an impressive feat for someone as pale as Nathan already was. I put my hand on an unskinned portion of his leg and gave him a squeeze. "It's not like the last time."

He took a deep breath that trembled when he released it. "I know. And I trust you."

Since he couldn't actually lie on his stomach, I used pillows and balled up towels to prop him on his side, exposing his back. The marks from where he'd been scourged were missing now. I traced my finger over one of the lines I remembered, and for a moment, I almost lost my nerve. I didn't know if I could cut into Nathan's skin, if I could deal with causing, if not pain, damage to his body.

Suck it up and get on with it. Let's see some blood, Dahlia said in my brain, sounding incredibly bored with the whole proceeding. I wished I could somehow blindfold her so she would take no pleasure in what I would do. But I found it was simply better not to think of her at all.

I took a syringe and the vial of local anesthetic and set to work injecting Nathan and ignoring his flinching when I did so.

"Can you feel that?" I asked when I was done, sticking him a little with the needle. I jabbed a little perimeter around the injection sites where he indicated the skin was numb, then took a Sharpie marker and drew a rough rectangle within the numbed area. Taking a deep breath, I picked up the scalpel and started to cut.

It was the most difficult thing I'd ever done. Harder than giving stitches to a squirming two-year-old, harder than cleaning pebbles out of a motorcyclist's leg while he panted and turned gray from the pain. Cutting into someone I knew, someone I loved, even knowing it was for the best and they were going to be fine and feel no pain, was the worst thing. Ever.

Just when I thought it would go better if I started talking to distract myself, Nathan decided on the same tactic. "Is Ziggy okay?"

Thank you, I sent to him over the blood tie. "Yes. He's out at Club Cite, trying to get us a new donor."

Nathan made a noise of acknowledgment, then was silent for a moment. When he spoke, his voice was quieter. "Did Bill die?"

He had to give me an opening, didn't he? I sighed and pulled the flap of skin I'd excised free. I laid it over Nathan's side for safekeeping and he squirmed and groaned in pure disgust. "Sorry," I said quickly, moving the piece to rest on his plastic-wrapped thigh. "Funny thing about Bill. He's um…"

"Ziggy turned him, didn't he?" Nathan didn't need me to answer his question, judging from the agitation that sizzled across the blood tie. "Great. I suppose he loves him?"

"It would be pretty soon in their relationship to say *love*, I think." I started working on another strip of skin. "Besides, you don't have to love someone to change them."

"Yes, you do." Nathan reached slowly to scratch behind his ear. "Otherwise, there would be a hell of a lot more vampires in the world."

My heart caught a little bit at what he'd said. "Well, it can't be true. Because you turned me after Cyrus killed me. And you weren't in love with me then."

The little boost I'd gotten deflated when Nathan said, "Well, I didn't know I was going to turn you, did I? I thought it was more a blood transfusion than a siring."

"That's true," I agreed quietly, hoping he thought my change in tone was due to focused concentration. But, to be honest, after eight chicken breasts, I could skin anything in the dark with my eyes closed while answering SAT questions.

He turned a little, hesitant because of the knife at his

back, I was sure, and looked at me until I was forced to make eye contact with him. "Carrie, I think I loved you from the second I saw you."

"No, you didn't." But even though I honestly believed he hadn't, I couldn't help the flip-flop in my chest. I dipped my head and smiled, pulling another strip of skin free. *How romantic.*

"You think I'm lying to make you feel good." He laughed quietly, and I smiled with him. He laid his head back down on the pillow and closed his eyes. "No. I think that most people are in love at first sight. They don't know it until after, of course. But I try to remember what it felt like not to be in love with you and I can't."

I paused in my work, then remembered the time limit on local anesthetic. Right now, blood was rushing its merry way to the deadened area, and soon all the pain-killer would be washed way with it.

I came away with three small strips of skin. I waited until the areas I'd excised showed signs of healing, then I covered them with gauze and rolled Nathan onto his back. "If all goes as planned, those will heal up before you feel them," I reassured him. After I pulled back the makeshift bandages I'd used to cover his chest, I put the few flaps of skin against the left edge of his wound. The seam between them closed up almost immediately, and I wanted to jump for joy at my success.

"Going that well, hmm?" Nathan asked through clenched teeth.

I pressed the back of my hand to his clammy forehead. "Hurts that much?"

All he could do in response was nod. I thought it would

be better if we waited to try again when he'd had some blood, and more rest. But now, after this slight repair, his injury seemed greater somehow. It was as though we were close to the finish line and had hit the wall.

"You're naturally impatient," he said, some of the color coming back into his face as I covered his wound again. "Just give it time. It's not like I'm going to go anywhere."

I chewed my lip. "There is that to think of, you know. How are we going to get you back to Chicago?"

"We won't." His words were cloaked in trademark Nathan steel.

Shaking my head, I started to gather up my medical supplies. "You're irrational from the pain."

"I'm not." He grabbed my arm to stop me moving around the room. "Carrie, we're not going back there."

I hesitated. While I was glad to be back home, in our home, staying would be suicide. I told him as much, both through the blood tie and out loud, and he sighed.

"They know where we are. They came right into the apartment to get me. But the same could happen in Chicago. And this is my home." He shifted on the bed and grunted a little in pain. "Your plan has failed. My back stings horrible."

"It's waking up," I explained offhandedly. "At least in Chicago, we have distance between us. And better security than a dead bolt and a chain lock."

"And here we have four perfectly capable vampires to guard me. And one of them is a Soul Eater with a witch's blood." Nathan wasn't going to let that point go anytime soon. Not that I could blame him, but it was devastating to my argument. Still, he plunged on, further destroying my objections. "Do you think, from a tactical standpoint, that being as far away from the enemy as possible is a really smart idea?"

"I'm not a tactical thinker. I'm a survival thinker," I sniped, tossing the vial of anesthetic into the med kit. "Why is this our responsibility? Why do we need to take care of all this…crap?"

"Because it is. And if we don't, no one will, and he'll win." He knew he'd just repeated the same thing I'd told myself over and over. "We stay," he started again, his tone gentle. "We stay. And we fight. And if we can't fight, then…"

"Then we die knowing we didn't just wimp out." I leaned down and kissed him. "Should we maybe put this in front of Max and Ziggy and Bill and see what they say?"

"Oh, we're including Bill in big decisions now?" The sarcasm fairly dripped off Nathan's words.

"If you were smart, you would." I didn't want to face his questions when he found out the circumstances surrounding Bill's change, but the longer I put it off, the worse it would be. "Bill has Ziggy's heart."

Nathan was quiet for a long time. "You did this?"

"I did. And you can yell at me about it all you want. But when you're done being pissed, you'll know why I did it." And then I braced myself for his outburst.

It never came. He might have been too tired. Or he might have, miracle of miracles, realized that he couldn't keep his son safe from every possible hurt in his life. But he did ask, "Did you know it would work? Or was Ziggy in danger?"

"He was in danger." I held out my hands helplessly. "I did what he asked me to. Out of respect for him."

"What about respect for me?" He closed his eyes and seemed to lose all the strength I thought he had. "Carrie, if I lost him again… I don't know."

"You might lose him again." I didn't say it to be cruel. "If not the Soul Eater, you'll lose him because you treat him like a child."

"If you had a child, you'd understand." The instant he said it, his eyes came open and they were full of grief. "You know I meant—"

I waved his words away. "I know what you meant. And you're right. I will never know what it's like to fear the loss of someone that close to me. But I do remember what it was like to be a young adult, trying to get out from under my father's expectations of me. I think I still am."

He beckoned me closer, and I knelt beside him and kissed him. He put his hands in my hair, ran his fingers down my neck, then groaned in frustration. "If Dahlia wasn't already dead, I would kill her," he swore.

"You won't be like this forever," I reminded him. "You're much better already. Yesterday night you could hardly talk, let alone move or think about sex."

I doubted he heard me. His eyes were sliding closed as I watched him. When he was deeply asleep, I went to the living room. Bill and Ziggy still hadn't returned, and for a weird moment it felt as though I stood in a different time. In a time before I had to worry about the Soul Eater, in a time before I'd even met Cyrus. It felt like the night I'd stood in this living room, listening to Nathan vow to kill me, still denying I was a vampire at all.

It hadn't been that long, less than a year, and it felt like a century away.

How had I gone from that person, who wanted nothing more than to return to her lonely apartment and pray for her old way of life back, to a person who made life-and-death decisions and damn the consequences. To a person who thought of all the truly terrifying things that lay ahead with some fear, but mostly with anger.

You should fear, Dahlia warned in my head. *You have no clue what he is capable of. What I'm capable of doing to you now.*

I went to the window and looked out on the town. The orange streetlights transformed the trees into shimmering, skeletal shadows against the dark voids of the buildings. At one time I would have worried about the things lurking out there, going bump in the night. But I'd seen them.

Dahlia's laugh rang through my head. *You haven't seen anything yet.*

"Bring it on, bitch," I whispered, my cold breath misting the window glass. "Bring it on."

Sixteen: A Shock

The club was just as loud and pathetic as Ziggy remembered it. Club Cite had never been one of his favorite places, but he'd endured it back when he'd been human in order to help Nate track vampires. It seemed like this was the first place vampires new to the city, or just plain new, ended up. And that was pathetic.

To get into Club Cite you had to find the place first, and it was intentionally nondescript. The building was brick, but someone used a really glossy exterior paint to cover it with black. The result was a brick building with peeling black blobs, and the whole thing reminded Ziggy of skin cancer. Once inside, the only place to go was down. He assumed there were offices upstairs, but the actual club was on the bottom level. It had a bar, but they only served alcohol on Thursday nights, the one night a week they didn't let in anyone under eighteen. The rest of the time, you could get coffee and French sodas from the Manson wannabe behind the counter.

The atmosphere was the same every night, though.

Frenetic, smoky, loud. Some generic metal song with wailing soprano vocals à la Nightwish blasted from the speakers, inexpertly coupled with an industrial beat. The tangle of bodies on the dance floor moved like *Soul Train* with a bad case of ennui: listless gyrations and half-hearted attempts to find the beat. It was depressing to think that people actually chose to spend their free time this way, all trying to out-goth each other with their Hot Topic wardrobes and grossly inflated attitudes of made-up depression. Ziggy leaned against the crescent-shaped back of the booth and tried to focus on the conversation Bill was having with a skinny punk in white face paint.

"And that was when I realized that my soul would be forever devoted to the Lord and Lady of the Darkness," the kid said, his hand trembling dramatically as he lifted his black-papered cigarette to his lips. "That I would wander forever. Lost in the darkness."

"Wow. Well, that's…" Bill looked at Ziggy, then back at the kid. "That's just fantastic. Did you hear that, Ziggy? The Lord and Lady of Darkness."

"Your sarcasm is not appreciated," the fishnet-shirt-wearing loser said with a dramatic flourish as he stood, almost knocking over the chair he'd pulled up to the table. Seating was at a premium. He took the chair with him.

"You're batting pretty low tonight," Ziggy observed with a smile. He touched the back of Bill's neck, tracing his hairline until he couldn't keep up his stoic expression and shivered a little.

He knocked Ziggy's hand away. "Stop that. We're supposed to be inconspicuous here, and making out in a room full of teenagers would definitely draw some attention."

Taking in Bill's appearance, Ziggy laughed. On an average street during daylight hours, Bill's gray T-shirt, tucked into his dark blue jeans, wouldn't look that out of place. But here, in the land of plastic pants and duct-taped-over nipples? He might as well have walked in naked. It would have drawn fewer stares. "Yeah, you look real inconspicuous."

"Hey, I tried. But we've got limited resources." He nodded to a girl with green streaks in her hip-length black hair who eyed them with some interest from the bar. "She looks like she'd be up for it. What's the story? Are we looking for a chick to bang in a threesome?"

"As long as we don't have to actually bang a chick in a threesome, yeah, fine." Ziggy wanted to drop his head to the table and cover his ears to block out any more of Bill's scheming. He had no idea—and really didn't want to know—how good Bill was at lying to people.

Before Bill could wave over their next mark, Max slid into the booth beside Ziggy. "Any luck?"

"No, but you're going to spoil our cover," Bill said, giving the girl at the bar an exaggerated wink. Her face contorted as if she was trying not to laugh, and she cocked her thumbs and forefingers like guns at Bill before turning away from him.

"Nice," Ziggy said, trying not to laugh himself. "How are you doing?"

Max shrugged. "Okay. I got a line on a group of 'real' vampires. You know, the kids who get together and drink about a teaspoon of each other's blood on the night of the full moon?" His eyes got big and he reached his hands out like Frankenstein's monster, then dropped them and laughed ruefully. "Most of them would shit themselves if they met a real vampire, but every now and then you find one who plays along. I got a few numbers."

"Bill's been using a line about us looking for a third, if you get my drift." Ziggy pulled out his cigarettes and lit one. "But so far, he's not having much luck."

Looking him up and down, Max grinned wryly. "Yeah, wonder why that is."

At least, Max had taken some initiative in the disguise department. They'd found a box of Ziggy's old clothes in the bookshop storeroom, and though Max was a few sizes too small and a few inches too tall to fit into most of the stuff, he'd at least embellished his black T-shirt and jeans ensemble with some heavy silver rings, rubber bracelets and a liberal amount of black eyeliner.

Bill had declined anything in the Mary Kay department.

"This music is killing me," Max groaned, covering his ears. "If we've got nothing now, chances are things won't improve. Let's get back to the apartment before I go deaf."

"You know, I really do find this kind of thing fascinating," Bill shouted to Ziggy as they pushed their way across the dance floor and toward the exit. "The whole 'look at my dark soul' thing going on here. I can almost take this better than eternally upbeat people."

"What, like you?" Ziggy chided back, but when he turned his head to see Bill's reaction, he froze.

You didn't forget the face of someone who'd done to you what that son of a bitch had done to him. And you definitely noticed when someone who's supposed to be dead is walking around in one of his old haunts.

It didn't seem possible, even though Ziggy knew it was. Still, seeing Cyrus there almost knocked him out.

"Max!" He turned and reached blindly, but it wasn't Max he grabbed. It was a painfully thin girl with blue hair in long braids who gave him a look that said she was ten heartbeats away from screaming rape. "Sorry," he said, distracted by the sight of Max moving through the crowd, toward Cyrus. "Bill, turn around, go that way!" Ziggy shouted over the music.

The creep was in one of the large corner booths, far enough away from the dance floor that the light was dimmer, and the cigarette haze in the air was thicker than the shadows. But there was no mistaking Cyrus, his nearly white-blond hair, his perpetual sneer. His black silk shirt, open almost to his navel, revealed one hell of a scar down his muscled chest.

Ziggy had to shake himself away from the memories that crashed into him. Mental scenes that were shameful and degrading and somehow so, so hot at the same time. He hadn't had much contact with Cyrus since Carrie had killed him. He'd accidentally answered a few of his phone calls to Dahlia and gotten the hell off the line. But he wasn't sure Cyrus had realized it was him. In fact, he wasn't sure Cyrus remembered him at all. And that hurt somehow. If someone did terrible things to you—no matter how nice he was to you after the fact, and how much you actually bought into that nice act before he ripped your throat out—you wanted them to remember you.

There were other people in the booth, too, young kids lining up to get a taste of what Ziggy had already experienced. Worse actually, because they wouldn't have someone to protect them. Ziggy knew without a doubt that if it hadn't been for Carrie's intervention, Cyrus would have thought nothing of killing him that first night in the mansion.

Cyrus saw Max first. His eyes flared wide with something that looked like fear, then narrowed into an expression of forced indifference. He didn't speak above a whisper. "If it isn't the father of the sword. How is the whelp doing?"

Max took a step forward, as if he would jump across the whole table to get at Cyrus, but Bill put up a hand to stop him. "Bouncers," he said meekly, looking like someone who really didn't want to be stuck between two vampires if they were going to go toe-to-toe.

"It's okay." Ziggy knew he didn't have to say it out loud, knew he could use the tie between himself and Bill, but he couldn't stand there any longer, waiting for Cyrus to notice him. It was like torture.

Bill felt the thought. At least, Ziggy was sure he must have, because he looked at him sharply and then away just as fast.

"It's okay," Ziggy repeated, clapping a hand on Bill's shoulder. "This guy's a total pussy. He isn't going to bother Max."

"It wasn't Max I was worried about," Bill grumbled.

At last, Cyrus noticed Ziggy. It was a blow to the heart when he said, "Ah, you're Nolen's son! You know, father has been extremely cross with you. With all of you, in fact."

"I don't give a damn if he is," Bill said, moving as though he would stand between Cyrus and Ziggy.

Calm down. He's harmless. Ziggy tried to project as

much sincere feeling into the message as possible, but an uninvited image of Cyrus, naked and pale and gleaming in candlelight, flashed into his mind. He knew Bill saw it, and that shamed him more than the memory.

Bill didn't flinch or look at him, but kept his anger trained directly on Cyrus. "How is your dad, by the way? I hear Carrie did a real number on him."

Cyrus flinched at Carrie's name. Ziggy filed that away to keep in his back pocket for later. Right now, though, there were too many people around, fragile, human people who could really wind up in a bad way if an all-out fight broke out. "Let's take a walk."

"Yes, a fine idea. You all take a walk, and leave me to enjoy my evening and—" he reached to touch one of his companions, tugging on one of the kid's blond curls "—my company."

"How about we tell the cops sitting down the street about your 'company' and you talk it over with them?" Max asked, lifting an eyebrow. "Or do you really think that kid is eighteen?"

"Jail cells can get awfully sunny," Bill added.

With an annoyed glance at the boy beside him, Cyrus slid around the table and out of the booth. Somehow, he managed to do it gracefully. The guy was obnoxiously like a vampire out of the movies.

They left the club as inconspicuously as possible, but Bill drew attention to himself by being too normal, and Cyrus drew attention by being too damn glamorous. When they got up the stairs and to the street, Cyrus didn't run, which was a relief. He followed them to the alley and leaned against the peeling, painted-over brick wall, arms crossed. "Well, you have me. Now, what will you do with me?"

Max put on an act of thinking really hard before he said, "I'd like to bash your skull in and rip out your heart, but history has proven that killing you doesn't seem to stick."

"We need information, though," Bill said pragmatically. "And if you really didn't want to give it to us, you would have gotten out of that club before you did."

"Or not shown up at all," Ziggy added, feeling weirdly like a tagalong. "Jacob has been really concerned with this ritual lately. Let's start there."

"Fine. Could we discuss this somewhere more comfortable? I do have a mansion—"

"No." Ziggy shook his head. "We're not going anywhere with you. We'll probably get ambushed by guards the second we drive through the gates."

Cyrus's eyes narrowed and he leaned forward. "I really think we'll all be more comfortable sharing information there."

"Let's go," Bill said, suddenly looking around the alley as though it would come alive and swallow them.

Ziggy wanted to argue, but something in the urgency Bill, Max and Cyrus moved with warned him against it. Cyrus obviously thought he'd been followed, possibly that they were being watched. They passed a sleek black limo parked at the curb, and Cyrus ducked his head. The driver waiting inside was sleeping, though, so they slipped by unnoticed.

"Go, quickly," Cyrus ordered, once they were inside the van.

"What's going on? Are we in serious danger, or are you just paranoid?" Max demanded from the back of the van.

"Let us hope it is the latter. Turn here," he instructed Bill.

The mansion was every bit as fucking creepy as Ziggy remembered it. A long driveway led up the sprawling lawn to the front of a house that looked as though it was modeled directly on the Haunted Mansion at Disney World. No, the Haunted Mansion was less scary. This mansion was freaking terrifying if you knew what went on inside.

They parked the van in the shadows near the side of the house, up on the lawn, at Cyrus's insistence. Rather than entering through the front door, he led them to the kitchen entrance.

Ziggy put one foot over the threshold and shivered. He remembered vividly standing in this room, defending Cyrus to Carrie, certain that he was safe where he was. The cold, porcelain-tiled walls flickered with sinister shadows in the dim light of one buzzing neon tube overhead.

"Are you okay?" Bill asked, not quite whispering but not speaking loud enough that the others would hear him, even at their close proximity.

There isn't time to explain, Ziggy told him through the blood tie. *But this is easier than whispering to me.* Ziggy kept up with Cyrus, who led them through the kitchen to the dining room. A table was set for one, and Cyrus seated himself behind the place setting of a single crystal wineglass and napkin. "Please, sit. Are you gentlemen hungry? I'll have Clarence set another place."

"This isn't a social call," Max snapped. "Get to your fucking point and let us get the hell out of here."

Cyrus rang the little bell beside his glass anyway. "You were out looking for blood at the club. I'm not an idiot."

"That's debatable," Max said, but a little more politely, if possible. Maybe because now they were going to get fed, and he didn't want to insult their host.

"You're hoping to stop my father. I applaud you. Someone has to, and I don't have the strength." Cyrus looked down at the scar on his chest, and Ziggy noticed Bill touched his own chest in sympathy, then dropped his hand quickly. "However, if you're going to stop him, it will have to be soon."

Clarence appeared, as skinny and spiderlike as Ziggy remembered, in his overly formal clothes. He'd come with a tray and three extra glasses and napkins. Cyrus hadn't even had to ask for them.

He indicated to Clarence to lay the places for them. "The ritual is to take place at the time of the full moon. You have about twenty days. You've killed most of his damnable creatures off, so it shouldn't be too much of a strain on you to kill him in the days before the ritual."

Ziggy shook his head. "Not too close to it. Knowing Jacob, he'll have plenty of company coming so he's got someone on hand to worship him once he makes the transition from Soul Eater to god."

"Yes, he does enjoy the attention," Cyrus agreed. "Perhaps something in the next ten days would be best."

"And you're sharing this with us, why?" Bill looked from Ziggy to Max, then back to Cyrus. "I'm the new guy here—"

"And what is your name?" he interrupted smoothly.

That flustered Bill for a minute. As if he wasn't used

to being interrupted. "Bill. Like I was saying, why would you share this kind of information with us? This guy is your father—"

"And his sire," Max put in.

"Sure." Bill shifted uncomfortably. "It doesn't seem like the kind of thing a son would do."

"You're right," Cyrus agreed. "Perhaps you are too new to understand the nuances of this situation."

Clarence reappeared, this time from the kitchen, with a covered platter; Ziggy recoiled. He'd seen Cyrus eat enough dinners in his life to know that whatever was under that silver dome wouldn't be good. And judging from the size, it either wasn't a whole body, or it was a very, very small whole body.

Clarence set the tray on the table and whipped the dome off without much ceremony, considering the drumroll of dread in Ziggy's heart. Instead of some unspeakable horror, which had become the mealtime norm for the past six months of Ziggy's life, the tray just held a carafe of blood. Cyrus indicated that Clarence should pour it before continuing to speak.

"I have had a very enlightening year. I've been resurrected from the dead twice, turned into a vampire twice, lost two women who I loved very much, one more than once, and it has all been at my father's whim these things took place. I see the solution to my problems as simple, but unachievable without help. My father must die, and stay dead, for my life to return to normal."

"How normal could it possibly be, if you're a vampire who's been dead twice already?" There was a sadness in Bill's voice that Ziggy hadn't heard before, but he didn't feel it over the blood tie. Was Bill already learning to hide his emotions? That was fucking depressing.

Ziggy realized too late that Cyrus was staring at him. "Not as normal as it was in my past, I swear to you."

It was enough to make Ziggy's throat go dry. Good thing Clarence had just finished pouring his blood. He gulped it down, fast.

"I've got to admit, that worries me, too," Max said. "How do we know we're not just choosing the lesser evil?"

"Speak to your doctor friend." Cyrus's voice softened. "You've never cared for me, but I swear, I will not play you false. Not after all that has happened to me this year."

He leaned back in his chair and closed his eyes, long hands curling to fists on the tabletop. "I used to enjoy cruelty. Relish it. Now I can't find it in myself to kill my own father."

"Ten days?" Max asked, as if clarifying. "You stay in touch with us, keep us updated. Try to rally some more help and we'll do the same. And we'll take care of daddy dearest."

"We'll try," Ziggy corrected. "But we're going to need help. Specifically, blood."

"Yes, of course. Clarence will get you all you need and more before you leave here tonight." Cyrus looked at them all hopefully. "Please believe me when I say that I want this over with as much as you do. And I am not on my father's side."

Max drained his glass and stood. "Fine. Get your man to load up a cooler." He turned to Bill. "Drink that."

Bill paled and tried hard not to look at the blood in front of him. "No, I'm okay. I'm not exactly ready to—"

"I'm not ready to watch you chomp into an innocent pedestrian tonight, so you're going to drink that now." There was absolutely no question, hell, not even a please or a thank-you implied in Max's tone.

"You're disgusted by it now, but you'll get used to it." Cyrus lazily stroked the rim of his glass. "You'll find that sadly true of so much in your future."

Before he could stop himself, Ziggy remembered a torrent of violent, sexual images from his time with Cyrus, and he couldn't shield Bill from them. He saw that telltale tic in Bill's jaw, just before he picked up the cup, drained it in several long gulps, then slammed it back down so hard, Ziggy expected the stem to break. Bill's face shifted into the monster snout and sloping brow of a vampire, then shifted back just as quickly.

"There," he said breathlessly, wiping his mouth on the back of his hand. "Now we can get the hell out of here."

True to his word, Cyrus gave them the blood he'd promised. Max waited in the kitchen while Clarence packed the plastic collection bags in a foam cooler, and Bill, wordlessly, had pushed through the kitchen door, out into the yard.

"Follow him," Max had said, his face full of sympathy. "I'll help this guy out."

The second he made it outside, Bill yakked up all the blood he'd drunk into the bushes. He stayed hunched over, his hands braced on his thighs, as though he might do it again.

When it seemed safe, Ziggy ventured a, "You all right?"

Bill didn't answer right away. He stood, wiped his mouth on the bottom of his T-shirt and leaned against the van. "I really didn't want to drink that."

Ziggy went to him and put his arms around him, knowing he wouldn't resist. Bill hugged him tight, fingers digging into his back.

"You're going to have to get used to it." Ziggy turned his head slightly to kiss Bill's ear. "I wish I could tell you there was another way, but there isn't."

After a moment, Bill stepped back. He wiped his eyes and pinched the bridge of his nose, as if it was a switch to turn off his frustration. "I know. And I know I have to…drink blood. I'm so thirsty and hungry and tired and nothing helps. But I've spent so long on the other side of things. You know, when I found out about vampires, that they were real, that they were all around, that I could make money feeding them, I didn't believe it. And I feel a little bit of that feeling now. The horror, the feeling that my life had changed, the not remembering what it was like before I knew."

Ziggy nodded slowly. "I think every one of us went through that. I don't think anyone becomes a vampire without a shock."

"Yeah, a shock." Bill laughed bitterly. "Hey, at least I got a pretty decent sire, though, right? I mean, you got kind of a raw deal. At least I got sired by someone I don't mind being with."

The little flicker of hope in Ziggy's chest flared, and he quickly squashed it out. "Well, for now you don't. I mean, in the future—"

"Stop it." Bill came forward, like he would kiss him, then seemed to think better of it, considering what he'd just done in the bushes. Instead, he touched his cheek and pulled him close. "It's been too long a night. I just want to go home, get drunk enough to drink some blood and keep it down, and then climb into a warm bed with you."

"That might be a problem. I don't think there is a free bed. You might have to settle for the storeroom floor again." A nervous laugh bubbled in Ziggy's chest, and he coughed to hide it. He also stepped back, wanting to put a little space between them. "Can I ask you something?"

Mild surprise lit Bill's eyes. "I don't see why not."

Ziggy took a deep breath, and the question tumbled out on it. "When you say you want to be close to me like that, is it you, or is it the blood tie that makes you feel it?"

The silence between them was important. One of those silences right before something really significant happens.

That significant thing was Bill's shake of the head, and his quiet, "I don't know."

"What do you—"

"Okay, let's load 'em up and move 'em out," Max called, muscling two huge coolers out the door.

"Damn, guy, you got superstrength or something?" Bill hurried over and took one of the coolers from him. "It's going to be a tight ride back to the apartment."

Max agreed with a shake of the head. "And the first thing I do when we get back is to tear the top off of one of these suckers and go straight to town."

A cold dread squeezed Ziggy's chest. "No. It's not."

He turned to Bill and Max, not wanting to say the words, because the task was going to be so incredibly unpleasant.

"First, we have to tell Carrie."

Seventeen: Confession

While the guys were gone, I had time to think.

Scratch that. Dahlia had time to think.

Once, while I checked in on Nathan, I found myself standing over him with a stake in my hand. Luckily, I realized what I was doing. Equally lucky, he didn't wake up and see me standing there.

She was a constant presence in my mind, so much so that I had to second-guess everything I did. Did I really want a cup of coffee, or was that Dahlia? Was I really too tired to block her out of my consciousness, or was that what she wanted me to think? And once I had blocked her, was I sure she was gone? It was worse than before, when she'd invaded my head. Now, she didn't have anywhere else to go.

I felt an unexpected stab of, if not sympathy, at least understanding for the Soul Eater. How much of what he did was the product of the souls trapped inside of him, either through the madness they drove him to, or their conscious effort to manipulate him?

It occurred to me that I was excusing him in a way, and I knew then that all that sympathy and understanding had to have come from Dahlia, because I still wanted to rip out Jacob Seymour's throat with my teeth.

And then that mental image filled my head, and I wasn't sure if it was Dahlia, or myself. The scene was vivid: straddling Jacob's lap, pulling his face to mine for a searing kiss. His bony hands clutched at my back, ripped away my shirt. My own fingernails scored deep, gory lines down his bare arms, and when I pulled back to suck the blood from my fingers, his mouth was there, fighting mine for the sticky crimson coating my skin. I nipped his jaw, drawing more blood, then his ear. And then, as he groaned in pleasure and dug his hands in my hips, I bit into his neck, hard and deep, and tore. My fangs sank through skin and corded muscle. Pulled away veins and stringy nerves. Crushed esophagus and split trachea. And when the mass of it was free and dangling from my jaw, I saw the delicate vertebrae of his spinal column, the grayish-white of unbleached bone, gleaming out through the cold red torrent that bathed my lap.

The apartment door burst open, snapping me from my reverie. To my disgust, my heart beat fast and my body tingled as if from a sexual fantasy. I smoothed my palms down the tops of my denim-clad thighs, as if there would be a wrinkle there I could press out with my hands, and tried not to broadcast guilt from my expression. "Did you find some blood?"

"Oh ho, did we ever." Max dropped a large foam cooler triumphantly on the coffee table.

"And there's another just like it," Bill announced, setting the second one on the floor just inside the door. "Your friend helped us out."

"My friend?" I had no clue who he was talking about, until Ziggy walked through the door. "You know, then?" I sighed, and he nodded.

"And apparently, so do you," Max said, sitting on the couch beside me. "What are the odds?"

Bill interrupted by clearing his throat loudly. "Blood first. Well, for you guys. Blood for you, hard liquor for me, then we talk about this."

"Agreed." Max stood and went to the kitchen with Bill and the coolers. It would take a miracle to get all of that in the freezer, but I certainly didn't mind.

Ziggy lingered by the door, his stare accusing. I spread my hands helplessly. "I didn't know how to tell you. I didn't even know he was alive until last night. And then there was Bill...."

"I'm not mad." His body posture didn't indicate he was thrilled, though. He ran his finger along the books we'd returned to the shelves, located the large hardcover volume titled *Spirits* and brought it down. He turned back to me. "Anything left in this one?"

"As far as I know." I watched him open the book to lift the small metal flask out and unscrew the top. "Why?"

Ziggy took a quick swallow of the scotch inside the flask. "Bill can't drink blood yet. This might...fix the situation."

"Ah." I remembered the first time I'd drunk blood. From Dahlia, straight from her hot, human veins. I pushed the memory aside. "I really would have told you."

"I know. But that doesn't change the fact I found out

myself." He shook his head. "They must have brought him back after you guys got me. Because I know I would have noticed him lurking around."

"How is he?" I hated to ask, but I wanted to know. There it was. It wasn't pretty, but there it was.

"He's on our side. That's the only thing you need to worry about," Max said sternly from the kitchen. "Hey, where's your gray guy?"

I made a face. "His name is Henry. And he's down-stairs trying to make the back room of the shop more liv-able for Bill and Ziggy. You can sleep on the couch, if you want to. I can't imagine it was fun for you, sleeping down there yesterday."

Max stuck his head out from the kitchen. "I was fine. I'll probably keep sleeping in the hole, actually."

When the blood had been warmed on the stove and we all had a mug of it—though Bill didn't touch his, prefer-ring to stick to the contents of the flask—they told me what had happened with Cyrus.

"Ten days?" I shook my head, dread squeezing my heart. "There's no way. Nathan won't be better by then."

"Nathan might be out of the plan, as far as fighting goes." Max stood and stretched. "However, you can make those handy little gray guys. How many do you think you can come up with before then?"

I choked on the blood I'd swallowed. "You're kid-ding, right?"

"Cyrus said we'd taken out a lot of Jacob's human soldiers. But still, we're going to want backup," Ziggy seconded.

I looked at the grim faces of the men sitting around me

and sighed. "I don't know. Maybe five. Maybe. But it took a lot out of me to make just Henry."

It doesn't have to anymore, Dahlia reminded me. I shoved her aside.

"Well, you're the best we've got. And I'm out of ideas. I don't know about you guys," Max added, pacing to the bookshelves.

Tell him about me, Dahlia demanded, pushing so insistently to the front of my brain I could barely focus on my own thoughts. I opened my mouth to tell them that I would make copies of Henry, no problem, let's go kill the Soul Eater. What came out was, "I'm a Soul Eater."

I heard the words tumble from my lips and at the same time wondered if I'd even said them. Max, Bill and Ziggy didn't appear to react at first. Then Max said, slowly, "Wait, what?"

I didn't want to repeat myself, because it hadn't been my choice to tell them in the first place. "I'm a Soul Eater. When we went to rescue Nathan, Dahlia got in my way. I just wanted to kill her. Maybe not. I don't know. I wanted something. I wanted her to suffer. So I ate her soul."

The admission drained me. My hands trembled when I reached for the mug in front of me.

"Okay…" Bill shook his head. "No, not okay. What the hell does that mean, you're a Soul Eater?"

Ziggy explained for me, thank God. I didn't want to have to.

"Jacob became a Soul Eater by consuming the blood and souls of other vampires. It's part of what makes him so scary. It's also a part of what makes him weak. He needs more than blood to live. He needs souls, and he can't get them from humans." Ziggy eyed me with something that looked suspiciously, creepily, like admiration.

I forced the shiver crawling up my spine to retreat. "When I killed Dahlia, I did it by draining her blood. And at the end, I sort of…sucked up her soul. Without meaning to."

Liar! Dahlia's rage flowed over me until my hands clenched down so tight I shattered the mug I held. Blood flowed over my fingers, staining the rug below my feet. "Oops."

"Nice." Max turned away, but it didn't help hide his emotions. Even his back looked angry. "You knew Cyrus was alive. You knew you were a Soul Eater. Anything else you didn't plan on telling us?"

"It wasn't that I wasn't planning on telling you. It's just that directly after I became aware of those things, I had to do a heart transplant and a skin graft. I got a little distracted."

"How distracted?" Ziggy asked quietly. "I mean, did you tell Nate?"

"Did I tell him what?" I shook my head to try to clear it. "I mean, he knows I'm a Soul Eater. He doesn't know about Cyrus."

"None of us did. And he's usually the last person you're honest with," Max snapped.

"Hey, simmer down," Bill barked, and I was surprised at the authority in his voice.

More surprising was Max's grumbled, "Sorry." Max hardly ever listened to anyone who wasn't Max.

"It's okay," Bill said, barely sparing Max a glance. "But the important thing to remember right now is that we're on a tight schedule in terms of taking out the Soul

Eater. And Nathan is a part of this team, even if he can't participate."

"You're right," I agreed, but my timing was unfortunate.

Just as I finished my sentence, Bill said, "That's why you need to tell him everything, Carrie."

I looked to Ziggy. I don't know what I was expecting. Maybe for him to rescue me by telling me I didn't need to be a grown-up. It was a stupid expectation. There was a pitying expression on his face as he said, "He's right. You've got to tell him."

I sighed and stood. "I should take him something to eat before morning, anyway."

"We'll go downstairs," Bill volunteered. "Give the two of you some privacy."

Max followed them to the door. "And I'll be down there, too. Not that I don't want to sleep on a bloody couch, but the sleeping bag in the shelter wasn't the scene of an amateur heart transplant."

And then, just like that, I was alone. And I had to tell Nathan that Cyrus, that person he hated most in the world, more even than his sire, was alive and well again.

As I refilled the kettle and put it on the burner, I carefully planned what I was going to say. At least, that was my intention. In reality, I became overwhelmed by all that I knew I had to say and how it collided with what I wanted to say and how that would be received in complete contradiction to what I actually meant. My careful plan was blasted apart before I even got a chance to put it into action.

It wasn't just as simple as telling Nathan that Cyrus was alive again. I also had to make sure he knew that nothing between us had changed just because Cyrus was back. He wasn't my fledgling anymore. In fact, I was surprised at the change in my feelings myself. I shouldn't have been. I'd known Cyrus in so many incarnations. Cyrus the monster. Cyrus the human. Cyrus the wounded soul searching for something to make him better than what he was. Cyrus my fledgling. It shouldn't have come as such a shock that the Cyrus who'd stood before me in the Soul Eater's run-down farmhouse was a completely different man than the one I'd loved most recently.

Still, Nathan wouldn't see it that way. And if I were to blurt it out, just like that—"Don't worry, I won't leave you for him"—he would see just broaching the subject as an admission of guilt. Or maybe I would. It was too difficult a situation to understand the difference.

The teakettle whistled like a *bean sídhe* portending coming dread, and I resigned myself to whatever new emotional turmoil was to come. I poured some slightly burned blood into a mug and headed toward the bedroom.

When I opened the door, Nathan gave me a sleepy smile, and I wanted to do a cartwheel just from that simple expression. "You look so much better. Except for the part where you look half-butchered."

He made a sound that would have been a laugh if he'd had more strength. "I feel a bit better. Still sore. But it's the first real sleep I've had in a while."

I set the blood down on the nightstand and gingerly sat beside him. "Do you need something for the pain?"

He slowly shook his head. "No. I want to be clear-headed now. I just want a few moments with you when I'm not drugged. Or distracted by pain."

"It's nondistracting pain now?" I smoothed a few locks of his hair back from his forehead. "Well, that's good, I suppose."

"You're damn right it's good. Now all we need to do is cure the boredom." He leaned into my hand and kissed my palm.

I pulled my hand away. It seemed dishonest to lull him into a sense of security that I would just shatter.

His expression took on an oddly conflicted look. Resigned, that he knew the moment of peace was over too soon. Soft, that he knew it would be hard for me to leave the moment, as well. "Carrie, what's wrong?"

I'm not over him. Dahlia's words taunted me. She tried to force them out, but I pushed her back, hard. Imagined walling her up behind bricks and a layer of cement. "Just trying to adjust. To everything."

"To sharing your head with Dahlia," Nathan said, his tone sympathetic. "Sweetheart, if I could take it from you…"

"I wouldn't let you." I took his hand in mine, marveling at how whole it looked in comparison to the rest of him. "I'm not being totally honest. There's more."

"Oh?" He arched one eyebrow. "You've got a secret lesbian lover since I've been gone? I have to say, I won't put up too much of a fight about it, so long as you've also developed an exhibitionistic streak—"

"Har, har." It was good to hear him joke again. Such a change from a few hours earlier when he'd thought he was better off dead. "No, it's about Cyrus."

Nathan's demeanor changed immediately. "Ah."

"He's alive." Like ripping off a Band-Aid.

Nathan tried to sit up, and I stopped him with gentle

pressure on an intact piece of his shoulder. "Don't get upset about it. It's not a big deal."

"Not a big... Wait..." he sputtered. "When did this happen?"

"Must have been after we took Ziggy. He was as shocked as you are." I chewed my lip. "He told us some things."

"How did this happen?" he asked, oblivious to what I'd said. "He died. I saw him die. You...saw him die."

"I did." And even though he was alive again, I relived that moment in my nightmares. "But it's not like this is the first time something like this has happened."

Nathan sighed. "When did it start to be all right to bring people back from the dead? This never would have happened fifty years ago."

"Maybe it would have," I reasoned. "I mean, you weren't quite as connected to that social circle back then."

"Social circle?" He closed his eyes. "Fine. What are we doing about this?"

That was a good question. If I had all the answers where Cyrus was concerned, the past year would have been so much easier. "I guess we're not doing very much about it right now. I mean, he did give us Ziggy's heart back. I forgot to tell you about that. And he told the guys what the Soul Eater has planned."

"How much time do we have?" I knew then that Nathan was feeling more like his old self. He was so ready to go into battle, I could feel his tension reverberating across the blood tie between us.

Unfortunately, there was no way he'd be riding into the fray with guns blazing. Not in his state, and certainly not for a while. "Ten days. Less. I mean, I'm not entirely sure. Max and Bill and Ziggy told me the story, but it was sort of all at once, with a lot of excited gestures and curse words."

"I'm sure." He frowned, his fists clenched at his sides. "God, why do I have to be this way when you need me? I'm pathetic, I can't even punch a wall to get my frustration out."

"Hey, don't talk like that." I took one of his hands in mine and tried to soothe some of the tension out of it. "You're not pathetic. You were just skinned alive. Granted the timing was bad, but I'm not sure there's ever really a good time to be skinned."

"There's never a good time. Period." The defeat on his face was almost too much for me. "In ten days, this will all be over."

"For better or for worse." The sick irony of the words mocked me. "I mean—"

He gave me a bittersweet smile. "I know. It was an unfortunate slip. But if something does happen to one of us…"

"Well, nothing will happen to you. You'll be here." Could I not say anything right tonight? "What I meant was, you won't be in immediate danger."

"I will be." He squeezed my hand, then pulled it to his lips to kiss my fingers. "If anything happens to you, it happens to me, too."

I wanted to say, "Nothing is going to happen to me." But history had proven that "Nothing is going to happen to me" is such a stupid thing for me to say. Also, what if nothing happened to me? What if after the Soul Eater was dead, I wasn't? I was still a Soul Eater myself. What happened in a year or two, when I couldn't hold back Dahlia anymore? What happened when my body became brittle because I could no longer get by on just blood? What happened when I became pure evil?

What happened when I was the monster my friends were fighting against?

As much as these thoughts tormented me, I couldn't let Nathan think about them now. We'd cross that incredibly frightening bridge when we came to it, but for now I had him to concentrate on.

"If you want any chance of being in fighting shape— and believe me, the jury will be out on that one for a while—we need to work on your skinned-ness."

Nathan sighed. "I would rather we never, ever repeat that excruciating procedure again. But I would also rather be able to help when it's needed. So, go to work."

"I have to get my stuff. And medicate you. Heavily." I turned toward the door. He protested, but I cut him off with words and a stern glare. "It's not for you. It's for me. It's very difficult to do this to a loved one. I'd rather at least one of us was unconscious, and it would be better if that person wasn't the one with the scalpel."

I turned again to go and he reached out for me. I stepped back and let him take my hand. "I love you."

"I know you do." I squeezed his hand and let it fall. "I love you, too."

And then I walked away. I couldn't say my goodbyes now.

Eighteen: Rest in Peace

It was dark in the alley. Too dark. And quiet. Way, way too quiet.

Max pulled his stake from his pocket and crouched, half hiding, half preparing. The light of the nearly full moon prickled his skin. Made him want to run. Made him want to pull all of his clothes off and let the moonlight glaze him. Made him want to tackle someone, and take her, right there on the leaves and bracken of the forest floor. To pound into her mercilessly, to bite and push and scratch.

A full moon, and he wouldn't be with Bella.

"When you return, I will change with you. I will not be able to run, so you cannot chase me, but I will hide and you can find me. And it will be…more than you ever imagined," she'd promised him when he'd lamented their separation over the phone.

But it wasn't enough to know that they would eventually be together. He wanted her now. He wanted the assurance that he would be with her again, without the roadblocks her father could throw in his way.

And he was bitter about it, which shocked the hell out of him. In the past, he would have wanted to be all up in the fight. Hell, he would have seen it as his duty. But here he was, less than twenty hours from go time, and all he wanted was to go home and hold Bella.

Even knowing that a fight was coming up should have helped him get through the last few days, but it hadn't. After waiting and mulling over the information Cyrus had given them, they'd finally made a decision on what they should do. They would hit the Soul Eater three days before his intended ceremony, in order to avoid tangling with any of the guest list. In the time between then and now, they'd all been pacing like caged tigers.

Well, sort of. Bill and Ziggy had spent a lot of time alone. And that was fine. Max had a strict policy about same-sex relationships: do whatever the hell you want, so long as I don't have to see it. He bent the rules when it came to sexy lesbian twins, but that was as far as he went. If Ziggy and Bill wanted to work on their relationship or do whatever in that little back room, fine. Better there than on the couch Carrie kept compulsively cleaning in the vain hope of getting the bloodstains out.

Not that she'd had anything else to do. Max grimaced at the thought of all Carrie was dealing with. She'd nearly fixed Nathan's skin condition and continued with his care, created several new Henries, was on a manic and ongoing mission to wash Bill's blood out of the couch, and all while putting a friendly face on to reassure them she wasn't going to devour their souls.

Still, Max found himself clawing at the walls—figuratively—and wishing his friends would hurry up and get their fight on, so he wouldn't have to stick around much longer.

And now, it seemed there would be another delay.

There was a distant creak of brakes needing a shoe change, and a few moments later the sound of footsteps. Prissy, Italian-loafered footsteps. And Cyrus appeared in the mouth of the alley.

When it became apparent he was alone, Max twirled the stake in his palm and slid it into his back pocket. Like a gunslinger. Like Han Solo.

He reluctantly conceded he still might like the fighting a little bit.

"Very intimidating," Cyrus said, sniffing. "Why did we need to meet here? I think they stopped paying their garbage bill."

"I know. It's uncouth. I wanted to meet in a well-lit public area full of television cameras and wear matching We're Vampires T-shirts so your dad would be sure to find out we were meeting, but I decided against that." He rolled his eyes. "What was so damned important that we had to meet at all?"

Cyrus didn't pay any heed to Max's bullshit. It was a little bit admirable. "I don't know when you're planning to strike, and I don't want to know. But I thought I should tell you that father has upped his security."

"That's fine. We've got reinforcements." It sounded better than cursing out loud and punching a wall. Could nothing go easy for them?

"He has a necromancer." Cyrus actually managed to say it with a straight face.

Max kept his expression carefully neutral. "We'll be sure to bring our level twenty-six Elf Mage along."

Cyrus at least had the decency to laugh at that. "I understand your disbelief, but aren't you a lupin? Don't you believe in magic?"

"I know about magic," Max snapped, kind of hoping he'd cover up the fact that he didn't know all that much. "But a necromancer? What's he going to do, read the *Necronomicon* out loud and ruin my camping trip?"

"He's going to raise an army of the dead." Cyrus didn't even blink.

Max shook his head. "Well, aren't we fucked, then?"

Cyrus shrugged. "If you went after him now, you'd come up against a veritable army of human and vampire bodyguards. If you attack on the night of the ritual, they'll be dead."

And that was the last suspicious straw, right there. "So, the safest thing to do, in your opinion, is to march in as close to the time the Soul Eater becomes a god as possible?"

"No." The man was freaking obnoxious with his condescension. "I don't want to tell you what to do. That is up to you and the rest of your motley band of heroes to decide. I'm merely telling you what I know. He has vampires and humans in a force that outnumbers yours. They will be sacrificed to feed my father's ambitions and, more practically, his guests, but they will be gone by the night of the ritual. However, at that time he will have a necromancer at his disposal. He will not only be performing the ritual, but he could also raise any number of reanimated corpses to slay you. When you choose to strike is a choice that is thankfully out of my hands.

But I thought it only fair that you make an informed decision."

Damn. Cyrus was so much easier to hate when he was doing crappy things. When he did something decent, Max felt like a fool for disliking him. "Thanks. I'll pass that information along." A strong pang of that dislike spiked in him, and he indulged it. "And what about you?"

Cyrus appeared to be surprised by that, that he'd been thought of at all. "What about me?"

Fostering that spark of dislike to a healthy flame, Max folded his arms over his chest and leaned against the wall. "Where are you going to be when we bring on the fight? Are you going to be on your daddy's side, or are you going to be on ours?"

"I'm on my own side," he said simply, mimicking Max's pose with a more relaxed one on the opposite wall. He glanced down at his nails—as if he could see them in the dark—and then looked up, practiced surprise on his face.

"Your side?" Max sneered. "Yeah, you would be."

"Everyone is on their own side. Anyone who tells you differently is either lying to themselves, or to you."

Right. "Well, you have a good night, then, asshole." Max turned to walk away, every muscle in his body screaming that he should rip Cyrus apart with his bare hands. And to be honest, Max wasn't sure if that was his vampire self talking, or his werewolf self. Or, if it was just Max Harrison, intolerant of bullshit.

"Max, wait, please."

And there it was again, that voice that sounded like someone who gave a damn. But it was coming out of

Cyrus. It was a neat trick. Max turned, trying to broadcast his impatience more clearly. "What?"

"How is she?" Cyrus seemed to struggle to get the question out. "I mean, is she... God, is she happy?"

"Well, she's a Soul Eater. And her boyfriend got skinned alive. And the fledgling she was mourning is alive again." Max stopped himself. The guy clearly cared about Carrie. He deserved something. "But I'd say yeah, considering the circumstances, she's not as miserable as she could be."

Cyrus nodded slowly. "I'm glad for that. I don't want to see her in pain if she can avoid it."

"I'll pass along the good word." Max turned again toward the open end of the alley.

"Don't." Cyrus's voice stopped him. "Please, don't tell her I asked. It would be...easier...in the long run. If she didn't know I was asking about her."

Max was torn between wondering what the guy's game was and actually feeling sorry for him. But it was so easy to find an ulterior motive in almost anything he did. And that wasn't just prejudice on Max's part; he was sure of it.

"I won't tell her."

Cyrus didn't follow Max out of the alley. Hell, if he wanted to stay and enjoy the funky garbage smell, it was all his.

Max was going to take a run.

In the grand scheme of things, ten nights isn't that long. And when you break that down to six, one of which you've already wasted, the time goes by pretty fast.

It helps when you're busy, of course. I'd upped the rate at which I patched Nathan's skin. Right before he went to sleep in the morning, I cut strips of skin from his back and pasted them over his torso. Right after he woke up at night, I did the same thing. He spent those six days almost constantly drugged and in pain, but he healed faster than I would have ever anticipated. By the fifth day, he was sitting up in bed, reading a newspaper. I'm not sure how much of the newspaper he comprehended, considering all the morphine I'd given him, but he found it highly entertaining.

That night, Ziggy had gone—with Bill, under protest—to St. Mary's to steal a wheelchair. We cleared all the furniture to the outside walls of the living room so Nathan would have at least some mobility.

"It feels good to be up and about again," he said, wheeling past me to the living room. He parked next to his favorite chair, gazed at it longingly, and then manfully accepted his wheelchair-bound state.

"It's good to have you back, man," Bill said. He moved as though he would slap Nathan on the shoulder, but then extended his hand instead. When Nathan merely grunted the most borderline polite response possible and didn't take it, Bill let his arm drop.

"So…" Ziggy tried to defuse the awkwardness of the moment. "When do you get to lose the stylish bandages?"

Nathan glanced down at his bare torso as if surprised to see his chest patched with gauze. The bandages covered a thin strip that still hadn't completely healed that reached from his collarbones almost to the waistband of his pajama pants. What had healed looked shiny and pink and full of seams, like Frankenstein's monster à la Robert De Niro.

"It's better to keep the raw stuff bandaged, so it doesn't dry out." I rolled my eyes. "And of course, infection, but I know that's not an issue with us."

"I'm not going to be much help when you leave… what? Tonight?" He looked up at me, fearful and hopeful at once. "You should probably head out."

"We're waiting for Max to get back. He was getting the inside scoop on something." Ziggy looked at me, as if for confirmation that he should say it. "From Cyrus."

"Ah." Nathan nodded. "Well, perhaps I can be of use in a planning sense."

Bill hopped eagerly into the conversation. "It seems like it's all going to be pretty easy. We took out most of those superstrong humans when we came to get you. And according to Carrie, he can't make more on his own, he needed that witch." Bill paused. "That Carrie ate."

"Yes, I'm aware of what happened to Dahlia," Nathan said drily. "I assume Max will be finding out from Cyrus exactly what kind of reinforcements the Soul Eater has dreamed up."

"If any. I mean, he wasn't looking too good when we left." Ziggy looked guiltily toward me. "Well, at least that's what Carrie said."

I nodded. "You're right, he didn't. But that doesn't mean he doesn't have some bumbling henchmen to take care of security."

"It would be better if the bumbling henchmen *were* security." Bill looked to me. "How many Henries do we have?"

I'd been busy. Not just with Nathan, but with creating new golems.

All the power I'd had before had come from drinking just a little bit of Dahlia's blood. And that power had been impressive, at least, to me. Now, with all of Dahlia's blood and her soul, Dahlia's very essence, I also had all of her power. Creating Henry had taken so much out of me, I'd dreaded trying again. Creating Henry Two had taken a handful of dirt, a few drops of blood and the kind of concentration I would normally expend playing FreeCell. After that, it had gotten even easier. Unbelievably easy. I'd actually gotten bored of it at one point and experimented with the kinds of stuff I could make Henries out of. The first Henry had been made out of ash. For Henry Two, I'd used some gravel from a nearby driveway. Henry One turned out gray, while Henry Two was an oddly natural-looking taupe color. I used potting soil and the result was a weird dark brown with colorless specks where the vermiculite filler had been. I crushed up a shard of hot-pink sidewalk chalk I'd found outside and made a pink Henry I named Henrietta.

I'd experimented with using more material to try and make larger golems. They always came out the same size and shape, just somewhat more dense. In the physical sense. They were all still of the same intelligence.

I'd made thirty so far, and stored them under a canvas tarp in the far back corner of the bookshop.

When I told Ziggy and Bill, they blanched. "You mean we've been walking right past them every morning? Sleeping with them right by us?" Ziggy cracked his knuckles as he talked.

"They're harmless. Really." That was a stupid thing to say. They were so harmless, one of them had killed Bill. "Unless I give them some really, really stupid instructions."

"Let's steer clear of that this time, okay?" I was amazed at the lack of bitterness in Bill's tone. He'd either gotten over the shock of being made a vampire, or he was just too distracted to be mad at me.

Ziggy shrugged the comment off. "I just want to know how we're going to get thirty of them in the van. I mean, can we just tell them to stack themselves like cordwood?"

"We could. If I'd known what cordwood was when I made them. Which I don't, even now." I paused. "You could explain cordwood to me, and then I could make another Henry and ask him to stack the rest of them like cordwood."

"That's a good idea," Bill agreed. "I can't remember how high a cord of wood is—"

The door opened and Max entered, looking oddly flushed and out of breath for a vampire. It might have been a werewolf thing, which would also have explained the leaves and grass stuck to his clothes. He saw Nathan in the wheelchair and gave a start. "You're up."

Nathan smiled at him. "They were just debating how to pack thirty golems in the back of the van. Do you know how high a cord of wood is?"

"Forget that," Max ordered, halting only for a second to give us a look admonishing us for our strangeness. "We're not going in tonight."

Dread clutched in my stomach. "You're going to tell us something we're not going to want to hear."

He nodded grimly. "Cyrus told me that his father has a huge security force right now. And the good news is that they're all going to be eaten before the ritual. But the guy doing the ritual is capable of raising an army of the undead to attack us."

"A necromancer?" Nathan shifted in his wheelchair, a look of excitement on his face akin to the expression you'd see on a kid on the bus to Disneyland. "He's really got a necromancer?"

"I guess," Max said with a shrug. "Doesn't sound so great to me."

"It doesn't sound that great to me, either," Ziggy piped up. "I'm not a big fan of zombies."

"We've got thirty golems. Why not just stick to the plan?" Not that I was aching to possibly get killed. It just seemed terribly disappointing, that this was supposed to be the night the problem we've been worried about for the better part of the year got cleared up, and now we had to wait again.

"Thirty golems who fight just like you," Nathan pointed out. "Not exactly a crack fighting squad. They would actually be more suited against shambling zombies. If you go up against armed humans and vampires, you're going to run through the lot of them pretty fast."

I slapped the back of his head. "Thanks a lot."

"He's right, though," Bill said, quickly reaching to cover the back of his head. "Don't hit me, but he's right. If we don't know exactly how big a force he has, it would be a waste of our time and possibly our lives."

Max nodded. "And Cyrus didn't tell me how many bodyguards the Soul Eater has. Still, we also don't know how many zombies this necromancer guy can make."

"Only as many as there are dead bodies in the area." Nathan wheeled toward the window and parted the blinds, as if he could see the whole city.

Max groaned. "And Grand Rapids has more cemeteries than any other city on the planet, seems like. Fantastic."

Max was right. There were probably more dead people than living in Grand Rapids and its urban sprawl. If he managed to raise them all…

Ziggy looked from Nathan to me. "That's really simple, though. Carrie can make more Henries, send them out to the cemeteries and kill the zombies as they come out the gate."

"That's impractical," Nathan said, dismissing the idea with a wave of his hand.

"Impractical, but it might be our only solution." I covered my face with my hands. "Of course, we'll have to actually find and count all the cemeteries."

"And how many gates are in each one?" Bill added bleakly.

Or you morons could just ward the cemeteries and keep any magic from entering, Dahlia suggested in my head.

"What was that?" I asked, and all of the guys looked at me.

Ward. You. Idiot.

How do I do that? I hated asking her for anything, but if she was in the mood to be helpful, I wasn't going to question it.

No, wait, I was. *Why are you telling me this?*

Because if you get killed, I get free. And I think the only person strong enough to kill you is Jacob.

Fair enough, even if her assumption that I would die at the Soul Eater's hands didn't inspire a lot of confidence. "We can ward the cemeteries."

Bill, Max and Ziggy all responded with some variation of "What does that mean?" but Nathan turned his wheelchair. "That's an excellent idea."

"Okay, it's excellent, but what does that mean?" Max asked me.

Thankfully, before I could admit that I didn't have the foggiest clue what I was talking about, Nathan spoke up. "It means that we would do a spell that would work as a barrier between the necromancer's spell and the corpses he was trying to reanimate."

"How long is that going to take?" I didn't want to argue with my own suggestion, but we were unfortunately constrained by time. "I have all of Dahlia's powers—" *Maybe not all,* she seethed in my brain "—so I could do the spell no problem. But if it means we have to go to every single cemetery in the area, I don't know how we're going to make it."

"You wouldn't have to go." Nathan tapped his index finger against his lips. "I have at least seven warding spells we could take a look at tonight. Most of them involve doing a simple spell over ingredients and then sprinkling them around the perimeter of the area you want to ward."

"So, we could do the spell, and then split up and sprinkle the dust?" I brightened at that. "Max can go out in the daylight now. Whatever we don't cover, he can do."

"But I want to be there, as well," Nathan said quickly. The desperation he felt was written clearly across his face. "I'm not going to be able to help in the big fight. I want to at least be able to do this."

"Like Carrie said, we could split up," Bill interjected, rubbing the knees of his jeans nervously. "She could go with Ziggy and I could go with you."

"And I could pick up the day shift," Max finished for him. "Perfect. Let's make with the magic, guys."

Nathan wheeled forward, trying hard not to look at Bill. "Maybe I should go with Carrie. Assuming the spell even works to begin with. I'm still very fragile, and I'm sure she wouldn't want me to be—"

I saw through his plan. He wanted to avoid being alone with Bill. While I wasn't sure it would make him any more accepting of his son's relationship, it probably wouldn't hurt any, either. That's why I said, a little too enthusiastically, "No, it's fine! You'll be fine, I'm sure."

"Tell me what books you need, and I'll grab them," Max offered helpfully. "I have to go downstairs and call Bella anyway."

Nathan sighed heavily. "Get me a pen and I'll write them down."

Do you really think you can pull it off? Dahlia mocked in my mind.

I shoved her aside. *Remember, if you trip me up, I might just waltz through this thing alive. For your sake, you'd better cooperate, so Jacob can avenge you.*

She laughed. Or, at least, her soul trapped in me replicated the crazy sound of her laughter. In that moment I almost called off the entire idea of warding the cemeteries.

And then I wondered if that was what she wanted me to do all along.

Nineteen: Army of One

Though it was plenty warm in the bookstore, Max's blood pumped cold through his veins. "Could you repeat that?"

Bella sounded far too cheerful and way, way too oblivious to the implications of what she'd done as she explained. "My father has been deposed. After I informed several pack members of the situation with the Soul Eater, they called a special meeting of the council. They were enraged to find that my father had hidden this information from them, and I was correct in my assumption that they would view a vampire god as a threat to our continued existence. They voted, and cast my father out."

"My God, Bella, are you okay?" Max had never known his father, but he was pretty sure he'd take it hard if he had and some council had voted him into exile.

"Oh, yes." She sounded like someone talking about their breakfast, not their father. "He was not sentenced to death. He will probably retire to the Sanctuary, or perhaps meet with the outcast clan on Corsica. I will still be able to speak with him if necessary."

"You're taking this remarkably well." Almost too well. What if he was exiled somewhere? Wouldn't she be upset about it?

And then he remembered that he had been exiled, in a way. Worse, he'd been sent to die. And she hadn't been too demonstrably upset. But she had done something to ensure his return, as much as something like that could be ensured. If she'd done this to her own father, she'd thought far enough ahead to plan the best possible outcome.

That was his girl.

"I have had time to accept it. Now, do you wish to hear the council's decision on the Soul Eater?" She didn't give him time to answer her. "They are sending a core group of warriors to assassinate him. I, unfortunately, was not invited to go. But I will stay behind and perform the battle rites with the priestesses of the clan. Fighting would be an honor, but this is an honor greater than I have dreamed of."

"Pardon me if I don't immediately concentrate on that last part. You said they're sending warriors?"

"Yes. Fifty, perhaps more. They wish to make an example of him." She paused. "Max, this means you do not have to fight now."

Damn. That put him in a hard spot. There was no way in hell Carrie and Nathan weren't going to fight. They would argue that it would be too dangerous to leave it up to someone else. They had a responsibility to the world or something like that. And he had a responsibility to them, even if he wasn't entirely vampire anymore.

"I'm sorry. But I'm going to have to fight. You know they're not going to back down, and I'm not going to be able to let them go in on their own." He could feel her disapproval over the phone. "I promise to be careful. I'll stick to the fringes, all of that—"

"You are not one of them, Max. You are one of us."

"I know that. But I can't turn off my feelings for my friends like a faucet. They'll get themselves killed if I don't help out." He stopped, cold reality smacking him in the forehead. "If they're there, at the Soul Eater's house when the werewolves show up, they're going to die, aren't they?"

"Our soldiers will not distinguish one vampire from another," Bella admitted.

Rage boiled in Max's stomach. "You were going to tell me this when?"

"It does not affect you, Max. They know that you will be there and they will not harm you. But what description should I have given them of your friends? It would be impossible to tell one vampire from the next." Bella sounded exasperated and tired. "If they wish to stay and die, that is theirs to decide. But you have a responsibility. To me and to the pack, and to your child, as well. You must come home now."

It was the hardest thing he'd ever done, he was sure of it. He wanted so badly to return to her, to forget about the life he'd led as a vampire and start a new one. One where he didn't have to kill or battle mystic forces. Where the last year—hell, the last couple of decades—didn't exist.

But what kind of a man would that make him? Running from his friends in their time of need, when they were walking straight into a massacre. They didn't have many illusions about their survival, but at least they thought they stood a chance. Max had seen the warriors train and fight in practice. They would be lethal in battle, tearing through vampires without a thought about what they were doing.

The picture of blood and carnage that filled his mind made his mouth go dry and his cock grow hard. The sick thing was, he couldn't tell if it was the vampire in him or the werewolf that craved the destruction.

"Bella, I can't." The second he said it, he wondered what kind of moron he was that he actually went through with it. "I can't let my friends walk into this blindly."

She made a noise that could have been a sigh or a held-back sob. "Max, I am frightened for your life."

"I know you are. So am I. But I've come through worse things than this. I'm sure I have." He neglected to add that he wasn't entirely sure what worse situations those might be, because that would be unhelpful. "When will the warriors get here?"

"They plan to attack at the time of the full moon, but they will arrive a few days before. If you do not wish to come home, at least promise me you will go into battle with them, not with the vampires. Do not shame the pack." She was so sure, so goddamned sure that vampires were these evil, filthy creatures. Max wondered how she'd ever fallen in love with him.

He wondered if she would ever accept him for what he was, what he really was. A vampire who happened to get bitten by a werewolf. Would she ever admit to herself that he hadn't been born as she had, that he was something else? Or, would it become the thing they never spoke of, until one of them exploded?

His goodbyes to her were mechanical. Not cold, but

he didn't feel the longing for her as he had in the past. And when he hung up, he still felt that crushing pain of loneliness in his chest, but it was for a different reason.

They might save the world from a rampaging hell god. They might be able to fix everything that had gone so terribly wrong over the last year.

The way we decided what warding spell we would use was not as scientific or mystical as I thought it would be. We flipped through the books, wrote up ingredients lists and decided to use the one we had the most components for. After that, Nathan went to work crossreferencing magical substitutions by planetary influences, elemental correspondences and mythical connotations. I'll never stop being amazed that the same man who prayed the rosary every morning when he thought I was safely asleep knew more about witchcraft than any other person I had ever met.

Well, that wasn't entirely true. I was pretty intimately acquainted with Dahlia now, though I wished that wasn't the case. There were times I wanted to scream, just to drown out the sound of her in my head. Even if I blocked her from communicating with me, she was there, like a high-pitched frequency whine in my brain. Like water in my ear, rolling around and blocking out the sound of everything else until I wanted to claw it out to make it stop.

As it seemed not an entirely wise decision to claw my head to let the voices out, I would try to concentrate on something else. And luckily, Max gave me that exact distraction. I'd thought we'd seen the last of him for the night when he burst through the door looking like someone who'd just heard they needed a tooth pulled.

"Listen up, guys," he said, coming into the living room to shake Ziggy awake where he lay passed out on the end of the couch. "You're not going to believe this."

"Not going to believe what?" I had to poke Nathan to get his attention out of his book. "Now that we're all listening."

"We don't need any spell. We've got reinforcements." Max went on to explain about the pack Bella belonged to, and what she'd done for us. Just when I was about to be grateful to her, he added, "And she doesn't want you to fight."

"What?" I shrieked.

"Carrie, wait—" Max said, but it was too late. I was on a roll, fueled by the horrible crap going on in my head courtesy of Dahlia, and the horrible crap going on around us, courtesy of the Soul Eater.

I stood and marched up to Max, though I'm sure the effect was diminished somewhat by the fact that I'm several inches shorter than him. "We were here when this thing started. At least, some of us were. And we're going to stick it out until the end. Just because she doesn't understand what it means to be loyal—"

"I told her no," Max interrupted. "I told her there was no way you'd agree to sit at home and let someone else take care of it when there was so much on the line."

"So, when do we go?" Nathan left the book on the kitchen table and wheeled into the living room. "I'm ready."

"You're not going," I reminded him, but Max answered the question anyway.

"We're going in on the night of the ritual. It won't be

easy. For one, you guys will have to avoid the were-wolves. They'll kill any vampires they come across."

I cut him off. "But you'll be there. You can tell them—"

"I won't be able to tell them anything." He wouldn't look me in the eye. "It will be the full moon. I'll change. The warriors will change, too. But I…I don't know how much I'll remember. About you guys or anything. Just make sure you stay clear of anything even remotely wolflike."

"There's more to it than just running in and saving the day, though," Bill pointed out. "If this Soul Eater guy is a big nasty, how do we fight him?"

"I think fifty werewolves can handle him," Max said, almost contemptuously.

"I don't." Nathan looked around the room, making eye contact with everyone. "In any situation where a crowd gathers intent on destroying him, what happens?"

A chill of memory crept up my spine. "He gets away."

"He uses the confusion as a distraction," Ziggy added.

Nathan nodded. "Our odds are better if, in the confusion, one person goes after him specifically. And only one person here has the kind of power to kill him."

It was a weird feeling. I wanted to yell at Nathan for wanting to send me into danger, but in the past, when he'd wanted to stop me from getting involved in something for my own good, I've yelled at him for that. It was a true case of "be careful what you wish for," I guess.

"Come on, man. That's stupid," Max said quietly, fulfilling his role as the person who spoke reason on my behalf.

I didn't have the conviction to argue. "At least having Dahlia trapped in my head will end happy. Not entirely happy. I mean, she'll still be trapped in my head. But at least I'll be able to use her for something."

Use me. That sounds so dirty. And so unlike poor, pure little you.

I bombarded her with images of Cyrus and I together, that first time, when I'd torn at his throat with my human teeth and reveled in the pain we'd caused each other. It wasn't mature, but for some reason I wanted her to know that I was better than her, and a hundred times better than she ever was, at anything she was proud of.

"Carrie, are you okay?" Nathan's voice came to me as if through a fog. "Carrie?"

I snapped myself back to reality. Unfortunately, in reality, I'd clenched my fists so tightly my nails had dug into my palms hard enough to draw blood, which now dripped onto my clothes.

"Sorry," I said, smoothing my shirt down out of nervous habit. The blood from my hands stained the cloth and I crossed my arms over my stomach to hide it. "What were we talking about?"

"We need exact details of what the ritual will entail," Max said, eyeing me warily. "Only Cyrus can give us that information. Unfortunately, he's only speaking to us in riddles right now. Maybe you could…"

"Of course, I'll talk to him." I didn't want to sound as though I was jumping at the chance to see him again, though maybe I was. "He'll be honest with me. At least, as honest as he feels like being."

"I'll call him and set it up." Max turned toward the door.

"Wait, can't we—" Nathan stopped himself. "Never mind. This way will work."

Thank you, I sent him silently, but he looked away.

"I guess we'll go downstairs, then," Ziggy said awkwardly.

Bill stumbled as he stood. "Leg's asleep," he said sheepishly, following Ziggy.

Alone with Nathan, I could barely face him.

"You know what I saw, Carrie." The words scraped out of his throat as if they were coated with razors. As if it was physically painful for him to speak.

I couldn't deny it. He had an all-access pass to my head and I'd just been replaying "Carrie and Cyrus's Greatest Hits" in my mind. There was no hiding anything from him. "I know."

"When is this going to end?"

I had a horrible feeling that I knew the answer, but I couldn't say it out loud. Instead, I asked him if he wanted a cup of tea, and he said he'd love one, and we pretended that nothing had happened, nothing was happening, and nothing would happen.

It was a pretty fairy tale for a few hours, at least.

Max called Cyrus and arranged to meet him at midnight, in the old section of the sprawling graveyard on the east side of town. It wasn't a terribly long walk from the apartment, and I wondered if Cyrus suspected I might show up.

The night was cooling off rapidly, and fog hung in the air, shrouding the ground. Half-sunken gravestones thrust up from the ground like broken teeth biting at the thick haze. I felt as though I'd wandered into a cheesy vampire movie.

Cyrus stood with his back to the path I stumbled down, his hand gripping the foot of a cement angel perched just above his shoulder. In the dim light I saw he wore a red brocade robe, like the ones he'd worn when I'd first met him. His hair was shorter now, and the effect wasn't quite the same as it had been then. Now, he looked a little like those kids Ziggy had known, who dressed up to play vampire.

"Kind of a cliché, isn't it?" I asked, but not with the mocking I would have directed toward him in the past. "You know, meeting in a cemetery at midnight?"

His back stiffened at the sound of my voice, and he spun, pure rage in his face. "Where is your werewolf? Baying at the moon?"

"No need to be nasty," I admonished, coming to stand in front of him. "I wanted to come. I wanted to see you."

"Why?" He turned away and stalked toward a leaning crypt. "So you can tell me that it's me you want? That it's me you love? And then change your mind when it becomes convenient to love someone else?"

"I'm not the only one guilty of that," I said, my limbs trembling with rage. "You ran back to Dahlia as fast as your little legs could carry you, didn't you?"

"I did what I had to in order to survive!" He stabbed a finger at his chest and advanced on me. "It's all I've been doing since you came into my life!"

"So you blame me?" I tossed up my hands and laughed bitterly. "It's all my fault your life has been miserable for the past year. Well, I never asked you to attack me in that morgue. I never asked you to make me a vampire. And I never asked anyone to bring you back."

"I know!" He gripped my upper arms and pushed me into the base of the cement angel. Concrete chips fluttered from behind me and I heard the angel, apparently attached only by its weight and gravity, rock on its pedestal.

Cyrus didn't seem to notice that we were about to be killed by a falling monument. His face was inches from mine, teeth bared, features crumpled into his vampire form. "You didn't bring me back! You had Dahlia's spell book! You could have brought me back!"

It took me a moment to decipher his words, choked by anger and hindered by his vampire face. His features morphed into his smooth, human visage and he stepped back, still trembling with rage. I stood by, my hands clenching and unclenching as I tried to think of something to say.

I didn't get the chance. He uttered a sound of disgust and strode away from me, down the path.

"Wait!" I jogged after him. "You mean, I could have brought you back instead of your father?" I didn't know whether to be insulted that he expected me to in the first place, or feel bad that I hadn't thought to do it myself. "You're back. Why does it matter who did it?"

"Why does it matter?" he repeated, wrath and bewilderment plain on his features. "My father pulled me back to sacrifice me. I'll be going back to that damnable blue world and there's nothing I can do to stop it."

He grabbed me again, but this time I was ready for him. He wasn't as strong in this incarnation as he had been in the past, and I pushed him off me, hard. He fell back, and I loomed over him. "You want to stop it? Than quit whining and help us! Help us without doing it on your own terms and worrying about your hurt feelings!"

"Do you really want that?" He pulled himself up,

warily. "Do you really want me to be in your life again? Won't it destroy the perfect solution I provided you with my death?"

My heart lurched in my chest. "You think I wanted you dead?"

He couldn't meet my eyes. "It certainly made your choice easier. Which one to pick, your sire or your fledgling?"

It felt as though I'd had the wind knocked out of me. My heart raced and I became dizzy. But I didn't collapse or lose my balance. I'd had a revelation.

"Cyrus, even if you had never died…there wouldn't have been any choice. I don't love you."

Now I knew exactly what people meant when they said the weight of their world was lifted off their shoulders. It was true, I didn't love Cyrus. I was drawn to him, inexplicably, but I could never be happy with him. I could only be happy with Nathan. Whatever feelings I had for Cyrus had been a result of the blood ties we'd shared, or nostalgia for those feelings. But Nathan…I'd had feelings for Nathan almost immediately, before we ever shared a blood tie. They'd been lost amid the physical attraction and my desperation to learn about the world I'd been thrust helplessly into, but they had been there all along. Nathan was right; there was such a thing as love at first sight. No other kind existed.

And I wasn't the only one who knew it. Cyrus knew it. I saw it cross his face as he watched me. I hadn't loved him, just as he had never loved me. What a fine pair we'd made.

Hanging his head in defeat, he laughed. "You're right. You're right. You don't love me, and I'm doomed. This has turned out to be a merry meeting, indeed."

My breath escaped me on a guttural exhalation. "Stop with the self-pity. Why would your father bring you back just to kill you again?"

"He's finally streamlined the ritual he needs. Remember Dahlia's pleasant little trick of including all sorts of impossible ingredients and tasks in her spells? It seems that's not an original idea. He didn't need the souls of all of his fledglings. The ones who'd been killed either at his own hand or due to their own misdeeds won't be missed in the metaphysics of the ritual. But he does need a certain number, and to reach that number, he now needs two of us."

I shook my head. "But why you? He could have picked up a drifter and turned him and used him. Why go to all the trouble of raising the dead?"

"To punish me." He sighed heavily and pinched the bridge of his nose, tilting his head back. When he opened his eyes, they shone with tears like the stars we couldn't see beyond the city's light pollution. But Cyrus wouldn't cry in front of me. Not now, when he was so vulnerable in other ways. "He gave me life, not just once. And he believes I wasted those lives. He wants to punish me, and to send a message that my weakness can't be tolerated."

"And you were going to go along with it?" We started to walk down the gravel path. The graveyard seemed somewhat less sinister, though nothing about the physical atmosphere had changed.

He took my hand in his as we walked. "He has my heart. Whether I 'go along with it' or not, it doesn't matter."

"It didn't occur to you to just…escape?" True, the Soul Eater had his heart, but if he wanted Cyrus for the ritual, he wouldn't stake him. "Unless he only needed your heart, you'd be free and clear."

"He'd find me." Cyrus shook his head. "And besides, as much as I hate being dead, I hate being alive much more these days."

It killed me to hear him say this. I might not have loved him, but I certainly didn't want him to suffer this way. "It doesn't matter, anyway. He still needs another fledgling, right? Unless he's got one willing to go to the slaughter, he can't do the ritual."

"He has one. Or a part of one, at least." Cyrus gave me a pointed look. "I'm sure you'll figure this part out. You're a smart girl."

A splinter of confused panic lodged in my chest. He couldn't mean Ziggy's heart, because Bill had that. And he couldn't mean Nathan's heart, because I'd actually seen that with my own eyes as it beat in his chest. "I don't—"

"His skin, Carrie." Cyrus sounded as if he would gag on the word. "Dahlia is an inventive torturer, but I can't believe she would have thought that up on her own."

The marks. The symbols carved into Nathan's body. "The spell was called 'The Dark Night Of The Soul,'" I stammered. "Does that mean…"

"My father has access to call Nolen's soul back. It's how the spell was done in the first place. Whatever you did to free him of the spell freed his soul and returned it to him. But my father can use those symbols to call it back. All he has to do is consume the symbols and Nathan's soul is his, forever."

My stomach heaved at the thought of the Soul Eater tucking in to eat Nathan's discarded skin, but I held back the vomit. "So, Nathan will die, then, if your father completes the ritual?"

"No." Cyrus said it matter-of-factly. "He would go on living, I suppose, until he did finally die. And then, instead of going into that blue world, he would go into my father. Or, wherever the souls consumed by him will go after he's become a god."

The idea of Nathan's soul being taken from him was something so horrific and wholly unacceptable that I bypassed anger and went straight into cold, calculated fury.

"We're planning to attack during the ritual. Whatever information you can give me would be helpful. And I can either try to save you, or—"

"Oh, there are all kinds of details father has delighted in torturing me with. Who will be there, what it will entail." He stopped walking and faced me. "It's going to be dangerous, Carrie. I'd rather not see you get hurt."

"I'm not going to back down from a fight, you know that. Can you be on my side? Maybe sneak me in? When I…ate Dahlia's soul, that made me the most powerful of our little group. I'm going to fight your father myself." I shrugged, suddenly feeling foolish. "Not that I'm trying to sound invincible here. I will still need help."

He clucked his tongue mockingly. "Now, now. If you're so sure you'll fail before you even start, you've doomed your entire enterprise."

We resumed our walk, but we didn't speak for a long time. It was a comfortable silence, until he stopped again to look at me. "There are times that I wish I could have done things so much differently with you."

"Is this one of those times?" I knew that sounded too

prying, but I couldn't stop myself. "What would you have done?"

"I wouldn't have tried to dominate you. And I wouldn't have tried to seduce you. I wouldn't have tried at all." He laughed softly. "I think you recognized that. That I was trying. And you resented it."

"That's very insightful of you." The way I felt about Cyrus, my sire, wouldn't have been quite as forgiving as the portrayal he'd given himself, but I let him keep his delusion, a little. "You could also have toned down the psychotic narcissism."

"Yes, that has always been my downfall in relationships." He leaned forward as if he would kiss me, then stopped himself a hairbreadth from my lips. "No, that would be a bad idea."

I couldn't help my breathlessness when I whispered back, "I'm glad one of us remembers that."

He straightened and looked up at the sky. "I miss the stars. After this is all over, I'm going to go someplace where I can see stars."

"After this is all over, I'll be dead." The words slipped out as if finally freed. I couldn't have said it to Nathan. I would have worried about upsetting him. And maybe that was the true difference between the two men. Nathan, I could love and yet not speak the truth to, not all the time, especially not if it would hurt him. I couldn't love Cyrus, but I could be selfish and self-focused with him. When I'd thought I loved Cyrus, I'd just loved the way I could be around him. It was a little sad.

Cyrus didn't argue with my sudden, fatalistic turn.

"It's really what will be best for you. You'll go crazy, spending eternity with Dahlia."

Now that it was spoken out in the open, I wanted to cry. I didn't want to die, and yet I'd said the words and sealed my fate. I felt suddenly tired and overly emotional. I choked down my sobs. "I have to get back to Nathan. He was pretty damaged when I took him from your father's place."

"I want you to know I had nothing to do with that," Cyrus said, quickly and earnestly. "She tried to get me to join in, but I fear I disappointed her. In truth, I didn't want to see Nolen, and I didn't want him to see me."

"That's fine." I didn't want to hear any more, in case he told me a lie. I couldn't take any more lies from him. "Tell me how you can help me."

"I can get you into the ritual. The participants will all be dressed the same, so it won't be difficult for you to go unnoticed once you're inside. From there, I assume you'll have your own plan?"

I nodded. "We'll think of something."

"And you can help me, if I wanted it?" I could tell he tried to keep the hope from his voice, so I responded noncommittally, telling him I would do what I could. He seemed to accept this and said, "Very well. I will send you a disguise. On the night, you should be able to enter unmolested."

"Thank you." We shook hands awkwardly, and I turned away from him.

I was a few steps up the path when he called after me. "Carrie. There was something, wasn't there? I mean, we did have some part of each other?"

I couldn't look at him. It was too much to know that

months from now, we might pass each other in that weird, blue-spirit realm and not recognize who the other was. After all we'd shared, we would be ultimately alone.

"Yes. I think we did."

Unlike Orpheus, I didn't look back as I left the land of the dead. But the end of the story would have been the same, either way.

Twenty: Loose Ends; Further Unraveling

~~~ ❧❧❧ ~~~

When I came through the door, Nathan was waiting for me in the dark living room.

I tried to keep my voice light. "Where is everyone?"

"Downstairs." He didn't humor me by pretending nothing was wrong. "I want to talk to you."

I sat in the armchair, and I didn't bother to turn on the lights. I knew what he wanted to talk about. There was no way I'd reached the conclusion I had in the graveyard on my own. Left alone, it was only a matter of time before we could no longer avoid thinking beyond the problem at hand.

"Nathan," I began, trying to find the impossible way to cushion the words. "There was a reason that Dahlia… did what she did to you."

He nodded, resigned, as he looked at where the tight, transplanted skin met the unblemished part of his arm. "I can't say I didn't wonder about that, myself."

I wondered what else had been tormenting Nathan

while I assumed he was just concentrating on healing. "Cyrus thinks that his father will consume the symbols and take your soul back. Nothing would happen to you, at least, until you died. But he would be able to complete the ritual."

"Nothing would happen to me," he repeated softly. "I would lose my soul."

"Nathan—" I began, but what was I going to say? That he didn't need a soul? I wasn't a spiritual person and I still wanted mine. And Nathan owned a New Age book-store and was still a devout Roman Catholic, even if he couldn't go to Sunday-morning mass. That was more than a conflict of interest. It was a clear sign that he was still searching for something. Whether he shared those feel-ings with anyone or not, he clearly still valued his soul.

"What will happen after you kill the Soul Eater?" There was a tension in his voice I'd never heard before.

The only answer I had for him was, "I don't know."

"I think you know." Slowly, painfully, he pulled him-self up from the wheelchair and stood, leaning with one hand on the back of the couch for support. "At least, you're afraid of what will happen."

"I'm afraid of dying. That I know for sure. And I'm afraid I'll fail, and I'm afraid I'll be too late and the world will suffer for it. And I'm afraid that I'll succeed and I won't be able to stop myself…" I cleared my throat and tried to hold back tears. "I'm afraid I won't be able to stop myself from draining him and taking all of that evil into me."

"And even if you do manage to kill the Soul Eater and you don't feel the compulsion to take his soul, you'll still be a Soul Eater. You'll need to feed again. And I don't think you'll be able to," he finished for me, grimly. "And if you can…I'm not sure what I'll do if you go down that road."

My breath caught in my throat. "What are you suggesting?"

"Only what you thought of on your own." He sounded angry and tired.

"So, what do I do?" I stood and paced the living room. "Kill the Soul Eater and then let someone kill me? It's not like they can stake me."

"Maybe one of the Henries could cut off your head," Nathan said, sitting heavily back into the wheelchair. "Or we could entrust Ziggy to do it—"

"Stop!" I covered my face with my hands and stretched my tired skin out of shape. "I can't sit here and listen to the man I love talk about ways to kill me!"

"Do you think it's something I want to talk about? In terms of ways to spend our last days together, it's pretty fucking low on my list!" He struck the arm of the wheelchair and the hard plastic armrest shattered. "I don't want you to die!"

My mind raced toward some indefinite point, but I knew I had to get there. "Wait! Wait! We have Dahlia's book! It has the spell that brought Cyrus back! We could—"

Nathan shook his head vehemently. "No, no, I'm not going to do that. I'm not going to count on something to bring you back when I don't know if it's going to work!"

Rage, such as I'd never felt before, propelled me toward him, and I slapped him across the face so hard I heard a bone in my hand crack. "Then that's it? You just kill me, and what? Life goes on because you don't want to get your hopes up? Fuck you!"

I watched, aching to hit him again, wanting to hit anything just to make the pain in my chest go away, as he slumped over, cradling his jaw.

My hand hurt. My heart hurt. All of the energy drained out of me and into the floor, and I followed it. It felt good to lie there, unmoving. It was actually taxing to speak, but it helped some. "I can't believe we're discussing the way I'm going to die."

For the moment, we didn't. I listened to the clock ticking in the kitchen. I'd noticed that morning that it didn't show the correct time anymore.

Finally, I lifted my head and said, quietly, "You could stake me." When Nathan didn't say anything, I continued. "I know the box is soldered shut, but it's not like we can't get the tools to open it. You could wait until I killed the Soul Eater—you could tell through the blood tie—and then you could stake me."

"And what am I supposed to do then?" He lifted his head slowly, and when he looked me in the eyes, he let all the pain and anger he felt wash over me. "You say I'm going to go on with my life. What do you suggest I do? Find someone else? Maybe some human woman to ease my pain? Isn't that what they write about in all of those stupid romance novels?"

He stood and took a few, shuffling steps out of the living room. In the back of my mind I noted that some of his strength had returned. Not to the point that he would be any help to us when the fight came, but enough that I would be assured he would be all right when I was gone.

"That's a fairy tale, Carrie," he said, turning just

enough to look at me over his shoulder. "When you're gone…I might as well be, too."

I stayed where I was. Nathan was too pissed at me, at himself, at the world, for me to follow him. I lay on the floor, my head blessedly empty of thoughts, until the sun came up and my aching back forced me to retreat.

Nathan was in the bedroom, but he wasn't sleeping. He sat on the side of the bed, still dressed, most likely still in the pose he'd been in when he'd first sat down. I sat beside him, not touching him, and he didn't look at me.

"I don't like the thought of you going on with your life, either. But you will. You're like that, Nathan. No matter how bad you think you are at it, you survive. And you've definitely survived worse than this." I stopped, feeling tears well up and forcing them away. "Maybe this is happening for a reason. Maybe I happened for a reason. If I'd just stayed on my own, tried to deal with being a vampire all alone, maybe I would have never met you or Cyrus and never learned about the Soul Eater. I would never have been around to help destroy him."

"Well, forgive me if I don't praise God for your divine purpose." Bitterness dripped from his words like poison. "You're right, I did survive through killing the woman I loved once. I never thought I'd have to survive it again."

He stood up, stumbled, then regained his footing and limped weakly to the dresser, where he braced his hands on the top of it. "I went seventy years between Marianne and you. I love you, Carrie. Maybe more than I ever loved my wife. And not just because of the blood tie, and not because I'm a different man now. I love you and I don't think

I'll be able to move on after this. I can't imagine being with another woman, not even physically, and have no interest in the idea. It makes me sick to think that one day, I'm supposed to be holding some stranger the way I hold you. Touching her, telling her I love her. It's not possible."

"It will be." I couldn't believe I was endorsing the prospect, but it was the truth. "Someday, it will be."

"No." He turned, still supporting himself on the dresser. "You're the second woman I've said those words to. After everything went so wrong with Marianne, not just her death, but everything that went wrong between us before she died, I never thought I would be able to love someone again. And now I have you, and I can't believe how blind I was back then. But what we have is different, Carrie. I won't get another chance at this."

"You'll try the spell," I said, willing him to trust the words I didn't quite believe myself. "You'll try it and if it works everything will be the way it was. And if it doesn't work, you'll go on. And you'll never stop missing me, just like you'll never stop missing Marianne. And it will hurt and you'll suffer, but, Nathan, you'll live forever. You'll have another chance."

He came to the bed and sat down beside me. "I'll live until something else like this happens. Until another witch skins me alive."

"Then you'll have to choose your dates more carefully."

We laughed. It would have been masochistic to resist the break in tension. He kissed me, holding my face between his palms, and I covered his hands with my own. When he pulled away, he linked our fingers on the bed between us and rested his forehead against mine. "There won't be any others. I mean it, Carrie. I'll spend the rest of my life trying to bring you back if I have to."

I didn't argue with him. He meant for his words to be a comfort, but if bringing people back from the dead were a simple thing, there would be more dead people walking around.

You have no idea how hard it is, Dahlia hissed. *You're not coming back.*

I didn't need her to tell me that. I could feel it.

Nathan kissed me again, this time with a much different intention. I laid a palm flat against the tight, shiny skin of his healing chest and pushed him back gently. "You're not better yet."

"Then you'll have to be gentle with me."

And it was more gentle than we'd ever been with each other, slower and much, much longer. I'm sure he felt the same urgency I did in the face of the uncertainty ahead, but it created an incredible tension to have that urgency denied. But the biggest difference was that this time, for the first time, when he told me he loved me, it didn't sound forced for my benefit.

Afterward, when he lay in an exhausted sleep beside me, I thought about what he'd said. He loved me, maybe more than he'd loved Marianne. Selfishly, I'd wanted to hear that. Now, when it was the thing that would make it most difficult to give him up, now was the time I heard it.

It wasn't fair, but I would take it.

The night of the Soul Eater's ritual came too quickly. Of course, Ziggy was fairly certain a death row inmate's execution date came too soon, too. But that was negative thinking, and Bill had been trying, in the short time they'd been together so far, to break him of that.

Bill half woke and rolled over. "You're still awake?"

"Can't sleep. I guess I'm just so damned excited." Ziggy scooted down on the pile of blankets. "Like a kid on Christmas morning."

"We never had big Christmas mornings when I was growing up." Bill rolled to face away from him again. "Try to get some sleep."

Ziggy lay down beside him and looped one arm across Bill's waist. "I don't want to waste the entire day sleeping. What if one of us dies tomorrow?"

"Look, I'm really tired. But as arguments for sex go, yours is pretty strong." Sleepily, Bill turned to Ziggy and leaned his head against his neck, nibbling the skin there.

Ziggy pushed him away. "That's not what I meant."

"And I woke up for nothing," Bill quipped, sliding his hand down Ziggy's stomach.

"Wait, wait." Ziggy gripped Bill's wrist, even though his mind was changing fast on the sex issue. "I don't want to go and get killed and not have said…some things."

"Oh, you mean you don't want to get killed without telling me goodbye? In that case, I really did wake up for nothing." Bill tried to turn over, and Ziggy stopped him.

"I don't want to say goodbye. If you get killed, it's not like we'll be separated for that long." Ziggy sighed in frustration. "I just want to make sure you know some stuff, in case."

Bill shook his head. "It's the same thing. But go ahead. Whatever you have to say, I'm listening."

Now that he had the go-ahead, Ziggy wasn't sure

where to start. He might be Bill's sire, but they still hadn't known each other that long, and it wasn't as if they'd made great strides in their relationship beyond memorizing who liked what where in bed.

So how did he say what he wanted to say without sounding like a psycho? How did he launch into a long, long list of all the things he liked about Bill, from the in-between color of his hair to the way he pronounced the letter *R,* without turning into that really clingy guy who goes out on one date and then decides to start naming their children?

"I love you," he blurted, and then he realized that maybe the laundry list of cool things about Bill might have been a better way to go.

"I see." Bill didn't look him in the eye. "Well, that's a stupid thing to say, considering."

Ziggy flopped onto his back and stared up at the exposed beams of the floor above and tried to ignore the sound of Pac-Man dying, which currently echoed through his head. "Yeah. That's me. Stupid guy."

Bill didn't seem to hear him. "I mean, when I was almost killed, you gave me your heart without having any idea how I would deal with it or what would happen if we didn't end up together. And you've been hurt so many times in the past by people, it would have made more sense just to let me die and protect yourself. But you didn't. And the stupidest thing is, you thought you had to tell me you love me for me to know it."

The knot in Ziggy's stomach relaxed and he covered his face, unsure whether to laugh or cry. He chose laughter. "Don't you ever fucking do that to me again."

When he uncovered his face, Bill had risen up on one

elbow and looked down at him. He smoothed some of Ziggy's hair away from his face and let his hand linger at his jaw. "I know you love me. And I know how lucky I am to have somebody like you in my life, even if we did find each other in really strange circumstances. And I hope you stay in my life. So I'm not going to tell you that I love you, because no matter what you call it, before a thing like this, it's goodbye. And I don't want to tell you goodbye."

It should have made him feel better to know he'd said it, Ziggy thought later as, still sleepless, he held Bill and stroked the tight muscles of his back. But the truth was, Bill had been right. It felt more like *goodbye* than *I love you,* and Ziggy wasn't ready to tell him goodbye, either.

The sun was almost down. Max could feel it under his skin, like something wanting to get out. He'd been too keyed up to sleep, and he definitely hadn't wanted to listen to Ziggy and Bill doing it in the back room, so he'd come upstairs to the apartment to ignore Carrie and Nathan doing it in their bedroom. Now, he was trying to figure out the best way to say "See ya later—forever" in a note so he could take off and join up with his kind.

His kind. God, he hated that. Bella had a point, and he knew it. He wasn't just a vampire anymore. He could spend time with vampires and try to live like a vampire, but he just wasn't one anymore.

Still, he wasn't a werewolf. He was a lupin. And he knew Bella wanted him to forget the vampire side of himself because it was the very thing that made him a lupin. It seemed as though his only option was to choose one half of himself and run with it.

And of course he would choose the half with Bella. That was a no-brainer. It just seemed so unfair that he had to choose at all.

Growling low in his chest, he ripped the first page of the notebook off and wadded it up. He didn't want to write a stupid note. He wanted to see the moon and become the beast that was rampaging through his veins. He wanted to run and hunt and howl. He wanted to get the big fight over with so he could go home to Bella. He wanted…hell, he just *wanted*.

"You're up early." Carrie came down the hall, tying the belt of Nathan's ratty old bathrobe.

"Same to you," Max said, trying hard not to smile at the picture she presented with her bare feet and badly mussed hair. "And it didn't sound very restful in there."

She blushed and looked away, smoothing her hair. "We weren't loud."

"No, but the bed was." Max chuckled. "I'm sorry, I shouldn't tease you."

Carrie dropped into the armchair and moved a rumpled-up ball of paper with her toe. "Great American novel not going well?"

Sheepishly, Max crouched down and picked up the trash. "Not exactly *Moby Dick*. More like a Dear John. Or Dear Carrie, Nathan, Ziggy and Bill. I'm leaving."

"I didn't think you'd be sticking around." Carrie's voice held a note of sadness, as though she was trying hard to be brave.

It was exactly the reaction he hadn't wanted to face, and the reason he'd wanted to be out of the house when they all found out. "Yeah. That's the thing about the family life, you know. Not as much time for running around with your old college buddies."

"Well, there is that. And the fact that when night falls you'll be a vampire-killing machine." She tried to smile, and it faded too quickly. "You aren't coming back again, are you?"

"I don't know." And he really didn't. It probably would have been better to let them think he wouldn't, then surprise the hell out of them ten years later. "To be honest, I'm not even sure you'll be here to come back to."

Her face went ashen, but she visibly forced the expression away. "Yeah, well. I mean, I hope you'll check. I mean, I hope you'll be there for Nathan if something happened to me. God forbid."

"I wouldn't worry about Nathan. For one, nothing is going to happen to you. And for two, he's got Ziggy. And Bill now." Though Max was pretty sure he knew how Nathan felt about that. If Max was uncomfortable thinking of the kid getting it on with a guy at least a decade older than him, he could guess that Nathan was even less enthusiastic about it.

Carrie laughed. "Yeah, I'm sure that will be a real comfort for him."

They fell silent, until she said, "Max, I'm going to miss you."

"Hey, you might see me again. You never know." But it seemed like a lie.

She didn't play along, either. "No. I won't."

He had the strongest urge to hug her. And who was he to deny that urge?

She stood when he came over to her and squeezed

him so hard he was pretty sure she would break his neck. "No funny business," he assured her. "I'm not going to try anything."

"Because you're not drunk." He heard tears in her laugher, and he buried his face in her shoulder.

He should have been sadder when he left. Maybe he should have looked back over his shoulder. But by the time his feet hit the pavement, his muscles bunched to run, ready to find the warriors through the call of the wild in his veins, his vampire life was already behind him.

Twenty-One: Battle Lines

◆━━◇◆◇━━◆

True to his word, Cyrus sent me a disguise. The sun had just set when a shaking, frightened teenager knocked on the door bearing a package wrapped in brown paper. I took it from him and advised him not to return to his master, but whether he did or not was out of my hands.

A lot of things were out of my hands now.

"What is it?" Nathan asked grimly, looking up from the unpleasant task he was working on. When he'd packed away my heart for safekeeping, he'd put it in a box and padlocked it, not bothering to retain the key for any reason. He'd been sawing through the padlock for a while now, with very little progress to show for it. If I were going to be alive after this, I would definitely purchase more of that company's locks in the future.

I set the package on the table and carefully untied it. A glimpse of vibrant purple peeked from between the edges of the paper. "I think it's my disguise for tonight."

The Soul Eater, like his son, had very ornate tastes. The costume for the ritual was apparently a floor-length-and-then-some, hooded, purple brocade robe. The pattern woven into the fabric was a near-exact rendering of Jacob Seymour's personal symbol, a serpentine dragon wound around a huge gem. Lilies were bizarrely incorporated into the design, and I turned the fabric this way and that, hoping the pattern looked less tacky from a different angle. "This is not exactly the look I imagined for my funeral clothes."

"Don't say that," Nathan said quietly. He reached for the golden mask that had come lovingly wrapped in the robe. "Does this fit?"

The mask was smooth and featureless, a perfect, generic oval with two holes roughly where a person's eyes would be. Definitely not a "one size fits all" situation, but obviously meant to be. I raised it to my face, ignoring the stab of dread in my stomach, and tied the leather thongs behind my head. "I think there are going to be some very uncomfortable people at this ritual."

"Probably more uncomfortable when they're ripped limb from limb by werewolves." Nathan went back to work on the box. "Get that out of my sight. I don't want to see it again."

I did as he asked, tucking the robe and the mask into the open bag of weapons he'd prepared for Ziggy and Bill. "Where are they?" I asked, knowing Nathan would know who I spoke of. "We need to leave soon."

"Don't be in too much of a hurry." Nathan didn't look at me as he spoke. "I'm certainly not looking forward to it."

I took one of his hands in mine. He didn't resist me. "This is not hopeless."

"Let's not talk about it." He pulled his arm away. "I'm not ready to say my goodbyes just yet."

Ziggy and Bill came upstairs, and Nathan and I both put on masks of indifference, as though we were just waiting to get the fight started. We'd agreed that telling Ziggy and Bill what was about to happen would only cause another argument, and we didn't have time for it. We let them in on the part where I infiltrated the ritual, but kept a tight lid on the fact that after I went in, I wouldn't be coming out.

"The van is in some rough shape," Bill said, wiping his hands on a grease-streaked towel. "The stuff I can fix, I don't have the equipment for. The stuff I can't fix, I just don't know how to."

"But will it get us there? All of us?" I thought of the Henries. They would certainly look a little strange walking as one big group toward the Soul Eater's farm. Not exactly something the Soul Eater's goons could overlook.

"There, but maybe not back," Bill answered grimly.

"Maybe we should set up a place to meet after the whole thing goes down, and Nate can come pick us up?" Ziggy asked, looking from me to Nathan.

Nathan didn't even look up from his work on the box. "No. I'm still too weak to drive."

"You don't look very weak with that hacksaw," Ziggy said, nodding toward the table. "What are you doing with that, anyway?"

"There's something inside that Carrie needs to fight the Soul Eater. Something I stole from him when I left Brazil, after he sired me," Nathan lied smoothly. "I lost the keys for the padlock."

Ziggy didn't look as if he believed him, but he didn't argue. "Well, that was smooth. So, should we figure out a place to meet?"

"How about an 'every man for himself' scenario?" I suggested, mentally crossing my fingers that they wouldn't sense something was wrong. "It's such a long way…maybe we'll say that if the van still works, whoever gets there first drives to a predecided location and waits for the rest of the group. And then gives them until two hours before sunrise to show up. That way, if the van stops working on the way back, there will still be time to call a cab and get back before the sun fries everyone."

"But what about the Henries?" Bill appeared to be honestly concerned about them. "Are we just leaving them?"

I hadn't thought of what we would do with them, once they had served their purpose. "I guess I can tell them to find their way back here. As long as they don't do it in a group. Then, they can store themselves in the shop, where they have been." I bit my lip. "Is that okay with you, Nathan?"

"Doesn't matter," he grunted, sawing at the padlock with renewed vigor.

"What about Max?" Ziggy asked, looking around the apartment. "I thought he would be up here, raring to go."

I looked at Nathan and, seeing that he would be no help, sighed. "He left this morning. To find the warriors Bella sent. He won't be coming back."

"That's a hell of a thing," Bill said quietly.

"It's a traitorous thing. Kind of." Ziggy shrugged. "I mean, just taking off. Even if he is on our side."

"No, I think we just can't understand." Bill's face took on a look of momentary panic, expecting us, I suppose, to tell him that we understood and not to call us stupid. When he didn't get that reaction, he went on. "His life has been turned upside down. He's been a vampire for over twenty years and now he's suddenly a werewolf. Think about what it felt like being turned into a vampire. He just did that again. His entire life just changed. And it's going to change again when his wife back in Italy pops their kid out, right?"

I hadn't tried to look at it that way. I really hadn't tried to look at it from any way except how it affected me. "You're right. It's probably better, anyway. He's pretty sure that when the full moon hits him, he won't be able to remember who we are and keep from killing us."

"It's probably a good thing he stays with his own kind, then," Ziggy agreed.

There was a clank, and Nathan swore. "I got the lock off."

Covering his laugh with a faked cough, Ziggy said, "Great. You can grab whatever it is you need from Nathan, and then we can get moving."

"Not quite." Nathan came to the living room, his expression sober. "Carrie, why don't you and Bill start stacking the Henries into the van. Did you ever find out how tall a cord of wood was?"

"Very funny." I knew what he wanted. He wanted to tell Ziggy goodbye. I motioned to the door. "Come on, Bill. We've got some Henries to wrangle."

The Henries were downstairs, just as I'd left them. Bill stayed by the van and let me go down to give the orders. I pulled the tarp off and stood back. "Listen to me, all of you. Form a single-file line and head to the door. The first one of you will go straight up the stairs, to the van parked at the curb. Bill will be there to put you in the van. Do everything Bill tells you. When Bill calls for you, the next in line goes. Do not go up the stairs until Bill calls for you."

I watched them file up the stairs, one after the other, and prayed no one driving by would notice the precise stream of identical humanoids issuing from the bookshop. It took at least an hour to get them all packed in, maybe more. The entire time I wondered what was going on upstairs.

Technically, I didn't have to wonder. I knew what was going on. Nathan was spending what could be the last moments he had with the son he'd already lost once. I could imagine him there, trying to be brave and reassuring in the face of uncertainty, but failing miserably. I'd realized once that if eyes were the windows to the soul, Nathan's were floor-to-ceiling. He was so easy to read, it seemed almost unfair to look at him when he had secrets I knew he wanted to keep.

Ziggy came down to help us just as Bill loaded the last Henry in. His eyes were swollen and red, but he shrugged off any of Bill's attempts to find out what had happened.

"It's nothing," he said finally, giving Bill a quick hug. "I appreciate you being concerned, but really, it's just what you'd expect, okay?"

Bill accepted this reluctantly, and I had a real stab of sympathy for him. I knew what it was like to love someone who kept things secret when they didn't have to, when it was unhealthy for them. I wanted to tell him that things would get better, because they would, but it wasn't the time.

"Listen, Nate probably wants to see you, before we go." Ziggy's expression was surprisingly understanding. Sometimes, I let his "tough teenager" exterior fool me.

Upstairs, I found Nathan in the bedroom. He sat on the bed with the box that contained my heart. It was open, but I couldn't actually see the contents beyond the protective layers of bubble wrap. Bubble wrap. I suppressed a laugh at the low-tech, cheap-plastic solution to the mysterious occult problem of guarding my life.

He didn't look at me as I sat beside him, and then I noticed the wooden stake lying on the quilt next to him. A chill of the "someone just walked over my grave" variety went up my spine, and I tried not to stare at the object of my imminent destruction with horrified fascination.

"We're ready to go," I said quietly, praying my last few words to him wouldn't be met with catatonic response. "Nathan, I—"

He turned and pulled me into his arms, covered my mouth with his. The kiss was almost painful in his desperation. His arms crushed me too tightly. When he released me, he trembled. "I can't let you go. I can't do this."

I closed my eyes and felt a cold tear slide down my cheek, mimicking the ones on Nathan's face. I didn't tell him he could do it, or that everything would be okay. So, I just said, "You have to."

He nodded, grief still contorting his face with a painful grimace, and he let out a ragged sob.

I put my arms around him and then my tears came in earnest. His body felt so solid and comforting next to mine, so familiar. To think that in a few hours, maybe less, I wouldn't be able to do this. I couldn't even comfort my-

self with the knowledge that I might be brought back—
I had no doubt Nathan would try, but no guarantee that it
would work, either—or any illusion that I would carry
this memory into the afterlife. I had been there. I had seen
what it meant to be dead, at least by vampire standards.
By the next morning, I wouldn't remember who Nathan
was. I wouldn't remember who I was.

It took more strength than I ever would have given myself credit for to let go of Nathan. Everything in me
screamed that I should keep holding him, give him another kiss, tell him I loved him just one more time. But I
knew that after I did, there would be another "just one
more time" and another and another, and that wouldn't
help either of us. He knew it, too, and he didn't try to stop
me as I left.

"Are you okay?" Bill asked when I emerged, and I tried
hard to keep my inner turmoil from showing on my face.
"I'm fine. It's just hard to walk out and not know if I'm
coming back."

"You're coming back," Ziggy said, taking my hand in
his and squeezing it. It was a shock—he hardly ever
touched anyone. And then I felt like a liar.

"Let's go," I said, turning away from them. "Get this
thing over with."

The Soul Eater's farm looked a little bit better spruced
up for the ritual. Nothing could make it look homey, in
Ziggy's opinion, but the torches lighting the driveway at
least made it look a little less forbidding.

"There are people walking up the drive. That's a
comfort," Carrie said, pulling on her creepy gold mask.

"As long as I'm not the only one strolling in on foot, I should be okay."

They'd thought of that on the way. "Remember the vampire New Year party? Cyrus had valet parking," Ziggy had pointed out. "I think somebody will recognize this van if we pull up in it. Then, game over, man."

"Let's not panic until we get there, okay?" Bill had said. He'd had those tense little crinkle lines at the corners of his eyes that he often had. Maybe he had them all the time, and Ziggy just hadn't known him long enough to realize what an uptight son of a bitch he was.

He laughed. He couldn't help himself.

"Is this funny to you?" Carrie asked, muffled behind her mask, and he laughed harder.

"I'm sorry. I'm sorry. I'm just…tense." He noticed from the corner of his eye that Bill had his chin to his chest, eyes closed, shoulders shaking with laughter he tried to hold back.

"Great." Carrie pulled her hood up and climbed out of the car. "The Henries will do whatever you say, Bill. I'm going to head down."

"Carrie, wait!" Ziggy hopped out after her, ignoring Bill's fiercely whispered pleas to get back in and keep a low profile. There were no cars on the dirt road, no low, soft rumble preceding one, so he decided it was safe. Carrie stood on the edge of the dirt road, her long purple robe draping awkwardly over the ankle-high umbrella of the mayapples growing on the shoulder.

What should he say to her? He didn't want to give her another long goodbye. They'd both had one too many of those tonight. So he didn't say anything. He just threw his arms around her in a quick, totally not re-grettable hug. When they both made it through this, and they had to, they wouldn't have a lot of crazy "I think you're going to die, so I'm going to spill my guts" type confession of feeling between them. And life could go on that way.

Her eyes widened, ice-cold blue behind the gold mask. There was no way Jacob would miss that it was her. He'd raged endlessly at the many horrible ways he'd like to kill her, reflecting often on her "pitiless eyes." It was her eyes he'd fixated on, and Ziggy prayed Jacob would be too pre-occupied with his ritual to recognize them.

"When the werewolves show up, release the Henries and hang back. Don't get into the middle of things unless it's a last resort. And when the battle is over, get the hell out of here."

"What about you?" he called after her.

She didn't turn around. Her robed figure looked like a shadow slinking down the moonlit road. "Every man for himself. Don't wait for me."

"But—" He stopped himself. It wasn't the time to argue.

In the van, Bill's laughing fit had definitely passed. "What do you think?"

"I don't know." He shook his head. "She said to let the Henries go in. First wave kind of thing, I think. And if we need to bat cleanup, so be it."

Bill stared out the windshield, as if he would be able to see better in the dark the longer he stared. "Sounds reasonable."

They sat in silence for a few minutes, and a nagging, itching feeling formed in the back of his brain. "Carrie told me we should leave without her. Kind of. She said, 'every man for himself.'"

Bill nodded. "That's what we talked about earlier."

"I know, it's just…" Something seemed very strange, the way a movie seems strange right before the hero's best friend is revealed to be the supervillain. "It seemed weird, the way she said it. And Nate said…ah, it's probably nothing."

There was a distant howl, and Ziggy noticed he wasn't the only one in the car that jumped.

"Do you think that's one of them?" Bill asked, his face gone suddenly pale. He hadn't been a vampire long enough yet, Ziggy realized, to be pale all the time.

He put a reassuring hand on Bill's knee. "This is all going to work out. Mark my words, I have a good feeling about this."

And then he said a quick, silent prayer that the last thing he said to Bill wouldn't be that lie.

I held my head up as high as I could as I walked down the driveway. *Project an aura of "supposed to be here,"* I told myself. I looked up at the house, which seemed oddly slanted against the horizon. The sagging roof seemed to sag worse. If I were the Soul Eater, I would be praying that the place wouldn't collapse on my little party.

A black car rolled slowly past me down the drive, and a gold-masked face peered out from the lightly tinted back window. I fought the urge to look away. Instead, I nodded to the figure inside the car, who nodded in reply and looked straight ahead.

Two other attendees walked ahead of me, their purple

robes trailing the dusty ground. I measured my pace carefully, not wanting to catch up with them. If I did, I wasn't sure if I should say anything, or if that secretive nod that had worked on the person in the car would work again. Best to stay by myself, since I didn't know exactly what the tone of the event was. A spiritual gathering? A celebration? An orgy? If I judged it based just on the costumes that seemed to have been taken straight from *Eyes Wide Shut,* it was the latter of the three. But I really, really hoped I was mistaken.

As I got nearer to the house, I saw the gathering through the windows. There didn't appear to be any electric light on in the house. In the yard in front of the porch, two gigantic bonfires lit up the night, and inside were more candles than could be found in a Gothic cathedral. I followed the two figures in front of me up the stairs, wondering how I would find Cyrus among the identically garbed throng.

A hand grabbed my wrist, low beside my body, not calling attention to the movement. The gold, featureless head jerked almost imperceptibly toward the yard, and I followed back down the steps and around the corner of the house, where we were hidden by some dying bushes.

Cyrus took off his mask, but indicated I should keep mine on. "I just wanted you to know I'm here. Stay close to me."

"How did you know it was me?" I asked, my whisper distorted ridiculously by the mask.

His jaw clenched, and he looked away. "Stay close. I'll do what I can for you. Promise you'll do what you can for me."

I nodded, not wanting to speak with the mask encumbering me.

"I hope that whatever plan you might have comes to fruition before my father kills me. If not, you might consider…not letting him kill me." His expression changed to one of disgust. "I can't believe this is my life."

I can't believe this is mine, either. I didn't say it. I took his hand in mine and squeezed it, then motioned back to the house. He replaced his mask and we walked inside.

The last time I'd been in the farmhouse, there had been a dead body rotting in the dining room and various dark and sinister shadows lurking in the corners. Now it was bright, there weren't any dead bodies immediately visible, but it was still frightening. The bottom floor had been crudely gutted. It looked as though someone had just taken a sledgehammer to the bits of wall they could reach and left everything else behind, including the staircase. Two steps hung like a half-severed limb from the upper floor. Overhead, wires that probably hadn't had electricity running through them for twenty years dangled from the broken plaster skeleton of the former rooms.

In the middle of the newly open space, a large circle was drawn on the floor. The robed figures in attendance stayed well outside of the perimeter, whispering to each other in small clusters.

Only one person stood within the circle. He was a tall, thin man, wearing the same purple garb as everyone else, but no mask obscured his pinched, hook-nosed face. A thin mustache, the same oily black as his slicked-down hair, quivered above his lips as they twitched in a mumble we couldn't hear. He stood over a black-draped altar, lifting objects and turning them this way and that. Behind the altar, a huge, carved wooden chair—a throne, really, there were no other words to describe it—was positioned under a hanging oil lamp with a single flame.

"That's the necromancer," Cyrus said quietly, nodding toward the man in the circle.

"He'll perform the ritual?" I asked, thinking too late that disguising my voice might be a good idea. The necromancer raised up a sword, the blade glinting sinister silver in the golden light of the room.

"That's him," Cyrus said mechanically. "And that's the blade that will split my heart and kill me."

I wanted to reassure him that I would do whatever I could to keep him safe, but the chance was too great that someone would overhear. I put on a tone of disinterest. "Seems a bit big. Overkill, and all."

The door behind us slammed shut just as the ominous chime of a grandfather clock somewhere in the room sounded midnight.

Cyrus's hand found mine, hidden in the voluminous folds of my sleeve, and he gripped it hard. The back door, previously down the hallway, now directly across the cavernous room, opened on screeching hinges. In walked Jacob Seymour. The Soul Eater.

My breath caught in my throat, then tried to force itself out on a nervous giggle I had to fight hard to suppress. The Soul Eater was, for the very first time I could remember, wearing modern clothes. Ultramodern, in fact, a single-breasted black suit with clean lines that had a slight sheen to it, and highly polished black dress shoes. His long, white-blond hair lay stick-straight over his shoulders, and a golden laurel wreath crowned his head.

I don't know what was more ridiculous, that he'd eschewed his flowing, medieval garments on the night they would have been most appropriate, or the laurel wreath, but I bit the inside of my lip to keep my laughter in.

His appearance caused a ripple of excitement through the crowd, and they applauded him wildly. He bowed once, stiffly, then settled into the large throne behind the altar. His expression was serious, but I saw the quirk of a shrewd smile at the corner of his mouth. "My God. He's going to kill these people," I realized out loud, my remaining heart pounding erratically in fear.

Cyrus jerked my hand hard and placed one finger on his gold mask where his lips would be, to hush me.

You included, Dahlia laughed delightedly in my head.

Over the celebratory noises, a loud, foreboding howl echoed outside. The Soul Eater stood, nearly tipping the oil lamp—I was momentarily disappointed that he didn't; accidental immolation would have solved so many of my problems at this point—his face a tight, pinched mask of rage.

He knew, I realized. He knew that resistance was inevitable.

Another howl raised the hair at the back of my neck.

The werewolves were here.

Twenty-Two: Ain't No Party

It happened so fast. One minute the small clearing was crowded with men. Naked men, which Max was less than comfortable with, but clothing wasn't such a hot idea in wolf form.

The nightmare of the gym class locker room hadn't lasted long. The leader, a guy Max had seen around the pack compound but had never talked to on account of his snooty, Euro-trash appearance, had thrown back his head and howled. His face had been the first thing to change, his lips pulling back from an O shape to stretch over elongating jaws. His hair, black and long and pulled back into a ponytail, broke loose from its tie and appeared to grow longer, until it was a veritable blanket wrapping around him. He fell to his hands and knees, and then those were obscured by his hair, which moved like one solid piece to coat his limbs. His arms twisted at the shoulder until the elbows faced out and popped into knees. His hands and feet shrank into themselves with a wet, popping sound that brought Max's lunch up to his throat.

Then, like a flash, it was done, and standing where the leader had been was the largest wolf Max had ever seen.

He'd expected it to be black. Bella was black when she was a wolf. He wasn't sure of himself, on account of the fact there were no mirrors out in the woods, but he'd assumed they would all look alike. Not this one. It was a snowy gray.

According to Hollywood, werewolves didn't look like wolves or dogs at all. Just guys who were considerably more hirsute. The first time Max had changed, he'd thought of *An American Werewolf in London* and he'd momentarily worried that whoever he might kill while hunting would be condemned to living death, following him around and popping up at the worst possible moments. But, like most things, Hollywood had the werewolf thing all wrong. When Max had first watched Bella change, moments before he'd changed for the first time, himself, he'd learned that werewolves were truly wolves, not just humans with bad body hair.

Once their leader changed, they all started changing. Max stood there for a long moment, the urge he'd been feeling all week—the primal urges to hunt and fight and fuck and kill all rolled into one big, confusing, pushing need—grew in him to unmanageable proportions. His chest tightened. He couldn't breathe. He fell to his knees, tried to clutch at the burning pain in his ribs that seemed to spread out to his limbs, only to find that he couldn't quite bend his arms the way they used to.

Not as bad as last time. It was an oddly calm thought to have when he felt as though his body was being ripped limb from limb. He looked down at his ruined hand and saw it in stark black-and-white, the edges kind of fuzzy. It shrank to a wide, flat paw, half of it missing.

The pain passed, and he tried to stand, realizing belatedly that he was standing, but on his wolf legs and feet. He wasn't sure he would like being so short in a fight.

The leader barked, and the pack surged forward. Another dog, a steel-colored one with mismatched eyes of gray and blue, snarled at him and he cowered instinctively, then hated himself for doing it. But the wolf was appeased, and moved in front of him.

They ran, and Max found himself straining to outpace the whole pack. Only real, conscious effort kept him from running off wildly into the woods around them. He had a goal. The details of it were a little murky now, but he knew he had to stay the course.

Something in the air changed. He could smell it. It was a bright, crisp note of ozone, like after a lightning strike. It smelled like magic. He didn't know how, but it did.

The pack sped up, bursting through the trees into a wide, open lawn. Nothing was there. Nothing to fight. No chance to rend some enemy's flesh and feast on his innards.

A low rumble shook the ground, growing in intensity. The leader turned and growled at them. It wasn't Patton, but it was as inspiring a prebattle speech as could be accomplished by a dog.

Cracks appeared in the ground. The enemy was here. They were just early.

"They're here. Raise them!" The Soul Eater's lips were white with fury as he shouted at the necromancer. "The rest of you, get out there and protect me!"

The purple-robed attendants looked at each other from behind their faceless gold masks. A ripple of fear went through them. Obviously, they weren't prepared or inspired to fight.

"Do it," the necromancer commanded. "Or I can finish you all off!"

They crowded toward the front door, and Cyrus pulled me after him.

"Not you, Cyrus," the Soul Eater called. "We'll need you."

He stopped, still clutching my hand. His eyes were large and pleading behind his mask, but I shook off his hold. If I stayed, the Soul Eater would know, and he'd be able to call his minions back to kick my ass. Once they were outside and distracted by their own fight, it would be safe to begin mine. I just hoped I could think of a way to save Cyrus in the meantime.

I turned away from him and followed the crush.

The vampires all stopped in a cluster at the bottom of the stairs. I looked in the same direction they all stared. Forty or fifty werewolves, in wolf form, stood, visible only from their shimmering eyes, at the trees lining the edge of the yard.

The vampires began to whip off their masks, and I panicked. If I took off mine, the Soul Eater could recognize me. Or, maybe one of the goons here would recognize me. I'd been to the vampire New Year party, and I'd been in March's brothel. The chance that some of these vampires might have seen me on either occasion was slim, but disturbingly real.

I didn't have long to worry about it. The ground at our

feet began to rumble, and I staggered for balance as it began to shake and split. The house behind us creaked and groaned, and I wondered what would be safer, running toward the werewolves or staying right next to a collapsing house. From the steaming fissures that formed in the ground, the stench of sulfur and something worse, something unspeakably disgusting, rose up.

A skeletal hand appeared, clawing at the ground, pulling an arm swathed in tattered flesh and fabric. And from every other crack in the trembling ground, body parts in varying states of decay emerged.

We'd warded the cemeteries, but we'd never thought about what might have been buried around the house.

The zombies were barely out of the ground when the werewolves rushed to attack. I turned toward the driveway, looking to the trees lining the road. My eyes only had to scan back and forth twice before I saw the Henries marching down the lawn in militaristic rank and file. I knew who I could thank for that.

"What the hell are those?" a vampire next to me shouted, drawing the attention of the others to the lines of Henries, who broke file and ran, shouting, oddly uniform, as they rushed the vampires.

The werewolves tore into the zombies, breaking bones in their jaws and spitting out putrid flesh. But the parts of corpses that fell didn't die. They just fought harder.

Above the occasional yip of an injured dog or a scream of a vampire falling to either the Henries or the wolves or the zombies—who didn't seem to know or care what side they were on—I noticed a strange silence from the house. It seemed like there should be, I didn't know, chanting or something. I didn't see anyone through the windows, and I needed to get back to Cyrus and kill the Soul Eater before he became a god.

I edged my way back to the porch steps and had one foot up when someone pulled me back. I looked down in horror at the hand grasping the hem of my robe. Rotting red flesh with a few hanging tags of green skin still clinging to it half covered stained finger bones like a tattered glove. The long bones of the forearm appeared to be fused together, until I noticed that it was soil and grass impacted between them. A large, mucus-covered white larva curled out of it and fell to the ground.

The arm, horrible as it was, was nothing compared to the creature it was attached to, a zombie missing half its skull and the rest of its body beneath the rib cage. The piece of head that was left had slipped down the spinal column and hung there like a grim necklace, a rotting black eye held in the socket by bloated facial skin.

The thing held me with its one arm, trying to climb up my robe, dragging its decomposed body behind it. I pulled the purple velvet over my head, shaking the grasping fingers free of my leg beneath the fabric. I lurched up the steps, then realized too late that I didn't have a weapon.

It was part of the plan Nathan had objected to and that I had insisted on. Not knowing if there would be security measures at the door, I hadn't wanted to walk in strapped with weapons only to blow the whole plan the second someone checked me for them.

Unfortunately, this left me with some difficulty. While it seemed the vampires around me hadn't thought twice about bringing knives and stakes and swords, it wasn't as if there were vampires dying all around me and leaving me with anything I could use. I considered pulling a piece of the porch rail up to use as a stake, but I wanted something with a longer range.

At the corner of the porch, a vampire with long, red hair wielded a sword clumsily against a snarling werewolf. I made my move fast, before she could actually hurt the animal. I pulled myself up to stand on the rail and launched myself onto her, praying I'd miss the sword. The werewolf backed down a little, obviously surprised, and she turned, face frozen in an unflattering expression of confusion. We both tumbled to the ground, and either her inexperience or lack of preparedness caused her to drop the sword. I grabbed it and while she still scrambled for my hands, turned it and speared it through her chest. She exploded into a puff of flame and ash, and I jumped back up, brushing myself off. My hair flew wildly around my face, and I realized that in the confusion my mask had been knocked off.

The werewolf regarded me for a moment, then, apparently deciding that I was on its side, turned its attention to a shambling zombie.

A vampire near me had seen what I'd done. He still wore his mask and robe, but I could tell from his height and build that he would be trouble. He charged at me, and I ran, around the side of the house facing the woods, and prayed no more wolves waited in the trees. The vampire in the mask pursued me, and he was fast. Faster than I was. He overtook me by a few crucial steps, picked me up and slammed me into the neglected rosebushes at the side of the house.

The impact knocked the wind out of me, otherwise I would have shouted at the pain of the thorns pricking through my clothes. I tried to pull my double vision into focus as the vampire removed his mask and shrugged back the hood of his cloak.

"Remember me?" he purred, his face twisted into his vampiric visage.

I couldn't tell from his face, but his long blond hair and his body seemed familiar. He was muscular now, but he'd been even more so when I'd met him at March's brothel. The disease that had been killing him had obviously taken a toll before he'd been changed. "Evan."

He laughed, the sound demonic due to his twisted face.

"You got turned," I said, shrugging helplessly in his grasp. "Congratulations."

"No thanks to you." He flashed his teeth. "You were going to let me die."

I forced myself into feeding mode and snapped my jaws at him. "So what? So, I didn't turn you into a vampire. Waaah. I don't have time for your stupid personal vendetta."

"Why, because you have to kill the Soul Eater?" He shoved me hard against the siding. "I saw you kill that other vampire."

"And you're not going to let me get away with killing Jacob blah blah blah." I punctuated my sentence with a sharp head butt that forced him to drop me.

The sword lay on the ground where I'd dropped it, and I dived after it. He recovered quickly, and made his own dive for the sword. I got my hands on it first, but he got his hands on me, preventing me from getting up. He crawled over my body, toward the sword clutched in my outstretched hands. I tried to turn over and smash him with it, but he was too close for me to do much with the blade, and I knew if he got it, I was as good as skewered.

Still, I had to try. As I flipped onto my back, trying to wriggle free and still keep the sword out of his grasp, he screamed. And then he lifted off me. I watched as he flew at least six feet off the ground. He crashed back down, and his assailant was upon him again.

It was a werewolf, a dirty, yellowish-gray werewolf. It loomed over him, biting down on his throat to keep him from screaming.

I took my chance and climbed to my feet, scooping up the sword. As I turned to run, the wolf howled, and I turned, ready to strike him down if I had to. "I'm one of the good guys," I reassured it, and it pawed at Evan's motionless chest. I looked down, and saw that the paw was little more than a ruined stump. And it was where Max's maimed hand would have been.

I covered my mouth and dropped the sword in shock. I knew, of course, that he would be here. I just hadn't thought I would see him in his wolf form. It was bizarre, and I was torn between wanting to pet him and thinking of how strange vampire-form Max would have found that.

He barked at me, then trotted away from Evan's immobile form. I wondered how long it would take Evan to heal, and hoped the werewolves weren't just doing half their job out there. But I didn't have time to worry about that. I hurried to Evan's side. He was still unconscious, which made it much easier to line up the point of the blade with his chest and jam it down without resistance. I didn't stay to watch his ashes settle into the grass.

The backyard was oddly calm, considering what was happening in the front yard. At the farthest back corner I spotted a crude graveyard, evidenced by dark, humped mounds of dirt. They appeared undisturbed, though, and I wondered if the necromancer had been able to raise just the corpses in the front yard, without disturbing the ones in the backyard.

The back door was on another, smaller porch, so I didn't see until I was actually up the steps that there was no one inside the house. The circle on the floor was exactly as it was before, and the altar was set up exactly as it had been. They had left. And they'd also left behind all of their impressive-looking tools.

As if I was being sucked backward into the blood tie, my own memories rampaged through my mind. I thought of all the spells I'd cast from Dahlia's book, all of the flashy ingredients that had been meant to throw people off the track of actually completing the spell.

They were doing the ritual somewhere else. I spun, scanning the yard helplessly.

The barn!

The side yard between the barn and the house was littered with body parts, but there was no immediate fight to impede me. My feet pounded on the hard earth, so loud I was sure the Soul Eater would hear me coming. I forced myself to slow and creep the last few feet. A short earthen rise angled up to the doors, one of which was open a crack. Light and a terrible smell leaked out. I covered my mouth with my shirtsleeve and tried not to gag as I peeked through the opening.

One glance inside revealed where the smell was coming from. All of the Soul Eater's human victims—and those of his guests—must have been stored here for later disposal. Rotting bodies, bloated from the heat and the early stages of decay, were stacked around the perimeter of the barn like sandbags. They created walls at least six feet high. It was a good thing the necromancer hadn't animated these corpses, or the werewolves and the Henries would have been overcome way too easily.

Then I realized this might be the last line of defense, the reserves, so to speak, and I wanted to make a run for it.

Then I saw the proceedings inside, and I knew I had to do something.

Cyrus lay spread-eagled on the ground, staked out with short ropes. His robes were gone, and his pale chest was bare above the waist of his black trousers. The Soul Eater sat on a throne, much like the one in the house, but this one appeared to be made out of human limbs and torsos. He was at ease on the grisly pile, actually smiling as he watched the necromancer dip a large stick tipped with a bundled-up rag into a simmering cauldron. When he removed it, the rag dripped with something tarry and black. He slapped it onto Cyrus's chest, painting it over his skin in a scalding line. He grimaced and strained against the ropes, but they held.

This is all flash, Dahlia informed me witheringly. *This guy thinks he's David Copperfield or something. All Jacob has to do is drink the potion, then drink Cyrus, then release all the other souls trapped in him. Then this necromancer guy has to worship him, and then it's done.*

The necromancer just has to worship him? Weren't there already enough babbling sycophants who worshipped Jacob Seymour? *What stopped him from being a god before?*

He had to perform certain tasks first. You know, like when a saint has to do three miracles to become a saint? Guided by Dahlia, I saw Jacob instructing her to give Cyrus the potion that had been intended to create a natural-born vampire. He'd achieved that goal easily. Then, I saw Dahlia snarling and rounding up five vampires— March, the vampire madam, among them—so that Jacob could destroy his own vampire progeny. And finally, she showed me Jacob clutching a dried-up, withered object in his fist and plunging it into an eerie green flame leaping out of a cauldron. The same cauldron, I realized, as the one in the barn right now.

Forge the sword, spill your own blood, and then the test of fire. He's not a vampire anymore. He's more like... more like a god in waiting.

So, he'll be harder to kill? I didn't need her to answer the question. I dried my hands on my jeans, then gripped the sword in one hand and braced the other one on the door. *What about Nathan's skin? The symbols on it, to call his soul back.*

What do you think is in the cauldron? Besides various herbs and holy water, of course.

Mentally, I shushed her. *It's showtime now. Are you with me, or against me?*

Against you, she responded with no hesitation. *But lucky for you, that means I'm going to help you.*

I'd never pretended to understand Dahlia in the past. "Whatever," I said under my breath, fully prepared to weather a change in her mood that might lead to me fighting her internally, and the Soul Eater externally.

I pushed the door open. Both the Soul Eater and the necromancer looked up at once. Cyrus, still writhing in pain from the burning, tarry potion on him, took longer to notice me. When he did, his face slid from a pinched expression of agony to an exhausted smile of relief.

"Jacob Seymour!" I shouted, raising the sword in both hands, ready for the fight. I couldn't believe that was my voice, loud and echoing off the walls of the barn.

The Soul Eater stood, his eyes blazing with fury. "By order of the Voluntary Vampire Extinction Movement, which is no longer functioning, I am sentenced to death for my crimes against humanity. I've heard it all before."

"I'm not here for them." I tightened my grip. "This is all for me."

Twenty-Three: Endgame

‿✺‿✺‿

"How's it look?"

Ziggy lowered the binoculars and passed them to Bill, so he could see for himself. "The zombies are almost gone. Some of the Henries are having problems with the vampires, but I don't see too many dead werewolves. One or two, at the most."

"Guess they won't be needing our help after all." Bill sounded disappointed at that. "Not that I really need to go in and start killing people left and right. But it would have been nice to get my hands a little dirty."

"It's not over yet," Ziggy reminded him. "Carrie might need our help, still."

Though she had said over and over that it was every man for himself, he and Bill had agreed that it would be stupid to let her get killed when they might be able to save her.

Nate had said something along those lines, too, now that Ziggy had a chance to slow down and think about their talk back at the apartment.

"Carrie knows what she has to do. Don't get yourself

killed trying to save her. Let her do what she has to. And let me do what I have to, okay?"

He'd agreed then, thinking it sounded a little bit like a mother scolding her kid for climbing too high on the jungle gym at the playground, but he'd really just said the words to make Nate feel better.

Ziggy leaned back in his seat, pressing his knuckles to his mouth. The torn leather of his fingerless gloves scraped his lip. "Bill, what do you think Carrie's chances are? Of doing this thing alone, I mean?"

"Not good." The answer came fast, and Bill lowered the binoculars, looking a little guilty at pronouncing her dead on arrival. "I mean, that's why we agreed to go after her, right?"

Ziggy nodded slowly. "Yeah. But she wasn't the only one who said we shouldn't meddle in the fight. Nate said it, too. He said we needed to let her do what she needed to do, and let him do what he needed to do. What do you think about that?"

"I think it sounds kind of fatalistic," Bill said with blunt honesty. "It sounds like they don't want to be responsible for leading lambs to the slaughter."

"That's what I thought, too." Ziggy shook his head. "I think there's something going on."

As Bill looked through the binoculars again, Ziggy thought of all the possible scenarios he could come up with. Did it have something to do with the fact Carrie was a Soul Eater now? He'd never actually seen Jacob fight. Was it possible that Soul Eaters became demonic killing machines, and Nate and Carrie knew this and didn't want Bill and him to get caught in the cross fire?

What about the werewolves down there? Max had said he didn't know if he would recognize them in his wolf form. Maybe Carrie had done a spell to make her recognizable as a good guy, but she just didn't have enough juice left to cast the same spell on two other people? And that was why they needed to stay out of the fight?

Or, it could have been that they would be a distraction. Ziggy knew how hard Carrie would fight to protect another person. She'd done it when they were trapped in Cyrus's mansion together. She'd done it when she'd agreed to put Ziggy's heart in Bill. It seemed as if she cared too much about everyone, and Nate was afraid she'd be too busy protecting them to fight.

That seemed more reasonable than any of the other possibilities. He absently scratched his chest through his T-shirt, feeling the bumpy ridges of his scar beneath.

Then, he remembered the box. And Nathan's secrecy regarding it. And he felt more stupid than he had in a long, long time.

"I need you to know before you leave here tonight that I love you. You might not be my flesh and blood, but you're my son. And I've been so stupid, letting you think I would reject you over something as trivial as…who you go to bed with. No matter what happens tonight, I need you to know that I love you, and that I have always been proud to call you my son."

"We've got to get back to the apartment," Ziggy said, sitting up in the seat and snatching the binoculars out of Bill's hand.

"What? Why?" Bill at least started the van while arguing. "What's going on?"

It took a lot of Ziggy's effort to keep the tears from coming out when he said, "I think Carrie is going to die. And I think Nate is going to be the one who does it."

The Soul Eater's eyes sparkled with genuine amusement as he stalked toward me. "What a wonderful performance. Remind me to thank Nolen for sending you along. You have such a flair for the dramatic."

"As do you," I said, nodding to the throne made of people parts. "But I didn't come here to banter with you."

"No, you came here to kill me." He chuckled. "It's a pity that you won't succeed—"

"Because you have some grand plan and I'm too late and you're going to tell me all about it before putting it into action and you have never, ever seen a single movie in your whole life, otherwise we wouldn't be having this discussion." I wouldn't have normally wasted the time I just had, either, but my irreverence in the face of his grand act seemed to infuriate him even more, and odds seemed to be more in my favor if I could incapacitate him with rage before striking.

"Fine," he said with false graciousness. He nodded at the necromancer. "Kill her."

I rushed at him. He raised his hands. I cut one of them off.

I'd meant to kill him outright, but it was harder to aim my strikes than I'd anticipated. I'd never used a sword before. By the time I got the blade back under control, he shouted a spell.

You're so dead, Dahlia giggled in my head.

The rows of dead bodies wriggled and squirmed, coming to life before my eyes. I didn't give them a chance to get to me. I held out my hands and screamed, "Apart!"

I saw the word leave me like a sonic boom that spread across the air in the barn. It knocked the necromancer to the ground. It even tossed the Soul Eater back into his now-reanimated throne of flesh. The wave of disruption hit the bloated bodies, exploding them to a shower of meaty, putrid sand that rained wetly over all of us.

Cyrus made a noise of disgust and thrashed, spitting, against his restraints. One arm came free. Blood poured from nearly a dozen wounds on his chest and face, probably because I hadn't thought to exclude him from the spell that had just obliterated the would-be zombies around us.

"Nicolas, say the words!" the Soul Eater screamed, lurching for Cyrus. His teeth sank into Cyrus's shoulder. The necromancer began to chant.

I could leave Cyrus to be devoured in an instant by his father, or stop the Soul Eater's transformation by killing the necromancer.

I knew I would regret it. But I went for Cyrus.

My sword sank into the Soul Eater's back and shoulder, and he released Cyrus immediately, blood dripping from his mouth.

Cyrus was too weak to get away. I was awed at how fast the Soul Eater had drained him. His lips were blue— I had no idea we could look like that—and he trembled as he tried to crawl to safety.

While the Soul Eater struggled to remove the sword from his body, I pulled Cyrus to his feet and helped him limp to the door of the barn, where he collapsed against it. "Don't go out. There are still vampires."

He nodded that he understood and I spun, weapon-less, ready to attack the necromancer, hoping I would be in time.

The necromancer was still chanting, cradling the stump where his hand used to be in his robe. I charged him and he faltered in his chanting, backing away from me.

"Don't stop, you fool!" the Soul Eater ordered.

Nicolas the necromancer was a much more loyal henchman than I'd ever seen. He sputtered in fear, but he kept chanting. I made a grab for him and he dodged me, running behind the bubbling cauldron. I charged around it, but he managed to keep the distance between us. I saw only one option. I dived across the cauldron, grabbed him by the head and pushed him in.

I screamed as my arms sank into the boiling tar, but I held him down. I saw chunks of skin float to the surface and prayed it wasn't mine, then nearly vomited at the thought it could be Nathan's. But I didn't let go, not until Nicolas stopped thrashing.

"Carrie!" I heard Cyrus scream, and I pulled my scalded arms from the cauldron, shaking as much of the boiling potion off of them as I could.

The Soul Eater was suspended in the air, glowing an eerie green-gold that seemed to dim the candlelight in the barn. He'd thrown his head back, a rapturous expression serenely gilding his face. His clothes melted away. His hair fell in shimmering, green-gold strands that floated to the ground and disappeared. His skin turned paper white. When he opened his eyes, they were bloodred. No pupils, no iris. Just a curtain of blood.

He looked the way the Oracle had looked. I wondered

if she'd been on the path to godhood, and had just been interrupted. It seemed so logical now.

"Cyrus, get out of here," I commanded. When I spoke, a huge wind blew through the barn, tumbling me over the hard, slippery ground.

"No!" he screamed back, trying to get to his feet. "Carrie, run! Don't stay here with him!"

You know what you have to do, Carrie. It was Nathan's voice, across the blood tie. *He's a god. Dahlia can tell you what to do. You can invoke him. Bring him into you.*

"How do I do that?" I asked aloud, shouting over the raging wind.

"Carrie!" Cyrus screamed. I saw him clinging to the doors. Tears streaked his face. I wondered what he was crying about, until I looked down at my hands.

The skin was gone. Some of the muscle. I saw a chunk of blond hair rip free and fly into the maelstrom surrounding the Soul Eater. I was literally blowing away.

"Cyrus, get out of here!" I shouted back, struggling to my feet. My jeans were tattered and ripping apart fiber by fiber. I stumbled closer to the Soul Eater. He didn't appear to see me, but the wind increased and knocked me down.

Carrie, try. Try to invoke him. Nathan's words were infuriating, because I had no clue what they meant.

Dahlia didn't tell me anything. But I pried her memories away from her. I saw her standing, naked, in a grove of trees. She was much younger, maybe thirteen or fourteen. There was no makeup on her face, and her red hair hung down her back in softly brushed waves, except for the beaded braids at her temples.

"Mother Goddess! Mother Goddess! Mother God-

dess!" she called out, stretching her arms wide. *"I humbly beg that you join with me, merge your energies with mine!"*

I pulled myself to my feet again, raising my arms against the onslaught of debris that sanded the flesh off my bones. "Jacob Seymour!"

He looked at me then, a truly evil smile on his face.

"Jacob Seymour! Jacob Seymour!" I took a huge breath, and when I spoke, I imagined the words surrounding him. "I humbly beg that you join with me. No, fuck that! I order you to merge your energy with me! Do it, goddamn it!"

The green-gold energy that surrounded him sucked into me, and I drew it in. Reveled in it. I felt drunk. I felt invincible.

The Soul Eater's body fell to the floor, wrinkled, pale and useless. "No!" he shouted, pounding at the hard-packed dirt like a child throwing a temper fit.

I wanted to stay just as I was, swaying in the currents of the awesome power I'd pulled into myself. But I knew in the back of my power-drunk mind that I had to end it.

I staggered to the sword lying on the ground. It glinted ethereal white, but it might have been because everything in my vision had a strange aura around it.

"No," the Soul Eater rasped as I approached him. "No, please. Take pity...."

I thought of all the people he had hurt in his life, those I knew of and those I didn't. And I thought of what he'd done to Nathan. I thought of Nathan's face as he held his dead wife. And the rage that built up in me wasn't my own. It was Nathan's, pouring through the blood tie. When I raised the sword and screamed, it was with

Nathan's rage and pain. It was Nathan's hand that struck Jacob Seymour, cleaving his head from his neck in one stroke. It was Nathan who raised the bloody sword in his hand and screamed to the sky in triumph.

It's done, I told him, though there was no need. But it felt good to give the signal myself.

I love you, he told me. I already felt the pain in my chest, where my heart should have been.

It wasn't as bad as I thought it would be. I heard Cyrus screaming my name, felt my body falling to ash around me. But the last thing I knew was Nathan telling me again, over and over, that he loved me.

And then it was only peace and the endless, murky blue.

"Nate!" Ziggy heard the panic in his voice as he crashed through the apartment door. Bill stumbled across the felled wood after him, but he didn't stop. "Nate!"

He tore down the hall. The light was on in the bedroom. He shouldered that door down, as well. Nate didn't say anything or even look at him. He had a stake in his hands, the tip positioned against his bare chest.

"Dad!" Ziggy screamed, but it didn't seem to penetrate Nate's brain. He shoved hard, embedding the stake in his chest. He exploded into ash, all but his heart, which flamed blue for a moment before falling to the bed in another puff of ash.

Ziggy fell. He didn't feel the floor beneath him. He barely felt Bill's arms around him. Nate was dead. The only man who'd ever truly loved him like a son, the first person to care for him without expectations in return…was gone.

"Ziggy!" Bill shouted, but he could barely hear him. Then Ziggy realized it was because he was screaming and sobbing.

"I can't believe it! I can't fucking believe it!" He pushed Bill away and fell full on the floor. It seemed as if the flatter he got, the less it hurt.

Bill picked something up from the bed. A book.

It took a long minute for Ziggy to realize what it was.

Bill's eyes were rimmed in red, and his voice trembled as he turned it so the pages faced out. "I don't think he intends to stay dead, Ziggy."

Max followed the warriors back to Italy. He wasn't sure what had happened to Carrie and the guys. He was more shocked to realize that it wasn't his problem.

The plane touched down on the pack's private runway just after dusk. He helped unload the wounded, left the others to unload the body bags of those who hadn't made it through the battle. He needed to see Bella.

The change in attitude at the compound was apparent immediately. The first people Max saw spoke to him in English—he'd been suspicious that they could, but just hadn't wanted to—and they spoke warmly of Bella and how glad she would be to see him back.

A lingering anger at Julian burned through his veins, but he pushed it away. He didn't want to see Bella that way. He felt as though he'd come home, and he wanted her to feel that way, too.

The door to their room was unlocked. He pushed it open and found it empty, but the curtains over the balcony door wafted in a soft breeze, and he knew he would find her there.

She didn't look at him when he stepped onto the balcony. She sat in her wheelchair, facing the mirror black of the lake. "Max. You have returned."

"Yeah. Don't sound too enthused." Great. He'd wanted to show her how different things were, now that he knew where he belonged. Now that he knew his place in the world, and that it was with her. All he'd done was fall back on sarcasm just as he'd always done.

Bella's hands grasped the arms of her chair, and she pushed as though she would stand. But it was impossible. Wasn't it?

She did stand, and Max felt hot tears coursing down his face.

"I was worried that you would not live," she said, her voice choked on her own tears. "I never thought I would see you again."

"I'm here now, baby," he said quietly, not wanting to take a step toward her, not wanting to do anything that might ruin this moment.

But there was something he had to say to her. "I'm glad you can stand up. That is the best present I could have possibly come back to. But I think you should sit down."

Her brow creased with confusion, but she did as he asked, and wheeled her chair around to face him. "Max?"

"I need to tell you something. And I have to be honest with you. And it's going to be hard, because I haven't been honest with myself."

"All right." She smoothed down the ivory silk of her nightgown. He noticed that her hair was loose around her shoulders, but the top was pulled back, held away from her face with combs. He loved when she wore it like that. She must have known they were returning this evening. She'd done it in the hopes he would be coming back, he realized.

Brutally suppressing the urge to take her in his arms and make love to her until neither one of them could move, he cleared his throat. "I'm a vampire."

She laughed, and it was like music to him. "I know this. Max, you are behaving very strangely. You used to be a vampire, I know."

"No." He shook his head vehemently. "I am a vampire. I will always be a vampire. But I will always be a werewolf, too."

How to explain it to her, the woman who was content to accept his unfortunate disability and spend the rest of her life with him? How could he make her understand?

"I'll never be just a werewolf. There will always be a part of me that doesn't fit in. But I know where I belong. For the first time, maybe in my whole life, I know where I belong. And it's with you. Not because I'm a werewolf or a vampire, just because I'm me. And I want you to love me because I'm me, not because someday I'll forget what I was or where I came from." He stopped himself, before he sounded like a total wuss. "Can you do that?"

There were tears in Bella's eyes, and she wheeled a little closer to him. "Max, I had no idea you felt this way. I do not love you because I believe that one day you will no longer be a vampire. I loved you when you were a vampire and nothing more. I would love you if you were a human. I would love you if it meant I had to leave my pack behind. I would love you if it meant I must sacrifice my very life."

He caught her up then, and whirled her around. Then he set her on her feet, but she was too weak from her earlier display of her progress, and he had to support her. He carried her inside and laid her on the bed. It was almost more than he could endure not to rip the nightgown from her body and have her, right then. He ran his hands down her sides, then smoothed one palm over her expanded abdomen.

A tiny, hard lump brushed his palm and retreated, and his breath froze in his body. Torn between a feeling of wonder and disgust, he could only laugh. "That's the baby? It's really in there?"

Bella nodded and pulled his face to hers, kissing his stubbled cheek. "Yes, it is really in there."

He pulled away from her and pressed his cheek to her stomach. "That's kind of gross. And kind of cool."

They both laughed then, Bella stroking his hair as he waited for another tiny wriggle, his child, proving it was there.

"We could leave, if you wish to return to your old life," Bella said, and it wasn't just to appease him. She meant it, in every syllable she meant it.

"No." He pulled himself up the bed to nestle his head in her neck. "No, my home is where you are. And you're here."

He meant it. Frightening as it was, he meant it. And even more frightening, he knew he wouldn't miss his old life.

He had a new one, and it was right here.

Twenty-Four: And They All Lived...

I don't know how long I drifted in the blank blue, gliding over other souls, hungry for life but not remembering a moment of my own. But then I saw life, shining, grasping, reaching for me, and I reached for it with my formless, lost soul. The second it touched me, I remembered who I was, and I was terrified of losing it. I clutched at it, babbling, and only after I felt real, human hands pry mine off whatever it was I clung to, did the desperation leave me.

"Carrie!" It was Nathan's voice, but I didn't see him. My vision was fuzzy and the bright light hurt my eyes. I knew it was Nathan holding me, because I heard his voice rumble through his chest, but there was something different about him. Something about him I'd never seen before.

"Nathan?" I managed through chattering teeth. A blanket, rough and scratchy, draped around my naked shoulders. "Nathan, you're human."

Then everything was black.

* * *

I woke in a room full of sunlight. The blinds were open and it streamed in from all sides, over the blankets covering me, over my vulnerable, exposed skin. I shrieked, beating back flames that should have been there, but weren't.

Nathan was at my side, and he pulled me against him, trying to comfort me and praise the heavens all at once.

"The sun!" I finally managed to shout.

"It won't hurt you," he assured me, and I thought he sounded like a crazy person. "Sweetheart, we're fine. We're fine. We're human."

I took a deep breath and felt my heart beating in my chest. My real heart, not some deformed digestive organ. And I had a temperature. Not a fever, but my skin actually felt warm. And I had to pee. Badly.

I scrambled over Nathan and raced toward the bathroom. I was human? It seemed so incredibly unlikely. My stomach rumbled, and I didn't crave blood. I wanted…waffles. And cheese-smothered hash browns. And Diet Coke.

I sat on the toilet and sobbed. I was human. The memory of my fight with the Soul Eater rushed back to me, and even as I reconstructed the weird events that had brought me to this place, I wanted to push them as far from my mind as possible.

I was human again. Nathan was human again.

He knocked on the door, and I realized that until this very moment, bathroom protocol had never, ever come up. I finished up and wiped off, then stood on shaking legs and opened the door. He looked worried and terribly, terribly mortal.

"Are you okay?" He reached a hand out and smoothed the hair away from my face.

I looked in the mirror. Blotchy skin, bags under my eyes. I loved it. I wanted to kiss my reflection. "I'm a human again."

I collapsed to the floor, sobbing in relief and joy.

Later, after Nathan had cooked the biggest breakfast in recorded human history, he explained what had happened after the night I defeated the Soul Eater.

"It took them almost a year to bring me back." He poured me a cup of boiling water from the teapot that used to warm blood. He dunked in a tea bag and set the steaming pot aside. "They were waiting for a priest to die, so they could use his hand. It's in the spell. When they brought me back, I explained how Dahlia used exotic ingredients to throw people off track."

I smiled, but I wasn't up to laughter. Not about this. Not yet. "How long has it been?"

"For you?" Nathan asked, as if he truly didn't understand what I was asking. "Six months more. We tried. Believe me, we tried. But we could never find you."

"You found me." I reached across the table and took his hand in mine. It seemed more intimate, now that we were human. Now that we had time ticking away against us. "Nathan, why did you do it?"

He sucked in a huge breath and pushed a banana-nut muffin toward me. "I couldn't live without you." When I raised an eyebrow in disbelief, he insisted, "I couldn't! Ask Ziggy and Bill. When they brought me back, the first thing I asked was if they'd brought you back."

I thought of Nathan, when he was my sire, ruled by the pain of the blood tie, and I realized that now we didn't have that to rely on to keep us together. "And now?"

He pulled my hand to his lips, kissing each knuckle reverently. "Now, it's the same. I love you, Carrie. I want to spend the rest of my life with you, mortal or vampire."

That caught my attention. "Do you want to be a vampire again?"

He gave an embarrassed laugh. "Ziggy offered to turn me, but I wanted to see…what you would want. I've been a vampire for over seventy years. It's more normal than human life to me now, but…"

"But?" I prodded.

He smiled. "But I like the idea of a clean slate. Being able to start over, brand-new. With you."

There was a long silence. I looked into his eyes, familiar gray, yet unfamiliar in their humanity. What would it be like, to grow old with him as a human? To make love to him as a human? To get married, have children, live the life that had been denied to me when Cyrus had attacked me what was now over two years ago?

"What do you want, Carrie?" Nathan asked, his expression a mixture of hope and fear.

"I want…" I spoke slowly. There was no going back from this moment. And it was a giddy feeling in my stomach. "I want to go to Vegas and get married."

Nathan looked surprised at this, but he said nothing.

"And I want to move out of this apartment, into a real house." I was on a roll now, and I had to rein myself in. "And I want to try to…have a child. Maybe more than one. With you. I want to have a human life with you. In twenty years, maybe we'll decide to let Ziggy turn us. Maybe not. But right now, I want to try for my happily ever after."

Nathan nodded, tears welling up in his eyes. I didn't get to finish my breakfast. We made love for the first time as humans, right there on the kitchen floor. And he told me he loved me, and I knew it wasn't because of the blood tie, because that wasn't a part of my reality anymore. He loved me.

It's a strange world we live in. The lines between death and life aren't as cut-and-dried as we like to believe. Neither are good and evil.

I had to experience both extremes for myself. Extreme strength and extreme powerlessness. Love and hate. Life and death. But I know now.

No one's place in this world is guaranteed. Not everyone is going to get a happy ending. But life isn't about how it ends. It's about the moments between. It's about the small things. The way our loved ones laugh. The sight of a butterfly in the sunlight after a year or two in the darkness.

The love and support of an old friend. They might not be with us in body, but they are with us in spirit.

The feeling of something we'd thought lost to us forever returned in a single, life-changing moment. Yes, that is simple, even though it might be momentous to us as individuals.

Because every day, on this planet, people are born and people die and stranger things happen. But I know my place now, and my purpose. And no matter what trial you have to endure to find that out…

It's worth it.

Turn the page for a preview of
LIGHTWORLD/DARKWORLD
By Jennifer Armintrout
Coming in August 2009

One

In the Darkworld, the filth made it difficult to fly. Faery wings were far too gossamer and fragile to withstand the moisture that dripped from the murky blackness overhead or the clinging grime that coated everything, even sentient things, that dared cross over the Darkworld border.

Ayla knelt in the mire, searching the mucky concrete ground for signs of her quarry. She'd had no problem tracking the werewolf this far, though she rarely ventured this deep into Darkworld. Her wings, not delicately made, but leathery flaps of nearly human skin, thick boned and heavy against her back, had given her the speed to track the rampaging beast on his home turf. But they had made her too conspicuous. As she tracked the wolf, something tracked her.

She heard it, lurking behind her. Whatever followed had wings, feathered, if she guessed correctly from the rustling that echoed through the tunnel like tiny thunder. Perhaps it thought she wouldn't hear it. Or couldn't.

The chill that raced up her spine had little to do with

the gusts of cold air that blew through the tunnels. She knew the beast that followed her. She'd heard it spoken of in hushed tones in the Assassin's Guild training rooms. It was a Death Angel.

The stories were too numerous to sort fact from fiction. Some claimed an Angel had the powers of the Vanished Gods. Some dismissed them as no more powerful than a Faery or Elf. And some insisted that to look upon one was death to any creature, mortal or Fae. Once, not long after Ayla had begun her formal Guild training, an Assassin was lost. His body was recovered, impaled upon his own sword, wings ripped from his back. She'd seen him, though Garret, her mentor, had tried to shield her. The marks on the Faery's ashen flesh indicated he had not been cut, but torn, as if by large, clawed hands. The killing blow had come as a mercy.

The blood pounded in her veins as she forced herself to focus on resuming the trail of her wolf. Pursued or not, she had an assignment to carry out. Until the Death Angel struck, she would ignore his presence.

Closing her eyes, Ayla called up the training she'd received. She reached out with her sightless senses. She could not smell the wolf, not above the stench of the sewer. She could not hear it. The irritated buzz of her antennae, an involuntary reaction to the tension vibrating through her body, coupled with the rustling of the Death Angel's wings in the shadows behind her, drowned out all other noise. She reached her hands out, feeling blindly across the pocked concrete of the tunnel wall. Deep gouges scored the surface, filled with fading rage. Her fingers brushed the residual energy and her mind lit up with a flare of red. The wolf had passed this way.

Rising to her feet slowly, she traced the walls with her hands. Here was a splash of blood, blossoming with a neon-bright flare of pain behind her closed eyelids. Innocent, simple blood. There would be a body.

In a crouch, she moved through the tunnel, her arms low to the ground, trailing through the congealed filth there. Something dripped farther down the tunnel. It was audible, like a drop falling from a spigot to a full bucket. There was water ahead. Dirty water, no doubt contaminated by waste from the human world above, but a carcass would float there. It would be easier to find the wolf's victim.

She followed the trail of blood and pain, the water rising to her knees, then to her waist. Something brushed her bare skin below the leather of her vest, and her eyes flew open. Floating beside her, split neck to groin, the empty skin of a rat.

Summoning energy from her chest, she directed it into a ball in her palm. The orb flared bright, and she tossed it above her head to illuminate the space. To her left, another tunnel led deeper into the Darkworld. Another opened ahead of her. In the yolk of the three tunnels, hundreds of eviscerated rats bobbed in the stinking tide.

Rats. My life is forfeit for the sake of rats.

Wading through the sewage, she made her way to a low ledge. Another body waited there. The werewolf, already twisted and stiff in death, caught between his wolf and human states. The grinning rictus of his human mouth below his half-transformed snout gave testimony to the poison that had killed him, would have killed the rats if he'd not gotten to them first.

It was said among the assassins of the Lightworld that Death Angels wait in the shadows for the souls of mortal creatures. The one that had followed her would find no such soul.

It was then she realized she'd been trapped.

She spun to face the Death Angel, caught sight of it in her rapidly fading light. Paper-white skin stretched over a hard, muscular body that could have been human but for the claws at its hands and feet. It hung upside down, somehow gripping the smooth ceiling of the tunnel, its eyes sightless black mirrors that reflected her terrified face. It hissed, spreading its wings, and sprang for her.

Gulping as much of the fetid air as her lungs could hold, Ayla dived into the water. The echo of the creature's body disturbing the surface rippled around her, urging her to swim faster, but her wings twisted in the currents, slowing her and sending shocks of pain through her bones. She propelled herself upward and broke into the air gasping.

In a moment, the creature had her, his claws twisting in her loosened braid. He jerked her head back, growling a warning in a harsh, guttural language. He disentangled his claws from her hair and gripped her shoulder in one massive fist, his other hand raised to strike.

The moment his palm fell on her bare shoulder, she saw the change come over him. Red tentacles of energy climbed like ivy over his fingers, gaining his wrist, twining around his thick muscled forearm. His hand spasmed and flexed on her arm but he was unable to let go, tied to her by the insidious red veins.

That was another rumor she'd heard about Death Angels. Though they craved mortal souls, the touch of a creature with mortal blood was bitter poison.

With a gasp of disbelief and satisfaction, she raised her eyes to the face of the Death Angel. His eyes, occluded with blood, fixed on her as the veins crept up his neck, covering his face.

"I am half human," she said with a cruel laugh of relief. Whether the creature understood her or not, she did not care. He opened his mouth and screamed, his voice twisting from a fierce, spectral cry to a human wail of pain and horror. Ayla's heart thundered in her chest and she closed her eyes, dragging air into her painfully constricted lungs. In her mind she saw the tree of her life force, its roots anchoring her feet, its branches reaching into her arms and head. Great, round sparks of energy raced to the Angel's touch, where her life force pulsed angry red. The pace of the moving energy quickened with her heartbeat, growing impossibly rapid, building and swelling within her until she could no longer withstand the assault. She wrenched her shoulder free and staggered back, slipping to her knees in the water, sputtering as the foulness invaded her mouth.

The Death Angel stood as if frozen in place, twisting in agony. The stark red faded into his preternaturally white skin. His bloody, empty eyes washed with white, then a dot of color pierced their center. Mortal eyes, mortal color. A mortal body. Ayla clambered to her feet and stared in shock, the rush of her blood and energy still filling her ears. All at once it stopped, and the Death Angel collapsed, disappearing below the water.

In the deathly still of the tunnel, Ayla listened for any other presence. Only the gentle lapping of the water against the curved walls of the tunnel could be heard, no fearsome rustling of wings. Would another Death Angel come for him, now that he was to die a mortal death?

He burst up through the water with a pitiable cry, arms flailing. Ayla screamed, jumping immediately to an attack stance, twin blades drawn. She relaxed when the now-mortal creature dragged himself from the water with shaking arms to collapse on the ledge. His chest heaved with each jerky breath of his newborn lungs, and his limbs trembled with exhaustion. He was no immediate threat.

Curiosity overcame Ayla's training, which dictated she should kill the Darkling where he lay. How many Assassins had the chance to survey their prey this closely? How many had the chance to destroy a Death Angel? Her weapons still at the ready, still poised to carry her into legend with the kill, she moved closer.

The Angel lay on his back, his ebony feathered wings folded beneath him. His hair, impossibly long, lay matted and wet on the cement, dipping into the water. The fierce muscle structure that had made him so strong remained, but his body twitched, sapped of strength.

It seemed wrong, cowardly to kill him in such a state.

An assassin knows no honor. An assassin knows no pity. An assassin is no judge to bestow mercy, but the executioner of those who have already been sentenced, those Darklings who shun the truth of Light. The gies, seared into her brain through hours of endless repetition, burned her anew, and she lifted her knives to deliver the killing blow. His eyes slid open, flickered over her hands and the weapons she held.

With a deep breath and a whispered prayer, Ayla closed her eyes. "Badb, Macha, Nemain, guide my hand that you might collect your trophy sooner than later."

He made no noise as her daggers fell. If he had, perhaps she would have been able to finish the job. But when she opened her eyes, saw the flashing blades poised to pierce his throat and sever his spine, saw his face impassive…

Her hands opened and the knives clattered on the ledge. She did not retrieve them. Let him have something to defend himself from the creatures that would come for him, the ones who would not kill him as quickly as she would have, if she had been mindful of the geis. She had never broken an oath in her life, but no power on earth or in the long dissipated astral realms could turn her head to look on him again or stop her as she waded into the tunnel that had brought her there.

He cried out then, when she was out of sight, but it was not to her. Probably to his One God, begging for help. But there had never been a God or Goddess in the Underground. Ayla knew she alone heard his prayer, and it haunted her all the way to the Lightworld.

NEW YORK TIMES BESTSELLING AUTHOR

KAT MARTIN

Neither sister can explain her "lost day." Julie worries that
Laura's hypochondria is spreading to her, given the stress
she's been under since the Donovan Real Estate takeover.

Patrick Donovan would be a catch if not for his playboy
lifestyle. But when a cocaine-fueled heart attack nearly
kills him, Patrick makes an astonishing recovery. Julie
barely recognizes Patrick as the same man she once
struggled to resist. Maybe it's her strange experience at
the beach that has her feeling off-kilter….

As Julie's feelings for Patrick intensify, her sister's health
declines. Now she's about to discover what the day on the
beach really meant….

SEASON OF STRANGERS

"An edgy and intense example of romantic suspense with
plenty of twists and turns."
—*Paranormal Romance Writers* on *The Summit*

*Available the first week of June 2008
wherever books are sold!*

MIRA®

MKM2554

From The Last Stand trilogy

BRENDA NOVAK

Four years ago Skye was attacked in her own bed.
She managed to fend off Dr. Oliver Burke, but
the trauma changed everything.

And now her would-be rapist is out of prison.

Detective David Willis believes Burke
is a clear and present danger—and
guilty of at least two unsolved murders.

But now Burke is free to terrorize Skye
again. Unless David can stop him.
Unless Skye can fight back. Because
Oliver Burke has every intention
of finishing what he started.
And that's a promise. Trust me.

TRUST
Me

"Brenda Novak's
seamless plotting,
emotional intensity
and true-to-life
characters...make her
books completely
satisfying. Novak
is simply a great
storyteller."
—*New York Times*
bestselling author
Allison Brennan

*Available the first week of June 2008
wherever books are sold!*

MIRA®

www.MIRABooks.com

MBN2412

New York Times bestselling author

MAGGIE SHAYNE

Before she joined Reaper in hunting Gregor's gang of
rogue bloodsuckers, Topaz was gunning for just one vamp:
Jack Heart. The gorgeous con man had charmed his way
into her bed, her heart and her bank account.

Now she and Jack are supposedly on the same side.
As Reaper's ragtag outfit scatters, Topaz sets out to solve
her mystery: what really happened to her mother, who
died when Topaz was a baby? And what stake does
Jack have in discovering the truth about her past?
Topaz is sure he's up to something—but her suspicions
are at war with her desires....

LOVER'S BITE